1

SUBJECT: QUESTION

From: Elizabeth Lambert

To: Jack Mathews

Date: Friday April 10, 2020 at 15:46

Are you the Jack Mathews I met in Avalon, Santa Catalina, 21 years ago?

Elizabeth (Swanson)

———

EVERYTHING ELIZABETH HAD EVER OWNED HAD BEEN sold, given away, or packed up and taped down in cardboard boxes. Columns of them lined the hallway, ochre against the setting sun like the foreboding façade of an ancient burial chamber waiting for the storage people to take them somewhere cool and dark, for another time, another place, another Elizabeth.

FRAGILE!!!

Elizabeth glided over the freshly waxed parquet floors as she closed the shutters of her Provençal home. This was it. Now all she needed to do was drop off the keys with the agents, fly to Paris for a late-night send-off dinner with girlfriends and the next morning she'd be crossing the Atlantic about the same time as the new homeowners were opening the doors to the next chapters in their lives.

By then, Elizabeth would be arriving in Felicidad, California.

By then, she'd be with Jack.

Elizabeth caught sight of herself in the mirror above the fireplace, arms outstretched, unfurling around beams of bronzed light.

Her team called her Titania—or 'Tits' to Magnus, her creative director—because she created magical worlds, but all those spaces Elizabeth had transformed, the audacious colors, arousing textures, breakthrough touches that made her clients cry out with joy, were disguises for the sadness that welled around her heart. Like a blister, it hurt; tender every time she breathed.

Now, the child who'd hidden, crouched in fear and cramped in pain, could smash through the store-front windows. The designer-dressed drama-in-demand who woke at five thirty to do her meditation before taking her daughter to school and jogging back to her desk as her assistant brought her green juice and a stick of celery—#lunch. The svelte blonde flying first class to building sites all over the world where she'd seduce investors to win bids for bigger, better projects. The socialite who referred to a man as 'my husband' but winced every time he walked in the room. That was the past.

Had Jack remembered to fill the refrigerator with Finé water? She'd text him again once he got to work, something extra spicy to mark the last day they were separated by time zones.

One suitcase and a weekend bag. The same amount she'd arrived in France with. This was the final shedding of two decades. Everything not packed would be left behind: the wine, the Le Creuset set and rococo patio furniture. That was Elizabeth, too nice, because the new buyers had tried to screw her over the house price—people do that when a nasty divorce is in the air, aim to shoot you in the back as you're running.

．　．　．

HOMEWRECKED

RUBY SOAMES

ZB
Zeitkin Books

For Jon, Bluebell & Edison

Three hours ago, Elizabeth's daughter, Cosima, had left with her father for her grandmother's home in the Luberon. The child hadn't even tried to conceal her impatience to get away, wriggling in her mother's arms when Elizabeth kissed her goodbye. Mis-feeding the buttons on her daughter's jacket, Elizabeth told Cosima that she loved her, but she knew the words didn't mean anything to kids; it's you being there that puts you in credit. We can feel the love we have to give, but who can really feel it coming back? Maybe that's why when someone says they love you, it never feels like it should.

Cosima broke free from Elizabeth's strangle-hold hug and ran to her father's Porsche Cayenne in the driveway.

Elizabeth had had to make three trips through the main doors to bring out all her daughter's cases to her ex-husband's car. They were heavier than she'd thought, or she was weaker. Bruno didn't move to help. He sat back in his laundered jeans, not looking at the house or Elizabeth, just the bobbing heads of agapanthuses lining the way to the pool. Even after everything, Elizabeth couldn't help feeling disarmed by the Brutalist architecture of his face and the careless way he left one hand on the steering wheel, the other stroking the top of his daughter's head.

The trunk opened. Elizabeth wrapped her hair around her neck and filled it with Cosima's belongings. She ignored Bruno's eyes in the rear-view mirror looking down her shirt every time she leant in. The last bag nestled next to his brown suede monogrammed Hermes holdall: a birthday gift she'd given him during lockdown to excite him for future travel—two days before she'd first written to Jack.

It was Bruno who'd pushed her to send that first email. The afternoon he'd walked into Elizabeth's bathroom and leered at her legs resting on the side of the tub above the crackling bubbles—one of the lockdown perks: a bath at teatime, what decadence! He'd been out all night, despite the 'Stay Home, Save Lives' messages. He'd smelt of cigars, cognac and many different kinds of perfume. 'You'll be forty in a few years, *Chérie',* he said, his fingertips closing around her big toe. 'I could never fuck a woman over forty, by that age, *elles sont toutes cuites.'*

Cuite—cooked through.

Elizabeth was careful of her nails while maneuvering the luggage around the stack of professionally wrapped boxes. Gifts for their Cosima. A whole summer's worth. But Cosima was already in her papa's arms, the best present of all.

Raising her daughter in a life Elizabeth had no experience of was the most she could have ever given; after that, it had been pretty much hit and miss. Probably more misses.

Bruno had let Cosima beep the horn, delighted the sound made Elizabeth jump.

Elizabeth had hoped that because of their Cosie, and that her business had supported Bruno all those years, he would be fair, be bigger than that, that he might actually surprise her, but he was not a nice person.

Elizabeth picked up Smudge who'd been pawing at the passenger's door.

'Bye, little guy.' She kissed the cushiony, velour patch between his ears before placing him on her daughter's lap.

'No. *Non.* I'm not taking him.'

'Bruno!'

'Not with the horses, and sheeps and tics. Is your fucking dog, *hein? Ah, non.'*

'But I'm going to the States for three months! You said—'

'And you said a lot of things, Lili. *Adieu!'*

'Fine. We'll talk every day my baby.' She kissed her daughter again. 'Wait—let me just check I packed your school bag—remember, just do a little bit every day.'

Bruno rolled his eyes, clicked open the trunk again as Elizabeth rummaged around the back pretending to look for something while lifting up the dog and settling him in between the suitcases.

'All good!'

Doors closed, engine on.

Cosima's after-thought wave, the crunch of gravel under Bruno's wheels, and they were gone until September.

Standing on the porch, blowing kisses at the back of her little girl's head, tears sluiced through Elizabeth's vision.

Nobody knew how hard Elizabeth had fought to provide this enchanted life for her daughter to take for granted.

Listening out for the fading buzz of Bruno's car on the country roads, snatching at the flashes of chrome through the cypress trees, Elizabeth held on to the very last seconds of having a family until the time came when all she heard was a woodpecker drilling into a tree-trunk behind her.

2

SUBJECT: ANSWER

From: Jack Mathews

To: Elizabeth Lambert

Date: Tuesday April 14, 2020 at 10:09

Only if you are the beautifull, green-eyed, 15yr old mermaid I found swept up on the shore that summer... Yes! Jack x

———

THREE YEARS and one month after that first email, Jack sat in his car outside the house Elizabeth had taken for the summer.

He flipped his cellphone from one hand to the other.

The For Rent sign was no longer pitched outside the gates and, in a few hours, the listings agent would be driving up with a van full of half-blooming peonies to arrange in white vases of equal size around the house. A chef from Kyoto was due that afternoon to stock the kitchen with the ingredients for vegetarian, gluten-free Japanese meals. The four-poster bed Elizabeth had designed for them had already arrived and been made up to her exact specifications. The metaphor wasn't lost on Jack. Elizabeth had finalized her divorce, sent her daughter away, cleared her work schedule, and packed up her life to be with him—now you lie in it.

Lie to your wife and kids from this fabulous five-bedroomed Hacienda-style property on Paloma Drive. Quiet, but for birdsong and the occasional splash of someone somewhere cooling off. Protected by clouds of bougainvillea, parasol pines, muscle-bound palm trees, and private security firms. Some said this was the best road in Felicidad, California, in fact, *he'*d said it was the best road in Felicidad.

He'd started this, but he never meant...

It was just a remark he'd made a few months before, early one morning when he and his dog, Tip, had been running up to Paloma Heights and saw the property. Its elegance, mystery, views right out to sea—some said even to Mexico, *he'*d said even to Mexico—all seemed so *Elizabeth.* So he sent her a photo of the house and the realty sign in front of it. And he jogged on.

I'll take it, she'd texted back.

Huh? he'd asked himself, walking through his garage to drop his burner phone into a plastic tub marked *Super-Strong Bonding Putty.*

Jack stared at his phone screen.

Call the agent.

And now, this weekend, she was landing at San Diego International Airport to pick up the keys.

Three years and one month and you blow up your life.

Psssst-pssst. The sprinklers started up, pissing out arcs of sodden rainbows over the just-cut grass.

Psssst. A swift slalomed between the myrtle blossoms.

Jack had the right to take his sneakers off, skid through those whirling jets, make himself a whiskey sour at the bar. Hell, he could even spend the rest of the day floating in the pool on that inflatable unicorn.

But he couldn't even get out of his car.

So close now. Elizabeth would be at the window, her blonde hair lapping at her shoulders, flour on her hands because she'd be making something for him, a low-cal high-fiber cake maybe. She'd look up, smile with her starbright eyes, she'd rush towards him, barefoot, in a long white nightdress like the ones in those British costume dramas Jude liked to watch. One shoulder strap slipping down. Nothing but bare skin under the cool cotton. The white glades of her breastbone rise right to the points of her hardening nipples. Flour dusts his hair, his palms would press against her thighs, and she is wild, tearful, there, on the floor. He wouldn't even have time to get his pants down.

If Jack packed a bag and left Jude a goodbye note now while she was at work, he'd be coming home to wanton pleasures like that every single night. He took his damp hands off the steering wheel to re-adjust where his shorts had tightened.

He needed to move on before someone reported a suspicious man sitting in a beat-up Nissan truck casing a house someone like him had no right to be near. Jack didn't belong there. He had his own driveway to sit in, his own home to go to, his own family. But then Elizabeth said he had a right to be happy.

Sure, he had a right to be happy, and yet, did he have a right to make others unhappy?

The cellphone in his hand vibrated.

Jude.

"Bentley said you weren't at work yet?"

Jack huddled over the phone, turning his back on the house.

"Nuh. Stuff." Jack had become a master of the vague and elusive answer having learnt that making up lists of non-existent errands only prompted her first-response instinct which was to try and help. Anyway, how was he ever to break free when she tracked his every move? "How did assembly go?"

"This time I'd had nothing prepared—nothing!—and I was driving in thinking I'd have to repeat something from years back, which I swore I'd never do, and then—get this—on the radio there was a report about an elephant and a goose at San Diego Zoo who are best friends. Isn't that wild?"

"An elephant and a *goose*?"

"Right? They go everywhere together—*inseparable*. They look out for each other and when one of them is sick, the other gets depressed. So cute! Two boys from eighth grade helped me download clips of the zoo workers washing down the elephant with the goose flapping in the water and the two of them having meals from the same plate. We put it to a soundtrack, hooked up my iPad to the projector and I spun it into an allegory of how we can love each other despite differences, blah blah. A few of the Senior Highs…"

Jack looked over at the radiating hologram of Elizabeth at the window, maybe this time she lifted her dress, teased him by touching herself like she'd done the other night on FaceTime.

"You still there?"

"Y'always come up with something, Juju. Elephant and a goose—that's nuts."

"I was lucky. Talking of animals, what did we forget?"

"I dunno. What?"

"Come on… this weekend: what?"

"Give up."

"Sweetheart…?"

Jude—always on the winning team at quiz nights—liked to make him guess. She called it *eliciting* information; he called it making him look stupid.

Jack ran through the ways Jude might have found out that his lover was landing on US soil in forty-eight hours.

"This isn't *Jeopardy*, just tell me or I gotta go."

If Jack was as unpleasant as possible, telling her he was leaving might be easier. Could even look like it was her idea. Either way, she'd be relieved to be free of her grouchy, priapic, amnesiac other half.

Being hunched up with the phone to his ear was starting to crimp the nerves at the back of his neck.

"Sunday of Memorial Day Weekend—that mean anything?" Jude asked.

Of course it meant something. *Sunday, May 28th, 2023.* Elizabeth was expecting him to meet her at the arrivals lounge then carry her over the threshold and make love to her on the bed *she'd* designed for them to lie in for the rest of their lives.

Psssst, went the sprinklers: *Tell her.*

Jack pummeled his cervical vertebrae.

Once he said it, the worst would be over.

He dragged a sticky hand across all four corners of his face, ground his teeth and took in the very air that would transform into the words he'd been rehearsing for the past three years.

"I'm—"

"Tip's birthday!" said Jude. "Our puppy's going double digits."

Jack laughed like a madman or someone at a job interview.

Tip. Their Australian shepherd pup, now geriatric.

"Let's go to the lake, hike a bit, picnic… We need to stop by Mom's anyway to check on the place, pick up any mail, what d'you say?"

"What about Aimee?"

"I told you last night. She's staying at Savannah's after—" An electronic bell chimed. "Wait." Jude shut her office door against the clamor of high-school kids making their way to class. "That's why I thought, *just* us. Blanket on the grass, bottle of chilled Sauvignon... We haven't done anything like that for so long." Jack heard her breathe in. "See, I feel I'm coming through this grief thing, and know what? We could go to the little trattoria that just opened."

"Not sure Tip's gonna dig the Italian vibe."

"For us, Jack. Let's start doing fun things for us."

"Yeah, but if it's Tip's birthday, shouldn't we focus on him?"

"Whatever. How about I make a cake out of—"

"Not chicken 'cause that gives him the runs."

"Chuck steak?"

"Could work."

"Another thing. Hear me out. Maybe I should sell my half of Mom's house to Dahlia? If we go up on the weekend, we could meet with an agent and—"

"You're cutting out—" Jack turned the ignition. "What?" He revved the engine. "I have someone driving up my ass … later … I'll—"

He switched off his phone, lifted his foot from the accelerator and cut the motor.

Psssst-pssst. Jack watched a hummingbird suspended right at the point where the water spray evaporated into mist.

A forty-one-year-old man in a car, not going anywhere, windows up because he was afraid people would hear his thoughts. *He* was afraid to hear his thoughts.

Picnic blanket.

A text. Elizabeth's PA, Emily, reminding him to fill the fridge with some weird, impossible-to-find bottled water.

Steak cake.

God, he loved his wife.

Psssst.

This was the sign.

God, make this house go away.

Tachycardia. Tendons twisted and tight like chains around his bones. He was sweating, his pupils were freakishly dilated. He'd lost his appetite—forget about sleep. How he envied Jude her ignorance.

Now, on top of everything, he had to buy his dog a birthday present.

He opened the window, gasped for air, let the droplets scatter across his face.

Elizabeth said the hardest part of leaving someone was telling them: so, could he tell *her*? He had to get back to what was essential, protect his collateral, take cover from the maelstrom. He needed to sacrifice her: save five people—six, if you counted Tip—to Elizabeth's *one*.

One marriage ending, another beginning, but *which* one?

God, make Elizabeth fall out of the sky in a terrible plane crash. No survivors.

3

SUBJECT: HEY YOU. ME, AGAIN

From: Elizabeth Lambert

To: Jack Mathews

Date: Friday April 17, 2020 at15:46

Really? That you? Jack Mathews? Jack from Avalon, summer 1999? I googled you and thought it had to be. I was about to DM you but then saw your company website which seemed less intrusive—and hey, I might want to buy a car off you! I'm not a stalker, I promise! I was just curious to find out how your life turned out. OMG! Such a long time ago—before we could legally drink, before cellphones or the internet—before Covid 19! You managing to stay healthy and sane through all this?

That summer was the most beautiful and the most painful of my life and only you know why. Anyway, I was just looking up old friends in between homeschooling, doom scrolling and cake baking and it was so great to see your face. You don't look a day older, BTW! Still devastatingly handsome!

Hope you don't mind me saying hello after all these years.

Hello.

Elizabeth x

———

JUDE LOOKED up from her desk to see Callie's silver nails curling around her door.

"Boo!" Callie bounced into Jude's office, stood in front of her and tilted her head to one side. "Break for lunch and take a spinning class?"

Jude regretted confiding in Callie how much the post-pandemic weight gain had got her down, because now, every time she writhed on her bed pulling up her secret support girdle —so tight she thought she'd bring on a nosebleed—she could hear Callie's voice reminding her, 'You're not going to get the butt you want by sitting on it.'

"Come on, it's a beautiful day and the instructor's super-hot. His name's Aristotle." Callie checked the school corridor was clear before whispering, "He has those nipple rings."

"Black Lycra shorts?"

"The tightest."

"Tempting, but I'm just not fit enough for a fitness class."

"Crap!"

"I haven't finished processing next fall's intakes and there's Ethan Malokov's transfer papers, preparing for next week's state budget meeting plus we're leaving tonight for the cabin. Next time. Promise."

Jude had hired Callie five years before to run the About U Wellness Program at Orange Flower Park High but they'd also managed to build a friendship despite Jude being her boss. Jude had been disappointed, even hurt, when after returning as principal to Orange Park, where she'd spent fifteen years as a science teacher, her old friends ranged from obsequious to diffident towards her. Her new role made them uncomfortable. No one wanted to sit with their boss at lunch until Callie arrived. She was much more interested in competing in Spartan Mud Race championships, her boyfriend PJ, and a side-line breeding Dobermans than school politics. And when she and Jude both lost their mothers the year before, their bond was sealed.

"Why, Mrs. Mathews..." said Callie, her blonde ponytail swishing against the nape of her neck, "you look *different*. You're..." she twirled her index finger in the direction of Jude's face, "beaming." Callie dropped into the chair across Jude's desk. "Nobody should look that good at the end of the week."

"Well," Jude lowered her head into her clasped hands, "Jack and I have... y'know... been *closer* lately. Did I tell you Bentley's moved in with Maxxie? And Aimee's been staying at Savannah's to practise their end-of-year hip hop thing and suddenly there's time for us. It's been really exciting."

"Good for you!"

"That's why I want to get all this done before the long weekend."

"So what *exciting* stuff you guys got planned—or should I not ask judging by the smile on your face?"

"Is it that obvious?" Jude covered her cheeks with her hands, her large hands that she'd spent her twenties feeling embarrassed about. "We're gonna stay at Mom's—the lake house—hey, you guys must come for a weekend, the dogs would love it." Jude took a few seconds to collect herself. "I haven't been back there since..." Jude rotated her mother's wedding ring which she wore under her own. "We're going to start using it more. Mom so wanted us to enjoy her home. And it's time, y'know?"

"Good for you."

"Sounds corny but it's like we're falling in love all over again. Jack's been so attentive, romantic. Last night he got this idea we go around the world—but he wanted to leave right there and then! He was jumping around the room, taking clothes out of the closet, looking for his foil jacket, downloading sailing apps. At one point he was actually pulling me out of bed to leave in the middle of the night! Nuts—but adorable. Of course I never stopped loving him but the *in love* part, it's like the tide, close then far, far then close. Just gotta ride them waves."

"That's deep, Principal."

"*And* it's Tip's tenth birthday. Guess we're all growing up! What you guys got planned?"

"Heading out to PJ's folks for the parade. No romance for me! Just fielding the interrogation, *When you gonna have kids? When you gonna buy a home? When you*—" The reminder alert on Callie's watch started beeping. "Got to run. If I don't see you, have a great weekend with lots of sunshine and—"

"—passionate sex by the lake?"

"Principal Mathews! Next week, girlfriend, you bring your sneakers, no excuses. You're gonna need exercise classes for all that humpin' and pump—Oh hi, Grace."

Grace Mitchell, music educator and longest-serving member of staff, gave a peremptory nod to both Callie and Jude before stepping into the center of the room as if it were an auditorium.

"I have something *very* disturbing to report," she said, her tremulous fingers adjusting her glasses on one of the terraced ledges under her milky eyes. "There's been a theft. Here. At the school."

"Oh no! What happened?" asked Jude.

"Jesus Menendez. He stole my cookies. Right outta my locker. And they're expensive cookies too. *Specifically* for diabetics. And there's only one health-food store that sells them."

"Mrs, Mitchell, you sit down and tell Jude *all* about it," Callie invited. "Enjoy your weekend, ladies," she added, twerking a few times before closing the principal's door.

4

SUBJECT: AFTER ALL THESE YEARS

From: Jack Mathews

To: Elizabeth Lambert

Date: Saturday April 18, 2020 at 15:46

Can't believe we found each other after all these years! Marcie my secretary created the 'Mathews Motors PR Department' (just so she could spend even more time on social media!) but thanks to this crazy pandemic I'm finally getting round to clearing my inbox, and saw your email!!! Dang—gonna have to give her that pay rise she's been asking for! Was I ever 18?! Remember that mane of golden hair? Gone. And that six-pack? Despite running 3 times a week and watching the cheesecake, I'm a few cans short! But I'm still the same boy at heart. How come you haven't changed a bit? You been hiding out in a cryogenerator since 1999? You live in France!!! Bonjour! Me and the guys are always talking about hitting the vineyards there one summer after we did an awesome wine trail last year in Baja… what I remember of it 😂! I'm still flipping cars, remember I was doing that before college in my parents garage and now I own Mathews Motors right here in Felicidad! If ever you come over we could give you a great deal 😏 I'm married to a wonderfull lady called Jude. Just celebrated twenty years of marriage. We got 3 kids. Preston, in his last year of school, Bentley, two years younger, who made $700 on an ol' Pontiac last weekend (he has his pop's talent for junk metal). After that, we have Aimee but we call her Beanie cause she's like a Mexican bean, always jumping. Still awake??? This is the longest thing I've written since high school!

Love from Your Old and now New (I hope!) friend, Jack xx

"Guess y'see places like this all the time," said Megan, searching for a reason why Elizabeth Lambert showed not even the tiniest appreciation for one of Buena Vista Realty's most prestigious listings. "Of course, there are more architecturally *out-there* properties, but they're not as homey, authentic, y'know?"

"I thought we agreed the wall hanging would go."

"The Native American tapestry—you don't like it?"

"No."

Her client didn't look up from her phone.

"OK. I'll get Esme to take it down. Can you wait till morning?"

Without an answer, Megan decided to continue the tour. She opened the garden doors and walked into the balmy evening.

"Flores takes care of everything out here but I know you are also a keen gardener so you guys will really hit it off. I reckon there's isn't one color missing in those flower beds! And you got all of Felicidad laid out for you. That's the reservoir, modern art museum, if you like beer, that's the brewery. Orange Flower Park is just—Mrs. Lambert?"

Megan stepped back into the main room where her client was standing by the child-sized vase of peonies that had taken the agent over a fortnight to source.

"The upstairs master bedroom suite is to die for. Mr. Mathews said you liked the sound of the Jacuzzi tub, I'll just take you through—"

Elizabeth made a stop sign with her hand, squinted at a message.

"You don't want to see—"

"Really." Elizabeth yawned.

"About the bed. Esme wasn't sure she'd made it up right, she used your diagrams, but—" Megan noticed Elizabeth's right eye twitching. "Mrs. Lambert, I've been gabbling away and you must be exhausted."

"Very."

"Jack Mathews signed off on all the paperwork, all in the folder there." Saying that name, *Jack Mathews*, shortened her breath, warmed her cheeks. *Rein it in, girl.* "Bet you noticed the kitchen island already?"

The listing agent wondered what it would be like to have a face like Elizabeth's, a face which needed nothing to be drawn on, colored in or covered up. "It's Carrara marble—cost like 25,000 dollars."

Elizabeth's phone buzzed with a message she swiped to delete.

"The contract states you've two sets of keys—Esme and Flores have theirs—they also have their own alarm codes so we can check when they come and go. You got all my details in the email, and my card."

"Thank-you. And I appreciate you coming all the way out to collect me, especially on a holiday weekend."

Collect me. Holiday. Megan repeated the words in her mind. Elizabeth spoke in a soft voice with a strange accent; Megan wondered if she'd appear more interesting to men if she too carried the same rounded vowel sounds.

"It's not something we do for clients, but *this* house, and *you.*"

"It's been a long journey." Elizabeth backed Megan towards the front door.

"Oh, the pool house, I—"

"Do you mind? I really need to freshen up, I'm expecting someone."

"Freshen up? I wish I could look like you after a long-haul flight is all I can say!"

The agent made clicking noises with her mouth as she grappled for her car keys in the cobalt-blue Lanvin bag she'd bought with part of the commission from the rental. She'd imagined it was the sort of bag Elizabeth might have chosen, now she realized Elizabeth would have gone for the taupe.

"Esme will be here tomorrow. I said that already. Well! It's been a real privilege meeting you. I am a huge fan of your work! My dream is to go to London one day and stay at the Cave—or the hotel in Paris—gotta find a rich guy to take me first!"

Elizabeth held the front door open, leaving Megan little choice but to shuffle towards her car.

"Can I ask one thing? If you take any photos of the place on social media, could you remember to add the hashtag Buena Vista Realty? Any little mention would—"

"I'll do that," said Elizabeth, stretching out her lower back.

"Hey, me and a group of gals go out to Barebacks Bar'n'-Grill Friday nights—it's off the tourist track even though the mixologist there was famous in New York before he moved here. They do lobster rolls, *the* best salted-caramel brownie ever. Weekends there's a live band. You're very welcome to—"

"No, thank you."

Had Megan heard that correctly?

"So that's everything, then. Enjoy your new home," she said, but didn't mean.

Glacial, Megan thought of Mrs. Lambert. And just rude. On the way home, in the car, she would cry. And not having a reason to speak with Jack Mathews again was a big part of it. She might even take the purse back to the store.

5

SUBJECT: STOP THE WORLD, JACK'S BACK

From: Elizabeth Lambert
To: Jack Mathews
Date: Sunday April 19, 2020 at 11:46

Living by the sea, wife, kids, car business—all your dreams came true! You want to know more about my life, huh? For the last twenty years I've been building up Lambert Interiors (brochure attached—I can also give you a special price!). My business is based in London though not for long, thanks Brexit, but we live in Paris, yes, I speak French but my favorite language is Japanese which I learnt working in Tokyo and since lockdown have been brushing up on, thanks, Duolingo!

I'm married to a French guy, Bruno. We have one daughter, Cosima, who's 10 years old. She's an angel except when she's fencing! My husband's family have a hotel in Aix-en-Provence that Bruno runs and we are blessed with a holiday home nearby which is where we are right now. The three of us stuck in a Paris apartment would be unbearable!

Jack, I guess you worked out that I stole your $2400 college savings. Now I'm in a position to pay you back and today's equivalent is around $6000. Please send your bank details so I can make that transfer.

Je t'embrasse. Stay safe.
Elizabeth xx

———

WITH THE CORNER of her skirt, Elizabeth wiped a smear of cleaning fluid from the corner of the sill. How could Megan have missed that?

She took off her sandals and stepped onto the lawn as little birds sprang back to their nests.

Home ground.

Sunday evening.

Jack had said he'd tell Jude over the weekend, but the weekend was almost over—almost. There was still time.

The rushing sound of the plane's engine was still in Elizabeth's head, and for a moment, she missed the estate agent's chatter and tuberose perfume.

Elizabeth's toes combed through the sticky grass. Her fingers spread out as if steadied by invisible threads. She breathed it all in: the cooling pines, birdsong, hills turning the color of moths' wings, and breathed it all out: the stuffy airplane, traffic, Megan's inane patter, her disappointment that Jack hadn't been there to meet her and her fear that he never would.

Lungs full. Lungs empty.

She should shower, change into the new silk pajamas she'd bought. Brush her teeth again.

A volt of electricity nearly lifted her off the ground when she heard the double beep of a text message.

> You put the fucking little dog in my car. Very dangerous and he shit on my tennis racket.

Elizabeth saw herself on a world map with a big red arrow pointing down at her—Paloma Drive. Felicidad, San Diego, California, USA: *You Are Here.*

But where is Jack?

6

SUBJECT: FRIENDS REUNITED

From: Jack Mathews

To: Elizabeth Lambert

Date: Monday April 20, 2020 at 7:52

I always hoped you were out there, somewhere, making beautiful things and doing mermaid stuff, but your website! Wowzer!!! Those places are extraordinary! I'm gonna send you some pix of cars I've worked on over the years. I'm not much of a house guy but I built our sun deck and a skating ramp for Bentley but the neighbors complained about the noise so he wasn't allowed to use it. Gonna write more later but it's Monday morning so I gotta jump on Zoom for our Team Meeting. Can you work those goddam break-out rooms? Don't worry about the money, please! Just buy me a drink next time you're in California. That's if there's a way out of the apocalypse. Another thing: cause we're all using the same computer at home and everything's kinda linked up to my family, hope it's OK if we continue using this old work email you found me on? Found some of your modelling shots! AND you wrote two books??? Got them coming from Amazon!!! You too stay safe island girl xxx

———

"Guess where I'm calling from?" Elizabeth asked. "Jack?"

After what sounded like a torrent of air and the jangle of keys, he cleared his throat the way he often did before they spoke. Jack's sneaky peep through the curtains before stepping onto their stage. It wasn't the noise in her eardrum that irritated her as much as the fact she still scared him.

"Hey," he said, before grating his larynx again.

"Guess where I'm calling from?"

"Huh?"

"Where. Am. I. Calling from?"

It didn't sound so cute the third time around.

"San Diego?"

"No… Paloma Heights!"

"I thought you were gonna stay in San Diego a day or two before coming down?"

Elizabeth trained her ears on the crunch of his footsteps on dry grass.

"You didn't get my texts?" she asked. "Megan picked me up from the airport."

"She's a doll, ain't she?"

"She can talk. Gave me a migraine." Elizabeth blew out her cheeks. "I thought you'd be there."

"Wish I coulda … there to … but … here…"

"You're breaking up." Elizabeth stabbed her toe into the earth—she couldn't bear speaking to people who didn't give her their full attention. "You've never been nearer but you sound miles away."

"So you like the house? That cactus out front is crazy, huh?"

"I haven't even been up to the bedroom yet, I was kinda hoping—"

"You checked out the lights in the shower room?"

"You sound like Megan. So, you coming over or what? I mean, you're only twenty-four years late."

"Thing is, I'm not in Feliz. I'm like eighty miles north at the cabin. That's why the reception's so lousy."

Breathe out. Maybe he'd told his wife and was now waiting out in the mountains like an exiled bandito.

"How did it go, telling her?"

She heard a branch snapping under his foot.

"Who?"

"Your wife."

"It's a holiday weekend. And... and tonight's... complicated."

"Complicated?"

"It's been emotional for her being here since her mom passed, and see, there's a lot of stuff needs doing—the electrics are crazy, you wouldn't believe! And our dog turned ten. But like in the evenings Jude swims across the lake—it's her *thing* —and someone has to help her out of the water 'cause the steps down from the jetty are very loose, I didn't have time to repair them. Probably best I skip the Sunday night traffic and hit town tomorrow morning." Elizabeth heard a dog bark and Jack whispering, "Wait. Just wait now..."

"You talking to me or the dog?"

"Tip lost his present, this rubber 'pizza' thing we—*I*— found. It actually smells of... still there? Hey, I'm gonna be over real soon to be near my sexiest neighbor. It's just—"

"When?"

"Okay, so Monday we have our team meeting, then I have to collect an engine in the city. Tuesday and Wednesday I'm in Chula Vista, then—"

"Just to get this straight, you haven't mentioned anything to your wife, have you? Like at *all*?"

Jack spoke before his throat had fully cleared so the 'Not exactly' came out as a croak.

"So you've said *something*?"

"I already explained this to you. I'm drip feeding the information. I know what I'm doing. I'll tell her when we're back in Felicidad and then I'll be right over. Babe?"

"OK, but... I was thinking, I'd like to meet somewhere completely new, somewhere neither of us has ever been."

"So you don't like the house."

"I do, but, I want a honeymoon."

"My crazy girl!"

"I have a friend who goes to a great spa hotel on the coast. I'll ask for the name."

"Aren't spas for women and gay guys? Nothing 'gainst

either, just—hey, it's a great idea. Thursday I gotta open up Kids Call and I've a bunch of stuff to—"

"I don't want to put you out."

"No, no, you're not, it's just—"

"I'll book something up. Something with 'free cancellation'."

"Gotcha."

Elizabeth rolled her eyes to herself because she was the only one in the couple who appreciated irony.

"No contact till you're ready, I mean it, Jack, I—"

A cough. A click. And he was gone.

7

SUBJECT: UR A STAR & I'M STRUCK!

From: Jack Mathews

To: Elizabeth Lambert

Date: Tuesday April 21, 2020 at 14:45

I have to admit something or I'll feel a little creepy—for an afternoon I forgot about the world collapsing around us and read up on you. You're one amazing lady! How's Danny? Ur mom? My dad left for Tampa with mom's bridge partner. She never got over it, then 5 yrs ago she got Alzheimers. In a home now. You ever track down your real dad? Aimee's just finished her last class so we're gonna walk our dog. Always, Jack xxx

———

"HE HASN'T TOLD HER." Magnus sighed, the arch of his bald head filling the top half of Elizabeth's iPad screen.

"Tomorrow. Monday. In the morning."

"Oh, he's put that down in his diary, has he? Well, check it's not written in pencil."

"Stop it!" Elizabeth giggled, nibbling at a cuticle.

"Just saying, Tits. He's had a few years now, but whatever. Helena, don't shake your umbrella inside the office. Jeepers-creepers—don't tell me those are crossed swords on the wall behind you?"

"It's 'Hacienda style'."

"There's an oxymoron for you." Magnus clicked his fingers at one of the girls. "Where's Emily with the samples? And Pinks are outside trying to make the delivery, get down there. Now. So when's the big Jack-reveal day?"

"Friday. At the hotel."

Magnus lowered his voice. "Well if he's a no-show you can comfort yourself with a facial and God knows you need to eat something, little bird, there's nothing on you."

"Can you ask Emily to double check the reservations?"

"Remind me why *you're* booking and paying for a dirty weekend?"

"I want it to be just us, no distractions, no stuff. And it's romantic."

"Hope so, duckie-doodle." Magnus lowered his voice, "Any news on your father?"

Elizabeth licked where she'd caused her finger to bleed. "I'll get more info from my aunt, apparently she has intel."

"Meanwhile, I'm not feeling good about the Sapphire Group renewing. Word is they also asked Davinka to submit along with two others, my spies are sniffing around their underpants right now."

"Can we schedule a team meeting for tomorrow afternoon to prep this? Do we have anyone on the inside who could give us a heads-up on Davinka's ideas?"

"On it. Meanwhile send over the 3D plans of Lady Bevan's home."

"I made some final adjustments on the plane, but they're ready."

Magnus began unwrapping an iced donut.

"You're already sounding American, come back before the wind changes. By the way, I'm going for drinks at Belgrave Square tonight, I have to show her something. Lady Bevan wants it all done by the time they get back from St Kitts." Elizabeth loved Magnus too much to let his rampant snobbishness irk her.

"Did we hear back from that barber's in Shoreditch?"

Elizabeth dreaded the call ending and being left alone with

the sound of laughter from the pool party going on next door, but more than anything, the piercing, pulsing terror that she might have masterfully and enthusiastically engineered her own downfall.

"No. Hipsters, what d'you expect," Magnus answered, lapping the sugar from his fingers and tossing his cup into the wastepaper basket. "Take a sleeping pill. Big sloppy kiss."

8

SUBJECT: MISTY WATER-COLORED MEMORIES

From: Elizabeth Lambert

To: Jack Mathews

Date: Wednesday April 22, 2020 at 3:47

Over two decades and 30,000 miles between us but I feel so close to you. Yes, I've traveled to many beautiful places but sometimes it's like only the backdrop's changed and I never stopped being that gawky trailer-park kid, just got better at faking it. You were right about my life being a fairy tale, too like a fairy tale, dark side and all. You asked about my sweet, special half-brother, Danny. The night I left Catalina, he went to live with his dad in Oregon, (a guy my mom had got pregnant from in rehab). But we'd kept in touch over the years. The last time we spoke was the night I was celebrating my engagement to Bruno. I was 24, in Paris, so nervous to impress Bruno's friends, we were leaving for a club when I picked up my clutch purse that cost all my savings and saw Danny's number on my phone screen. I didn't want to answer but another part of me longed to share my news with family. But Dan was calling with good news —he'd been sentenced to a state penitentiary rather than a federal prison. I put the phone down as he was saying he wanted to see the Eiffel Tower. A few days later, aunt Maribeth phoned to say he'd overdosed the night before jail.

It really meant a lot that you remembered that gentle soul. As for my mom, I never saw after that night in Catalina but I heard she died in a trailer fire. Remember that low-life husband of hers, Vince? When Maribeth called to ask about a funeral he said there was no point as she'd already cremated herself. Funny guy.

Your over-sharing friend, Elizabeth xxx

———

ELIZABETH HAD FALLEN asleep on the loveseat, phone in hand looking at photos of Cosima. She stretched and went back inside the house to put a sweater on. While running over how to phrase an email to a client, Elizabeth made a pot of matcha tea and broke into the family pack of Swiss chocolate she bought at Duty Free forgetting that she no longer had that kind of family.

Jack had that kind of family.

To crack the jet lag she had to push past midnight so she sat on the sofa scrolling through TikTok reels, willing Jack to drive over, save this day. There was still time.

Half waiting, half dozing, Elizabeth could hear the wild dogs scratching through the trash and the kids next door kicking a deflated ball in front of the Anaheim trailer park where she'd lived with her mother and brother. Elizabeth had already been up drinking a glass of lemon juice—a beauty tip she'd picked up in a magazine—when her mother swung her bedroom door open and took unsteady steps towards her. She put two hands against the wall as if about to be frisked, swallowed fast to stop herself throwing up. Queenie made an 'urgh' sound in her throat, wincing at unspecified pains. The tilt of her chin let Elizabeth know she was still drunk from the night before. Her hair was a self-assembled lump of tumbleweed, her eyes were sealed by clumps of mascara and a white paste collected itself at either side of her mouth.

People called her Queenie because she'd once fronted a punk band, Queen Mab but now she sang Country covers in bars and sometimes events. But no singing that morning, though. Vince had introduced her to crack cocaine only a few months before and already her skin was pitted with scabby craters and the bristles of her toothbrush were dyed red from her bleeding gums.

'Say hello to Mrs. Rufflington.'

'Who's Mrs. Rufflington?'

'You're lookin' at her. Las Vegas. Pass me those beers. Why aren't you at school?'

'It's Saturday.'

'Already?'

A beer can in each hand, *Mrs. Rufflington* sloped back to the bedroom in a long Snoopy T-shirt she'd worn since she was a teenager.

'Gonna consummate this thing or what?'

Elizabeth was outside the trailer, sanding down a cabinet she'd dragged from a dumpster. The site had been one of the longest places they'd ever stayed—three years—and in that time she'd set up a little workshop in the shade of a willow tree revamping furniture she'd found in the trash or garage sales. Recently people had started bringing stuff to her to repair or revamp—découpage, tortoiseshell veneers or neon glosses, rewiring or framing, she took on whatever was offered. Twice she'd negotiated a free month's rent after upholstering a few of the trailers.

Vince took a piss. He never flushed. Elizabeth heard the click of her mother's Zippo lighting his first joint of the day. The smoke twirled past her as he blew rings into her hair. Elizabeth fixed her eyes on the sign for 'FunTimes Trailers' though these days, since Vince had appeared in their lives, had been anything but fun.

Elizabeth felt Vince's big toe nudging itself between her buttocks and the doorstep. He lowered the joint to her lips, tapped her shoulder with his wrist. She shrugged his hand away, trying not to breathe in the smoke and his cheap cologne. He brushed the back of his fingers over her shoulder. 'Say, good morning, *Daddy*.' He stroked the top of her head as he chased down a glob of mucus. 'And get packing 'cause we're going on our honeymoon to Catalina Island.'

9
SUBJECT: HEARTBROKEN

From: Jack Mathews

To: Elizabeth Lambert

Date: Friday April 24, 2020 at 11:46

I'm heartbroken to hear about Danny and honored you trusted me with his story. That morning when I got back to Catalina from Newport Beach and you weren't there is still the worst day of my life. You were younger but way more experienced than me so I kept asking myself, was I a terrible kisser? My dad and the guys went all over the island searching for you but you, your mom, Vince and Danny had just disappeared. The manager of the club where your mom sang warned us not to go to the police cause of all the crazy stuff Vince was mixed up in. I never told Dad about the missing money, said I'd lost it on a dud car. Every day I thought you'd call or come find me and eventually I believed that for whatever reason, you didn't want to be found. Sometimes, I feared the worst. Ten years ago I sold a car to Al who's now one of my best buddies. His daughter ran away from home and ended up murdered, he dealt with his pain by setting up a call center for kids who need to talk, 'Kids Call'. That's what I do every Thursday night—now it's lockdown the calls are diverted to our phones so someone can answer any time, day or night. One of the reasons I did it is because I thought maybe you or Danny would call. Pasta boiling over, gotta go.

JUDE WIPED the kitchen counter with a damp dishcloth, stopping to scratch at a triangle of onion skin grafted onto the side of the work surface, reloading, over and over, the conversation she'd just had with Jack.

'I might not be back for a while.'

'How long?'

'I need to pick up a part down south, play some golf and think and—since when d'you need to sign off on my timetable, for Chrissakes!'

'I'm just asking where you'll be.'

'I don't know. Al's, maybe. Or an Airbnb.'

'Will you pick Beanie up from hip hop Friday?'

'Of course.'

'So you'll be back for the weekend?'

'No. Yes. I can't say.'

Jude had tried to catch Jack's eye, slow him down as he fitted his phone and wallet in his pockets and grasped on to the straps of a holdall.

'What's going on?'

'I said, I'm just not sure I want to be in this marriage anymore.'

Jack had opened out his palms to Jude, exasperated, as though she were forcing him to repeatedly explain something very simple—but this was the first she'd heard of it. Sunday, he'd suggested they try for another kid and then Tuesday morning these words came out of nowhere, like the overnight bag: pre-packed and stashed under the stairs.

The dishcloth in her hand was heating up with the energy of spores multiplying at an excitable rate. The mitosis stink traveled up her arm and accumulated in her chest until she threw the cloth into the sink and rinsed her hands with hot water. Was he saying their marriage was over? Shouldn't there have been an end? Or had they been living in it so long she hadn't noticed the scenery change?

Jude ached to call her mother, hear that mischievous, rasping voice ask, *Jujinsky, what's up, baby?*

What *was* up?

Marriage is a machine made up of so many parts. There's always a reason to check, to tinker, replace what was worn.

Jack, who salvaged broken vehicles for a living, of all people should know that. And they were vintage now! This was the time to applaud: they'd seen the babies through to adult life, ridden out the recession, a pandemic, Jack had only just finished building the Lantern pergola—he'd called it her Taj Mahal. They'd superseded all their parents' aspirations and seen two of them sifted into cremation urns. They'd nursed many of their friends through cancer, bankruptcy, divorce, alcoholism, all kinds of stuff. *Jack 'n' Jude*: always there, together, the constant, the example that two people could make a marriage work. If she'd repeated to anyone what Jack had just said, no one would have believed it. No one.

Marriage is a machine—how did theirs get broken?

10

SUBJECT: LOST SOULS

From: Elizabeth Lambert

To: Jack Mathews

Date: Saturday April 25, 2020 at 18:05

Hate to think what you found out about me on the internet! So cringe hearing me sound deep about fabric linings and toilet holders but I gotta say, if you want more lifestyle porn, check out my friend Céline's house in St Barthes!

So it was you who bought my books! The first book, A Crazy American Girl in Paris came out of a blog I was writing the year we were refurbishing our Paris apartment. In AmeriZen I wanted to define my style and how it relates to my travels in Japan. At least this lockdown is giving me the chance to work on something new.

Jack, you helping kids like Danny touched me so much. I also founded an organization to provide grants for art schools for under-privileged students. I hope in some way his suffering wasn't for nothing.

That singing mermaid again xx

PS You were anything but a lousy kisser ;)

———

TUESDAY MORNING after the long weekend and Jude still had *life* to do. Normally she and Aimee went in together but as she had an 11'o clock meeting on 'Security in the School Environment' in San Diego, she planned to leave from home. It struck her that her change in routine might have taken Jack by surprise, possibly why he'd been so shifty, defensive. But the weekend at the cabin… Had it been a parting gift? A homemade pastiche of perimenopausal romance to buoy her up while he decided whether to sign up for another quarter of a century of marriage? The last seventy-two hours had been some of the best they'd had in years. Saturday, they'd walked the dog before settling down on a blanket for a picnic lunch and, after a little too much fresh air and wine, Jack had covered them with his jacket, put his hands down her jeans and they'd made love, intense— discreet—so as not to be seen by hikers or Tip who tended to get overexcited at those moments. She'd slept on his chest until he'd nudged her awake to see a double-crested cormorant on the lake. After that, they'd headed back to her mother's cabin, all the time talking about changes they'd make to the place. Sunday evening, when Jude had returned from her sunset swim, Jack had waited for her with a towel he'd warmed on the rocks. He'd urged her to stay over Sunday night so he could check the flue and build a fire while she graded papers—never had he mentioned booking an Airbnb and needing time out to work on his backswing.

His leftover orange juice swilled down the sink, Jude picked up the damn dishcloth again, and wiped the table, half punching it as if to obliterate the morning and get back to last Sunday when Jack had cooked them breakfast and defrosted the freezer, he'd even used a hairdryer and cotton buds to clean out the corners of the ice compartment—not exactly the actions of a prisoner planning his escape.

The dishwasher clunked and churned with the plates they'd used for dinner the night before. A perfectly typical evening— they'd FaceTimed Preston, checked over Aimee's homework, and she'd spent the last of the daylight watering some of the newly repotted plants. Is that when he'd packed his bag?

The dishwasher went from a smooth hum to a grind. What had Jack been saying of late: 'Sweatpants again, Juju?' Grind. Grind, grind. The *You nevers*, the *You always*, the *Why don't yous*...? The paper cuts on the skin of their marriage, or had these lesions been signs of something more malignant?

Jude used the banister to lever herself up the stairs to the bedroom, her lips moving as she talked through what she had to do next.

Getting dressed was something she did quickly, like after a doctor's examination, and her clothing choices were less about what was fashionable or flattering and more about what wouldn't dig in, pinch, or show up sweat patches. She'd whole-heartedly adopted the elasticated waistbands of lockdown and still wasn't ready to shift back to the fuss of belts, zippers and buttons.

Later that afternoon there was a committee meeting with the school site team, after that, interviews, more late admissions, and not forgetting her AP science class for which she still had twenty-four papers to grade. Then there was Grace Mitchell's retirement party where she'd be expected to say a little something—

Back downstairs with another coffee, Jude lugged her workbag onto the dining-room table. In the middle of pulling out the folder she needed, she stopped. Jack would never have said those things, he'd never even packed his own case before and he had never left without kissing her goodbye. Jack Mathews hadn't left: he'd been stolen.

11

SUBJECT: PAINTIN' THEM
GRAY SKIES BLUE

From: Jack Mathews

To: Elizabeth Lambert

Date: Tuesday April 28, 2020 at 2:06

…is what I'm doing with a hot little Mercedes-Benz I picked up at the weekend. This is going to be a pet project for me while I'm still not able to open the garage. Just ordered Aimee and me a sushi lunch. Yup, I'm starting to like the stuff mostly coz with every bite, I think of you. I'm really a burritos guy but maki isn't bad, better with ketchup though 😋

———

THEY KNUCKLE BUMPED, Jack and Al, over the phones at Kids Call, in the makeshift counseling center at the back of the Organic Orgasm, a New Age store run by Al's girlfriend, Tammy.

"Bro, we need to talk. She's here," Jack whispered out of earshot of two trainees on another table. "Arrived Sunday when Jude and I were away for the weekend."

Al rolled a chilled Coke can over to his friend. "Oh boy."

"Friday we meet at a hotel on the coast, Elizabeth wants us to have, like, this vacation together. There's a spa, room service…"

"You forget you're married, dude?"

"It's all I think about."

"Jude's been calling Tammy. I'm feeling pretty sleazy knowing stuff, I told you already, I won't be a repository for other people's secrets."

"Jude's giving me space to think. I'm gonna head out to the cabin now and, after the weekend, Jude and I will talk."

Al opened his pouch of tobacco on the tabletop, pinched out a clump of tarnished fibers.

"So when you're tired of getting your rocks off, the 'little mermaid' just high dives back into the ocean, that it?"

One of the advantages of the Kids Call offices was that Jack could use their computers to write to Elizabeth. Once, Al had read the line *Good morning, Little Mermaid* over Jack's shoulder, after that, the name had stuck, though when Al said it, the inflection wasn't affectionate.

"Nothing's happened *yet*. You could still back out of this."

One of the trainees looked up at him from her sudoku puzzle, so he had to whisper. "But she's *here*. Now. The timing's awful. Jude has prize giving and the budget meeting and—what?"

"I'm laughing 'cause it sounds like you actually expect your girlfriend to check your wife's appointment diary for a convenient time to destroy her entire world!"

"Just saying, I need more time."

"You've had years, and now peony girl is up there in the Heights good to go. No judgment, but the only person you owe anything to is Jude. Still comin' in Thursday?"

Jack nodded as Al tossed his unlit roll-up into his mouth and headed out back to smoke it.

12

SUBJECT: KER-CHING!

From: Jack Mathews

To: Elizabeth Lambert

Date: Wednesday May 6, 2020 at 6:36

Ker-ching! Why? Coz I all ready sold four cars this week—just when I thought I never would again! On top of that, a guy came by with a piece of junk that looked like it'd been buried in a sand dune—people had finger-drawn cocks on every window but hey, only 35k on the clock. He wanted a quick sale so he could make it to his family before they close the borders. Gonna clean it up and sell it to a lady friend of mine who's looking for something for her daughter's 21st b-day. T-Bird—that's Traci, my assistant—she's gonna find a red ribbon to tie a bow around it to surprise the girl. Why isn't the world a better place when doing good feels so great? While I was waiting on the phone ordering parts I did some more deep internet research into the life of Elizabeth Lambert. Love that picture of you meditating with Steve Jobs in Kyoto. Respect! Your no.1 fan, Jack xxx

———

OFF FELIZ CENTRAL PARKWAY, on Pine Street and West 10th Avenue, where toilet-brush palms rustled over a wide road that circled back to the freeway, behind advertising panels for domestic appliances and discount warehouses, was a board on which six faces formed a corona around a picture of Jack

Mathews grinning with dazzling teeth and sky-blue eyes. *Mathews Motors. Don't let buying a car drive you crazy!*

The Uber rolled away from Elizabeth, leaving her alone on the forecourt that Jack walked across every day. She'd imagined his life so often, and now, these were his diesel fumes, the cars he had bought and hoped to sell, the dream team he called his *family elect*. She walked passed the 'Diagnostic Lab' and a washed-out sign showing the team in medical coats and stethoscopes surrounding a vintage rally car, entitled, 'Intensive Car Unit!'

This was the life he had chosen instead of being with her.

Elizabeth's eyes adjusted to the dark space of Mathews Motors.

A woman well-past retirement age, dressed in tight black lace apart from fluorescent yellow pumps trotted out from a back room.

"Yeah?" Must be Marcie, Jack's secretary. The one he called the Licorice Stick. The one who couldn't even take the simplest message. "Can I help you, ma'am?" she asked, tossing back her mauve braids.

"I'm looking to buy a car."

"Let's see... a car? A car... huh? I don't know about that... Just kidding!" She managed a low growl of a laugh while chomping down on a piece of chewing gum. "Bentley! Bentley." She grinned. "See that's his name." Elizabeth and the receptionist waited for someone to appear. "Shame he's not as fast as a Bentley! Hold on a—" Marcie took ostrich-like strides across the showroom floor.

When Jack had described the car showroom, Elizabeth's imagination had superimposed the white marble expanse from where Bruno used to trade-in their cars. Jack had once joked about how the place could do with a makeover but Elizabeth had never pictured how badly. She caught the eye of a man in a string-vest and shorts with hair like black onyx whose arms and legs were black with tattoos. Draxx, thought Elizabeth. And there was Ramirez, Elizabeth laughed to herself, Ramirez with the lisp and nine kids. She looked around for Traci, and the one called 'Good-Looking'.

"Here he is," said Marcie, retreating to the back office.

"I'd like to buy that car."

Elizabeth squinted at Bentley, seeing double: a clammy, chubby boy with thin lips and dirty feet in flip flops, but at the same time, the jawline, the shape of his eyes were Jack's at eighteen, the age they'd met in Catalina.

"The Mercedes 190SL?"

Elizabeth nodded, her focus away from the scree of blackheads pitting the sides of his nose.

"She's on reserve, but I can show you something else."

"I want that one."

Bentley crossed his large arms over his chest. "It's kinda not for sale is what I'm saying."

13
SUBJECT: OUR STORY

From: Jack Mathews
To: Elizabeth Lambert
Date: Friday May 8, 2020 at 5:46

Your books arrived today! I wanted to rip the packages open and lick every photo (of you!!!) but I'm waiting for some quiet time to get down to studying! It got me thinking maybe I should write something about the life of a used-car dealer. There are so many tips 'n' tricks I could teach people, what d'you think? Gotta go, it's poker night with the guys tonite—don't worry— all online now.

———

BENTLEY CHECKED her driver's license, the sinews in his biceps jumped under a tight anthracite T-shirt. No smile lines creased those gun-metal eyes.

"Know much 'bout vintage cars?" The boy's top lip pinched up into his front teeth, he'd tell her anyway. "That particular SL190 is a 1.9-liter engine with inline four cylinders, SOHC. All matching numbers and she's only done 29,109 miles in sixty years." He waited for her to show she was paying attention before going on. "She's a collector's car. My dad's been working on her a long time." Elizabeth continued to stare ahead at him. "But," he let his two palms drop to the table, "if that's what the lady wants." With a sniff, his fingers slid into the thatch of hair that formed an overhanging ledge over his forehead.

While the boy pressed one index finger over each letter key —possibly the same keyboard on which Jack composed most of his emails to her, Elizabeth listened to an instrumental version of *Grease* being piped through the speakers. It was the jet lag, not having eaten and the smell of gasoline mixed with floor bleach that made her feel nauseous. It was also the boy. The clash of arrogance against having absolutely nothing to justify it. Jack had once said that his sons would be like big brothers to Cosie but all she could imagine were her daughter's little bones being crushed between those knuckled jaws.

"The carburetors are dual Solex, she has a four-speed manual. You can trace her history back to the first purchase and its 1962 registration. Mr. Mathews actually met the grandson who was selling it. This car comes with the build sheet, the original owner's manual and the Mercedes sales brochures. This was someone's baby. Same money but for some bite you got the Ford Shelby GT500, a two-door coupé with a 5.4-liter, supercharged eight-cylinder engine and a six-speed manual transmission, or there's a cute two-year-old Porsche 911." He dug the end of a biro into a block of Post-it notes.

"I love the colors, the blue and red."

"The 'colors'. Gotcha. How wide d'you think the tires are? They're 6.50-13. Those, ma'am, are Coker classics. See at Mathews Motors, we restore to the highest specifications. You saw the tinted sun visors, Becker radio and the undercarriage— not a scratch. Mr. Mathews spent almost a year matching the hubcaps and the trim rings. What kind of finance plan are you looking at?"

"Cash."

Bentley dropped back into his seat, patted the chair arms.

"Planning on any trips?" asked Bentley. "You said you were here on vacation—news to me we have tourists in Felicidad. Mission beach, Pacific beach, La Jolla, but... here?"

"From what I've seen so far, it's a beautiful town with very friendly people."

"You've not been here long. You work out?"

"I have a personal trainer back home."

"Thought so," he said. "Your arms."

Marcie appeared at the door.

"Bentley? Your dad—I mean, Mr. Mathews—just called. He's at an auction till late afternoon. He said whatever you do don't sell the Mercedes."

"Too bad. Just sold."

Marcie and Elizabeth covered their ears at the sound of a car alarm piercing through the room.

"Jeez! What's that noise?"

Bentley picked up his phone.

"Who has a ringtone like that? Good lord!" Marcie cried as Bentley connected his phone.

"Not right now. I'm with a client." The tone was unmistakably one of a teenage son with his mother. "Uh. Marcie said. She *said*. Auction then driving details to a client..." Elizabeth felt her skin sticking to the plastic chair under her. "No, I said I'm—" Bentley cut the call before tapping rapidly at the keyboard.

Elizabeth could feel the heat from Marcie's breath against her cheek. "We've spoken on the phone a few times, right?" Elizabeth's heart jump-started. "I recognize your accent."

"They call it 'transatlantic'. I'm actually from California."

"Love those shoes," said Marcie.

"Hope I can drive in them."

"Marcie, Mrs. Lambert's taking the Merc."

"*Fay-lee-si-ta-ssi-yons*! Ain't that French for *mazeltov*? That car's a hot little number. Lotta people don't know what car is right for them. You read *Getting to Know you, Getting to Love You?*" Elizabeth shook her head. "See, I'm just here helping Mr. Matthews out but actually, I'm a life coach. Here's my card if you want a discovery session—first half-hour's free."

A blonde girl in a white suit stood in the doorway with her arms crossed against her chest.

"Traci, get me the keys for the 190SL."

"Mr. Mathews said no one was to take that car."

"Keys, Traci."

"Aren't those the keys?" She pointed at a small plastic bag containing two car keys attached by a piece of string. Bentley slapped his hands over the keys, afraid she'd grab them first but Traci was already out the door.

"Traci says females should only be taken out by other ladies 'cause a... toxic wokism and stuff, but you're OK with me, right? Not gonna sue or nothin'?"

14

SUBJECT: MY VERY OWN
SUPERHERO!

From: Elizabeth Lambert

To: Jack Mathews

Date: Sunday May 10, 2020 at 15:46

I love the sound of your life and your family are beautiful. Hope that's not weird—it was either

that or Worldometer! Oh Jack, since we've reconnected, I've been talking to you ALL THE

TIME in my head. So much to say. But can't write more as need to log into Cosie's virtual

piano practice. Keep making this crazy world a better place, Elizabeth xx

PS You really never worked out why I took off that night?

―――――

"WHEN YOU WANNA TAKE over the wheel, just say. OK. So here's Orange Park. And that's a skate park, there. I came 9th in the San Diego under 16s. Type my name in YouTube and you can see me. Shoulda been 5th. And my mom's the principal here. It was a dump before, now it's, like, OK."

Elizabeth examined the fake-Corinthian pillars and fluttering sign: *Orange Park High School.*

He slowed at the traffic lights and grinned, bearing a line of straight white teeth: evidence of his parents' commitment. Elizabeth too had a perfect smile, but it'd cost her the same as a small apartment and the best part of six months of her adult life.

"I'll show you a different side of San Diego, different from what you're used to anyways."

Leaving the town's center, Bentley passed signs for the Interstate before hitting rows of soot-fronted houses and burnt-out cars. A lot of dry grass and then a creek until they came to rows of houses with front yards and basketball hoops and signs to slow down your speed.

"I live down there," he said, pointing vaguely at tree-lined street. "Now she's nicely warmed up, you could drive from here. You OK?"

"I need to eat. How about we stop at a grocery store, buy food and you drive me home?"

They sat by Elizabeth's pool. Bentley, hunched over his plate like he was about to play the bongos with his cutlery.

"This place is incredible. I can't believe you have someone to cook for you," he said, his mouth even fuller this time with salami and ham. She picked at her alfalfa and avocado. "I'm on the Paleo diet—I only eat what men ate between two and a half million to ten thousand years ago. I also weight train twice a day. If you want, I can take you to my gym."

"Don't you have to be back at work?"

"Dad's away till Thursday. Traci's in charge, or she *thinks* she is."

"You don't like Traci."

"T-Bird? She treats me like I'm just the boss's son, which I am, I get that, but I been working there since I was fourteen, weekends, every vacation. She's in love with Dad."

"She is? And does your father like her?"

"Not like *that*, no way." His mouth twisted up like the knot in a party balloon. "Dad wouldn't look at another woman but Mom."

"They'd never separate?"

"Hell no! Actually, they're thinking of adopting a Ukrainian baby."

Bentley looked up from his tower of salami. "Feel better?

Sometimes you look spacey, but most of the time, you're very beautiful, Mrs. Lambert. Can I ask what you're doing here in Feliz?"

Elizabeth searched the low-lying clouds over Felicidad.

"Coming face to face with what I dread most."

Bentley shrugged. "Whassat?"

"Being 'underwhelmed'."

He put down his knife and fork and said, "Welcome to my world."

For the first time since arriving in America, she laughed.

Elizabeth noticed him staring into her lap, she stroked her upper thighs.

Bentley's eyes watered from not letting himself blink in case he missed a second of her moving her hips in slow circles.

"Those shorts are getting pretty tight."

Bentley swallowed with difficulty. "I haven't had a boner for 'bout six months. I thought it was the medication."

Elizabeth took a sip of her drink as a message appeared on her phone:

Mermaid – ready to start this thing or what?

"I have a meeting. Esme will show you out."

15

SUBJECT: I'M SORRY

From: Jack Mathews

To: Elizabeth Lambert

Date: Wednesday May 13, 2020 at 11:42

I guessed you took off because I hadn't been honest with you about Jude. I'd only just started dating her before I met you. I was a dumb, immature idiot and shoulda said something.

————

JACK HAD PLANNED that the moment he cut himself loose from his marriage, he'd go up to the cabin and take his boat out on the lake. So that's where he was when he tapped out the text to Elizabeth before lying back on the deck, staring up at the sleek new leaves.

A breeze nudged Jude's sunhat perched on top of a garden shovel like a low-flying UFO. She'd taken it off, handed it to him on Monday evening before gliding into the water. He'd stood there, waving her off, restraining himself from jumping in and pushing her out of sight. Just as she'd started picking up speed past the neighbor's dried-out willow tree, Jack leapt down, sprinted back through the driveway and climbed to the clearing which had the best phone reception to see if Elizabeth had landed. Elizabeth had wanted to tell him all about her trip and, of course, hear when he was coming over. He'd needed to get her off the phone as fast as possible without a scene so he could be back at the jetty by the time Jude appeared at the reeds on her return journey. He'd only just made it. The moment his wife was in sight, languidly swimming back, he was there with a fresh towel, wearing her sun hat and swinging his legs, Tip by his side. He even added a sleepy gaze, like, *Oh, there you are.* Sometimes he wanted to *whoop!* out loud because he was so proud of himself for pulling off these stunts. It was such a shame that no one was around to congratulate him on his tactical planning and fine execution, let alone the acting. Jack pondered on how sad it was that probably most people's best feats are never seen by others.

'Not every girl has her own personal lifeguard,' he'd whispered in Jude's ear, leaving a kiss on her cool shoulder where her skin was a galaxy of freckles; a reminder of the time she was seven and her father had taken her out to sea on his boat, got drunk, knocked himself unconscious and she'd had to steer the two of them back to the harbor before being taken to hospital for burns.

"Finally," said Elizabeth, an unreadable expression on the face filling Jack's phone screen. Well, unreadable to him.

"How about finally and *forever*, mermaid?"

"Not long enough."

And now she was smiling.

"Friday night, babe, I'm gonna—"

"Marcie's a character."

"Marcie? You met Marcie?"

"Didn't you promise me a car? I needed wheels, so I thought I'd save you some time and go pick it up myself."

"You went to my *work*?"

"Uh-huh. Wasn't a problem, was it?"

He had that feeling again—he was burning the bridges faster than he could ever get across them.

Now she'd stopped smiling.

"'Course not. Just feels weird you turning up there, anyone could've been there."

"Like your wife? The one you're adopting a baby with?"

Jack lunged forward.

"You met Bentley? Bentley—my *son*?"

"Why not? Your marriage is over, right?"

"The baby thing, I told you Jude was crazy."

Jack lent back into the creaking wicker chair. He wanted to talk to playful kitten Elizabeth, not this out-for-blood tiger.

"Am I supposed to just wait around for you in the shadows like I did in Catalina?"

"No, it's just... I was gonna give you the car, as a gift. I wanted to surprise you with it."

"I don't like surprises."

He wasn't wild about them either so Elizabeth springing up at the garage was doing crazy things to his blood pressure.

"Well thank you, ma'am, now I can say I made a sale!"

"Bentley's cash sale. And he earned it, took me for a drive around your 'hood, even helped me buy groceries."

It wasn't the first time he questioned how dangerous Elizabeth could be. Possible bunny boiler. You hear these stories, right?

"When we meet, how do you want me to kiss you—or should I just shake your hand, like you're a new client?"

She giggled, and he could breathe again now they were back on the road to their twenty minutes of kisses back and forth until a conference call took Elizabeth away.

Jack cracked open a beer, stretched his feet up on the porch, and toasted his new life. The water in front of him cooled, solidifying into piles of silver coins glistening in the moonlight. In the reeds, frogs and crickets cranked up their mating calls. She went to his garage? Met Bentley? Bought a car?

Jack soothed himself by counting only three days till he would have his mermaid again. And a yacht, and a home with a panoramic view and a private chef. He'd have vacations where he didn't have to worry about the cost of every ice cream and taxi ride. He would be meeting people who were pleased to see him, far from the clients who accused him of incompetence and overcharging.

He finished the can. From this night—he slapped a mosquito against his forearm—it all begins.

16

SUBJECT: LOVE IN THE TIME OF COVID19

From: Elizabeth Lambert

To: Jack Mathews

Date: Friday May 15, 2020 at 12:30

It's almost two months since the world stopped and yet someone I did work for two years ago is freaking out about the sofa coverings not conforming to EU fire regulations. Two of my team are off with Covid, one in hospital, and the Italian quarry we use is shutting down indefinitely. Yes. I loved you, Jack, more than I could ever imagine a girl loved a boy, and we'd talked about me coming back to live with you and us settling down, one day having a family, and then just by chance I learnt you had a date planned with a girl back home. Your dad had scribbled down a phone message, left it out for you to see. I took the money and then some bad stuff happened. I'm a moving forward kinda person so shall we leave all those feelings back in Avalon?

———

"WELCOME, Mrs. Lambert, to the Cove Hotel and Spa."

The manager had come out especially to greet Elizabeth and give her a tour of the hotel through a face mask adorned with the hotel's emblem.

"If there's anything you want, do not hesitate to call for me. We are extremely privileged to have you staying with us. Your friend Mr. Mathews arrived a few hours ago. Would you like us to call ahead to the room?"

They tried the number, no answer.

"Let me accompany you to the Catalina Suite. Carter will follow with your suitcase."

Elizabeth was at her most contented in a hotel. Any hotel, but the more luxurious, the happier she was.

As a kid when they'd had money, her mother would treat them to a few nights—sometimes weeks—in a motel. Some had pools, ping-pong tables or a diner attached which she and Danny could steal food from. But what Elizabeth appreciated most was being out of the back seat of a car. And people were, in general, nice, or in the case of the pits they stayed in, at least not outwardly hostile.

Soon as she was old enough to go off on her own, she found herself sneaking into hotel lobbies to study the way people walked in their expensive shoes, lounged on banquettes talking loudly on their phones, their luxury baggage abandoned in hallways for anyone in a uniform to take care of. Rich people can't do anything for themselves, she observed. This was the crack where she'd start drilling down for her fortune, and when she met Bruno and heard about his family's struggling hotel business, she struck oil. But even when she had homes—plural—of her own to go to, there were nights during her marriage that Elizabeth would check herself into a hotel with just her handbag and mascara-smudged eyes. And it crossed her mind that maybe, after all, living in one room was what made her feel safest.

There was a short caddy ride from reception to their private lodge. The porter slipped the card in and out of the slot and opened the door to their hallway.

Roses. Red roses everywhere. In vases, laying across the surfaces and on the bed where the petals have been gathered to form the shape of a heart.

"Datsa lodda flowers, ma'am." The porter grinned as his colleague shuffled past him to lay the suitcase on a stool.

"Could you have someone put them in a big vase out on the balcony?"

"Allergies?"

Elizabeth didn't tell him that red roses reminded her of the years she was a call-girl and occasionally long-term clients liked to pretend to themselves they were in a relationship. She passed the porter a fifty-dollar bill, guaranteeing his devotion for the rest of her stay.

There was a black, plastic sports bag in the corner and, was that Jack's aftershave she could smell?

Elizabeth used her nail to slice off the head of one of the roses and crushed the petals in her fingers. She couldn't stand clichés or drugstore aftershave.

17
SUBJECT: ARMAGEDDIN' OUTTA HERE

From: Jack Mathews

To: Elizabeth Lambert

Date: Wednesday May 20, 2020 at 21:45

Took a while getting back to you. Everyone's on the PC at home. Sounds like Europe is pretty serious about this pandemic while no one knows WTF's going on around here—absolutely no friggin' direction and the numbers are going up but I don't want to get into all that. What I want to tell you is that today a few of us came in to work to do some FILMING! Traci had this idea that when we sell a big-ticket car we make an infomercial about it. I'm sending you my debut performance—remember this was all done social distancing! I think you'll agree, no Oscars yet! BTW Traci only acts like my wife, she's not my wife, I mean, she's only 24 years old! Check it out! Gotta go, my friend Scott who I run with has just come by—he wants us to train for a marathon. Don't worry—I'm being real careful but man, feels great to get out. Super big kisses, J xxx

———

ELIZABETH HAD EXPECTED the spa area to be cleared for her in advance but there were people milling around in dressing gowns and two men in the jacuzzi, one of them was Jack.

Elizabeth watched him nodding at the other's burbling self-important narrative. Where at eighteen years old each cheek had a dimple when he smiled, he now had two permanent indentations. It was an attractive, worn-in feature; she couldn't have designed him better herself.

The other two tubs were empty, so why had the man sat with Jack? Or had Jack sought out company? Elizabeth had never anticipated other people in her fantasies of re-meeting Jack—and there'd been a lot of fantasies.

Jack's hair was thinner than it had appeared on her laptop screen. His chest was more cushion than mattress. He lay back with his arms spread out, looking up at the sky, holding that smile until she heard him laugh. A salesman's laugh.

Elizabeth grasped both sides of the belt of her dressing gown like the reins of a horse she could at any moment bolt away on.

The water would frizz up her hair which she'd got done the day before to be perfect for him. Was he worth it? The grass-green retro 1950s bikini that she saw in a magazine and had sent over in a taxi was too showy and the straps dug into her shoulders. Jack looked at her—for a second, it was like he was trying to place her.

"Here she is!" Jack said.

Jack waded over, leant halfway out of the Jacuzzi to take her hand as she immersed herself into the water, trusting Jack's strength to keep her steady. When Jack's face was directly in front of her, intent, reaching into an Elizabeth only known to him, she dissolved, reduced to a universal vibration. Jack pulled a face in the direction of the other guy. Elizabeth giggled, looking down at the top of the water.

"This is my Elizabeth."

"Bob. Bob Applebaum, nice to meet you." Bob's hand emerged from the foam for Elizabeth to shake.

"Bob's a cosmetic surgeon."

Bubbles around her, bubbles inside her.

"Elizabeth just flew in from France."

"France! Never been. My wife's always dreamt of visiting Paris. Long journey. You got jet lag?"

"I travel a lot so…" Jack's fingers moved over her ribs, Elizabeth lost the power of speech.

"Me?" said Jack, looking into Elizabeth's eyes and flattening his palm into the small of her waist. "I had a jet lag of twenty-four years."

"Jack told me you were sweethearts a long time ago so you'll need to make up for lost time, and I'm truly hard-boiled now. I imagine Elsa will be back from her shopping trip. Might get in another round of golf before dinner." The man waded towards the steps.

Foam nipped at the top of Elizabeth's shoulders as she started to panic at the thought of being alone with Jack. He must have felt it too because she heard him say, "Please don't leave on our account."

"Nonsense," he said, water cascading down his trunks. "I'm sending over a bucket of champagne. He told me all about your work. Lambert Interiors. My wife and I just bought a place in Santa Barbara, Jack said you guys would come out and give us some ideas about doing it up?"

"Bob's wife is a child psychologist," said Jack.

Elizabeth gave a practiced smile to mask a spark of indignation that Jack would volunteer her services without asking her.

"I have to say, you guys, you look *perfect* together. I wish you both all the luck in the world, all the luck..."

"We don't need luck," said Jack, rocking Elizabeth side to side against him.

Elizabeth wondered if Bob would ever leave as he waited for more water to drain down his legs.

"To love!" And he mimed toasting with an imaginary cup while nodding at Elizabeth's breasts.

"Funny guy," said Jack as they watched him plod back to the hotel's main building. "Elsa's not his wife by the way. She's one of his nurses."

"He has a nurse?"

"He told you, he's a cosmetic surgeon!"

"Sorry! I had other things on my mind."

"And on your body?"

Elizabeth slid behind Jack, the tops of her feet curling against the backs of his ankles. Jack ran his palm over the side of her head down to her throat where he left it, taking in the throb of her racing pulse. His other hand traced the features of her face with his fingers, she kissed the tip of each one—daring to lick the ends and leave his little finger in her mouth, only stopping when she noticed he was wearing a wedding ring.

"Tell me how you like the sound of the Mercedes's engine? I pushed her to 122mph, but the factory claim—you are *so* beautiful."

Jack lent into her, about to kiss her lips when they heard a little cough and the clinking of glasses. The waiter averted his eyes while setting down a tray of two champagne glasses and a bottle of champagne.

"With Mr. Applebaum's compliments."

"Thank you," said Jack, looking around for the man to thank. "This champagne's not cheap! Nice guy, huh?"

They each took a glass.

"To our first friend!"

"Nearly enough for a dinner party."

"OK, so, a toast—to first love!" Elizabeth threaded her fingers through his. "Jack, was it OK? Telling her?"

He kissed each of her knuckles. "Riding here on my bike I felt connected to the sky and waves, the gulls, sea lions, conifers and the Milky Way and the next galaxy and—man, sounds crazy—but I can't remember ever feeling so *alive* and it's because of what I feel for you babe."

Elizabeth kissed him, a show of her own vivacity.

"Let's grab the bottle, head to our…" said Jack, in between breaths, "room before we get thrown out of the hotel."

18

SUBJECT: SPRING RAIN

From: Elizabeth Lambert

To: Jack Mathews

Date: Friday May 22, 2020 at 12:47

Another week of cabin fever and existential angst. How did the planet get so quiet and empty and yet I'm rushing from room to room on meetings, taking calls, ordering food deliveries, scrolling the news. Now counting 27 WhatsApp groups. My daughter's not going to finish her school year so we're looking for a tutor, meanwhile, my accountant is working out how long we can manage on our company reserves… But I LOVED the video of you guys, I think you missed a career in the movies. Your colleague Traci is quite a stunner and it's pretty clear she's in love with you. I can't believe you guys can meet together like that—in France we have to print out a letter saying where we are going and for how long for the cops to check—even for a dog walk or food run! Will watch that video just once more, thank you, Mr Mathews of Mathews Motors, for bringing out the sunshine! Super big kisses to you too—say, you flirting with me, Mr M?

———

HEADS LOCKED in each other's arms, limbs molten with desire, Jack and Elizabeth leant against the doorframe of their hotel room as he opened the door to their suite.

The lights had been dimmed and the roses put on the terrace

as instructed with a bottle of champagne, chocolates wrapped in gold paper and two flutes on the center table.

"Y'know, this place is bigger than my entire house."

"When I heard they had a 'Catalina Lodge', we had to have it," Elizabeth whispered.

"This terrace is 260 square feet alone. I met you when you lived in a trailer."

Elizabeth stood behind Jack, holding him as they swayed in time with the waves.

"I told you I was gonna make it. You didn't believe me."

Jack knitted her tight against him as they two-stepped to the bedroom where Elizabeth fell back on the bed.

"My beautiful little mermaid," he whispered as her legs hooked themselves around his. "Bet even you never seen a bed so big—jeez, it's a Californian king, that's 72 by 84!" He passed his arm under the arch of her back; she was so slight compared to Jude. He kissed her vanilla-and-chlorine scented hair, nuzzled his mouth into the right angle of her neck and shoulder blades. Elizabeth returned his kisses, at first softly, then harder as she allowed herself to feel how much she wanted him. She spoke quietly in his ear, "One moment," then wriggled out from under him. She went into the bathroom and closed the door.

Jack rolled over on his back, stretched out like a star in the universe of their bed. He tapped the space she had left, missing her already. When he heard water running, he slid over to his jacket and pulled out his phone. There were over twenty messages—the first group from Aimee about driving her and Savannah to the beach for an end-of-year school party after their hip-hop class. *Yo!? Where R U?* to more frantic *DAD!!! Are you coming? ANSWER!!! Answer PLEASE!!!* Jack had no idea what party she was referring to but Friday he always collected her from hip hop which was downtown. He'd meant to ask Bentley to collect her but with all that was going on, he'd forgotten.

Messages from Jude had begun curt, officious. Is Aimee back from hip hop? Friday night-pizza night. Something about references for an internship Preston was applying for. Then the messages escalated in urgency until all that was left were paragraphs in block capitals and exclamations marks. And then Bentley had questions about the Bonneville. There was something from the bank about Preston's student loan. His running team were planning something they called a 'Happy Tracking' weekend to do with cocktails, was he in? Jack helped himself to a Belgian chocolate while listening to Marcie's incantation of calls he should return and the sound of Elizabeth brushing her teeth. On the team's WhatsApp group, Traci asked him to sign off on a couple's loan and to say Good-Looking asked for an advance to pay for his daughter's Prom dress that weekend. Lots of celebration emojis. Traci had also messaged him privately to say that Bentley had helped himself to the Cadillac. Again.

Jack rubbed his eyes, the bathroom door clicked and Elizabeth was there, a baby-pink lace negligée, her hair brushed out over her shoulders, the sea reflected in the bathroom mirror behind her.

"Avalon, 1999. You broke my heart. Now you start making it up to me."

19

SUBJECT: SEAN-PAUL SARTRE

From: Jack Mathews

To: Elizabeth Lambert

Date: Saturday May 23, 2020 at 9:52

Existential, *quoi*? Thanks for sending me to Wikipedia to get me some education. "Dude, trading in your car at Mathews Motors was the right existential choice!" I think this sale technique might work for me, eh? Yeah, Traci's hot and I love her—like a daughter!!!—you got nothing to worry about 😜 BTW you mention Magnus, alot! Should I be worried about competition there? And what about all those hunky builders you work with? I'm going to Lake Feliz tonight, about an hour and a half away from here and where Jude's mom has a cabin house. All I want is to get my boat out on the lake and away from all this talk about disease and death! But it means I won't be in contact for a while. Will you miss me? BTW we're celebrating this weekend because Preston got into San Diego State University to study Political Science. Let's hope they get that vaccine ready meanwhile I'm gonna have to sell a lot of cars to pay for the next four years, but we're dang proud!!! Existentially, Jack

———

JUDE WAS ALREADY CRYING when Preston opened the door to his student accommodation.

"This is just so inappropriate! So inappropriate. I should have called. I know…" Jude clung to her eldest son. "I just don't know what to do. I just—"

"What's happened?"

The worry in her boy's eyes made it all worse.

"It's nothing bad, sweetheart." She took out her tissue. "I mean, it's *bad*, not serious. Nothing's happened to Beanie or Bentley, but... that's it—I don't know!"

Not knowing was the worst, and the brewing summer heat, the end-of-year workload, the timer on the sprinkler system going crazy so that every time Jude came out of the house she was hosed down but then at night it sputtered like a garrotted soldier on their lawn. Aimee asked where her father was every two minutes. 'He's in Chula Vista,' 'He's at a factory,' 'Out playing golf.' Nothing stopped the questions until Jude had shouted, 'I have no fucking idea where your dad is!' Aimee had slammed the door to her room, reappeared minutes later with a bag and plans to stay with Bentley and Maxxie. 'Come on, Beanie, Dad'll pick you up from hip hop Friday, we'll have pizza night, watch a movie...' And then he didn't.

Preston led his mother into the apartment he shared with his friend Chadiki and two girls. 'Apartment'—more a corridor with dark, plasticized doors with small lightless bedrooms and one leaking cave of a shower room. But the September before, when Jack and Jude had arrived before the others to move their son in, they'd covered the yellow wipeable walls with posters and wall hangings and disguised the peeling linoleum floors with cheap rugs. Jack had rigged up LED lighting on the bookshelves which looked super cool at night and Jude had repainted the kitchen, changed the cupboard doors and filled the window ledges with herbs and plants, most of which had now turned brown and powdery. The lease was coming to its end, two of the other students were going abroad, and this space would soon be catalogued under Preston's college-day memories.

"So you like that sweater I got you," she said, tugging at his sleeves.

"I wear it almost every day," said Preston, sliding piles of sports equipment across the floor to clear a path to a black corduroy sofa that resigned itself to taking up their combined weight.

"So what's up?"

"Tuesday morning your father said he was going off to think about things. He left the house, deactivated the GPS on his phone and I haven't heard from him since."

"But he's been to the garage?"

"A little." Jude tore into the tissue. "He delivered a car to Coronado. He was in Chula Vista. Went to Kids Call last night, and then, when I was doing the grocery shopping after work, Aimee rang frantic because he didn't collect her from dance. I spoke to a few people. Mike told me the garage is struggling and that Jack's over-extended on loans. Marcie says he sits in his office listening to music through headphones for hours. That's weird, right? Scott—remember the guy he was training for the marathon with? —he said they hadn't been out together for months, and yet, Jack runs out the house most nights. Tammy insinuated that something was up, but kept saying I should ask him—"

"Tammy?"

"Al's wife."

"The hippy-crystals chick."

"Uh-huh. This morning I left him another message reminding him about pizza night after he returned from hip hop but got nothing back."

"Think about what?"

"What? Oh. Think about our marriage." Jude's deductive reasoning battled against a rampant panic. Stick to the facts. "He packed an overnight bag. You know in all the years we've been married I've always done his packing, even for overnight stays, and then... He didn't even give me a chance to—"

"It doesn't sound like Dad, does it?"

"No! Something—or someone—has forced him to go dark. Is it creditors? Is he depressed? Remember Ted? He got like that before—"

"Dad would never—"

"Forget pizza night? No way. And he left his fourteen-year-old daughter waiting on the curb. That area is dangerous, even in daytime!"

"How did she—"

"Bentley. He took her to Bree's, she's got Aimee tonight, I'll have Savannah tomorrow. It's not ideal because the girls are in some fight so it's—it's awkward." Jude let out an exasperated half laugh-half cry. "Another thing, Bentley's not been right since he moved out to live with Maxxie. I'm worried."

"How not right?"

"Bentley's voice. It's like when we had the 'bad time'. Snappy, inconsistent, even when I ask about the axolotls or his gym routine and now I think that maybe it's because he's covering up for your—for Jack. He must know something, or suspect, he could even be in on it—they work together all the time."

"You live together all the time."

Preston walked to a cupboard, took out two beers, handed one to his mother.

"The fridge died. Sorry, warm and no glasses. Student life."

Jude raised her can to her son.

"He missed his dental checkup. He didn't turn up to Connor's house when he said he'd have a look at his truck and not calling you kids...? We're talking about your father."

"It's Patty's seventieth birthday Sunday. He wouldn't miss his mother's own—"

"What do I say when Clare calls? And Sharon needs us to confirm Greg's retirement party at the golf club. Summer vacation in two weeks and still no plans."

Preston pulled his cell out of his pocket and pressed redial. "His voicemail box is full."

Against a background of ringtones, shouts in the hallways and toilets being flushed, they were quiet, puzzling out a best-fit context for Jack's behaviour. Nothing came to mind.

20

SUBJECT: GROSSES BISES FROM LONDON

From: Elizabeth Lambert

To: Jack Mathews

Date: Sunday May 24, 2020 at 2:47

I know it's family time and I never want to be in the way of that but just had to tell you, I managed to escape France for London! Just got back from dancing the night away at a 'private' club—yeah, testing and facemasks and we probably drank more hand gel than anything else, but oh to be normal again! And I deserved it after this week of rain and cancellations, what a 'bummer' as the Brits say. Back in my hotel room packing. Traveling is a nightmare and SO expensive but I won't bore you with all the tests and papers Emily has to deal with for me, etc. And BTW Magnus is totally gay so you don't have to worry about competition—y'know, Mr Mathews, you still got it going on ;) But tell me about your secretary—she looks like a real character!

Great news about your son, wow, political sciences! Can't write more as I'm going to pass out. I'll show you some of my plans, tell me what you think.

Bises—that's 'kisses' in French xxx

———

"HE COULD BE HAVING AN AFFAIR. Sorry, Mom."

Jude nodded, Occam's razor. "Bentley says Traci's crazy

68

about him. She's gorgeous, twenty-four, ambitious—could he resist if she…?"

"Traci's engaged to some hot entrepreneur, remember? The guy who bought that old Spitfire."

"The nights he works at Kids Call, he gets back late, doesn't want to talk, takes a long shower…"

"Most of the time it's just him and Al, and though Al rocks the goatee beard, not Dad's type."

"But y'know what's weird? Over the last year, Jack's been hanging out a lot with Al because apparently he and Tammy are on the verge of splitting. Serious financial problems, her kids, his depression…" She grimaced. "*Sex.* Jack would say Al needed to talk through stuff—remember he lost his daughter? But when I spoke to Tammy, she didn't say anything about it."

"Maybe she didn't want you to know?"

"Or Jack was lying."

They ruminated on this. Jude wondered how Preston, always so organized and neat, could stand living in such squalor but he had a way of adapting to any situation, unlike Bentley and Beanie, who needed life to be a certain way for them to even start thinking about participating in it.

Preston spoke softly. "I've seen Dad talk to girls, flirt, tease, he's a salesman. But he's… he's kinda lazy. Whatever he's doing, he'll be back because he can't live without you. It's probably just what he said, re-evaluating stuff."

"So I just wait till he wanders down from the mountaintop with news of the Lord?"

"Got any other options?"

His mother swigged at the beer.

"Mom," he said, moving closer to her. "This could be terrible timing, but I have to tell you something."

"You're dropping out of college?"

"No, in fact, I'm applying for master's—"

"STDs?"

"Can I speak?"

Jude drew her fingers across her lips, zipped up.

"I've wanted to tell you something for a while now but you're always so busy and—"

"We talk almost every day!"

"Mom!"

She knew what he was going to say, had known it since he was a child.

"I told you about Chadiki, my housemate. Well, he's more of a *room*mate."

"You're in love! Why did it take you so long to tell me?"

"Because I... it took so long for *me*. And then, I didn't want to tell you and ask you not to say anything to Dad and Bentley, but... you knew?"

"Always. But then, when you had that girlfriend in middle school I did start to wonder."

"The one with the hot brother!"

Jude clapped her hands, laughing.

"It's all new, we only got together in January."

"That's six months ago!"

"Well, once you come out as gay, it stops being personal and gets so political. It's navigating the whole lifestyle. We're meeting soon at a place that does the best *Quesabirria*, come with us."

A few hours later, Jude was in a restaurant where Preston and Chadiki debated the best dishes to order for her.

"So he finally told you!" Chadiki said, putting a hand on Preston's shoulder. "Not that I can talk, I haven't said anything to my parents."

"Dad's the one I worry about the most," said Preston. "He's kinda latent homophobic, right, Mom?"

"That's not fair, he's not!" said Jude. "He's..."

And the conversation turned from Chadiki's family to the enigma of Jack Mathews.

"Mid-life crisis," concluded Chadiki—*Chad*, he preferred.

"I just want to kill him right now."

"In Nigeria we say, 'In a moment of crisis, the wise build bridges while the foolish build dams.'"

The three of them were then joined by more of Preston's friends and Jude found herself laughing so much she forgot why she'd come all the way out to see her son. After a late-night visit to the grocery store to fill Preston's bare kitchen cupboards, she stood by her car, hugging Preston way too hard and long.

"I would never have done this tonight if I'd been with your dad. Maybe that's what he wanted, that we open up to new stuff?"

"Maybe. Drive carefully."

That's what it was. Jack was searching for spontaneity, change, something different and, as she joined the Interstate, she realised she needed some too. So Jack had made his point. She got it. Now he needed to come back.

21

SUBJECT: HEALTH WARNING

From: Jack Mathews

To: Elizabeth Lambert

Date: Tuesday May 26, 2020 at 17:54

I drove all the way back from Lake Feliz into work just to say I really hate it that you're out there while people are dying—you have changed my life a second time, sweet Elizabeth, and I need you in it.

PS I will have to tell Marcie you thought she was hot! She is 71 yrs old going on 14!

PSS Thank you for that French kiss from London ;) AND… Beeeeezzzzzzuuuuuz from a sweaty car mechanic from Feliz! MWOAH—that's a Californian kiss!

STROBES OF LATE-MORNING sun and searing apprehension broke into the hotel suite on Jack and Elizabeth's last day.

Elizabeth lay on her back, arms outstretched over her head, listening to the rumble of suitcases being rolled over to check-out. She nudged Jack with her foot. He groaned, plodded to the bathroom. Her bladder, too, was full, pressing down into where she was raw, itchy. They'd been up almost all night until only a few hours before and the room still smelled of sex and sea water and the M&Ms discovered in the minibar.

Jack returned from the bathroom. "Breakfast ends in twenty minutes." He kissed her shoulder. "Babe?"

"Call for it," she groaned, as Jack moved around the room, picking up clothes and sniffing them to check if they were passable for another day's wear.

"We said we'd go down then swim in the pool, seems a waste when we've paid for it."

Elizabeth's gaze followed Jack as he threw clothes in the direction of his holdall, humming.

In the bathroom, Elizabeth sat on the toilet, screwed up her sore eyes because it stung when she peed. Her hair was matted, springy, brittle and her skin felt like tissue paper. She needed a few hours to shower, moisturize and blow-dry her hair to start feeling human again, but Jack was already pacing the room re-reading the breakfast menu.

They'd spent the day before in bed until late afternoon when Elizabeth and Jack had had to organize a little photoshoot to justify her half-price stay at the hotel. After that, they'd taken a walk along the coast, stopping to swim in the sea, re-enacting their time as teenage lovers before drinking cocktails in a bar watching the sunset. But that morning, Elizabeth stared at herself in the bathroom mirror wondering where the endorphins and optimism had gone.

The face staring back at her was a scared fifteen-year-old girl.

"Ready? I'm starving." Jack opened the door, slipping the key card in his pocket.

"Hope we don't run into Mr. Applebaum again," Elizabeth whispered.

"I thought he was nice—might have some work for you."

Elizabeth was about to snap at him that as the Sapphire Hotel Group's main designer, she was some way from soliciting work from random strangers, but Jack was already overtaking the other guests as they shuffled, giddy with greed, from one platter to the next.

"Hey! They have honeydew melon! Wanna start with that?"

"Coffee."

A waitress seated them midway between the buffet and the shore, regretting she couldn't get them closer to the sea.

"You having cooked?" Jack asked. "I'm sure there's a vegetarian option, I'll ask the—"

"I said, *coffee.*"

"She's coming with it." Jack stroked Elizabeth's cheek. "You mind if I have the bacon? I won't if...? Just that this breakfast is forty-seven dollars per person and they have the maple—"

Elizabeth turned sharply as a man knocked into her chair.

"I gotta get some fruit and muesli, want some? You not drinking your coffee, princess?"

Elizabeth had forgotten how revolting filter coffee could be. She was aware Jack wasn't moving, just waiting for an answer.

"You should leave here and go back to your life."

"Now? Can I at least finish my sausages?"

"You've had your dirty weekend. That's all you wanted, not reality, not me..."

Jack saw tears seeping out from behind her sunglasses.

"What's all this? I'm not leaving you, hear me? I'm gonna ask them to do you a cappuccino. For the price they're charging, I think they can manage that. Try the blueberries, filled with antioxidants. And this smoked salmon is delicious."

Elizabeth let Jack coerce her into eating half a croissant with her cappuccino. She didn't speak until they were back in their room, Elizabeth wrestling Jack onto the bed, using all her weight against him, finding his mouth with hers, hard and deep, the Jack she'd fallen in love with that summer in 1999 had to be in there somewhere.

Jack flipped Elizabeth over, grappled with the buckle of his belt.

"You in a hurry, Captain?"

"Babe, checkout's midday."

Jack timed his orgasm for 11:42, after which they lay on their backs, steaming.

"Tell me you love me again."

He was new to all the love talk. Jude had never been into

that stuff: pet names, commentating during sex and finding metaphors to describe the quality of their connection. Jude was a scientist, a feminist post-modernist girl who would've quoted some article from the *National Geographic* at him, but Elizabeth, she just looked at him with those viridescent eyes and said, "We share the same heart." *That*, he understood.

"What are you doing?"

"Calling reception—I'm telling them we need another two hours," she said.

"But there'll be a charge! They said—"

"Well, Mr Mathews, just make damn sure you're worth it."

"Would madame like some food brought up?" the receptionist asked. Elizabeth reeled off a few dishes from the food menu despite Jack having made rolls for them at breakfast and smuggled them out wrapped in a napkin. It's what Jude had always done in hotels for him and the kids. He remembered Aimee and Bentley being on the lookout, filling their pockets with miniature jam jars and cheese slices—the excitement of a picnic later and a win for Jude's anti-capitalist streak.

Elizabeth put the phone down and buried her head in his chest.

"I'd like to start a family," he said.

"We can do anything, *anything*. We're free now."

The idea of impregnating her set off an urgency in him he'd never felt before. The sun was on his back, the room ablaze. There was no embarrassment, no 'not now!' the way Jude reacted whenever he said he wanted to do it. 'Ja-ack, *not* now!' she'd say, as if he wanted to take a piss at a supermarket checkout counter.

"It's two thirty, baby, I'll go down, settle up," Elizabeth said, collecting her hair into a sunhat.

"Let me. I won't be a kept man."

"Sure?"

Jack drummed his fingers on the wall. "I sold a car this

week, little blue Mercedes, remember? Come down when you're ready."

Elizabeth sat, alone, on the bed, replaying the last three days, waiting for the energy to start packing everything up. She saw a light flashing in the corner of the room. It was Jack's phone inside his jacket pocket. The light flashed again.

Elizabeth knelt down, eye level with the phone. Next thing, it was in her hand and without waiting to justify herself, she pressed the 'OK' button. On the screen were the names and first lines of text messages: Aimee (17) Bentley (5) Preston (2) Mickey Wheels (3), Halcyon Days Nursing Home (5), Mike (3), Drax (2), Dr Schwartz (2), Clare (2) and Jude (14) Jude, missed calls (29).

Elizabeth had already seen Jack put in his password: 0000. Typical. She scrolled down to Jude's name and read the first few lines of her messages but there were so many.

> What time u coming home 2 night?

> I'll bring the cake for Patty's b-day but could

> Where are you? Please get back to me ASAP

22

SUBJECT: OH CAPTAIN!

From: Elizabeth Lambert

To: Jack Mathews

Date: Wednesday May 27, 2020 at 14:48

Fret not! I'm taking super care of myself. Very touched by you being there for me these last six weeks, from my heart, soul and… er… my *mind*—what did you think I'd say? I'm in an Uber now, will write later. Are we the last people to use email? It's been so wonderful to see your emails among the demands for hotel reviews, penis enlargements and promotions. I saw you 'hearted' all those photos on Instagram, I was so hoping you'd see them when we did the shoot. Did I tell you someone offered me a job writing a lifestyle column for one of the UK weekend papers? All of it xxx

———

JACK AND ELIZABETH stood at the hotel's entrance looking straight ahead, like actors waiting for a curtain call. The porter rattled the trolley through with Elizabeth's cases at the same time as her Mercedes and his motorbike appeared.

"And there she is," Jack said, looking at Elizabeth's car. "That kitten can purr. Almost built from scratch, for you."

Elizabeth ground her teeth and pulled her cap over her eyes.

"Come on, what's up?"

"I didn't know you had dinner plans."

"What?"

"Isn't your wife expecting you home tonight?"

"What are talking about?" Jack gripped her arm, tried to turn her towards him.

"She's been texting you all weekend!"

Jack ushered Elizabeth away from where the doorman was standing. He read from his phone.

"It's my mother's seventieth birthday. Jude went with the kids to visit her. No big deal."

Elizabeth squinted her eyes shut like people do when they don't want to witness an accident. He read his messages fast, moving his lips in sync with the words. A friend from college was coming into town with his family over the summer and wondered if they could hang out. Al. The running club. He'd missed his annual dental checkup but would be charged the full amount; could he re-make an appointment as soon as possible as Dr. Schwartz was taking the month of August off? Clare and Preston. A retirement party. Halcyon Days nursing home. On the family WhatsApp group chat, *The Famous Five*, he learnt that Bentley had had to pick Aimee up from hip hop after she'd been left on the curb. All punctuated by Jude asking him to call.

"OK. So Jude had this idea I'd be back at the weekend... I don't know why she thought that."

"Because you haven't told her you won't be?"

"Not *yet*..." Jack looked around, aware of the people passing them. "I'm staggering the information, disarming the potential for dramas."

"You're *lying*."

"No—future proofing! Jude can be volatile. It's a long-term strategy."

"*Long-term*? We've been having an affair for three years!"

"Not—" Jack stopped himself.

"What? What were you going to say?"

They were the only two people standing still amongst the porters and valets who moved back and forth with suitcases while guests loaded up their golf clubs and three young children raced around hitting each other with their parents' tennis rackets.

"Can we...?" Jack lead Elizabeth further into the gardens but when he tried to take her arm, she yanked it away.

"My marriage to Jude was over a long time ago. She's going to realize that and it'll come from *both* of us."

"I'm getting serious *déjà vu.*"

"What's that?"

"I've been here before and I don't like it."

Jack looked around for some way to reassure Elizabeth before noticing the two car valets were still standing by their vehicles.

"At ease, gentlemen," Jack said. "She's a beauty, eh? Yeah, I know, talking about the car." The boys laughed. "My... er..." Jack looked to the ground, rolled over some gravel, "*friend* and I need a little more time to... er..."

Elizabeth whispered, "They're waiting to be paid."

"Oh, right." Jack put his hands in his pockets and brought out two dollars for the valet.

"Two dollars?"

"It's all I had." He wiped an arc of sweat between his brow and his hairline.

"Here." Elizabeth stepped forward, plucking two twenty-dollar bills from her wallet to put in each of their palms. "Turn the engines off and make sure they're not in the sun."

"Yes, ma'am. Thank *you.*"

Jack followed Elizabeth's funereal footsteps to a garden table under a honey-suckle plant. She took out her bottle of water from her purse, sipped it.

"You lied to me. That's why I'm upset, you get that?"

"Excuse me, I hope I'm not disturbing you?"

Both Jack and Elizabeth were startled by a woman crouching under the tree as she approached them. She held on to the top of her blouse and bent down to Elizabeth's face. "I just had to say I totally love what you're wearing—you have exquisite style. My girlfriends and I wondered where you got that—"

"Not now."

The girl yelped, took a small step backwards bowing at Elizabeth as she returned to her friends.

"Babe, that wasn't nice."

Jack's phone started ringing, he'd unthinkingly switched the sound on.

"It's my sister."

Elizabeth shrugged. Jack brought the phone to his ear.

"Yup. Send 'em from both of us… I'll settle up from work tomorrow. You decide. Marigolds and whatever you said sound great."

Elizabeth's arms were tight against her chest.

"Clare. She's sending flowers to our mom. Wanted the money upfront. She never has any." Jack tried to hold Elizabeth's hands but she scraped her chair back from him.

"You're the love of my life and it kills me I have to convince you of it." Jack shuffled his chair closer to her. "I understand you're upset. And why and all that, but these are just final details. Sweetheart, it's like when you buy a car, even the car of your dreams, you still gotta do the paperwork and wait for delivery."

"You saying I'm a *car*?"

"No! I'm saying… there's a process. But if you want, I'll go, tell her now and I'll come over to the house after. Would that make you feel better?"

Elizabeth watched Mr. Applebaum walking across the lawn with a sack of golf clubs over his shoulder and a young redhead trotting behind him crying.

"I'm going back to Paloma Drive. *Alone.* Find me when you're serious about us."

After Elizabeth watched Jack speed away on his bike, she made a few Google searches and left a message with the Federal Trade Commission.

"Hi, I really don't want to cause trouble but the other day I was sold a car at a Mathews Motors in Feliz and I had a weird feeling about it. They wanted all cash, said something about it being 'off their books.' I don't know what that means, but…?"

23

SUBJECT: A PROMOTION!

From: Jack Mathews

To: Elizabeth Lambert

Date: Friday May 29, 2020 at 9:36

This is your captain speaking: Fasten your seat belt and hold on tight! I'm glad you got my ads for penis enlargements, I sure don't need 'em ;) I was reading up on France—lockdown has made me crazy to travel! What a lot of public holidays they have there—no wonder you like it! This year—in normal life—I'd be working every day 8am–10pm even Sundays, even national holidays! Usually chained to my phone cause most of our sales come from people texting or calling about ads they see on websites and then they just ask random, stupid questions about cars they know they'll never buy. Remember the night we broke in to the casino? Stay in contact coz I seriously can't last without you!!! Over and out, xxx

---

JACK PARKED his car behind Jude's and, out of habit, and just for a second, he had that *ahhhh, home* feeling. Then dread pricked through his pores and the inside of his mouth tasted of old coins. His lips stung, raw and chapped from all the kissing. He gulped from the bottle of mineral water he'd taken from the hotel room. Before closing his car window, he listened to the same Sunday evening soundtrack his street had been playing for years. Folks scraping dishes while a dog barked for leftover bones, older kids finishing off homework and parents careening toddlers into baths or story time. BBQ grills being scrubbed. Someone dropping sacks of trash next to newly cleaned cars. Just another Sunday in Felicidad.

After leaving the hotel, Jack had sped ahead of Elizabeth to the garage so he could exchange the motorbike for his car as he wanted to pick up some stuff. He also told himself he needed to check on the building, see how they'd left the place after closing Saturday, but more than that, he needed space in between Elizabeth and Jude, a change of mental costume.

No. 5734 North Cedar Drive. The one place on the planet where he'd always felt safe, and loved, and a somebody to all the somebodies who lived there. He caught sight of Mouse's silhouette slinking across the road and tried to get her attention by waving, but the cat didn't even look his way.

Not even a week after he'd closed the door behind him and he was already on the outside. Whatever was going on under that roof, he wasn't a part of it: he would never be a part of it again, not wholly, not as an equal stakeholder. There were many points in the last two years he could have turned back—many times he'd tried. This was the last.

The first stars were working up a shine and all Jack wanted was a full night's sleep in his own bed.

He thought twice about using his key. It was half his house. It wasn't like she'd dug out a moat and installed a drawbridge over the weekend. Jack opened the door alerting Tip he was home. The dog slouched over, unimpressed. He smelt his crotch, examining the new set of pheromones.

"Hey, boy."

The hall was almost as Jack had left it: the pictures he'd hung nearly twenty years ago, the rug they'd bought in Bali with the mulled-wine stain his father had made one Christmas party. The bulb in the lamp he hadn't got round to replacing was still dead. Tip trotted around his calves. Jack clasped the dog's ears, looked into those cuprous eyes and patted him with disproportionate gratitude. They both sniffed the air: cigarette smoke.

Jack walked into the living room without putting on the light. It was the same room, although it seemed someone had come along and shaken it all up, put it back slightly tumbled. The right things but not in the right places.

Through the garden doors and across Jude's vegetable patch and the make-shift greenhouse where Jude nurtured saplings, sickly plants and grafted orchids from her already impressive collection, he saw a dim light in the pergola.

Jude was sitting in her reading chair, the back of her head tilted like maybe she was sleeping. Their pergola. The construction he'd built off their kitchen during lockdown to commemorate their twentieth wedding anniversary. 'This is my Taj Mahal to you,' he'd said.

Tip lapped up water in the kitchen with exaggerated gusto while Jack walked past him through to where Jude was—not working on plants—but faced away from him, one leg tucked under her, the other bouncing, outstretched in front. She had a pile of essays on her lap and a red pen in her fingers. Jack had never seen Jude grading papers there before, surrounded by bags of earth, glass jars, creeping tomato plants and those triffid-like things that were almost breaking through the glass ceiling.

Having thought of little else than this moment for thirty-eight months, Jack still wasn't prepared. And just as he considered turning and running out, Tip dropped down at the foot of Jude's chair and, as she bent down to pat him, she saw Jack. He resisted the urge to rush up, drop to her ankles and join Tip for a good, homely pat. He longed for her to say, *Go back to sleep, it was all just a bad dream.*

24

SUBJECT: COUCOU FROM THE RIVIERA

From: Elizabeth Lambert

To: Jack Mathews

Date: Thursday June 4, 2020 at 7:34

Dis me knee-deep in rubble (see photo) and that's little Cosima beside me, my new assistant! What a house, eh? I'm in Cap d'Ail with a skeleton crew. Check out this stunning little enclave just next to Monaco on Google Earth. At the end of the garden is a private beach and heli-pad! The people who own the house will probably only use it for a few days a year but no expense spared. Today, I was deciding where to put the saltwater pool and I thought, what would Jack say? It's like you're always by my side. Did you bag the client with the Cobra?

———

"You're smoking," Jack said.

Jude looked at the cigarette as if it were a prop someone had slid between her fingers.

"How's all the *thinking* working out for you?"

A part of him—a big part of him—had wanted Jude to make it harder for him so he could just make himself a sandwich and go to bed, text Elizabeth in the morning to say he was sorry but... but Jude had this way of speaking to him like he was some kind of joke. Just like that, 'thinking,' as if he wasn't capable.

Jack lowered himself onto the edge of an upturned crate, brushing off clumps of spider web that stuck to his fingers.

"Could you put down the cigarette, someone might see you?"

"It was your mother's birthday today. She'd had a fall on Friday, apparently the hospital left a message but you didn't call back and—"

"She get the flowers Clare and I sent?"

Jude blinked a few times, continued, "For the first time in... I don't know how long, she asked 'Where's Jack—why isn't Jack with you?' She's in diapers, thinks she was a Bolshoi ballet dancer and doesn't know the word for an 'orange' let alone that it was her birthday, but she knew something wasn't right. 'Is Jack coming?' We were all looking at each other and no one knew what to say." A wine glass tilted in her hand. "How do I explain why you didn't pick up Aimee from hip hop, or even call? Marcie couldn't reach you when Bentley had a buyer for that fancy bike you took, he was counting on that commission." Jude looked straight at him but the effort to control her expression forced her lips up into her gums; a face that Tip made when he didn't like another dog. "Talk to me."

"Life's short," Jack said, focusing on a guidebook to Peru under an obese cactus.

"Uh-huh?" She rotated her wrist as a signal for him to move on.

"I feel there could be another life out there for me."

She took in a deep, exasperated breath. "There's also another life for *us* here, in this marriage—did you think of that? Did you ever—" she stopped, restarted in a softer tone. "Patty's illness, my mother, the school, the garage losing money—all that, I admit, it wasn't *fun*, but—"

"Juju, don't. It's not your fault."

"Jeez, thanks, Jack."

"Living with teenagers, man, it can take you to the brink."

Jude took Jack's hand, pulled him closer. "Raising a family, making a living, losing parents, it's hard, that's why people marry, for those tough times. Weren't you paying any attention when the priest read our vows?"

Jack drew his hand away. "People change an awful lot from being just out of school. It's twenty-two—"

"—*three*—"

"—years later. It's too much to ask."

"Not from me it wasn't."

"Well, there you go."

"No, there *you* go."

"There I go," said Jack, rubbing at where the cigarette smoke made his nose itch.

Jude didn't stop him as he turned away back through the living room, past a watchful Tip and up the stairs which had never felt so steep, so lacking in suspension. Who was the man who skipped down them every day for the last twenty-three years?

Their bed. Only one side slept in. A bottle of Ambien and a can of Diet Coke on the bedside table. At least she got to sleep.

Did Jack dare think it was easier to make love to Jude than Elizabeth? The way sometimes in the night she put her buttocks up to him, slid him inside and moved until they both came and fell back asleep without a word; the way Jude just took care of her own pleasure, letting him get on with his. It takes twenty-two—*three*—years to render down to a few minutes of unspoken complicity.

Their bed was a king-size, brass. They'd seen it at Macy's when they were living in San Diego and Jude was pregnant with Preston. Jack had hummed Dylan's 'Lay Lady Lay' and Graham Bedwell—naturally they'd tittered at his name—asked them if they knew how much time was lost at work because people suffered from back trouble, sleeplessness, depression? It was the perfect sales pitch for a young science teacher and her mechanic husband. Jude pictured kids piling in with armfuls of toys on Sunday mornings; Jack pictured himself tied to the bedposts with neck ties… They could repay in ten instalments —Jude's share coming from her first paycheck.

Bentley's Spiderman figurine, which he'd left on their

windowsill five years before, must have sprung a web over Jack because he could not move.

Jude had been through his stuff alright. There were clothes of his he hadn't seen for years spread out over the floor. Boxes taken down, shoes in a heap and drawers upturned. He made a quick mental search of his covert operations—Jude could never have deciphered the password to his private Gmail account, his pre-paid phone was in his car's glove compartment and the few things he'd paid for over the weekend had been with cash. He was way ahead of a game she'd only just started playing.

Jack opened the loft and pulled out the black canvas backpack Bentley used for snowboarding trips. He dragged the case into the bedroom, wincing as it scraped the stairs leaving a trail of dust. He ran through the things he'd need for his new life with Elizabeth—his wedding suit might come in useful for dinners out—after that he began loading in clothes, shoes, anything he could grab while Jude made her way up the stairs.

25

SUBJECT: HOT CHICK IN A HARD HAT

From: Jack Mathews

To: Elizabeth Lambert

Date: Friday June 5, 2020 at 21:54

That house is no way near as bootyful as you, all that rubber got me burning up! You got 37,539 likes on Insta—that's insane! Got back into Feliz this evening to take Aimee to hip hop but they called off all her classes till next September and we're not getting a refund cause Covid is 'extenuating circumstances.' I took the sailboat out yesterday on the lake—see photo of those ripped abs. Thought of you. Saw on FB you're designing a line of wallpapers—can never stop telling you how great you are! Beanie's here needing to use the computer so will write later. Beside you always, true dat xxx

———

"*Not* the bedside clock."

Jack returned the clock to the bedside table. It was technically his, she'd bought it for him as a birthday present in the days before smart phones. He opened a drawer, lifted out a pile of T-shirts that Jude had recently ironed and folded, all the time aware of her perched over the open suitcase.

"Skiing gloves? Dad's Bermudan shirt?" Jude flicked the items back and forth. "Why can't you tell me where you'll be?"

"You can't resent me for needing a little time out."

"No, honey, of course I don't, but why shut me out? I've never stopped you doing anything you wanted: camping with the boys, Scott's bachelor weekend, poker nights, Las Vegas for that work thing, the Baja wine trip. Just say, like, tonight where *exactly* will you be?"

"You can reach me on my cell."

"You know how many times I called over the weekend? *We* called. Put that back. Hey, answer me? It's nearly eight o'clock at night, don't tell me you have no idea—"

"I have no idea. I'm not sure about anything anymore, who I am, where I want to be? Who—"

"Aren't these questions Aimee or Bentley should be asking. Jack—back up—*who* do you want to be with?"

"You'll just talk to me like I'm some kid in sixth grade."

He found a hoodie he hadn't worn since college and thought it would be useful when he and Elizabeth went to Carmel, then he forced away that thought in case Jude grabbed it out of his head. She watched him struggle with the zipper—*let me*—and she handed it back to him, zipped up and folded for him to shove in the bag.

"Is this about a woman—women?"

He dropped a handful of socks in the case.

"It's about me. Me. Just me. Why can't you accept that?"

"If it's about you, then it's about me too," said Jude, placing her hand on his arm. Jack's eyes glanced around the room as his Pink Floyd T-shirt slunk from the bed onto the floor.

"I've been thinking too. For the last two years I've been living with grief: my parents' deaths, Preston leaving, Aimee not being a kid anymore, the stuff with Bentley and adjusting to the fact that more of your life is behind you than in front, y'know?" Jack didn't even allow his eyes to flicker in case he revealed something. "Anyway, I'm through it, and I feel optimistic that this is our time to harvest what we've put into this family, not burn it all down. I finish school in two weeks, why don't we go on a real vacation—safari, cycling tours, river rafting—or we can camp out at the lake house, or we could sell the lake house? Get a new boat, sail around the world? Nothing is more important than you and me, is it?"

She was saying all this, and it was important, but all he could concentrate on was not pulling away from her touch.

"I said I—" He lifted his palms to his temples and stepped back until he was out of her reach. "It's like I see this accident in front of me and I'm skidding forward and I've lost control of the vehicle, I can only crash now."

"Is it oxycodone? Francine's husband was—"

"No! I'm not an addict, or—what? Francine's husband? Nate? I play golf with him, Nate's a—"

"Jack, I'm saying I'd never let you crash. Me, the kids, Tip, our friends… we're all here for you."

Jude watched him close his suitcase and lift it up on the bed. He grasped the handle and was about to walk out the door when she suckered herself on to his back with all her weight, preventing him from taking another step.

"Slow down. Change gear. Pull over and stop—stop this!"

"Don't!" Jack yanked the case away from her. Bentley's name tag ripped off in her hand. He dragged it down the stairs —*bump-bump-bump*—Jude moving quickly behind him, her fingers batting the air so she could clasp on to any part of him until she hooked on to his jacket pocket.

Jack freed himself. "I'll call you in the week."

Jude made a final plunge towards Jack who twisted away so that she lost her balance, stumbled over the doorstep, giving him time to throw the suitcase in the back seat of his car, get in and put his key in the ignition.

"Aimee's parent-teacher conference is Thursday night. Please be there for her."

Jack reversed into the road, twisted the wheels and drove down his street as fast as he could in between the speed bumps.

"Thursday night—don't forget—and fix these goddamn sprinklers!"

26

SUBJECT: FROM A SILLY BOY

From: Jack Mathews

To: Elizabeth Lambert

Date: Tuesday June 9, 2020 at 14:53

I'm freaking out that I might have offended you with stuff I said. I was inappropriate and I stepped over the line. I am a man and you are a very attractive lady but I guess in this #metoo era we guys have to keep that in check. I get that you're mad but as I haven't heard from you for a while and people are dying all over the world so please let me know ur OK. Mermaid, please don't think because ur hot I don't take you seriously or respect you as a wife, mother and professional. Thing is, you can't see my smiles and winks when you read my words on a screen 😉. Now that we've found each other, I'm kinda living for our email exchanges. All love from a silly, sorry boy, but your boy all the same xxx

———

JACK SANG loud to 'Under The Bridge,' Red Hot Chili Peppers, slapping the steering wheel with one hand, his free arm waving through the night breeze as Felicidad shrunk behind him in his rearview mirror.

Slowing at the bottom of Paloma Hill, he turned the volume down for his new neighbors.

The air tasted minty with the cool breath of eucalyptus trees.

Jack pulled up at the wrought iron gates of the house.

This is it.

A bat swooped over the pool which was lit up as if under luminol.

> Ur knight in shining armor is waiting outside the gates to save u. Whoooop!

> Jeez young sire, you took your time! Whoooop u 2!

A mechanical click. The sound of grinding metal. The gate doors trembled before opening their arms out to him.

Jack laughed with relief that Elizabeth hadn't changed her mind. He drove through, disappointed by the clouds of gnats congregating under the lantern outside the front door. But then Elizabeth appeared under the arch of the doorway, her face turning away as if she'd been slapped by his headlights. His mother used to stand like that: hair up, no makeup with a hand up to her forehead on the lookout for his late returns.

Jack didn't even switch the ignition off or close the car door before rushing out to Elizabeth and lifting her up as if she were drowning. He grappled at her hair, inhaling her skin as he pulled her down on the hall's marble tiles. This was just like he'd imagined so many times. His hands were searching the coolness of her buttocks when she moaned his name.

27

SUBJECT: SILHOUETTE OF MY LEFT BREAST AGAINST ST MALO SUNSET

From: Elizabeth Lambert

To: Jack Mathews

Date: Sunday June 14, 2020 at 21:05

I wasn't offended! You can treat me as a sex object all you want, knock yourself out. It's just been a crazy week traveling with my daughter to St. Malo, Brittany, to stay with clients/friends who've asked me to refurb their guest house. I just had to get away when NY fell through despite the endless tests and doctors and crazy expense! See photo of me with Lunar and Solar, their Labradors, on the beach. I've been walking about 25k a day, listening to music and re-living some of the moments we shared. The sea always reminds me of you. That hot mermaid you left on the beach all those years ago xxx

———

"GOOD MORNING, MR. LAMBERT," said the housemaid. "What can I make you for breakfast? Coffee, fresh fruit juice, cooked breakfast, maybe?" She was younger than Jack had imagined, wearing jeans and a red T-shirt, her black shiny hair twisted up on top of her head.

"All of that," he said with a laugh.

"Is Miss Elizabeth ready for her green tea?"

"She's still sleeping, jet lag."

"No problem, sir."

Jack sat on the terrace by the pool contemplating a swim when Esme brought out a plate of huevos rancheros, a bowl of fresh fruit, coffee and juice.

"Those are some eggs!"

"I hope that's how you like them. If not, let me know."

"Definitely how I like them."

As she served his food, Jack pointed beyond the horizon. "Beautiful day. So clear. See the sea?"

"Uh-uh."

"Think that's Mexico out there?"

She smiled. "Could be."

The sunlight caused her to screw up her nose and Jack could imagine exactly what she'd looked like as a little girl.

"You from Feliz?"

"Los Caminos, not far."

"Sure, 'bout fifteen-minute drive, ten if you pushed it. You born there?"

"Uh-huh," she answered, looking back to the white surfaces of the kitchen. She didn't want to talk about herself, but Jack wanted her to. This was the first morning of his new life and he had no time to lose in populating it with people who understood that he was not someone who expected to be waited on.

Jack looked at his plate again. "Thank you for this, Esme."

She opened her palms as an invitation for him to enjoy his eggs and cloudless view.

28

SUBJECT: A KISS FROM A ROSE

From: Jack Mathews

To: Elizabeth Lambert

Date: Monday June 15, 2020 at 7:46

Mighty relieved ur not mad at me checking out your booty. Please send more pics—maybe ur right breast so I can make an informed comparison? Or you in different outfits—ever do any nursing? 😄 I've decided to build a lantern pergola in our backyard to keep me from going crazy and an excuse to visit the lumberyard. Not gonna bother asking for planning permission right now, by the time we get through this, there won't be much left of the planet. Feliz is a scary ghost town with everybody hating on everybody and people goin crazy over the whole mask thing. A friend of ours was punched in the street. I know you wanted to go to NY but the number of cases are rocketing up and also I worry you might get burn-out, that happened to Mike, my partner. Just came in for our Zoom work meeting and wipe the dust off the cars but now need to bike up to Jude's mom who's got suspected Covid. So BTW, I'm worried about Bentley going through my email accounts—he has a lot of my passwords and the other day I got an invoice from some gaming company for $475 for apps he bought!!! Think we could set up something just us? Say if it's awkward. Maybe we could talk on the phone one day? I'm starting a list of questions to ask you, but first: what car do you drive?

————

"More fuel?" asked Vice-Principal Ramón, holding out the

coffee jug. "Don't look so worried, the Haydon meeting will go fine."

That's when Jude remembered Haydon Liverside was bringing in his family, lawyers and mental health team later that morning to decide if the school had responded appropriately to the minor's wish for a gender reassignment.

Jude toasted Ramón with her coffee mug. "Here's to a summer vacation at the end of the tunnel."

They sipped fast so they didn't have to taste the drinks.

"I'm really sorry but I have something I need to do this morning. I'll be back way before ten but *if* I'm late, start without me."

"This morning?"

"It's unavoidable."

The moment Jude heard Ramón start assembly, she texted her assistant, Liam, to say she had been called away and could he check Aimee had her gym bag?

Jude had to know Jack was OK, that's all.

She'd been selfish and insensitive when he'd come back on Sunday night to speak his heart. She'd badgered, patronized and threatened him when he said he was vulnerable and needed space. Now she understood why he was on the run. Each time she remembered the disappointed way he'd looked at her, she screwed up her eyes, held her breath. Cruel. She expected to mess up at work sometimes, leadership doesn't work retroactively: it's public, it's instant and the targets are constantly moving, and with her kids—it's easy to misread the turbulence of a teenager's psychotic universe—but with Jack, they couldn't be on opposing teams when all the prizes were joint. So when he'd got up to leave, *her* fear had superseded good judgment and compassion. What if—she'd asked herself at four that morning—the police came to the door and said he'd driven off Coronado Bridge? How would she explain that to the kids? No wonder he had been so fast loading that suitcase with the pile of clothes she'd put aside for the thrift shop.

She'd let him down.

She had to explain.

Ask forgiveness.

Jude took the road off Orange Flower Park and found herself creeping down Pine Street, passing Jack's face on the Mathews Motors' sign. At 8:19, there was only one mechanic smoking a joint by the body shop.

For all the reasons she loved her little MG sports car, the fact that it provided excellent camouflage for watching the Mathews Motors garage hadn't been one until then.

Traci and Draxx arrived at the same time with Draxx ambling over to the gates and unlocking the padlock to the forecourt while Traci tapped sunscreen onto her forehead. They didn't exchange a word, even between the conifers and the 7-11, Jude picked up on the tension between them.

Five guys wearing blue overalls got out of a car. Jude didn't like it that Jack paid cash to these men who appeared and disappeared from nowhere, often taking tools, petty cash, clients and parts with them, but Jack had argued that mechanics were near impossible to keep hold of: they didn't make them like Bob anymore. Bob, with the poppy-red mustache and OCD, who'd been chief mechanic at Mathews Motors after working at Jack's dad's boatyard for most of his life, was now dead.

So just as Jude was thinking about labor laws, Jack's Nissan turned into the garage. He'd come from the north, behind her, direction of the hills, not downtown or the shopping district or the residential Buena Vista area where Al and Tammy lived. Jude waited for him to get out of the car but he didn't. He was on the phone. His head leaning to one side, hair a little wet. He was clean-shaven and wearing a white shirt. She saw his shoulders bounce like he was laughing. Not a case for the psychiatric ward: Jack looked just fine. More than fine. She'd only wanted to know he was OK, but now she was there and had her speech ready, she reversed from her shady vantage point and parked right in front of him.

29

SUBJECT: NEPTUNE CALLING SALACIA

From: Neptune99

To: Salacia99

Date: Saturday June 20, 2020 at 6:21

Morning, beautiful Salacia! Can't believe we had our first call-date in the first-class lounge of JFK! D'you get to sleep on the plane? It was pretty emotional, huh? I get what you were saying about guilt but, goddess, no need to feel badly coz we're just old friends catching up but like I said, it's nothing sinister, just it's our world—the universe of Neptune and Salacia. Safe journey. The guy with the big trident xxx

———

"—SPINACH AND PAPAYA? GROSS!" Jack laughed as Elizabeth described some of the contents of her morning health drink. "I'm just parking up at the garage. Miss you bad already. I'll try to get back before eight so we can get in a naked swim together."

"Sure you can't come back for lunch?"

"No can do, took too much time off last week—I gotta sell some metal, keep my princess in the style she's accustomed to —and you got a bestseller to write." Jack pulled up the hand-brake. "I'm sorry I didn't wake you to say goodbye."

"Oh, I love it when you make that noise."

Jack chuckled into his collar. "The noise like this...?" He made a humming noise. "Again? Like this..." Jack and Elizabeth sighed in unison. "And hey," he said, tapping on the dashboard and watching Traci shine up the cars in the main window. "When I get back, we'll do our sunset meditation, those breathing exercises really h—"

Jude's face stared at him from the other side of his car window "Gotta go."

And Jack was out of the car with Jude clasping his wrists.

"You're OK. Thank God!" Jude closed her arms around Jack.

"Sure, why—?"

"Last night was awful. I was so wrong and I'm so sorry."

"That's OK."

"No. You were reaching out and I should have listened."

"Don't worry about it." Jack stepped back, tucking his phone into his back pocket.

"I should have been there for you, instead I-I was mean and —that a new shirt?"

"Ju, please, don't beat yourself up about it."

Jack pinched off bits of leaf that had stuck to her top.

"You wanted—*needed*—to talk but I didn't listen, I messed up."

Jack folded Jude into him, kissed the crown of her hot and prickly head.

"Shhhh, it's all alright, I wasn't mad at you."

"Oh, thank God," Jude fell against him, "'cause—"

Jack steadied her while asking, "Shouldn't you be at work?"

"I am. I'm *there*." She laughed, waving in the direction of Orange Flower Park High. "I just needed to see you're OK, and to say I totally support whatever it is you're doing. If you need me, I—"

"Thanks, but I'm fine."

"Really?"

Jack leant against his car, looked up at the sky, Jude watched the blue of his irises sharpen. "The truth is, I'm learning to meditate." Jude stepped back. Jack nodded. "Zen style. I didn't wanna say 'cause I thought you'd laugh."

Jude wore her most sincere, serious expression. "No... that's great. *Good* for you."

"I'm trying to access my authentic self, my Buddha nature, and for that, I have to detach for a while."

"Do you have any idea how long that's going to take?"

Jack shrugged, the hills beyond holding his gaze.

"Are you following a course? A temple... sect?"

"Nah." He scratched his chin with his car key. "It's called a Practice—I'd love to talk to you about it more, just we got the Monday meeting starting now."

30

SUBJECT: NEVER FORGOTTEN, NEVER LOST

From: Salacia99

To: Neptune99

Date: Wednesday June 24, 2020 at 14:46

SO great to hear your voice again—after all these years! And me too, had a million things to ask you! OK, you wanted more photos? This is a selfie of me by the Seine walking Cosie to school just before the 'confinement' as they call it here. I'm heading back to the South of France today because it's too freaky here. Even though, I'm never scared because I have you, my King of the Sea. Got the Gmail thing set up on my phone too so waiting for a photo of you, handsome.

───────

"GOOD MORNING, awesome people! A brand-new week starts today!" said Jack to a near-empty show-room.

Traci waved from the courtyard where she was talking to a client, Jack read her lips, *Yes, that's Jack Mathews.*

Bentley was at the coffee machine; he shouldn't drink coffee. The middle child, the one who shared Jack's looks but whose cynicism distorted them. Even at his best, a readiness to take offense was sprung tight. Stimulants twitched the trigger.

"Did I just see Mom here?"

Jack saluted his son. "Yup, she just dropped by."

Bentley stirred in five sugarcubes.

"I thought you guys weren't talking?"

"Team meeting. Get the word out."

Jack returned to his office, ignoring Marcie who was already tottering over to him with a list of phone messages.

"Give me ten," Jack said, closing his office door.

Jack was about to press the redial button to hear Elizabeth's voice one more time, when Bentley appeared in the seat opposite him, kicking out his studded boots.

"Sit properly, come on, champ. Whassup?"

"Y'tell me." Bentley loaded his cheeks before shooting it all out. "Mom called last night, woke me and Maxx up."

"Inconsiderate," said Jack, scrolling through the appointment diary.

"She thought you were gonna drive off Coronado Bridge."

"Your mom and I just talked, everything's fine."

"Good, 'cause she was like *convinced* I was hiding something about you, went on and on asking me stuff," Bentley scratched at the eagle's talons of his tattoo, "then this morning, she's *here*. So, you, like, leaving Mom, something like that?"

"I'm just takin' time out."

"So that's a 'yes'." Bentley interlaced his fingers behind his neck.

"No, it's what I said, a little me-time."

"So where was 'me-time' last week?"

"Up the coast visiting garages—yes, Traci?"

Traci stood at the door, holding out the specs for the red GT. Her voice always went into sing-song higher pitch when she was talking about clients in front of them.

"Mr. Mathews, I see you're busy, but is there any chance we could come down for a trade in and self-finance?"

"First client of the week—let's drop 800 dollars and offer an extra year's warranty. OK, Traci, *and* a complimentary car wash," said Jack.

Traci nodded but didn't move. "Could we talk?"

"Sure." Jack nodded to his son.

"Privately?"

"Be right back." Jack was loath to leave Bentley in his office but any hint of that would have set off warning signals.

Traci moved into a side office that no one used because it was full of boxes, filing cabinets with jammed drawers and a broken bubble machine. She squared up to Jack and said, "You sold the Mercedes, Mr. Mathews. I was saving for that car."

"You never said."

"I did, a whole bunch of times."

"I'll find another like it. Hey, T-Bird, come back!"

31
SUBJECT: ACTIVATED AND READY

From: Neptune99

To: Salacia99

Date: Monday June 29, 2020 at 9:36

Sunshine girl—it's like you got some remote control to my soul because wherever I am, I think of you and I am activated—totally turned on!!!

———

BACK IN HIS OFFICE, Jack's face was red and stinging.

"Make sure Traci wins a bottle of champagne end of the month."

"It's sparkling wine, Dad, but whatever. So, you met someone? You havin' some kind of breakdown? Transitioning?"

Jack watched Traci close her sale as he tried to answer his son. "Half of my life, *all* of my adult life, I've been married and sometimes in long-term relationships, the well just dries up."

"Dad, that's gross."

"Oh God, no, no, not like that, I mean—"

Jack watched Traci processing the registration forms.

"Mom said she'd see a counselor if you guys need to talk things through."

"Good idea."

"It was Maxxie's idea."

"Oh, you talked about it with Maxxie?"

"Everybody's talking about you, Dad. The Frankenfelds asked if you'd been radicalized. You know Mom started smoking again?"

Jack snapped open a can of Red Bull as Marcie tapped on the door.

"Hey, boys, it's that time of the week."

"Gotcha." Jack nodded, taking a sip from his can.

"After you took off last week, lady came by, snapped up the Mercedes sport. Dad? That rich-bitch blonde something to you?"

"Don't use that word about women."

"She didn't even look under the hood. I know what wanting 'space' means."

"I'm an old man, kid, let's mosey…"

Marcie emerged from the kitchen with a pitcher of iced water in each hand and what looked like leftover salad floating to the top.

"What's all that shit in the water?" asked Jack.

"Cucumber cleanses the kidneys."

Jack watched his team filling the meeting room—they always sat on the tables, never the chairs that were put out, a few mechanics were finishing their cigarettes outside and Traci was moving around the showroom with her distinctive after-sale walk.

"Traci's pissed she didn't get the foreign, isn't she, Dad? Is she the reason you're leaving Mom?"

"T-Bird's too smart to bang her boss." Jack's phone buzzed in his pocket. "I gotta take this call."

Jack back-kicked the door to his office picked up his phone.

"You have to come home—it's urgent."

Elizabeth's voice was low and breathless and made his heart thud. Jude had found out.

"What? Tell me!"

"I was just dressing, before Esme did the bedroom, and I picked up your T-shirt, the one that you wore on Saturday, I put it to my nose and oh God, get here now and fuck me. I *can't* wait till tonight."

"Baby, I'm just about to start our Monday motivation meeting. They're already pretty mad at—"

"*Now.*"

32

SUBJECT: ON STAND-BY

From: Neptune99

To: Salacia99

Date: Tuesday June 30, 2020 at 4:35

I'm at work creeping around in the dark because we are now officially closed but I just had to get some privacy because my wife's on the computer all day long looking up the spread of Covid cases and then her sister from New York facetiming every hour to announce some new crisis and then there's her book group, Zoom yoga class or Aimee's homework club. Time I buy myself a laptop and create a no-entry space in the house or craziness will kill me before Covid does.

———

JACK'S FACE was blanketed by Elizabeth's hair, his stomach against her back, his hands cupping her breasts. Every time he drew himself back rings of warm tight muscle enclosed around the tip of him, a pleasure so intense he edged in and out of consciousness. But he had to keep it together because they were on a public beach. Elizabeth undulated against him until Jack couldn't fight the build-up of desire that started at the arches of his feet, traveled through places he didn't know he had sensation, and came out as, "Aimee's Parent-Teacher Conference!"

Late. After all the reminder texts Jude had sent him. After all the notifications popping up on his phone. After all he'd said to Aimee. But Elizabeth had wanted to go to the beach that afternoon and then needed to be dropped back at the house which had lead him into the thick of rush-hour traffic. He was late by ten minutes—twenty—he re-calculated, as he neared the full car park. Right out in front was Jude's racing-green MGB 1979 Roadster. The wreck he'd towed from Nevada from a Brit who'd had his license revoked and was on his way to rehab. There it was in her parking space, over the white paint on the tarmac: *J M Principal.*

Miss Principles, he and Preston had called her the year she got the job. There had never been a doubt that Jude would move up through any school until she was in charge, but the position at Orange Flower Park High had been quite a jump from Head of Science in a small Escondido school. Needless to say, she'd managed to convince the board that though she was young with small kids, she was indefatigable, equipped with a Master's in Curriculum and Instruction from night school, was fluent in Spanish and committed to raising the place out of its slump. What they didn't know was that what motivated her most was avoiding her husband's imminent bankruptcy. When she came home to tell the family she'd got the job, Jack unveiled the sports car. The car was everything the job wasn't: flashy, impractical, sexy and un-American. And it only comfortably sat two—OK, not *totally* comfortably—but the car marked a new start for a young couple with places to go.

Jack raised the new Tom Ford shades Elizabeth had bought him to the top of his head and slid his key out of the ignition. He checked his rearview mirror praying there were a few guilty cars behind him, but it seemed he was alone in being waylaid by sex on the beach.

Aimee was outside the main door with a bunch of girls. The group huddled, all eyes on their phones, their fingers moving around the screens like mandibles over rotting fruit. When Philly saw Jack, she nudged Aimee with her knee. His daughter lifted her head before looking back to her screen. Ophelia stretched herself out on the handrails, "That's one DILF," she said, just loud enough for Jack to hear. Aimee attempted to slap her friend but Ophelia jumped aside and swung out her arms. "I present to you, Mr. Jude Mathews!" Some of the girls tittered, the rest didn't even look up. Jack had never liked Philly, *Ophelia*. He hadn't liked her dad who'd been a football star at school then married the class sweetheart when she returned from Hollywood after a canceled TV pilot. Their daughter, unfortunately, took after her dad: bulky, boorish, someone who was tickled by the discomfort of others.

"Howdy, Jellybean," Jack said.

"They're in the gym. Dad? That way."

Jack made his sheepish *I know-I know* face. Only that morning he'd texted Aimee to promise her that although he had to be away for a while, he loved her just as much as ever and that nothing between them would ever change. Jack put his hand out to stroke Aimee's head but she ducked, muttering, "New shades, huh?"

33

SUBJECT: LA VIE EST BAD

From: Neptune99

To: Salacia99

Date: Wednesday July 1 30, 2020 at 1:45

Me again. It's bad here and getting worse. One of Aimee's friend's dad died up in LA in the same hospital as the actor Nick Cordero. Love those photos you sent and love you calling me Neptune, so to live up to the name, here's some of me on my boat—you might want to check them out in private 😈 *Au revoir* for now, *ma belle*—here are some virtual red roses xxx

———

WELCOME *to Orange Flower Park High!* The multi-colored banner hung over the central hall. That bleach they used on the floor got Jack's nostrils every time. He passed a sign pointing to an exhibition of art projects, the end-of-yearbook behind a glass window, class photos and announcements about regular hand-washing that were now curling and yellow.

"Aimee's dad," Jack said, lightly squeezing the hand of a blushing girl who looked not much older than his daughter.

"Aimee's history teacher. Jane. Miss Gavet," Jude said, without looking at him.

Jude was all in black, her hair dirty and a blemish like dribbled fruit juice pitted her chin.

"I had a client…" He almost put his hand out to touch Jude before she turned her back on him. He directed his excuse to the teacher. "Someone professed to owning a vintage Oldsmobile, far outta town, the lady wouldn't let me go, and—"

"Is that sand in your hair?" Jude asked.

The teacher's mushroom-colored lips moved out of sync with her litany of Aimee's grades. Jack occasionally caught sight of his daughter through the windows with Philly and Savannah and a boy who Jack had been reminded repeatedly to refer to as 'They.'

"…it's just keeping her focused, she's easily distracted—"

Jack's fingers drummed against his thigh as he thought up ways he could prove to Jude he *had* gone to see someone about an Oldsmobile and then passed by Kids Call. It's just that he'd done those things before he'd picked Elizabeth up and gone to the beach, but still—

Jude nudged him. "D'you hear that?"

"Hm?"

"Short attention span, huh, wonder who she got that from!" Jude pretended to swipe the back of Jack's head. "Thanks, Jane." She stood up, checked her list of teachers, looked everywhere in the room but at Jack. "Mr. Dawson. Chemistry."

"I know you're mad I'm late but I was working."

"I'm mad because while I appreciate you are… going through something… no one's been able to reach you." Jude moved in front of a couple with a sharp, "Could we? We'll only be a moment; my husband was caught in traffic."

"Mrs Mathews, of course."

"She blown up the science lab yet?" asked Jack, shaking the man's hand.

"Not *yet*…" Mr. Dawson mumbled before setting a portable alarm to four minutes. "So, er… aside from what happened Tuesday… Aimee's failed this course. Four tickets for tardiness and in class she spends most of her time brushing her hair and chatting." He stopped to let Jude take notes. "It's a shame, she has potential for science—obviously it's in the family—but she needs to think hard about where she's heading."

Jack wondered if it was really necessary for the teacher to be wearing his lab coat after hours.

"But how are her grades?" asked Jack.

The teacher and Jude looked at each other. "Jack, we're beyond grades here, I mean, after the *incident*."

"Incident?"

"My husband's been on a personal development course these last two weeks, we haven't had a chance to talk."

"Have a good evening and let's hope next year will be a new start," the teacher said, resetting his alarm for the next parents.

In the corridor, Jack, like so many of the other parents, tried to get Jude's attention.

"What *incident*?"

Jude scanned the list of teachers while acknowledging the hellos and introductions surrounding her.

"Well, while you were on your mountain trying to reach nirvana or Nevada strip clubs, whichever, Aimee was caught with seven vials of nitrous oxide and two boys."

34

SUBJECT: IF YOU THINK YOU CAN READ MY MIND...

From: Elizabeth Lambert

To: Jack Mathews

Date: Thursday July 2, 2020 at 5:38

What am I thinking now?

"REMEMBER STEPHANIE?" hissed Jude. "Focus, Jack. Stephanie and Paul Brewster, we went to their daughter's wedding in Palm Springs, they sailed around the South Pacific islands."

"Sure, sure, *Sunseeker Manhattan 66*." Jack nodded. He remembered that wedding. The long weekend away from his computer, how he'd ached for Elizabeth all through the service and spent most of the afternoon texting her in the toilets and how Jude had fretted over him having food poisoning. By the time Jack tuned into what the teacher was saying, they were wrapping up the meeting and Jude was back moving into the crowd as parents angled for her attention.

"Were the boys hurting her?" he whispered.

"More the other way around." Jude shifted her bag on her shoulder. "We'll talk later."

The sky swirled with what looked like black ink over the hills where Elizabeth would be waiting for him to come home.

"Hey, Jack, how come our kids get older and the teachers get younger?" asked one of the dads.

"And prettier!" interjected another before covering his mouth with a hand his wife was slapping.

Standing around the juice pitchers they took mini tacos or brownies made by the kids from Home Ec. class.

"These are delicious. Going anywhere fun this summer?" asked a dad Jack remembered having the same conversation with every year.

Jude looked at Jack, one eyebrow raised. "Jack? What have we decided for this summer?"

"See what's left after all the extra tutoring we're gonna need for Aimee," he muttered into his drink.

"So we made it through another year, eh?" Sonia grimaced.

Jude opened out her arms and hugged her old friend. "You OK?"

"No, not really. He bifurcated on me."

"He what? Sounds like something you got adult-only websites for."

"Even more disgusting. *Loopholes for Assholes*—Bifurcation, in California state law, means Paolo can marry before divorcing me—and he did, he did! Went to Las Vegas and came back to move all his assets into *her* name. So now they are both in *my* house... and y'know what? He's not speaking to the kids because his new wife's hurt they didn't send a wedding present!"

"Mr. Ducas hates me, doesn't he?" Aimee asked, jumping off the hood of Jude's car.

Jude took her keys out of her purse.

Jack hung back.

"Dad, can we get a takeout?"

"G'night, Mrs. Mathews—exciting about being on TV tomorrow!"

Jude waved at the man who got into a jeep.

"What's that?" asked Jack.

"Our SD Unified District's cluster meeting is part of some election campaign thing for Hoffman."

"I *said*, can we get a takeout?"

"Sure, why not?" asked Jude, putting her arm around her daughter.

"OK, so, I'm gonna shoot," said Jack, raising his arms to envelop Aimee.

"Mom just said we can get a takeout!"

"I have to get going."

Jude stopped, turned, her keys pointing at him like a pistol.

"Tell her where you're going, Jack," said Jude in a hand-over-the-money tone.

"Dad?" Aimee brought her hands to his forearms.

"I'm real busy right now, Jellybean. I have a lot of exciting projects on with some interesting people and—"

The last stragglers came out raising their hands in a final good evening to Jude. She didn't respond, her focus locked on her husband.

"But what about food?"

"How about I come by in the morning and we'll do breakfast before school. How about, Jellybean, we—"

"Tell us where you're going?" repeated Jude, the question more pointed by the sound of a boy kicking a football into the school fence.

"Let's talk tomorrow."

"Where are you going? Dad? Where—?"

"I'll be over in the morning, blueberry pancakes at Swaggers!"

"I don't want to get up early tomorrow to see you, I want to go home with you both now!"

"We could grab lunch tomorrow?"

"What do you mean, lunch? I'm in school!"

"Jack? Please. Can't you...?" Jude lowered her voice. "We need to talk."

"Tomorrow. Breakfast. Swaggers."

Jude stabbed her keys in the lock and opened the door, but instead of getting into the car she came back for Jack swinging her briefcase at her side.

"I am trying to understand this, really I am, but... we are hurting. We are *hurting*."

Then Jude got in her car, stretched her seat belt across her. Jack saw the dials on the walnut dashboard light up. Jude turned out of the carpark, waited at the crossing and, when it was clear, she let that fiery engine roar towards their home.

35

SUBJECT: YOU'RE THINKING...

From: Jack Mathews

To: Elizabeth Lambert

Date: Friday July 3, 2020 at 10:34

If only Jack Mathews would come here and take me in his arms and kiss me?

————

ELIZABETH WAS by the pool in a silk leopard-print dress editing photos of herself on her iPad.

"That bad, huh?" She handed him a beer from the ice bucket next to her.

Jack twisted the top off, took a swig.

"You know what the best thing about me is?" asked Jack.

"Your cock?"

He sighed. "My wife."

Elizabeth sat up cross-legged.

"People meet me and they think, nice guy, good mechanic, could pass the time with him watching a game if I've nothing better to do. But then they meet Jude and they see me differently. They're like, oh, he must really have something to get a wife like that. A wife who's a scientist, put herself through college, raised three kids, led an entire school through the pandemic, made a rose garden from cuttings, tells funny stories —does accents and everything. She'll get up at dawn to bake a cake for someone who's going through a bad time. She'll spend half an hour with a pen in her mouth trying to find the right words to praise some good-for-nothing thirteen-year-old's shitty project on photosynthesis. She remembers people's birthdays, she's probably the only person left on the planet who still sends cards: *Good luck! Get well! Congratulations!* She has a whole pile of them for folks and their kids—and their kids' kids, there's always someone's baby to buy for! She's quick, you know, she gets things before other people do, before I *ever* do." Jack swigged, looked into the pale blue pool. "All I know of life is just a filtered down version of stuff Jude's told me. So when people meet her, they think there's something more to me, and there *is*, it's *her*."

"So what the fuck are you doing here with me?"

"Don't be mad," Jack held her foot, shook it a little.

Elizabeth sat up, faced Jack head on. "When I was fifteen years old, you chose Jude over me. Am I just a close second?"

"No! My Salacia, this is our time."

"You don't sound so sure."

Jack pulled Elizabeth to him and rolled her over so she was face down, he drew her nightdress over her buttocks and spanked her. She laughed, wriggled out from under him. "But tell me you made a mistake in Catalina."

"I was a stupid young boy and I'm going to make it all up to you."

"Yes. You are. But first…" Elizabeth reached down and brought her arm back up with something in her hand. "Tah-dah!" she said, handing it to him. "Open it."

Jack started opening the present, surprising himself with how excited he felt to be receiving something weighty and so intricately wrapped up. He stopped when he saw the Omega box.

"Babe, I…"

Elizabeth nudged him with her foot.

He opened it.

"It's the Seamaster Diver! Do you remember, in Catalina we saw one in a store... I wanted to get it for you so bad but we only had enough change for a can of Coke?" Elizabeth stroked his arm. "I never forgot you saying you liked it. You still do, don't you?"

Jack was afraid to take it out of the case. Elizabeth did that for him as he held out his arm.

"You can swim in it and when you do your flying lessons, it'll be great with all the—"

"But these... they cost..."

"Shh, don't think about that. You like it?" she asked again as he unhooked the Casio Bentley and Preston had bought him two Christmases ago.

"I'm... It's..."

Elizabeth held his wrist, looked into the watch face. "It's what we lost—*time*."

Jack's eyes caught the points of her nipples, his fingers pinched them as his mouth searched inside her nightgown. This body had meant *sex* to him since the age of eighteen. She opened her legs and lifted her hips up for him to run his fingers over what felt like warm oil inside her. Her arms fell back over her head, her hair splayed over the sofa, and there she was, his Elizabeth, his hot shining star.

36

SUBJECT: COWBOY TAKE
ME AWAY

From: Elizabeth Lambert
To: Jack Matthews
Date: Monday July 6, 2020

Just saying.

———

MOST MORNINGS JUDE woke at a quarter to six to capitalize on a portion of the day that was hers alone. Sometimes she'd take a coffee back to bed and read, or bathe, bake, but this time of year, with its blasting sunlight, birdsong and color, she spent it in the garden. That morning though, even with the sleeping pill she'd taken the night before, she wanted another hour in bed but Tip was anxious to get outside and Jack would soon be at the door to fetch Aimee.

Jude lumbered downstairs, the light from the windows seared her corneas as she kicked away shoes, jackets and skateboards piled up on her way to the kitchen.

Jude swallowed a Xanax with her first coffee and listened to Tip rustling in the bushes. She lit a cigarette. Just two weeks to get through before the end of school, then she had her permission to crack up.

This was the third summer they hadn't had anything planned. Three years ago, they were still hoping her mother might get better. Two years ago she died that June and the year before they were saving for Preston's time at college. She blew the smoke out slowly. But there had been a time... The moment Preston was old enough to appreciate traveling they'd gone to Indonesia, he'd even written about the experience in his college application statement. Five years ago they'd taken trains around Europe for three weeks, they'd spent every night for months before, the five of them, at the kitchen table with maps, guidebooks and laptops plotting out the entire vacation. There was Cancun with Dahlia and her asshole husband, Hawaii for the family reunion before Covid—hadn't there been happy times, Jack? *Jack?*

"You're talking to yourself. Creepy," said Aimee with her hand over her eyes.

Jude followed her back into the kitchen.

"Come here, Beanie." Aimee wrinkled her nose and shook her head. "I'm not going to..." she couldn't say it—*hug you, kiss you* "...it's just I noticed you scratching your head and—"

"Yup, lice. Philly has 'em too. They crawl across her forehead in class. She says she's training them."

"Aimee! Why didn't you say anything? Come here—*here* now! Who else knows about this?"

Aimee pulled away. "Mom!"

"This is serious. We should tell school nurse—stop moving. Parents should know... I can't deal with this now. We'll get some treatment, probably have some, somewhere..."

"He's not coming, is he?"

Jude looked at the kitchen clock, already 7:49, and fell into the nearest chair and scratched her own head.

"It's common for men to go through times of questioning who they are in life and—"

Aimee made that face, like she was placating a deluded, crazy person.

"He *said* he'd take me to Swaggers for breakfast and," she started up the stairs, "he's not here."

Jude re-loaded the coffee machine—her third—it'd make her pee all morning.

Aimee spun around the banisters and sat cupping her face in her palms. "Do you think all that psycho stuff last night helped —screaming at him?"

"I hardly *screamed*."

Jude sat down next to Aimee who traced her finger over imaginary circles on the wall. Tip followed with a huff, crossing his paws in front of him.

"He said he'd take me out for breakfast."

Jude put her hand out to her daughter who actually took it.

"I told you, this afternoon we're hosting the Annual SD Unified School meeting, but y'know what? I'm going to tell Liam to prepare without me while you and I go to Swaggers and order everything on the menu and we'll charge it to Dad's card, hmm?"

Aimee smiled; the little Jellybean smile Jude saw so rarely these days.

"He can't leave you. You're the best mom in the world," she said, dropping her head to her mom's shoulder.

"Maybe I haven't been the best wife in the world…"

Can you be the best mom and best wife?

"Let's see how many pancakes we can get through. Front door in three minutes. Go!"

Once Aimee was back in the bathroom, Jude picked up her phone and touched her first *Favorite* person: Jack *Home*. Although he was neither.

The phone clicked.

"You promised to take Aimee out for breakfast before school."

"I was just—"

"This is *not* OK!" She could hear him moving fast, doors closing and clothes rustling. "A no-show for your *daughter*?" Jude was as loud as she could be without Aimee hearing.

"Juju, I'm on my way."

"Be here. Today. Twelve thirty. This bullshit has to stop."

37

SUBJECT : LIVIN' LA VIDA LOCA!

From: Jack Mathews

To: Elizabeth Lambert

Date: Thursday July 9, 2020 at 17:07

Not using the Salacia/Neptune account as back in the office. On the phone to the hospital where Covid's ripping through Jude's mom's lungs. Started with a cough now she's got an oxygen mask and unsteady heart. Meanwhile, the health insurance bastards are messing with us. Also, I can't visit my mom so no idea how she's doing. Today been to three go-sees which were a complete waste of time although yesterday I made an offer on a Ram pickup I could do something with. More loco shit, Bentley threw black paint all over our living room after something went down at the online prize-giving at his school. Preston's working like crazy for his AP exams which were canceled but now happening online and Aimee's turned vegan. Remember dancing to that song? Have beautiful dreams of collecting perfect shells on perfect beaches xxxoooxxx

---

EVEN FROM THE OUTSIDE, the house was all wrong: doormat askew; letter box open; the grass on the lawn was yellow, brittle despite puddles on the path. The sprinkler settings were off again, Jack would've dealt with that had he not been paddleboarding with Elizabeth. The curtains in the bedroom were only half drawn across the windows, the hanging baskets outside the house had turned into expressionless faces sprouting straw hair to ward off strangers. Not the home he'd known for the last two decades—or was it that *he* had changed—got used to fresh paint, high ceilings, digital readouts and his 'n' hers dressing rooms.

Jack stopped the car outside the garage, turned it around for a fast getaway if needed. He stretched in the sun, opening his arms wide before feeling for his keys in his back pocket.

Tip was laying against the door so Jack had to push hard to get in. The dog leapt up, knocking into Jack's knees, his tail whipping back and forth, always optimistic for a big walk or the remains of a beef bone. 'Tip *smiles* like a dolphin!' Aimee used to say. Jack opened his hand for Tip to nuzzle into. Did he smell another woman on Jack's fingers?

Then he felt a weight heave against his coccyx as his sphincter dilated, shut tight, dilated, closed, opened and— "Oh boy." Jack moved fast to the top-floor bathroom.

He got his pants down just in time to sit and feel a week's worth of impacted waste funnel through his intestines and into his self-designated toilet. Mind, body and matter all worked in unison to pass out hundreds of dollars of *haute cuisine*. It left him weak, sweaty even. But there was more. Jack collapsed over his knees as if he'd finished a marathon.

When they'd bought the house, the top floor had been a large, open attic. Jack, with help from a friend who worked in construction, had turned half of it into an apartment with a large room built up into the eaves. Jack had put in skylights, wood laminate floor and the shower room. Originally the conversion had been to create a 'quiet' room for Jude, then Preston and Bentley wanted it for boys' sleepovers. Later, Bentley had ideas for a home gym so they made way for that as well as a guest area for family, friends and the occasional babysitter. They already had a small single room as a spare room but Jude had filled that with clothes, ski equipment and baby paraphernalia.

When Beanie came along, Preston had been given a Scalextric from Jack's dad so they set it up there, later joined by a Wii, Aimee's dressing-up box, PlayStations and a DJ set. Then there was a period when Jude and Aimee had got him to build a doll's house for them. Elbows on knees, Jack recalled all those weekends scouring eBay and yard sales for wallpaper and fabric offcuts, tiny things to put in the tiny rooms.

When Jude's dad died, when Dahlia moved to NY, when Clare left for BC and Preston for college, Jack and Jude had ended up being resentful depositories for all the things people said they'd come back for but never did. There were boxes full of extra bedding, shells, family board games, broken printers, an exercise bike, sacks of clothes, buggies stacked up against the walls, packaging from the Apple store and children's guitars, blow-up mattresses and where there was space, Mouse kept her own curation of dead animals.

Jude never got her quiet room.

But despite all those incarnations of their top-floor space, the attic's shower room had always been Jack's toilet. He went there, to his own litter, out of respect for Jude but also because he liked being up high, looking through the Velux windows over the tops of trees. There was an upturned box on which Jack had a pile of car magazines he liked to browse, there was a calendar he'd put up over ten years ago of classic cars that hung on the back door. During the pandemic, this bathroom had become his office—the only place no one would dream of colonizing.

The skylight continued to misdirect flies into the sink that hadn't been cleaned in years. The shower he and Jude had picked out the day President George W Bush was inaugurated was grimy, stiff and calcified. Preston's eleventh-grade biology books and a pair of Aimee's pajama bottoms from the days when she only wore pink stopped the door from slamming.

Jack's time on the toilet, in probably his favorite room in the world, came to a finale. Dizzy, it took him a little time to adjust to a standing position. He had expelled a feces the size of a small state. It almost deserved to be named. He wished there was someone he could show it to. He thought about calling Jude in to see it, she was always interested in unusual things.

He wondered what kind of a reaction he'd get if he posted it on Instagram.

He needed to pick up some more clothes, stuff that wasn't frayed or stained. Elizabeth had said she wanted to schedule time to take him clothes shopping which he understood to mean she wasn't happy with his wardrobe. And while he liked her standing in front of him contemplating what best suited him, he wasn't sure about the patterned shirts and designer jeans she nodded at in shop windows. But instead of the master bedroom, he found himself in Aimee's bedroom, lying on her bed, his legs dangling out the sides. He looked at the posters of rappers that had been stuck over the ones of dolphins. She'd made a wall of notes from friends: hearts and kisses, code words and emoticons. He put Beanie's pillow over his face and lay there until he heard Jude's car come to a stop behind his.

38

SUBJECT: NEW YORK CHEESECAKE ANYONE?

From: Salacia99

To: Neptune99

Date: Monday July 13, 2020 at 7:55

My naughty Neptune—(could you try to remember to write on this platform JIC?)

Here's me in Soho NY "quarantining" while I make plans to refurb this Brooklyn home—she's a UK-born model and he's an NFL player—I can reveal no more! Right now eating a delivered cheesecake—restaurants still not opening and the mask debate rages on. Y'hear a German Shepherd died of Covid last weekend?

Sorry to hear about Bentley. Everyone's speculating about the long-term mental health impact these last few months will make on all of us, but particularly teenagers. Cosima was in tears the other day after seeing on Snapchat some of her friends had got together without her. Heartbreaking.

I need to head back to Paris end of the week as we're leaving for Bruno's parents in the country, but first, got to get something for Cosie from FAO Schwartz! Word's out another lockdown is being planned once everyone returns from their little window of freedom. I'll be sad to leave the same continent as you!

Sexy Salacia, the one with the tail.

———

JACK WATCHED Jude from the landing as she got out of the car, grabbed her purse, dropped it, swore and picked it up again. All the time, muttering to herself. She lifted out a brown paper bag from the deli. Her face and neck were red inside a black linen suit that was bunched up at her elbows and hanging off apologetically. She ducked her head into her hand to hold back her hair and block out the light.

Jack could see purple-black patches under her arms as she lowered her sunglasses, only to lift them again, rub her eyes and squint. Wasn't that the black suit she'd bought for her mom's funeral?

You did this to her, he accused himself, and yet she still brought you lunch.

He was in the hall when Jude walked through the door. They both looked surprised to see each other standing in their own home.

"Hot out, huh?" he said.

Jude blinked, widened her eyes; the look Aimee made when she was embarrassed at things her parents said.

She walked past him to the kitchen and dumped the bags on the table.

"I've only got an hour."

Jack wondered what for.

"Why don't I do the lunch, you can shower and…?"

"It's the middle of the day, Jack—is this your new life now? Midday showers?" It was actually. She tugged at her top. "We're having lunch together, *no*?" She was almost shouting. "So let's *do* this."

Elizabeth almost always came home, slipped off her clothes and stepped into the shower before applying her lotions and brushing her hair and—

Jude turned her back on him, went to a shelf in the recess next to the fridge and brought out a bottle of red wine. She pulled out the plastic cork, grabbed a glass, filled it and knocked it back in three long gulps.

"Is this *your* new life now?"

"Fuck you."

"What happened with Aimee last week?"

"She was caught in an amatory situation with two boys having a little nitrous oxide party."

"Nitric what?"

"Laughing gas. Maxxie said lots of kids do it. Maxxie also said Bentley's being really weird, you noticed?"

"Can we just get back to Aimee. She was with *boys*?"

"She's fourteen. How's the meditation going? There's a sandwich in there," she said, pushing the Trader Joe bag over to him. She put her hand in her purse and lifted out a packet of cigarettes. With the other hand she rooted around for a lighter, lit a cigarette and blew smoke out of the window. "Last night was *very* upsetting. With Aimee. You get that? *Very* upsetting. Jack? You were late, all... *undone*... distracted. Aimee's parents' evening, Jack! *My* work. And you just get in your car at the end of the evening and *so long* like we'd only just met?" She hiccoughed. "You did *not* handle that right. Then you promised to take her for breakfast and never show up!"

"You zoomed off before I could firm up the plan!"

"A *plan*? To see your daughter?"

"Y'know what I mean."

"No. *No*, I really don't."

"It was a dick move," said Jack.

"You think?" Her hand fell to the table making the sandwiches jump. "How could you forget to take your own daughter to breakfast if you'd said you would?"

That morning, before Jude's calls, he and Elizabeth had lain in bed knotted up together, watching the birds out of the window and making up stories about their lives, giving them voices and imagining out loud what they might be saying to each other. A blissful calm after the frenzy of making love.

"Can we move this thing on? I got a meeting this afternoon."

Jack blinked away the smoke from his eyes and avoided asking what meeting.

"The last thing I want is to hurt Aimee. Or anyone. But I need to be able to work things out, *alone*."

"Fine. But why *now*? It's the high school prom next Friday. I have college applications, the science trip, my phone is flashing constantly with parents on hold. In the next two weeks we have budget meetings, academic review meetings, the zero-hours timetable, in-take meetings, new legislations committees —two members of staff have just handed in their notices, that's a violation, but what can I do? The head janitor has cancer—three months to live—four little kids, yeah, Ramón's cousin. Could you put whatever *this* is on hold?"

"I've been unhappy for a while now, sorry if my mental health messes with your work schedule."

"You were *that* unhappy?" she asked patiently. "Living here is *that* awful? How about, you meditate here? Hey, you could turn the top floor into a private sanctuary—incense and pan pipes. I'm… I'm really…" she slammed her hands down on the table, "fucked up by this, you know?" She looked at her watch again. "Goddam I have to—"

"I'm not coming back."

It was like everything inside that black skirt and red silk blouse turned to protoplasm. Tears like silver beads rolled down her shirt. Jack got off his chair, put his arms around her and heard her whisper, "I want my mom."

"I don't want to hurt you."

"So don't."

Jack tightened his hold, wishing he was the person being left.

"I will do everything to make this as easy and painless as I can. I love all of you just as much as ever—even Mouse." He smiled, hoping the joke about how he hated that cat would lighten the mood but Jude was in a kind of trance.

The room was quiet. Jack breathed out, relief evaporating off him—he wanted to run. And run and run. It would be fun to take Tip too. That reminded him, he needed to get back upstairs to pack his jogging shorts.

"Why?" Jude came alive in his arms, erupting like a

wounded dragon: red, smokey, with a strength that knocked him off balance. "You said you needed time to *think* and now you're *leaving*?" She made a grab for her bag, threw the cigarettes in and thrust the glass of wine to one side. Her fingers jabbed at his shoulder. "You need to be *you*, you!"

Standing in front of him, almost level in her power heels, her hair flaring out, she shook her fist at him with her index pointing out like a gun. "Go back to wherever you're hiding and *think* again." Her breathing was intense, fueling a livid energy. "You *don't* get to go! You *don't* get to be someone else! Be a *better you*. Here! Where *you* live! Where *you* live with *us*!" Jude poked at his chest, hard, enough for him to be knocked back against the doorframe. She grabbed her bag, pushed it over her shoulder, picked up the bottle and swallowed back the last of the red wine so that her mouth looked like she been ripping into a carcass then strode out of the kitchen, out of the house, slamming the door and snap-reversing out of the drive.

Jack was still leaning against the kitchen door after Jude had left. The flat of his hand against his chest, rubbing where she'd thumped him. Her wine glass was on the table, the chair she'd knocked over still upturned. Tip lay in the hall, facing the door, occasionally shifting position with a huff. The fridge buzzed. The kitchen clock ticked.

Jack's phone buzzed with a text from his server provider notifying him of his last payment: $392. What? He scrolled through the itemized bill to see most of the calls had been made from Jude's phone. The most expensive was a set of numbers that had been dialed repeatedly over the last week—one call from 4:48 in the morning. Who'd she been talking to? Lawyers? Private detectives?

He cut and pasted the number into his phone. Waited. It rang. Harp music played before a voice-recorded message:

"Welcome to Purple Path psychic readings, tarot forecasts

and oracle guidance. Please hold while your spirit guide finds you a messenger."

Jack changed the dog's water and closed the downstairs windows.

Tip tap danced at the door.

"No walk today, bro."

Jack had to move now to be at the garage before the gang lord arrived for his Shelby AC Cobra. The car wasn't ready; Jack had had to take it up to Cobra County where they confirmed he'd misdiagnosed the problem, now Jack was waiting on them to change the fuel-level sender.

A text came through from Elizabeth. She'd made an appointment for 10am to go house-hunting.

Next thing, Jack found himself wrapped around Tip on Aimee's bed again where he slept until he heard the neighbors' kids coming home from school.

39

SUBJECT: HOW YOU DOOOOIN?

From: Neptune99

To: Salacia99

Date: Wednesday July 15, 2020 at 9:03

You crazy, girl? I just read they got giant refrigerators on the streets of New York for the pilling up bodies. Get out of that place! This virus does not mess around—Jude's mom contracted it from the kid who delivered her groceries. I CARE A LOT ABOUT YOU!

BTW I do a killer Joey from *Friends* impression but it doesn't come out well on email—if you're bored isolating, maybe we could talk again? Leave a slice for me!

———

JUDE CURSED the day she'd campaigned to have speed bumps put on her road. With each mound, she was getting later and a new terror crashed over her.

They would have to sell the house.

She'd end up in a little studio filled with rescue cats that would try to wriggle out of her arms when she squeezed them too tight. She'd have to make do with window boxes. She would say Jack leaving her was the best thing that had ever happened while thick-matted gray hair spread down her thighs and she put up notices in the halls of her building reminding people not to slam the door after 9pm because *some people were sleeping!!!* She wouldn't even be able to afford to laminate them.

Her kids would make up excuses not to come by because she snapped, smelt rotten and took ages telling some story about a conversation she had at the laundromat.

Jude had eight minutes to get into a room filled with people who wanted to talk about funding, academic achievement and educational state law changes.

She'd die old, poor and alone.

No one would want the cats.

Had she just physically assaulted her husband?

Jude drew in the air from the A/C; held it in her lungs as if she were underwater. She blew out and in again, relished the relief of light-headedness. She repeated the sequence as it dislodged the pressure in her chest until she saw the top of the school peering through the trees in Orange Flower Park.

The traffic lights turned red so she pulled out a cigarette to calm herself. A woman waiting at the bus stop stared at her. It was a rare sight these days, someone smoking, maybe it was illegal.

When the lights changed, she heard her mother's voice, *Jujinsky, just do the next right thing, and don't forget to breathe.*

40

SUBJECT: SAUDADE

From: Elizabeth Lambert

To: Jack Mathews

Date: Tuesday July 28, 2020 at 2:52

Captain Jack! So love your voice! Feel SO close to you right now. Love the playlist and great news about your running times. And thanks for the podcast recommendations, will listen when on the plane. Teachable moment: just saw the definition of this word on the internet. 'Saudade'. It's Portuguese, means a longing for somewhere like home. It's the way I've felt ever since we parted that night.

———

JUDE SWERVED through the school gates, nearly crushing Bradley Orson holding up a sign saying *Valet Parking 'n' Deluxe Car Wash: You're British Service!*

"And if it isn't the lovely Lady M!" he called out, wiping his green jacket.

The year before Jude had made Bradley clean all the staff's cars as a punishment for repeatedly smearing the toilet walls with shit. A few of the teachers, seeing him labor over their vehicles, had given him a few dollars and Bradley got a taste for money so he set up the Valet, Vac 'n' Vash.

Brad pushed his yellow rag-doll curls up to her window. "I

say, have you been parking under a tree oozing lots of sticky stuff." He wiped his fingers on his Hawaiian shorts after opening her door for her. "Know what, m'lady? Why don't you let me give it a jolly good clean?" He opened out a pulpy red hand. "Keys? Oh, and I wondered if you'd had a chance to talk to Mr. M about me doing something at his garage?"

"Not yet…"

Bradley threw the keys up from behind his back, spun round and caught them.

"I gave a lift to a neighbor, big smoker, you have air freshener?"

"Absolutely chipper. This little baby will be tip-top and smelling of lavender by teatime."

"This meeting will go on late. Can you leave the keys with Liam if you don't see me."

Bradley saluted her, turned on the ignition and rolled the car away. "Have a spiffing afternoon."

Jude kept forgetting to ask why he spoke in that ridiculous British accent and to have Ramón look into the legalities of having a pupil make money on school property.

Tumbling into the staff toilets, Jude braced herself before peering at her face in the mirror. The door opened. Carole.

"Isn't this exciting, being televised? None of the other clusters have anything like that!"

Jude clenched the sides of the sink.

"You OK?" she asked, handing her a paper towel. "Hot flushes? Don't it just feel like a giant sweaty sumo wrestler picks you up, grabs you to his prickly breast for thirty seconds —squeeze, squeeze, squeeze—then he drops you down all sticky and cold? Sucks."

Jude screwed up the paper towel, tossed it in the trashcan while Carole stared at her reflection in the washroom mirror.

"Jack's leaving me."

Carole Green had been a newlywed, feisty and ambitious secretary at one of the first schools where Jude taught but when they re-met a decade later at Orange Flower High, she was a divorced, mother-of-two whose college education she couldn't afford without working nights at a fast-food restaurant.

"You guys will patch this up by tonight." She put her hand into her purse. "Try this foam foundation, it moisturizes and takes the shine out at the same time, here…" She unscrewed the tube; Jude closed her eyes and hoped the moment would pass quickly. But once Carole started pressing her cold fingers to her skin, she succumbed to a moment when someone was looking after her.

"Another woman?"

Jude didn't know how to answer when she heard voices in the corridor and the school bell ring for 2pm.

"You have a little bug in your hair—got it. Little color on the cheeks… So, what happened?"

"Last week he said he needed time to think and went off for the weekend, and then when he came back he needed more time to think—was doing meditation classes, but he took a big suit-case and his golf bag. Then today, he said he wasn't coming back."

"The 'I-need-time-to-think'? He's met someone, he wants to try them out a little before deciding… If you're not satisfied with your product, you can have your wife back after thirty days."

"He never said anything about another woman."

"He wouldn't. Judy, you won't believe this now, but Bruce leaving me was the best thing that ever happened to me. That's what made me realize I was an alcoholic. Today I have a spiritual program, friends, three cats and I'm growing—"

"I don't want to *grow*. I want *Jack*. Sorry, it's just… so hot!"

But despite the heat, Jude had to wear a jacket as the top underneath was too badly crumpled.

"Honey, there is a bright side—"

"A *bright* side?"

"Think of all the weight you'll lose."

41

JM: TUES 4 AUG 2020

Sorry couldn't talk. Still not able to visit Jude's intubated mom. Gonna buy iPad so kids can see her. Sorry sad news when ur on vacay. Gonna go 4 a run and listen to our playlist. Loud!

———

"Principal Mathews!" Frank Hoffman pushed himself up from his chair and waddled towards Jude as two camera operators captured the moment he bear hugged her. Frank was head of Felicidad school district and running for governor. Jude had known him for over twenty years yet she'd never once seen behind his dark glasses.

Liam came in rattling trays of iced water. Jude waved him over, took two bottles for herself and apologized again for having left him at lunch to set up the meeting.

"No worries. Here are your notes, the folder..." he said, tapping the piles of papers under her nose.

"How's Jack? The family?" bellowed Hoffman.

Jude saw Liam exchange a look with Carole—so, the news was already out.

Jude put the water to her lips and nodded with a smile to avoid lying.

"Frank Junior passed his driving test, so I'll go by the garage, see what your old man got." He stopped to wipe his forehead with a handkerchief from his breast pocket. "Great results this year, seventy-eight percent to college, five to Ivy Leagues, and that football team of yours! Pat's some trainer, huh? Sorry about the circus—" he gestured at the film crew, "politics! How's Dahlia, she still in New York?"

Turning to answer him, Jude noticed a smear of orange-colored foundation on his white shirt. She scratched her head again.

"She's fine, yeah, busy…"

Jude contemplated how she could discreetly wipe off the stain at the same time as realizing she might be giving the whole room headlice.

"Say hi from a future gov'nor to her." Frank had never blown out the torch he'd carried for Dahlia since kindergarten. Jude gestured to Ramón to turn up the air con, he signed back that it wasn't possible.

Jude stood up, tested the mic and started.

"Welcome, everyone, to Orange Flower Park High School, end of the school year 2022–2023—" She stopped for a few *Yays!* and applause. "We are very proud to be holding the third Annual State School Budgets and Monetary General meeting for our district cluster. Our team and board would like to give a special welcome to Frank Hoffman—" The room clapped for a man who most of them had been to school with and remembered as the prime target for bullies.

Jude picked up the sharpest looking pen and used it to scratch the back of her head as they worked through the agenda… all the while, Jude trained her eyes on the orange smear on Hoffman's collar. She raised a hand to acknowledge his praise of her initiative to start the school day later that year, listing the reduction in car accidents, truancy, lates and rise in grades. Despite a room full of people and cameras, she dipped her hand in her bag, felt for the foil of pills and squeezed out another diazepam. Pretending to cough, she flicked it to the back of her mouth. A gulp of water. Her gaze traveled to the cool of the hills. Jack was out there somewhere, but he wouldn't be home when she got in.

42

SUBJECT: C LA V

From: Salacia99

To: Neptune99

Date: Wednesday August 5, 2020 at 3:45

I was at the salvage plant when I heard your message, must have been devastating to tell the kids how ill their grandmother is. The more I know you, the more I appreciate what a great man, father and friend you are. E xxx And don't forget to VOTE—less than 100 days until the election—remember to register? Also, phone coms not private—private email accounts. WhatsApp better if poss and long to hear your voice again!

———

"AND AFTER ALL THOSE years you found each other..." Sherry-Ann drained off a tear from her lower lid.

Miguel nodded. "How romantic! So, we need something that isn't slutty, yet *totally* slutty."

The best thing about a new love affair was all the sex; the worst thing about a new love affair was all the sex. It was the third time in two weeks that Elizabeth had cystitis, which had sent her into town to pick up something from the pharmacy but once out, instead of finishing the introduction to her book that was due that Friday, she'd found herself in Victoria's Secret telling the shop assistants the story of her and Jack as she rotated in and out of the changing room. They decided on a crimson bra, gossamer lace matching panties and suspenders before Sherry-Ann had the inspiration to add a ribbon waist band.

"I'll take all these," she said as Miguel all but snatched her gold card from her Prada wallet.

As Elizabeth contorted herself around her shopping bags to reach for her car keys, there was yet another obstruction to getting home. Someone was standing by her car.

"Can I help you?"

"Oh, I was just admiring this…" The woman started to laugh. "Elizabeth?"

"Yes?"

"Megan. Megan of Buena Vista—"

Elizabeth gathered the last of her energy to look alive.

"Gorgeous car!"

"It is, yes, a gift from Jack. He actually rebuilt it—it was a wreck before."

"Jack Mathews?"

"Uh-huh. Anyway, nice seeing—"

Megan looked down at her feet, then reached for Elizabeth's arm.

"I know you guys are looking at property. I was kinda hurt you didn't go through me."

"We're looking to buy and you do rentals, right?"

"Well, that's the thing: I want to move from rentals into sales. And having you as a client, it could be life changing for someone like me."

"Oh please, I'm not that influential! But I'm sorry, I should have contacted you, and from now on, you will be our *numero uno* agent. Have a good—"

"Can I tell you something?"

Elizabeth nodded, her hand over her eyes, damning the girl for putting her in direct sunlight.

"Mrs. Mathews asked me to do an evaluation of her lake

house. Her sister might buy her out, death and taxes, blah blah, but when I was talking to her, I realized she doesn't have any idea Jack's up with you in the Heights."

"I assure you they've separated."

"Really? Cause she said they might sell both houses and sail around the world."

"How about our number one agent breaks the news to her?"

"Me? But—"

"I'd be really grateful to you. You're seeing her this weekend, you say?"

Megan nodded.

"Very grateful and then let's do lunch."

"Hi there, new neighbor!"

Elizabeth had just got out of her car as her gates were closing when a couple in matching running gear stepped through. He, tall, broad-chested in his fifties and her, doll-like, not long out of school. The man took one stride to his partner's three.

"Matt, Lindsay. We live next door," he said, pointing at his house.

"Elizabeth," she said, shaking hands with Lindsay whose eyes hid behind pink-rimmed shades.

"Look, we won't pretend that we don't know who you are, people talk—"

"Megan talks! Elizabeth Lambert, right? I'm a stylist and content creator, kind of thing," said Lindsay, clapping her hands. "I studied design in Rome."

"She's a fan," said Matt, rolling his eyes, lighting a cigar and then chugging out white balloons of smoke.

"Looks like someone's been shopping at Victoria's Secret!"

"Well, my husband had a tough day, so…"

"Sexy underwear and he'll forget all his problems," said Matt. "Hey, just wondering if you guys'd like to come over this weekend. Monday we leave again for Austin."

This was exactly what Elizabeth and Jack needed—to build a social life to compete with the one Jack missed.

"How about Sunday night?"

"Sure!" said Lindsay, bouncing up and down. "Have a..." she pointed at the VS bags, "special night!"

Inside the house, Elizabeth trode heavily up the stairs to her bed. Esme had done the laundry and changed all the sheets, so Elizabeth wasn't able to snuffle around the bed for little pockets of Jack's smell on the pillow. She re-read his message from the afternoon.

> Picking up Aimee from hip hop coz Jude's got work stuff till late then straight back to rip off those panties with my teeth, 🥢🥢🥢

43

SUBJECT: HOT STUFF

From: Elizabeth Lambert

To: Jack Mathews

Date: Friday August 7, 2020 at 21:45

Those are some sexy legs—how can I work when you're sending me these very distracting photos. OK—revenge—here's me in something very black and tight doing my Zoom yoga class but still wearing my mask!?

Here in Oxford, England, where we found a language school for Cosie.

BTW Just reading rock bios about the Seattle grunge years to see if any of those guys my mom hung around could be my dad.

Elizabeth—the First!

———

AGAIN, NO ANSWER. SHE IGNORED MAGNUS' email forwarding details of the Shoreditch project. Scrolled past Bruno's text asking when she'd take Cosima at the end of August. Her editor was asking again if she'd send over the chapters she'd promised. Another text came through, an old client asking about the search for her father and inviting her to stay at her house in Dana Point Harbor. But Elizabeth just lay there waiting for Jack like a machine on standby. Maybe this is how she'd always been since Avalon.

146

. . .

'Did I just see a mermaid stealing Pop Tarts from the store?'

Brother and sister froze. On home ground, their escape routes of back alleys, fire exits and climbable trees were second nature, but that Spring in 1999, they'd not had enough time on Catalina Island to work out their terrain.

Elizabeth turned to see a man: tall, strong with sand-colored hair flopping over blue laughing eyes. He was only a few years older than her, looked friendly, but she knew how quickly these things could turn.

Elizabeth put her hand in her jacket pocket, threw the packet down between them.

'It's cool,' he said, handing them back to her. 'No one saw but me. Here.' Jack held out a packet of cookies and a bottle of orangeade. Danny waited for Elizabeth's nod before taking them from him.

'You told the man in the store that *Double Trouble* was your boat,' said Danny. Jack laughed. The kid's percipience often threw people.

'I wish! I needed to make a ship-to-shore call, so I said it was *my boat* on behalf of the crew, not me personally. I'm just working on it.' Jack said, not letting on he'd noticed Elizabeth taking the food back and handing her brother a cookie. 'My dad and I picked up this wreck to do up for a guy over at Newport Beach. Should make quite a few bucks out of it to cover college, I start this fall. You local?'

The children looked to each other.

'Not my business,' Jack said.

'Our mom sings at the Salty Bear. They let us stay in their back room.'

'Sounds fun.' Though judging by the way the kids looked to each other, probably not.

'I'm Jack.'

'Danny, and my sister's Elizabeth.'

'Elizabeth. Like the queen,' said Jack with a wink.

'Lotta people say that,' said Danny.

'Yeah. Cause she's Elizabeth the *first*, right?'

The boy beamed, it was easier to talk to him because the sister wasn't like anything he'd ever seen. Hair of threaded gold, pale aquamarine eyes in a heart-shaped face just on the turn from child to woman, and he didn't want to linger too long on those tanned legs in cut-off shorts with a belt of feathers. She was shoeless and wore a lot of silver rings. 'Wanna see the work I'm doing in the cabins, have us a little deck picnic?'

Danny started to pull Jack towards the harbor, Jack pretended to stumble, cried out as though being kidnapped, the boy dragged him faster. And then Jack heard Elizabeth laugh and she felt the heat from his taut, rounded shoulders when he pointed to the boat. She moved close enough to see dust in his hair and paint on his flipflops as he leapt onto the boat.

'Here,' he said, reaching out for Elizabeth. She felt the strong clasp of his hand as he drew her aboard and into their story.

'You thought about treating the deck with a dark walnut varnish? It'd bring out the grain of wood and cover those stains?' she asked. No, he hadn't thought of that. It was like before he'd met her, he hadn't known anything about anything.

44

SUBJECT: SUMMER OF 99

From: Jack Mathews

To: Elizabeth Lambert

Date: Tuesday August 11, 2020 at 19:45

Thank you for the guided tour around Oxford yesterday, awesome! I'm sending you another two playlists to download. One is all the music we listened to in Avalon, summer '99 and the other is to bring you up with the music scene in the States right now. Coz of Aimee's dance thing I'm down with what's in – unfortunately, I also hear a lotta drill music from Bentley but I won't deafen you with that! Suddenly got super busy here with tons of folks taking their vacations in California cause they can't go anywhere else.

———

"GOOD EVENING, could you put me through to Madame Salacia?" Jack asked, pressing the phone to his ear.

Elizabeth let out a sleepy laugh. "I was just remembering the time we met."

"Huh. I like to focus on our future—like tonight. Who took those photos?"

"Why? Want her to join us?"

"Just you is plenty babe!"

"This velvet corset is so tight, how about you—"

"Stop! I just picked Aimee up from hip hop, dropping her

off at school then I'll be straight over to unlace you, so slowly until you're begging me to rip it all off."

"You didn't get back to me about the open-house tour, the house in Carlsbad?"

Jack coughed. "This weekend? I can't leave the garage. It's chaos. Bentley took off and—"

"Another time then."

"I wish I—"

The line went dead.

"Evening, sir."

Jack looked around to see where the voice came from.

"Bradley Orson, President of Valet, Vac 'n' Vash."

"*Vash?*"

"Alliteration, sir. I've been meaning to talk to you about a business proposition." The boy held out his hand, the other clutched a soapy bucket. "Lady M. said maybe I could set up my service at your garage, see, school closes till September and I'm saving for college."

"We have a car-cleaning service already, thanks."

"But I offer a valet service as well as vacuum, clean and polish any vehicle ship-shape-and-Bristol fashion—all *by hand*."

"OK well come by tomorrow afternoon. Don't you have a home to get to?" Jack asked before remembering Jude saying something about how he didn't.

45

SUBJECT: BIOPHILIA 4 EVAH!

From: Neptune99

To: Salacia99

Date: Thursday August 13, 2020 at 20:45

At Kids Call tonight. It's hard hearing the stuff kids are saying during this pandemic. You're now waking up to a new day, wish I was by your side. Could we 'chat' later when I walk Tip? Otherwise we'll have to wait a while coz Beanie's got three other girls over till Sunday. Just planning how to set up the showroom with your 'chromazone' idea from Pinterest! Hope the carpenter came back in the end!

———

THE PLYWOOD DOOR to Jude's office expanded in warm weather so to open it she had to synchronize a shoulder push and sharp kick. As the frame shuddered, she took two long heavy steps into the room and collapsed in her chair.

Only minutes before, the principal's suite had been filled with over-tired and excitable staff celebrating the end of the teaching year though there was still another week of sports activities and prize day to get through.

Jude gulped back some leftover orange juice from a plastic cup and tossed it in the direction of her overflowing trash. Since she'd been made Head, she had thrown an informal staff party in her office to thank everyone for their contributions to the year. They'd sipped, nibbled and spilled out stories of times gone by and hopes for the future. After an hour, Liam announced they had something for Jude and brought in a baby magnolia tree from all of them to her. In her thanks, she'd been on the verge of breaking down, less grateful than hysterical. It hadn't been a stirring speech, or party; it hadn't been a good year, and for her personal archives would only stand out as the one when her husband wanted to end their marriage and Aimee had been caught by the chemistry teacher having sex with two Grade 11 boys.

Jude texted Bentley:

> Could you come by the school this evening to help me take my gifts home? Chocolate and bath oils in it for you and Maxxie? Preston's coming tonight. Friday night-family-pizza-night!

The fan's blades whipped up the stale air as Jude read the school's prayer framed above her desk:

This is our school.
Let peace grow here,
Let these rooms be filled
with contentment,
And our hearts filled with love.
For as many hands build a house,
So many hearts make a school.

Jude had found the lines in an old library book and used it as part of the school's mission statement. But as much as she tried to inspire peace in her heart all she could see was her hands pushing Jack away from her the week before. Jude felt around in her handbag for a painkiller in the hope it might ease her lower back. She swallowed it down with flat warm Diet Coke from the can. *And breathe.*

There was a bang at the door.

"Mom!"

Jude gasped for air and wiped the sides of her mouth.

The door swung open as Aimee rolled into Jude's desk knocking a pile of papers to the floor.

"You look weird," she said, squinting into her mother's face. "Look what I found."

Another bang against the desk's leg.

"Stop it!"

"OK, OK…" Aimee lifted herself up. "I'm hungry, can we go now?"

"Just… *please.*" It came out as a plea because Jude had no strength to deal with Aimee in one of her hyper moods. "I thought you and Philly were at dance class?"

"Mom? It's after *nine*! We been helping Carole go through lost property. That's how we found this hoverboard."

"It's not yours."

"Is now."

"No!" Jude's heart was going off again. Aimee slid down to the floor.

"It was lost, what's the biggie?"

"You said 'we,' is Bentley with you?" Jude walked to the basin in the corner of her room and drank from the cup that she normally used to water the plants. "Beans. Please. I beg of you. Stop skating around in my room and—"

"Can I take this?" Aimee asked, holding up a basket of macaroons.

"No, not now."

"But I haven't eaten!"

"I need to make a list of who gave what first."

"Make a list," she said, opening the packet, "and whoever's left gave you these. I'll take some for dad too."

"Dad?"

Just then Jack's silhouette filled the frosted-panel window in her door. He tapped it then stepped into the room. That Jack smile. And he was looking in good shape: trim, with a haircut and new clothes. He shook his head at the plants, bottles, boxes of chocolates—then the magnolia tree.

"Must have been a bumper year," he said with a whistle, "or you're taking a lot of bribes these days."

"Oh yeah, I got those parents well trained." Jude held up a statue of a green frog in a tuxedo. "Who's gonna get this for Christmas?"

"Bentley!" said Aimee and Jack at the same time.

"Hey," said Jack, looking at a watch that Jude had never seen before. Looked expensive. "Let's help Mom close shop."

"OK, you can have the macaroons but *after* you put that skateboard thing back."

46

SUBJECT: IT'S JUST A LITTLE CRUSH

From: Elizabeth Lambert

To: Jack Mathews

Date: Friday August 14, 2020 at 17:55

Maybe a big crush 😊 Loved talking to you about your impressions of Paris when you came here with your family, still laughing at the image of you wearing a beret! Hey, I was thinking of coming out to see you in San Diego? I could also combine with the search for my dad...? What d'you think?

———

ELIZABETH POSITIONED herself in the bathroom wearing the VS panties and bra underneath one of Jack's open shirts. She lifted her phone over her head, let her hair cascade down her back catching the last of the day's sun and took a photograph. *Dressed or undressed?* She threw the shirt into the laundry now it had oil on it and stepped into a pair of silver thigh-length boots. She referenced a number of hashtags before sitting on the ledge of the upstairs window watching for Jack's car. As the streetlights came on, Jack texted that he needed to put Aimee to bed. *Back ASAP.* They were not going to have the sex session she'd been directing in her head all day. Elizabeth lay back on the hall carpet; put her fingers in her panties. Her orgasm was immediate, shallow, without pleasure.

Over 298 people reacted to her story several seconds later. The 'Likes' quadrupled after ten.

Her phone rang again.

"Yes?"

"Lizzy? *C'est toi alors!* How are you, my darling?"

Céline always talked in one slow strangulated note as if she were coming to take your hands at the end of a mutual friend's funeral. Everything was tragic, futile, but together you'd battle on for lunch.

"So last week, my darling, we had dinner with Bruno and a very pretty young Russian girl—stupid as anything—and he told me you were in California and next week I'll be in LA with friends on the coast, when are you free?"

"I'm in this weird, no-where place called Felicidad but I can get to La Jolla, although I'm behind on my book and—"

"Victoria will be with me; she'd love to see you! I'll be in touch."

It was already dark when Elizabeth put the phone down. It went again—no caller ID. The person hung up when she answered.

Elizabeth sat through another episode of *Love Island UK* and the phone rang again. Elizabeth was about to be rude when she heard a voice say her name.

"Miss Lambert, I'm sorry to bother you. It's Bentley again. From Mathews' Motors, I left a few messages and—"

"Bentley, please stop calling me."

"But in that Instagram photo—"

"Did you hear what I said? Don't call me again or I'm going to report you for harassment."

"But I need to—"

Elizabeth cut the line.

47

SUBJECT: MAKE MY HOTLINE BLING

From: Jack Mathews

To: Elizabeth Lambert

Date: Tuesday August 18, 2020 at 17:35

We got cut off when you got into the elevator. Relax! Of course I want you to come out—you crazy? It's just we're locked down, baby doll, and even if you could, you'd have to quarantine and test constantly, wouldn't you? And what if you got sick? Also, this BLM movement has made stuff pretty nuts out here. When I asked about video calls you seemed a little freaked. NO PRESSURE. It's just a way we can see each other without risk and riots. My sister, Clare, and her wife, Kendall, are driving down to stay cause we wanted to celebrate Preston's HS graduation—Kendall is a total freak about germs so they're gonna build a tent in the back yard! But it might not happen coz the travel rules change every day. Your lonesome sailor, J xxx

———

JACK FINISHED CARRYING in the last of Jude's end-of-year presents—even the magnolia tree which had left mounds of earth in the back of his pick-up and through the house to the backyard where he'd sat it in a black plastic bag filled with water. The petals reminded him of the skin on Elizabeth's buttocks. His shirt was damp and his underarms smelt of fermented yeast but he kept his jacket on so that as soon as he had a chance to slip out the family home he wouldn't lose a second.

After throwing stuff on a tray for Aimee to eat, and hearing, "Dad. *Vegan*," Jack stood, legs akimbo, hands on hips, under the porch light on the lookout for Jude's car to appear through the dark-red sky. He saluted Jerry, the dentist who lived opposite, who swung the door to his Hyundai Kona closed with one back-hand motion. *Asshole.* Jack and Jude had seen a lot of Jerry and his dental hygienist wife until some conflict had broken out between Bentley and their son. Jack swiped at a moth circling the new bulb he'd just put in. He considered opening the bottle of Jameson whiskey buried in Jude's booty pile. He sure deserved a shot for the road. In fact, he could take the whole bottle, share it with Elizabeth. Jude wouldn't know it was gone. She was drinking too much as it was; taking it would probably save her a liver transplant.

Aimee tugged at the end of his jacket. "Come see this TikTok reel, it's gonna make you laugh."

Aimee landed on her beanbag which Jude had ordered especially in her favorite color—*Chartreuse*—with the word *BEANIE* printed on it.

Aimee scanned her search results while patting Tip's head. "Just watch."

"OK but once mom's home, I gotta shoot."

Aimee's fingers tapped the keys of the laptop he'd given her Christmas 2020. Since that time it'd been covered in stickers and friends' initials written in blobs of different-colored nail polish. He remembered the debate about whether or not they should get it for her when most of her classes went online—and Jack was terrified she'd see something from Elizabeth if they continued to share. Everyone had an opinion: the boys, the neighbors, Jude's staffroom, of course, Marcie— the garage guru—had many. Governments could have deployed air strikes swifter than settling the question over whether Aimee was too young for such an extravagant present.

"Where d'you say you were going?"

"Visiting a client, who's also a friend," he answered, forcing out of his head the image of Elizabeth in suspenders.

Aimee raised her eyebrows and put on a Miss Marple voice: "And does the friend have a name?"

"Show me the clip again, that was funny."

"Thought you wanted to talk."

Just then, Jack saw a large white box in the corner of the room covered in cellophane and a picture of a brand-new iMac.

"Jellybean, is that a new computer?"

"Uh-huh. Mom's end-of-year present to us."

"When she get that?"

"Monday. After school. We popped some tags and had Chinese. Bentley bought Maxxie a Dyson hair straightener for her birthday which was kinda dumb as they broke up the next day. This elephant paints with his trunk, watch."

Jack stroked the back of her head, wondering if he could get away with putting his mountain bike in the car.

"Mom's right: something has changed about you."

"Nothing's changed about how much I love you. And Bentley and Preston—"

"And Mom. You love Mom too, right?"

"I love and respect your mom."

"She said you—"

They both looked up when Jude opened the door, her arms full of groceries. "Did you see the sunset? Wasn't it extraordinary?"

Through the open door, they could see Bentley parking his bike and Maxxie getting down from it.

"Maxxie's here," said Jack. "Thought you said they broke up?"

"Guess she wanted her gift," said Aimee, already riffling through the food bags.

Jude shrugged. "They just had a little fight, Jack, couples have them all the time, don't they?" Jack didn't return her gaze until she asked him, "Hon, could you make sure we have enough charcoal, we're gonna do a barbecue tonight, we'll be eight if Aimee wants to invite Savannah."

Bentley eclipsed the porch light before walking in and taking off his helmet. Maxxie followed, her eyes to the ground.

Aimee high-fived her brother and opened a packet of Doritos, offering some to Maxxie.

"Eight people?" asked Jack.

"Yeah. Preston's on his way with Chadiki."

"With what?" asked Bentley.

"Chadiki, his friend. I got some carne asada, sausages and salad. Beanie, come on, fairy lights!"

Preston and Jack bear hugged, slapping each other's backs.

"That's great about the internship—maybe they'll take you on, too."

"Dad, it's a crap-commission only thing. Meet Chad, my friend from college."

Jack took Chad's hand. "Preston's talked about you, welcome. You like meat? If not, we have other stuff."

"Sure do," he said, before Jude called out, "Jack? Stop Bentley putting chili sauce on everything—sorry, Chad!" She hugged Preston's friend. "We're nearly done. Beanie? Did you invite Savannah and Bree?"

"What's that?" asked Bentley, pointing at the barbecue.

"Beanie's vegan sausage. It's tofu, and—"

"Looks like an abortion," snarled Bentley.

"Maxxie, you OK?" Jack searched for her eyes under the bird's nest of indigo-colored hair. Eye contact with Maxxie was often an uncomfortable event because she suffered from trichotillomania and her gaze reminded Jack of a staring contest with one of Bentley's axolotls. "You kids know what you're going to do with the time off?"

Maxxie looked at Bentley. "Time off?"

"Dad's given me a break from the—"

Maxxie stood up and went back into the house. Bentley picked up his beer and followed her out with, "Gee *thanks*, Dad."

"Leave them," said Jude, holding up a bottle a champagne. She chinked her glass.

"Ladies and gentlemen, and Jack—joke—I propose we celebrate the end of this shitty day and this shitty year and having Chad with us tonight. Jack, wanna open this and Preston, maybe you'd like to make a toast?"

Jack popped the cork and handed the bottle back to his eldest son.

"We're celebrating the end of the school year, for Mom and Beanie. And, for me... I'd like to celebrate the beginning of—"

"That stick is for *my* Halloumi. No one touch it," threatened Aimee.

Jude put her hand on her arm. "Shhh... Preston, go on."

"We've got to the end of the school year. Mom, you're awesome. Dad too, and—"

"—and me and Bentley and Tip and Maxxie and... yeah, yeah, yeah," chanted Aimee.

Preston looked to his mother who nodded for him to go on. "So this is maybe a good moment to share with you a great thing in my life and, I hope, a great thing in our family's life..." Preston took the hand of his friend, Chadiki. "I—we—have something to announce to you all."

"Y'said that already," said Aimee, spooning a tortilla chip into the guacamole and dropping it onto her phone. "Savannah can't come, she's—"

"Ssh, Aimee," said Jude.

Jack, for the first time that night, exchanged a look with Jude that translated as, *Aimee's had too much sugar.*

"Well, Mom already knows and she's encouraged me to... come out... in front of you all and say..." He twisted his hand into Chadiki's palm. "Chadiki and I are moving in together next year."

"Thought you already shared an apartment?" asked Aimee.

"We do, but in the fall we'll live together *as a couple.*"

"Gotcha," she said, clamping down on her chip.

The relief left Preston breathing hard as Chadiki bumped against his shoulder.

"To the adorable couple!" said Jude, raising the bottle of champagne.

"Is this champagne?" said Maxxie, blinking at the bubbles.

"I'm pansexual," said Aimee, swirling her finger around the dip bowl. "Preston, why are you crying?"

Jude opened her arms out, ushered them all into her reach.

"Group hug!" announced Aimee, putting down her phone and jumping into the ring of locked arms.

"I love you all so much—Bentley, come on in!" Jude said, opening the circle for Bentley to lurch into.

"To the best ever family," said Preston, "and the best partner."

Seeing Tip nudging himself into the group, Aimee added, "And best dog!"

48

SUBJECT: LONDON'S BURNING

From: Elizabeth Lambert

To: Jack Mathews

Date: Wednesday August 19, 2020 at 22:54

Cheri amour, thanks for your sweet texts. So here's a photo of me on Europe's highest building! The designer award was just a little thing from a small magazine but the party was cool and I danced till sunrise! If you wanna see more, check out my IG. There's a photo of me talking to David 'n' Victoria Beckham? We're thinking of going to St Barthes to stay with our friends/clients as Bruno can't stand the idea of another 'confinement' in France but I'll still find away to reach you. PS My therapist suggests I take a DNA test.

THE EVENING PASSED as they filled up on food and family lore, Chad answering questions about his life, asking about theirs, Preston's account of his interview at the law firm and Aimee instructing them about who could eat what. Bentley hung back in the doorway sharing a T-bone with Tip, but when Aimee announced it was time for ice cream with warmed brownies, he turned back into the house and opened the front door.

"Bentley?" Jude called after him.

"Gonna grab some marshmallows to roast," he shouted back, slamming the door.

"What? Now?" Jude rolled her eyes at Maxxie who'd barely eaten. "*And* we have Daddy's favorite cheesecake, not Mom's homemade but still, pretty good," said Aimee. "I'll get it."

"I'll help you," said Maxxie.

"What's up with them?" whispered Jack to Jude.

"Maxxie found out Bentley had lunch with a client... a woman. She looked at his phone records, he's been calling someone—she thinks it's this person. He says he's not sure about things, needs space... sounds familiar, huh?" She widened her eyes and tutted. "Why are you looking like that? You know—"

"No," Jack snapped. "He only comes to work to drive our best cars away."

"I'm going to suggest he stays up at the cabin a while. I was surprised to see Maxxie tonight. You wouldn't do me an herbal tea, would you, a pot, with the mint from over there?"

Jack walked into the kitchen, the mint leaves bunched in his hand but stopped, mid-step, listening to Aimee going through her hip-hop routine with Chadiki whose knowledge of rap music rivaled hers. She squealed at songs he recommended she listen to, tapping the titles into her phone. Jude and Preston volleyed back and forth with views about some political event while Bentley closed the front door, walked through the house without marshmallows.

"Mr. Mathews?" Maxxie was standing behind him. "You forgotten what you came in here for?"

Jack turned, looked at the quizzical smile on that ashen face. He wanted to say, *Yes, I'd forgotten this. All this.*

"Beanie! Bed! Come on or you'll be all cranky tomorrow," called Jack again, catching Bentley feeding Tip the last of the sausages.

"You OK with that?" asked Bentley, jutting his head

towards the kitchen where Jude and Chadiki were scraping food into the compost.

"With what?"

"You know *what*, Preston," he said, curling his lip. "Aren't parents supposed to flip out when their son says he's gay?"

"In the 1950s maybe."

Bentley scratched his chin. "I know some people today that wouldn't like it. Not at all." He pushed at a plastic chair. "Mom's even making up a bed for them."

"And?"

"I had to date Maxxie for a year before she could 'sleep under your roof.'"

"You were sixteen."

Jack looked through the haze of lights over the city and back down at the grass that needed cutting. "Dude, what's up with you?"

"You mean quitting at your dumb garage to go into body-building? Cars are not my thing."

Jude came out with a sponge in her hand. "Take the phone away from her, Jack."

"But tomorrow's Saturday!"

"Beanie, no technology two hours before and after sleep!"

"Sounds fair," Jack said, protectively feeling for his own phone.

"No way does it *sound fair*!" Aimee lowered her baseball cap and crossed her arms in the defiant pose that had started her dance routine.

"Come on, missy!" said Jude, pulling her daughter up the stairs.

When Jude and Aimee were out of sight, Jack lay a hand on his son's shoulder.

"If you resign from the garage, go ahead, but there's a, like, way of doing it, a professional way. But right now, all I hear is *Where's Bentley?* and it's causing problems."

"All I hear is *Where's Jack?* So don't hang that on me. Draxx hates me, always—"

"Maybe think about treating his sister better."

Aimee hung over the banister waving her toothbrush out to Jack. "Can we all go to Swaggers for Saturday brunch? All of us, and Chadiki?"

"We'll see."

"And don't *forget* this time."

"Tomorrow afternoon we're making a series of videos about our cars for prospective buyers—how about you be in some?"

"Only if I can direct."

Jack followed Aimee to her room, smiling as she bunny-hopped into bed.

"Chad's cool, huh?"

"He's as smart and funny as he is handsome. If I were gay, I'd go for him too."

She giggled into her duvet and Jack suspected she was acting like a kid to keep his attention.

"Are you gay? That why you're leaving?"

"Chad's taken, so… no."

"And you *love* Mommy, right?"

"Of course, and I love you, Jumping Bean, our Aimee, our *loved one*."

Jack kissed the end of her messy braid. She looked at his jacket, the car keys in his hand.

"You really have to go?"

"I'm right here."

After leaving her room, he passed Preston's where he and Jude were making up the bed.

"Night, boys," he said.

In the hall, Jack zipped up his jacket, opened the door.

Jude called to him from the stairs. "You're *not* leaving, now? It's—"

The cool air rushed in.

"I'm just taking Tip for his walk."

"You'll need his leash then," Jude said, holding it out to him.

49

SUBJECT: HEY INFLUENCER!

From: Jack Mathews

To: Elizabeth Lambert

Date: Thursday August 20, 2020 at 22:14

Showed Traci your IG account and she said, oh, an 'influencer.' Then Marcie gets going about how she's also an 'influencer' because 37 'organic' people liked her recipe for quinoa, kale & mango salad. I'm like, yeah, right! I'm sitting in the supermarket lot listening to the French songs you sent and wishing you were here to sing them in my ear. I know I'm not as good-looking as David B but I am your No. 1 fan! You took a private jet to St Barthes? Have you heard anything about a global pandemic and cost-of-living crisis?

———

JUDE WAS LYING on their bed in a cream silk nightdress Jack had never seen before. Likely her mother's, he thought with a shudder. She was reading a book called *The Untethered Soul.*

"It was fun tonight, huh?"

She watched him as he fixed the window on the latch, looking out as Mouse sprang out from a hedge.

"Half-moon," he said. Jack sat next to Jude, aware of his bare legs so close to her hands.

"I drank way too much."

Jack took a few steps towards the door. "Want a glass of water?"

"Don't. Every chance, you go sneaking off."

There was no point denying it, so he sat back down.

"That thing, about Aimee and those boys, at school, I thought I should talk to her about it, we're not dealing with it and we should."

"*We* are not dealing with it? You stop by and start judging my parenting? You have a nerve to—"

"Ssssh, hey, I'm just asking what the strategy is?"

"Strategy is to keep the train on the track till school ends. She's a live wire and if we punish or criticise her it will send her in the wrong direction. Right now, they're all very uneasy about…" she rubbed her wrist, "this situation. But tonight, it was the right thing to show them we're a family and we can pull through anything."

"Yeah," he said, laying back next to her, his arm over his eyes.

"Because we love them," Jude said, stroking his hair. "And *we* love each other, right?"

"Hmm," answered Jack. "Bentley gave Tip way too many sausages."

Jude took a sip of her Coke, turned off the light, and lay back on her pillow watching the walls go from black to silver.

"My handsome boy," he heard her whimper. "I had such a crush on you when you dated Dahlia. I never thought you'd even look at me, let alone call, take me out… *marry* me. I never thought I'd be able to keep you. Turns out I couldn't. Are you in love with someone else?"

"Oh right, you really did drink too much."

Jude leant over, brought her lips to his mouth. She tasted of sugar, and toothpaste, and *Judeness.* She moved against him, folding her legs up around him, clasping him towards her. Her heat, her tears aroused him, and he lifted up the nightdress, smoothing his palm over her limbs.

He'd always loved Jude's body: her roundness, strength, the belly that had incubated his three children. He thought back to the first date, when he drove to the lake house to take her to dinner to spite Dahlia who'd refused to go steady with him. Over her pizza bianca she explained that white was, in fact, every color in the whole spectrum combined, and that night, twenty-five years ago when he drove her back to the cabin, he knew he'd marry her, even when a few months later all that went on with the girl in Catalina, it was always Jude he came back to.

50

SUBJECT: BABY, WHAT'S OUR SONG?

From: Salacia99

To: Neptune99

Date: Tuesday August 25, 2020 at 5:19

Here's me galloping on this beautiful stallion over the talcum-powder sands of St Barthes' coast, the other picture is Céline's boat—the sailing is top! So Emily, my London PA, set up this Spotify channel for Lambert Int to have soundtracks to go with our mood boards but she also set up another one for us—link below. The Françoise Hardy 'Message Personnel' reminded me to answer a question you asked the other day on the phone. What made me reach out to you after all these years? So many times I'd be in the middle of something—driving, a meeting, drawing or talking to a client—and I'd just stop dead in my tracks like I'd been shot through the heart because there was this gaping wound—you. I've always missed you, but most of time, it was like a recurring back pain or sense of constantly tripping over something, off-balance and lopsided cause I wasn't complete. And then when this pandemic hit, I thought I could die and you'd never know. It was worth the chance to ask if you'd ever felt the same. Did you?

———

ELIZABETH LEANT her head against the windowpane breathing to the even rhythm of Jack doing his morning laps in the pool. In Catalina they'd spent afternoons swimming together, when he'd called her his mermaid, and he the sailor who'd summoned her from the depths. And she still ached for him every time she saw the curve of his shoulders, the power in his muscles, the cool ripples gliding along the backs of his feet.

That Monday morning, there was no sun, no birdsong, even a chill in the air. Jack lifted himself out of the pool and used the waiting towel to pat himself dry, then dropped it back onto the lounger. Elizabeth thought, *He doesn't want to be here.*

"Shall I bring your breakfast out here, Mr. Jack?" asked Esme.

"Why not?"

The girl blushed as she placed Jack's orange juice on the table followed by, "Blueberry pancakes," she said. He punched the air and made her laugh more, shaking his head like a big dog, stretching out before he sat down to his meal.

Elizabeth told herself to keep it together until he left for work. She had done well so far, not making a scene when he came back on Saturday evening, talking about his work with no reference to the text he'd sent at one in the morning saying he might as well stay with his family because it was too late to leave. When she saw him, he'd acted as though it had been normal and so she acted as though it had been normal, even accepting his gift of an expensive bottle of whiskey and not breaking it over his head.

"Today's the big day—lunch at Gatton's with your partner's wife, right?" Jack said. "The folks you stayed with on St Barthes."

Elizabeth looked at the half melon Esme put down in front of her.

"They were fun, huh? Matt and Lindsay."

"Cute couple." Jack looked at his watch. "We have our Monday meeting in half an hour. Gotta shoot... so I'll come for you about twelve thirty."

"Sure?"

"I need to see Mack in La Jolla anyway, and then I'll join you ladies for coffee."

"Ladies?"

"Ladies who lunch."

"Funny, 'cause I'm sure I used to run a business…"

Jack wrapped his arms around Elizabeth, chomped on her neck, "And now you're just my little porcupine."

"Concubine."

"No, baby, I meant *porcupine*. You got those *ouch* little things that—*Ouch!* and *Ouch!* and—"

"Stop, my hair! The restaurant's booked, right?"

"I said already, yeah, yeah, yeah. And don't worry, it's fancy-shmancy enough. Love you." Jack bent to kiss her once more before making a thumbs up sign at the kitchen window. "Esme—thanks for the packed lunch. Have a great day!"

Jack's motorbike growled all the way down the hill.

Elizabeth closed her eyes to stop them prickling. She couldn't explain, even to herself, this sadness, this disappointment and the agony of missing Cosima. She'd call her. She'd meditate. The clouds would clear. She had a new dress to wear for Céline and hoped that when Jack said he'd booked a fancy restaurant for her Monegasque friend who had homes in Paris, Positano and St Barthes, two nannies for adult children and a husband who had financially backed Lambert Interiors, that Jack knew what *fancy* meant—even him using the word *fancy* was concerning. And she'd have to find a way of stopping him from wearing that ridiculous jacket.

"It's perfect" Elizabeth said, giving Jack a kiss on the cheek as they drove up to Gatton's in La Jolla. It was exactly what Elizabeth would have chosen for Céline: overlooking the sea, tablecloths like sails, diners speaking in hushed voices and holding the silverware like needlepoint.

"I came here for a wedding once, thought it was classy."

"And did I say you look particularly handsome today?"

Jack put his hand on Elizabeth's thigh, moved it higher. "Show me later what you do to handsome boys," he said before giving her a final affirmative pat. "You OK to go in there alone?"

"Alone? With Céline Beaujoin? I'm terrrrrrified!" Elizabeth tugged at his lapel. "You know, you probably don't need that jacket today, it's so warm."

"I need the pockets. So text me when you finish your main course, maybe after that, we'll go down to Mushroom Cove, dip our feet in the water, make love on the sand—if I can wait that long, otherwise it's over the back seat of my car again."

Instinctively he looked at his phone, a text from Jude: *We need to discuss summer plans.*

Jack looked up to see Elizabeth still standing in front of him.

"*Bon appétito,*" he said, driving away.

The last time Jack had been in La Jolla it'd been a cold day in February, when he'd spent hours texting Elizabeth with reasons why it wasn't a good time to tell Jude he wanted to leave the marriage. And here he was, driving down Prospect Street with his blonde in Gatton's waiting for him to join her and a deluxe watch on his wrist. A few hours before, Elizabeth had asked him what he thought about moving to London. *Never*, he thought, rolling down his window to watch kites gliding in the air, a fleet of sail boats cutting patterns on the sea and teenagers playing ball on the grass.

"How's tricks?" Mack had expected a thoughtless return of fine, fine, can't complain but seeing the concentration on Jack's face, he turned his phone to silent mode.

Mack had lived in San Diego all his life but refused to cede his Celtic ancestry even throwing in a Dublin lilt when he spoke. Jack was probably one of the few people who knew that

Mack had never been to Ireland and that his connection with the Emerald Isle had stopped at his grandmother.

"I think I'm going through a divorce."

"You *think*?"

Jack bobbed his head.

"Sorry to hear that, man. What did I read on Facebook this morning: 'Marriages come and go but divorce is for life!'" Mack chuckled, despite Jack not even breaking into a smile. "Come here." Mack opened up his arms as though his body was magnet plated. "Jude's a good woman." Mack slapped Jack's back. "Always liked her sister too, she was somethin', that Dahlia."

"Thing is, I met someone."

"Aha! The heart will go where it's gotta go, eh? Marie, two ice teas out here. How's business up there in Feliz?"

"Not what it was. You?"

Mack whisked his hand in the air. "Better, but…"

A group of young women gathered at the door hoping to make a quick getaway for their lunch.

"Hey, ladies! This one's single—grab him while you got the chance!"

"I said, Mack, I'm *taken*."

"Don't be crazy. You gotta test drive the newest models!" said Mack, leering at one of the women who looked very similar to his Italian wife, Marie, but thirty years younger.

Marie brought them some ice teas.

"Separating—Jack and Jude."

"No! Oh no. Jude!" Marie wrung her hands. "Jude make me laugh so much, remember, Mack? When she tell us about the little children she teach—I laugh and tears! —remember? The boy, who thought he was a pterodactyl?" Marie found it hard to talk through her laughter. "And over the summer vacation no one cleaned the fish tank and they had frogs all over the classroom—they jumpin' everywhere—all over school, frogs jumping, hop-hop!" She stopped laughing. "You send our love."

Jack's phone beeped. Elizabeth was midway through their main course.

"This woman, whoever she is, she's got ya. It's written all over your face, why don't you just do what you gotta do but don't get caught?"

"Elizabeth's special."

"Divorce is special—it's for life, my friend," he said, reaching to slap Marie's ass.

51

SUBJECT: THAT LITTLE BLACK DRESS

From: Neptune99

To: Salacia99

Date: Monday August 31, 2020 at 23:35

"Your head on my chest…" Taylor Swift, Tim Mcgraw. Our song, no? Out walking Tip. We're in the red-tier zone so, lucky to be out at all. Jude's mom's unresponsive. Dahlia couldn't come visit in the end. We're gonna have to take a loan on the house to cover a whole bunch of stuff. Can't sit still, can't follow a conversation, can't eat or sleep—can only think about you. Send more pix of you paddle boardin'. Wish I was there to rub oil on your…

———

JACK TOOK his time to cross Gatton's to observe Elizabeth with her friends *in the wild*, so to speak. He read the movement of her scarlet lips and was drawn to the way she used her hands to speak, flagging up those shiny red nails. Rouge Assassin, she'd told him the color was called.

Céline reminded him of his stepmother's Pekinese: bulging eyes and high rounded shoulders. The other woman was pert, with a short blonde bob and eyes that flickered from one friend to the other.

"Ladies," Jack said, with a mild salute.

"Lizzy, you didn't say how handsome he was!" said Céline, standing up and letting him kiss her on both cheeks as Elizabeth had instructed him that morning. He looked back at her tight skin and wondered if someone had pulled a plug from the back of her head and sucked everything out.

"Of course I didn't, otherwise everyone would want some." Elizabeth laughed. "Jack, this is Victoria. She has a company making the most divine Scottish linens from her home in Inverness."

Again, a two-cheek kiss on skin that looked so stretched it could snap.

"Thrilled to meet the enigmatic Jack, subject of our confabulations!" Victoria sounded like Bradley, the kid who cleaned cars at Jude's school. Shame he wasn't there to interpret.

Céline pulled up a chair for him, leaning just low enough for him to see the tops of her small breasts inside her navy-blue top. Before sitting down, Jack went to kiss Elizabeth but she drew back. Céline saw the rebuff; her snout twitched.

"Elizabeth says you deal in vintage cars, my husband's an irredeemable fanatic. All I care about are the toys—self-parking and heated, massaging seats."

"Well then, vintage would probably not be your thing."

"Bloody money pits." Céline poured him a glass of white. "The love of Nico's life is a 1933 Rolls Royce. Remember it, Lizzy?"

"Beautiful car."

"Looks like a glorified black taxi and it's always at the workshop, but it survived the war so let's hope it'll outlive Nico's driving!" Céline laughed. "Now to the business of summer plans, you're absolutely joining us all on the boat. We're doing the Cyclades, again. D'you like boats, Jack?"

"Got my first sailing license at twelve years old."

"Decided then! Elizabeth looks so dainty, but once she's on the ocean, quite a formidable sailor, aren't you, *ma puce*?"

"I think of her as a mermaid," said Jack, looking into her unfocused gaze. "So far we haven't had a chance to think about plans for this summer," said Jack. "I'm separating from my wife and…" He moved back for the waiter to put down their coffees "…things are… kind of in the air."

"Married!" Victoria said with a clap. "Knew he looked too good to be true." They all laughed, though Jack didn't see the joke.

"A lot of changes in front of us." He went to catch Elizabeth's fingers in his.

"Nothing a trip around the Aegean wouldn't sort out," said Céline, flicking her napkin. "You have children? Bring them! Elizabeth misses her Cosima bitterly and Bruno's a terrific friend of Nico's so he'll be bringing her to join us."

"OK," said Jack, experiencing a rush of blood to his neck.

"Hopefully you'll have left your wife by then!"

They all laughed again before Victoria asked, "Who's having pudding? Elizabeth, the usual?"

Céline looked to Jack who looked to Elizabeth.

"What's that, honey?"

"Don't you know? Our Lizzy always has the crème brûlée, I put on weight just looking at it. Do you have a sweet tooth, Jack?" The question made Victoria giggle into her napkin, and when Elizabeth blushed, he figured she'd told them about the other night when he'd covered her naked body with vanilla ice cream only to lick it all off.

Jack waved the waiter over. "I'll pass on dessert this time, need to stay trim now I'm stepping out with this glamour gal."

"Lizzy is glamorous, sure, but also enormously talented."

"Yeah, I know, she—"

"Let's have a little something with our coffees, shall we?"

Jack closed the menu. "Actually, I'll have a lemon tart."

"Who'd have thought, here we are, by the sea, in California, me looking at my darling friend and her dashing American hunk! Is it too late to make a toast? To holiday romances!"

The four of them chinked their glasses as Jack's phone buzzed in his pocket. He looked at the screen and saw *JUDE (Cell)*. It buzzed again.

He was about to switch his phone off when Céline raised an eyebrow.

"If it's important, don't mind us," she said, looking to Victoria.

"Excuse me, ladies," he said, taking his phone to the outside terrace.

52
EL: WED 2 SEPT 2020

I should never have written that first email, Jack. You should never have answered it. We should never have let this go so far. We're not teenagers but two married people with children and responsible lives. We are playing with fire—it's warm and seductive and fun—but neither of us want to see our homes in flames. I'm closing the account and deleting your number from my phone.

———

"JACK?" Jude's voice broke on the outbreath.

"Ju? Y'alright? Aimee OK? The boys—?"

"Can't. I… just… can't—"

Jack was at the front of the restaurant with the sea breeze flicking at his face. He pressed the phone hard against his ear.

"What? You can't what?"

"I can't—"

"Take a breath… release. Another… There… that's it."

An elderly man and woman sitting near him widened their eyes to each other and ate in silence, tuned in to Jack's conversation.

"You at work?"

"Yeah, I'm at work. In an important meeting," he said. The couple exchanged a look, forks suspended above their plates. "I can't hear you—just… what is it?"

Jack moved aside so the waiters could pass him. If he moved anymore he wouldn't be able to watch Elizabeth stirring her coffee.

"Juju, what's going on?"

He waited for her as she sniffed some more.

"I'm in Walmart, the El Mara one."

"Uh-huh."

"And I—I got all the shopping done."

"Good, good."

"And they're all waiting for—" Jude gulped for breath.

"Waiting for…?"

"Me! Jack, they're waiting for *me*. She rang all the groceries up. On the cash register. And they're all behind me, getting mad because—" A woman said something loudly to Jude. "I'm talking to my husband, OK?" he heard her snap. "I can't remember the number."

"Number?"

"My code."

"What code?"

"You know, the PIN thing. For the damn card."

Jack's eyes drifted over the horizon where he caught sight of a line of training sail boats down the coast. Preston and Bentley used to take sailing classes in Mission Bay on boats just like those. "It's… so… stupid, but—"

"Just walk away. Leave it and go back later."

"That's not the point, I can't remember my fucking PIN number!" she yelled before he heard her say, "Can you get here?"

Jack ran through all the four-digit codes to cards they shared: passwords, memorable dates, mother's maiden names.

"Is this to our joint account?"

She wailed, "No… *mine*." She didn't say anything for a few seconds, then asked, "What's happening to me?"

"You're doing great. Great… I got you," he said.

"Can you come over?"

"I'm in La Jolla."

"La Jolla? You said—"

"I'm with Mack. Juju, leave the shopping. It's not important."

"Beanie's in the car. First day of the summer vacation for her and she's already mad 'cause I said Savanah couldn't stay over because she has headlice—actually, we all do now, but I'm —Jack, I'm too ashamed to tell anyone with all that's going on. I feel awful, I just… I just can't deal with everything right now. I'm so tired, Jack, so tired."

"Let's breathe together. In for four…"

"Apparently Philly's had nits for weeks—she thinks they're cute! How many times have I talked about hair play in assembly?"

"Come on, breathe with me. Start again, in for four… Hold. Out for four…" He repeated the exercise, one they'd learned to calm Bentley's rages. "If the code doesn't come to you, walk away. People do that every day." He turned to see Elizabeth and her friends looking at him.

"The groceries are all bagged up, it came to 345 dollars. Can you believe it? But Preston and Chad are coming at the weekend. Bentley's moving back, it's not working out with Maxx. I wanted there to be food in the house… I thought, if there's food, thing's will be alright." The tension in Jack's shoulder was starting to release now that Jude was talking in actual sentences. "Shit! The ice cream is melting! Jack, you still there? So I put my card in… it starts with three," she whispered. "It's 3597. Or 3795. I know the numbers but… the order. There's a two in it. 32… 3297… 79? 79! …3579? Or 3279, maybe that's it. You still there?"

"Still here," Jack replied, watching three seagulls tussle over a bread roll.

"In La Jolla with Mack. You see Marie?" Before he answered, Jude said, "It's 3279. I'm sure… 3279." Jack held his breath before Jude exclaimed, "It worked!" He punched the air. "Told you."

"Come tonight. Preston and Chadiki are doing Mexican."

Jack ducked under a low-flying crow. "Gotta go."

"Is that a yes?"

"I have to go."

"Send my love to Mack and Marie. And sorry!"

"Will do, and hey, nothing to be sorry about."

"Love you."

"Bye."

"Jack?"

"Yeah?"

"Can I tell the kids you'll be over later tonight?"

Jack cut the connection.

"Excuse me, ladies," said Jack, returning to the table.

"Your dessert's cold," said Elizabeth.

It was, and the cream had turned the outer crust soggy.

There were only a few people left in the restaurant. Elizabeth's eyelids were heavy and most of her lipstick had come off apart from a dark outline. Céline spoke French to her, leaving Victoria to tell Jack about how friends of hers were building an eco-lodge. She threw out names—waiting a few beats for Jack to pick up on them—but he was too drained to pretend he understood what she was talking about. Céline called for the check, which arrived on a silver tray with three handmade chocolates and was placed in front of Jack.

Céline took out her credit card first. Elizabeth followed but Jack held up his hand. "Girls, please, my treat."

"Don't be ridiculous, Jack," said Céline, gripping his wrist. "I invited my friends. You were a bonus—an extra sweet *digestif*—and anyway, we *hardly* got to see you."

"It's my pleasure," Jack insisted.

"Lizzy, talk sense into your boy!"

"Jack's very generous," said Elizabeth.

"If you insist. *Très gallant*! And almost perfect!"

Jack dropped his card on the 450-dollar check. A hundred dollars more than Jude's entire grocery shop.

Almost?

Céline brought her warm coffee breath to his ear. "You just have to stop that wife of yours pushing you around."

Four hundred and fifty dollars for a cold tart, or was it *tarte?*

53

SUBJECT: THE TIES THAT BIND

From: Jack Mathews

To: Elizabeth Lambert

Date: Thursday September 3, 2020 at 22:32

Writing to ur private acc in case you closed the Salacia one. Don't ever regret writing to me. Man, that hurt. You gave me more than you'll ever know. At the beginning of every fall, it all comes back to me. That September, coming back to San Diego with all my friends going to college or jobs... everyone beginning their lives, but mine was over. You just took off and my heart was worse than broken, it was beyond repair. I respect your wish for no contact but I had a dream last night that you couldn't breathe and needed to reach me. A nightmare actually. So I just wanted you to know I will check our account every day in case you need me for anything.

J xx

"COASTAL ROUTE OR HIGHWAY?"

Elizabeth hunched herself up against the passenger door and didn't answer.

"Coastal," he said.

Jack distracted himself by racing a speedboat that was zooming across the ocean parallel to them. Elizabeth sulking, this was a new one.

"You want to go on this trip? I mean, she invited us."

"She wasn't inviting us."

He cocked his head. "She asked—"

"—she was taunting us. Rubbing in what I'd given up by leaving Bruno and their social set."

"But—"

"You are so naïve. Even a few days on a chartered yacht like that is a few thousand dollars—a *day*! And Bruno's there. It was an invitation to a *fuck you*."

Jack reached for Elizabeth's arm. "Some friend."

She sighed, her head still facing away from him.

"You shouldn't have taken that call. It looked weak."

"She was in trouble."

"You don't say? What kind of trouble was *she* in now? Being held up at gun point at the Mexican border? Double heart bypass surgery? You knew how much I wanted to avoid gossip. So? What was so urgent?"

Jack tapped the steering wheel and mumbled, "She forgot her PIN number at Walmart." He wouldn't mention the bugs-in-hair issue.

"Oh well! Something like that! *That's* worth Céline warning me off a man who's clearly never going to leave his wife." Her hands slapped her face as a tear came down. "Fucking humiliating!" She turned to Jack. "Since Friday night, when you didn't come home, something's really fucking off, Jack!"

Jack couldn't put it into words how it was sleeping next to Jude, their cubs around them, the dog snoring on the landing, watching over the house. Jude had slept through the night with Jack holding her, protecting her from the person who could hurt her the most, himself.

"It's Bentley," he said. "This drug dealer out in Pasadena left us his treasured car, been calling every day and making threats—even Draxx is scared of him. Now someone calls to say Bentley is riding around in it. He's quit the garage and broke up with Maxxie—after three years! That's why I needed to stay home, to talk to him."

Elizabeth kicked off her shoes, hugged her knees against her chest.

"Bentley's been calling me. Like, a lot."

Jack swerved.

"What?"

"Calling to check if I'm happy with the car, to ask if I need recommendations for gyms or doctors, calling me, obsessive a lot."

Jack's fingers went to smooth out the mountain range of pleats across his forehead.

"You don't think he's connected me with you?"

"Oh, I forgot this is all about you."

Jack sped up to overtake a car toeing a dinghy.

"You think you're so smart about people, little mermaid, but I'll tell you something about you: you're ashamed of me in front of your friends."

She lifted her palms up, shook her head and let them drop in an act of exasperation. "Ever thought I'm ashamed of them in front of you?"

Jack took a turn that led down to the sea where there were cars parked and an empty snack stall. He switched off the engine.

"Hit the back," he said.

Jack thought he'd self-combust with lust when he saw the flash of white flesh at the top of her thighs as she tumbled onto the back seat, headfirst, heels last. He got out of the car and in the back with her. He put his jacket over them before lowering his trousers and boxers down to his knees and in seconds she closed around him like a shell.

After releasing each other, rearranging their clothes and breathing regularly, they sat in the front listening to that week's favorite playlist.

"I wish we were the only people in the world."

"Me too,"Jack murmured. "Maybe I am weak. If weak is being sensitive to others' pain, if weak is seeing different perspectives and wanting to help where I can."

"I know, and I wouldn't love you so much if you could walk out of a relationship without thinking twice." She studied the lines on his palm. "And it scares me that I'm the reason you're having to make that choice."

Jack covered his face with the palm of her hand. "I don't have a choice."

54

JM: THURS 10 SEPT 2020

Please Elizabeth. We have to talk.

———

ELIZABETH SNAPPED a photo of the equal strips of land, sea and sky in front of them.

"How d'you meet Bruno anyway? Don't think you ever told me."

"I didn't."

Nor had she told him about her last night in Catalina.

"After Catalina…" Elizabeth waited till Jack looked away in shame, "I was in LA with Vince's friend who sent off some photos of me to magazines, model agents and *stuff*, and a woman got in touch, offering to wire me money for a ticket to Paris. She was called Chrystelle and twenty-six years old, had done an MBA in Switzerland, spoke lots of languages, invited me to stay at her place. Every time I asked about work, she said it was important to be seen at the right parties and meet the right people, travel all over. She lent me clothes, money—it made me uncomfortable, but she was like, you'll pay me back one day, don't worry about it."

"Good friend."

"Huh. When we were out together, she'd loop her arm around mine and tell me all about her miserable childhood in an English boarding school, her dad having affairs and her mean mother. But she adored her brother, looked out for him, and that reminded me of Danny. Then one night she called me from London to say there was a man coming over from Qatar who wanted to spend the night with me—he'd pay two thousand dollars. That's when I realized Chrystelle didn't run a model agency. From that night, I was called to men and parties all over the world including Tokyo where I met a famous interior designer."

Jack sniffed, looked away. "You had sex with men for money?"

Elizabeth's voice was barely audible. "You left me no choice."

"Me?"

"When I left Catalina that night, it was all I had to sell."

"Last I remember you had my college savings."

"I gave that money to my mother to get away from Vince."

"And did she?"

"Can we get back to me? Back to how when you betrayed me, I thought I'd never trust another man, so figured I might as well make money from them. And guess what? Bruno was Chrystelle's little brother. Yup. I helped her organize his twenty-fifth birthday in St. Tropez. We arrived by boat for lunch, partied all night: magnums of champagne, cocaine, girls and for his 'big' gift, he wanted me."

"Bruno fell in love with you?"

"That's the Cinderella version, but real life? When his mother insisted he get serious about running the family hotel in Aix-en-Provence, he agreed, but to show how pissed he was, he said he was going to marry someone *he* wanted. So I was a living *fuck you* to his mom. The funny thing was that the hotel was my first big project. After that, we had an understanding— I'd look after the business and he could do whatever he wanted. But he never let me forget how we met."

Jack held her face towards his. "Are you still mad at me for that night? I was a dumb kid who said a whole lot of stuff that I meant at the time but—"

"I understand, Jack. Jude was the kind of girl you could marry and have kids with, I was just poor white trash you could throw away when you were done. I get it."

55

SUBJECT: A SAILOR–LOST, NOW FOUND

From: Neptune99

To: Salacia99

Date: Friday September 18, 2020 at 17:34

Your voice came to me like a rescue craft to a man stranded on a desert island. Stop apologizing! We needed to suffer to realize this is bigger than the both of us. As you said, we're good people, we love our families, we're not criminals and what's wrong with two friends just riffing together?

"Mama!" Jude called out as she dropped her bags inside the cabin.

Tip was already running through his preliminary checks: sniffing the damp air, scratching at the corners of the rooms, batting his paws at something under the sofa. He sauntered back to Jude to report no immediate dangers.

"Jack?"

All week, Jude had imagined Jack there, meditating, getting back to nature, preparing the cabin for the summer.

She rested her hand on Tip's head, the two of them mesmerized by the miasma of dust particles suspended in the beams of light over their heads.

Jude hadn't heard from Jack since Monday when she'd called from the supermarket. He'd not been in touch with Aimee or the boys, hadn't offered any ideas about how they'd spend the summer or manage Preston's tuition for the following year. She'd worried when Marcie mentioned he'd barely been at the garage and Al had missed seeing him at Kids Call Thursday night.

Jude, needing to be at work another two weeks, got in touch with an ex-student who ran a scuba diving school in Coronado to ask if they'd take Aimee last minute. It had been expensive, not only the course, but supplying wet suit and equipment for two weeks' diving. Bentley had been uncharacteristically helpful, even driving Aimee to the camp in exchange for sports gear of his own. Jude charged it all up to Jack's card.

That Friday, before the traffic buildup, Jude had left for the cabin to talk to Jack. But he wasn't there. And her mother wasn't there. And the kids weren't there. And the loss made her want to scream.

Jude's mother had gone from a dry cough to an ambulance and never came home. Her last words to Jude had been on the telephone, 'I can't let you go.'

'We'll be fine, Mom.'

She'd never been a second in her life without her mother, so how could she even imagine what *fine* in a motherless world could mean?

Jude opened the doors and windows of the cabin where her parents had lived since they sold their city house and had the happiest years of their marriage. She checked light switches, listened out for mice and went in search of a broom, still expecting to find her mother dozing in a chair.

While her children had found it too hard to even spend a night in the house since Ma-May had died, the natural world had no qualms about moving right on in, Jude thought, blowing onto a windowsill carpeted in dead geranium leaves and little bits of what looked like dunes of grit but were actually very active little black bugs. There was so much to do before the listings estate agent came by the following day to value the property.

Jude flicked out giant moths from the windows and let the pine-tree air fill the house. She took out her phone to send Dahlia photos of what repairs were needed. If Dahlia was too busy in her Central Park office to help her throw buckets of black water out front every five minutes, she could at least be encouraging.

By the time the sky was buttery over the motionless lake, Jude unfolded herself from where she'd been crumpled up on her hands and knees. She pulled the plug on the soaking pans, rung out the dust cloths and hung them over the porch ledges to dry.

And the answer was there.

56

SUBJECT: WTF?

From: Jack Mathews

To: Elizabeth Lambert

Date: Tuesday September 22, 2020 at 19:34

Help me get this straight: we just broke up, made up and now you want to break up again? NO worries princess. America's Covid death toll is past 200,000 so what's our little drama worth against that? It's great you and your husband had a productive Skype counseling session. I'd NEVER stand between you. Can't believe you say you have island fever—I'm in ONE HOUSE with FIVE people and a BIG DOG and a FERAL CAT called MOUSE and it's been almost SIX MONTHS!!! But let me just ask you one thing, what do YOU really want in this life? If I'm anywhere in that picture, your landing pad awaits.

———

"That was an out-of-body experience, captain," Elizabeth hummed.

"Here's a kiss landing," said Jack. "You cried, baby."

"The places you take me." Elizabeth rotated her wrist above her head, seeking cooler air.

"We are one." He interlaced her fingers with his and heard his stomach rumble like the snapping of a guitar string. "Did Esme make a roast chicken?"

"I think so." Elizabeth kissed the wet nest of hair between his pectorals.

"I need to re-fuel before I take you out of that delicious body one more time," Jack said, smoothing his hand across one nipple then the other. Elizabeth arched her back, let her head fall back, her hair nearly reaching her heels behind her.

"Stay there, God of the Sea, and I will return with your chicken sandwich, a beer, vegetable chips *and* some extra sweet fellatio for dessert."

Jack stretched out on the bed, watched a single puff of cloud scud across an impossibly blue sky before he brought his Omega to his face and saw the time.

"Jesus—it's two thirty! I got four appointments this afternoon and interviewing a kid for Bentley's job, deliveries arriving and then meeting a guy who might loan me the—"

"It's *Saturday*."

"S'my busiest day!"

"You gotta eat," said Elizabeth from the hallway below. Jack switched his phone on.

Aimee Bean:

> Dad!!! Call me PLEASE

Draxx had texted every twenty minutes about an error code on the OBD reader. Marcie was having trouble holding off complaining clients especially a Mr. Elbaz who'd picked up his car only to return it a few hours later with a different problem. Traci WhatsApped asking for approval on a loan she was preparing. Someone was looking for Bentley and Good-Looking was asking to take a two-week summer vacation.

Jack looked back at a text he'd missed from Aimee the day before:

> DAD! WHERE ARE YOU??? Mom's crazy. She dumped me in a concentration camp for SMALL KIDS!!! COME GET ME!!!'

Jack tapped out a line to Aimee:

> Pin and send location ASAP will come get u

Jack fought his way out of the swathes of curtains surrounding his bed while leaving Aimee a voicemail: "Jelly-bean—I get you don't like the summer camp. Hang on in there."

An email notification at his work address with the subject line 'Aimee' popped up:

Mr Mathews, I was a junior camp counselor at Coronado Scuba Diving School. Aimee was placed in an incorrect class and suffering from anxiety issues. She said she'd kill herself. To keep her safe I brought her to my home. Coz I got involved like that, I been fired. She's here with my mom. I'm asking for further instructions, sir. I'm in a difficult position. Kenzo Gutierrez.

Then something from Draxx came in saying Geza had threatened if his car wasn't ready by that afternoon he was going to come down and 'deal with it himself'.

So Bentley still hadn't returned the car.

Jack put his hands on either side of his temples.

"I can't stay—"

When Jude had texted a few days before saying that Aimee was at summer camp he'd given himself permission to take his foot off the gas. Clearly he'd misjudged the speed at which catastrophe was hurtling towards him.

"Yo." A woman's voice.

"My name's Jack Mathews, I believe you have my daughter, Aimee Mathews."

"She here."

"OK so I need to bring her home."

"You do, do you?" The woman snorted. "You don't know waz goin' on, mister, do you?"

"Where is she?" He found himself raising his voice at the same time as hearing Elizabeth on the phone downstairs and a lawn mower start up in a neighbor's garden. He squeezed his eyes shut. Another text from Traci shot up on the screen.

"Hear me Mr. Mathews, my boy lost his job on account of y'daughter. She couldn't a stayed in that camp—"

Jack pressed the heel of his left hand into his eyeballs to restart his brain.

"Just tell me, is Aimee OK?"

"She's sleeping. I gave her a little something to calm down."

"You gave her *drugs*?"

"She gotta lotta energy."

Jack searched for his trousers. He could never find anything in this damn house because he was always tearing off his clothes in a hurry. He tossed the phone on the bed as if it were contaminated. He had definitely been *fiddling while Rome was burning*, an expression Jude used when Bentley had been a kid watching TV while the school bus was pulling up at the stop to collect him. Shirt buttoned up. He could hear Elizabeth in the kitchen preparing his food tray. It was too hot to wear the jacket.

His phone buzzed under the sheet and an email from Jude appeared. Jack skim read it: *…a message from my mother about how we can go forward … A solution to all our problems … We all live at the lake house … nature … tranquility … do up the old boat or buy a new one when Dahlia buys us out … guaranteed income and money left over to travel … Beanie can have a real play den … convert the garage … a home for us—*

A home for us. Lake. Sun. Family. Peace.

Go back, back. Candles and a crackling transistor radio. Chipmunks. Honey bacon sizzling and waffles. A wet dog and late-night board games.

The lake house.

Frogs croaking on the waterlilies at sunset. Blue birds. Afternoons he and Bentley spent making sailboats out of leaves and twigs to throw down one end of the creek and running as fast as they could to catch them at the next bridge. Fishing with Preston. The hammock. Trips out on his boat—and maybe a new boat, why not? The stars at night all crammed into the sky, wild, luminescent. Pizzas from the wood-burning stove he'd built into the garden wall for Jude's mom and dad. Aimee teaching herself Taylor Swift favorites on the guitar.

The Gutierrez woman's address appeared on his screen.

South-East San Diego.

Rome was black smoke.

Elizabeth stood at the bottom of the stairs with a tray of food in her hands and a glass of beer.

Timber was crashing down on the people he loved.

"Sweetheart, I gotta run."

"Where?" she asked, as if there were no other place in the world.

"Rome's burning."

"Rome?"

"It's an expression. Means everything's, like, totally fucked up."

Jack checked the clasp on his watch while twisting his heels into his sneakers. He was tempted to grab the sandwich off the plate but the look in Elizabeth's eyes was murderous.

"Aimee's been kidnapped."

"You have never once asked about my daughter."

"What? Sure I have. You talk about her all the time."

"You're not here all the time and she isn't here at all." There was a catch in her throat.

"Can we talk about this later?"

Elizabeth turned back towards the kitchen shaking her head. "And off he runs."

57

SUBJECT: BURNING UP FROM COVID FEVER, NOT FOREST FIRES

From: Jack Mathews

To: Elizabeth Lambert

Date: Wednesday September 23, 2020 at 22:34

————

"MRS. MATHEWS?" Megan called out as she walked towards the cabin.

As a rule, she changed from her driving shoes into heels but looking at the thrashes of straw-like grass and broken garden furniture, these were people who wouldn't mark her down for casual footwear.

A big dog lay stretched across the front porch, watching her.

"Hey there, Tip," she said. "You must be super-hot in that big fur coat."

The dog huffed in agreement, slouched over to her.

Megan had met Tip once before when, on viewing the Paloma Drive house a second time, Jack Mathews had brought the dog. Animals were strictly forbidden to enter prospective homes but there was something so irresistible about a hunky man—and in shorts! —with a devoted beast at his side so that when Jack wrapped his arms around the dog's neck and asked, 'Is this Okay?' Megan had answered, 'Sure!'

Megan looked at the wooden house and jetty where an old boat knocked gently against the dock. There wasn't anything she wanted to do more than strip off and throw herself into those waters for the rest of the afternoon.

"Where's your mommy?" she whispered, reaching out to the dog with the back of her hand like her mother had taught her as a child. "Hello?" Megan pushed open the screen door to see Jude asleep in the armchair opposite the fireplace "Mrs. Mathews?" Megan leveled with her client's face, the dog placing itself between them. "Megan Howell. Buena Vista Realty. I'm a little late, it was a jungle on the highway, you'd think on a Saturday afternoon…"

Jude wiped the corners of her mouth, screwed up and opened her eyes a few times.

"Do you need a little time? I can come back, I—"

"No, it's fine. I'm Jude." She yawned with a shake of the head. "I started cleaning at five this morning and just sat down and…" Jude's feet felt for a pair of flip flops. "It's the air here, knocks you out."

"Listen to those birds!" added Megan, cocking her ear to the cacophony of chirps. "Do you know how rare a place like this is?"

Jude looked at her watch: four thirty-five. After this she'd have to make it fast to get groceries as they closed early on Sundays.

"Was that a cuckoo?" squealed Megan.

"Uh-huh. And there are chipmunks out back."

"This is such a magical home, Mrs. Mathews," said Megan, spinning around the room. "There are so few of these properties left, you know. In the early eighties they forbade anyone to build on the lake. And you have private access. Wow! The one on the other side, the white house, that went for over six million dollars last summer."

"The Clarkes, yeah. I think she was the county judge," said Jude, watching the agent with her glossy chestnut hair and red jacket with brass buttons tapping at walls and counting wall heaters. Megan had already let Jude know she'd won Feliz's

Agent of the Year in 2022.

"But, er, there's work to do," said Megan.

Jude went to the kitchen, took out two of the cleanest glasses. "My parents never really changed it since the seventies when they added heating and the outside lighting, then after my dad died, the house was too much for my mom. My husband updated the kitchen a few years ago. We added the second garage to keep the boat, put in a new shower up—"

"Five bedrooms… about 2500 square feet, you reckon?"

"All in, yeah. Glass of water? I can't even offer you ice in it, but—"

"I'm good, thanks," answered Megan, not trusting anything coming out of those taps. "Oh!" Megan jumped.

"That's the cuckoo again."

"Sounds just like the clock," Megan giggled. "*Land* is what's important, Mrs. Mathews. New kitchens and all, easy, but it's the natural space. Oh my!"

"Natural space we got," said Jude, sweeping an exoskeleton from the tabletop.

"Must be hard, coming here after, y'know, your mom passing and all."

"It is. And isn't."

Megan made a sad clown face before clapping in the air and announcing, "So I need to measure up, which I do with this little machine here." She lifted her phone up and waited for a beep. "The photographer can come Monday morning or Thursday afternoon, so we need to talk about gaining access if you're not here."

Jude brushed dust from her hair as she reiterated. "But we just want an idea of value… sale *and* rent."

"You're fact finding—you said it, and I heard you."

Jude could see why Ms. Howell had hustled up so many votes for her award.

"So, y'know, on rentals we have a team who cover every-thing from staging to providing hand towels, gardening services and storage. We check—you're yawning, sorry, it's boring, I know. Here's all the T&Cs on that," she said, dropping a thick booklet on the table.

Jude clenched her teeth so that Megan wouldn't see another yawn coming.

"Can I?" She pointed to the stairs. "The management package is seriously worth considering."

Jude took her water to the porch.

Jack would have read the email she sent him describing how they would get their lives back and *better*. Saturdays were a bad day for him but he'd probably come over that night, and they would watch the sunset, maybe eat at the Italian where they'd gone on their first date. Tomorrow they'd swim, walk the dog, and make plans for their new life.

58

SUBJECT: DESERT-ISLAND DESPAIR

From: Elizabeth Lambert

To: Jack Mathews

Date: Friday September 25, 2020 at 23:45

Covid! OMG, are you OK? Sorry I hurt you. Yes, I'm in the most beautiful place on earth which claims 'no Covid cases' but my heart is breaking. It's not exactly paradise here with homeschooling, doing reels without a green screen or studio lighting and there's always having to act grateful to Céline and Nico, our hosts.

Bruno and I had a big fight after I was nominated for Designer of the Year, he said I only got nominated because all the talented people were staying at home. Céline weighed in, playing referee until finally Bruno agreed to Zoom sessions with the relationship therapist. We have to give our marriage our best shot for Cosie. You asked, what do I really want? I want to be 15 years old, in your arms, in that stinky little cabin on your boat and for that night never to have happened. Can you take me back there? Get better soon!

———

THE DOORBELL RANG. Elizabeth let out a laugh of relief that Jack had returned to apologize, but as she got up to answer the door, she saw the shape of a heavy-set man in black pacing up and down, then looking through the windows. Jack must have left the gate open.

Elizabeth didn't have time to lock all the doors and

windows. She didn't move, just waited for him to give up. He didn't. Instead, he pressed his face up to the glass and rang the bell again. Elizabeth stayed still, curled into the wide white armchair in the hall.

The man turned and started to stalk away from the house. Elizabeth moved low and fast up to the staircase window that looked over the drive. The pane was clear, not frosted like the ones downstairs. The man turned sharply, looked right at her.

"Mrs. Lambert? It's Bentley, Bentley Mathews? Mathews Motors. I was just passing and..." He stood at the bottom of the three stairs to the entrance. "Your gate was open. Shouldn't leave it like that."

"Noted."

"We talked about an after-sales follow-up." He coughed; same nervous cough his dad had. "And maybe I could take you out in my new car. An AC Cobra—100,000 bucks worth."

Elizabeth came down the stairs and opened the door, but not wide.

"I'm busy right now."

"That's the code, for the gate, right?" asked Bentley, pointing at a Post-it note written above the key hooks. "1999."

"Come," she said, leading him into the kitchen. "I made a sandwich but I'm not hungry." Elizabeth was aware her shirt dress was short and that she hadn't showered since having sex with the boy's dad.

The sun projected ripples from the pool onto the chrome pans, the knives and clock.

"How many bedrooms you got here?"

"Six—no, seven, I think. If you include the pool house."

"You don't even know?" he asked. "S'like something you see from the road and you wonder... what kind of princess lives there?"

"A slobby one," she said. "I'll bring the drinks out by the pool."

Once Bentley was in the garden, moving the parasols around, she allowed herself a moment to return her breathing to normal until she saw him lay down on his stomach and slither towards the shallow end of the pool. He opened his mouth, flattened his tongue on the top of the water and lapped at it like a big dog. Elizabeth looked around for Flores but the gardener had left already. She'd been through enough in her life, she told herself, to let a teenager scare her.

Sitting with their coffee milkshakes after Bentley had finished his father's abandoned sandwich, he grinned at her.

"That afternoon we spent together. It's cause of you I'm leaving my dad's company and making something of my life."

"Don't do anything because of me...what are you thinking?"

"Going pro body building." Bentley swallowed loudly, blushed. "If I do a competition, would you come watch? Mrs. Lambert, what are you really doing here in Feliz?"

"When I was fifteen years old we went to Catalina for my mom's honeymoon but it was really just a pretext for her deadbeat guy to set up some casino heist. My half brother and I were planning to run away, go to Oregon to live with his dad when out of the blue I met this handsome and caring boy who was there working on boats to save for college. I'd never let anyone close to me but he... he got through. I was actually happy! We had the island to ourselves, stars at night, lazy afternoons, midnight swims. Love. Crazy love. Crazy teenage love. The worst."

"So what happened?"

"I'd been fighting off my mom's boyfriends for years, but Vince, when he heard I was seeing someone, he got scary. Possessive. I was in danger and I told this boy. He swore he'd protect me, organized a little marriage ceremony behind a ruined chapel. We wrote vows, promised undying loyalty, I even wore a white bikini, found a stray dog to witness it. And after, we made love on the boat he was fixing up. It was my first time, in that little cabin. I felt I'd been given the keys to the universe. And then I went up on deck to get us some juice or something and saw a note by the phone from his dad asking him to call his girlfriend who couldn't wait to see him that weekend."

Bentley's shoulders twitched, Elizabeth wasn't so sure he was really following her story until he said, "You know Mrs Lambert, I could track him down and kill him."

"Thanks but I have better plans. I want him to be sorry, to be homeless, and alone, broke and wondering what the fuck happened." He held her stare, nodding. "Bentley, I have stuff to get on with this afternoon. Thanks for passing by."

And she followed his clumpy strides to the car on the drive. He got in, still shirtless, raised a hand.

"Nineteen ninety-nine, wasn't it?"

"Stay out of trouble," she said with a wave over the engine's blast.

59

JM: SUN 27 SEPT 2020

> First day up for me. Still coughing but I'll live.
> Your marriage comes first. I respect that and
> pray you both find a way to happiness.

———

OF ALL THE times of day to do this journey, whined Jack to himself, sitting behind a wall of RVs loaded up with mountain bikes and kayaks, long-haul trucks and family hatchbacks—just your usual weekend traffic buildup between Feliz and Coronado. He punched the address into the GPS. Should have been forty minutes, but it estimated one hour ten. He should have grabbed that chicken sandwich—he hadn't eaten since breakfast. Jack called the office hoping to catch Marcie before she left but Draxx answered the phone with, "Yo, this guy's really freakin' me out. First we couldn't find the part order and now the car's disappeared."

The order.

Geeza's AC Cobra.

Jack remembered thinking he must order the part. He actually remembered thinking how terrible—how *completely disastrous*—it would be if he forgot to order the part. And then he forgot.

"Do you have the order number?" asked Draxx.

Elizabeth called him Captain, what a joke.

"Er, no, not right now... Marcie left already?"

"She had a Tinder date lined up. And Mr. M, the MV50 book's gone missing—know anything that?"

Jack's throat was drying up from the blast of cold recycled air. "Just close up."

"Huh?"

"Take the afternoon off, all of you. Paid."

"But, like, Traci's with a client and the Ford's not starting —" Draxx stopped, realizing he was talking himself out of a free afternoon.

"Beat it. I got a family emergency."

Draxx asked: "Does the emergency concern Bentley?"

"No, why?"

"This Geeza guy, he's bad news. He loves that car and your son's driving around in it. But you want us to take off—I heard you right?"

"S'what I said."

Jack ended the call, scrolled down Jude's email on his phone: *...sell the Feliz house and the garage to buy Dahlia out and we move to the hills, you can work on cars privately... no mortgages, no loans, you can practice your meditation, it's so beautiful here and Aimee—*

"D'you get my email?" Jude asked, answering the second her phone had started to ring. "Us living here together?"

"I think there's some merit in your plan."

"Damn right!" she laughed. "We just have to love the life we have. It's all here!"

"Right now there's a more immediate issue—don't panic— but Aimee ran away from camp. I'm on my way to pick her up from some crazy lady's house—don't ask. I'll get her and come straight over."

"Straight over. I love you, Jack!"

Jack put his hands to the fan because he was sweating and they smelt of sex. He hadn't brushed his teeth and his GPS was proposing a short-cut that his gut told him made no sense at all.

60

SUBJECT: SIN-CHRONICITY

From: Jack Mathews

To: Elizabeth Lambert

Date: Friday October 2, 2020 at 15:45

Oh my sexy, luscious, mouth-watering mermaid. I swore to myself I wouldn't check my emails and then I missed you so much I wanted to re-live our moments and just as I opened the account, an email from you popped up RIGHT AT THE SAME TIME! Yes! Missing you sucked BIG TIME!

"THERE YOU ARE!" said Megan, startled to see Jude take a cigarette out of her mouth. "It's a charming house. I'll get back to the office, talk comparables with my colleagues then circle back to you with some figures so—"

"Megan," Jude moved her hair from her face. "I'm so sorry to disappoint you, but my husband and I have decided to keep this place, live here full time."

A dragonfly cut between them.

"I know you came all the way out here on a Saturday..."

"So you're not gonna sell, or rent, at *all*?"

"Jack and I are very excited about making this our home and—"

Megan looked down at the dust on her driving shoes then back at Jude. "You know Jack is living up in the hills with the lady from France."

Jude nodded, only vaguely listening.

"That must be another Jack, we don't—"

"Jack Mathews. He instructed me to take the place on Paloma Drive. I wouldn't forget a rental like that! Elizabeth only called this morning about a house on Ocean Beach they were looking to buy, Jack even—"

"Jack Mathews, Mathews Motors?"

"Uh-huh. The car guy. I showed him around the house— *twice*! The second time he came with the dog, that's why Tip recognised me."

Megan saw the look on Jude's face. She'd go to hell for this but it was too late to backtrack. And really, this nice woman needed to know what her husband was doing behind her back.

"Wait…" Jude darted back into the house and returned with a picture of Jack and Aimee on her phone.

Megan nodded. "That's him."

"When did the woman take the house?"

"Jack got in contact April and they signed on the property pretty soon after. She arrived Memorial Day weekend. Lemme get you a drink."

Megan came back with a Crème de Menthe in a mug that had

Best Grandma in the Universe emblazoned on it.

Jude sipped. "He left last month… *space*."

"He said he was going into *space*?"

Jude's lips—turned green by the drink—moved, but all Megan could catch was, "Send me the address."

61

EL: WED 7 OCT 2020

In Brittany but back in Paris Friday night.
Bruno's coming back next Monday so how
about a video-call this weekend? Wear
something tight and black!

———

SHE WAS a dead ringer for Gloria Estefan.

"Ma'am, you have my daughter, Aimee."

"First, we gotta talk."

Jack followed Gloria Estefan, without the Miami Sound
Machine, down a corridor, through clothes, boxes, cable wires
and bird cages, all the time listening out for his daughter's
voice. Gloria was in a paisley-patterned housecoat—a kind of
work uniform—although a furry bra peeked out from her
lapels.

"Can I just say hi to Aimee?"

"Kitchen. Sit."

Jack tried to date the house by counting the layers of wallpaper on the kitchen walls. So much stuff: fridges, computer
screens, goldfish bowls, snowshoes, keyboards, broken sports
equipment—how would he find Aimee in all this?

"Kenzo and I are getting ready for a garage sale dis weekend, me 'n' some girlfriends." And she made funny clicking noises like a dolphin with her mouth.

Mi Tierra. Jack and Jude had loved that album. They'd listened to it that whole summer when Preston was a baby and Jack had taken on the project of creating a backyard from a pile of breezeblocks. Estefan's voice brought back the smell of earth and the promise of grass seeds. They'd sung to it in the car buying diapers and watching Preston fall asleep in his bassinet. *Mi Tierra*—my homeland: first child, home and garden—all the things Jude had written about in her email.

Jack moved away from a chinchilla munching through a box of Cheerios.

"I see you're a pet lover," stated Jack.

"Pets?" she glared at him. "Don't use that word, mister. These are animals I happen to share my life with. Pets! Most are rescue animals. Abandoned, abused, tortured—that one," she pointed to something moving on top of the refrigerator. "Dat's Winston. Don't touch him, he's funny 'bout guys." Jack had no intention of going near whatever was under the bandages.

"Jesus, how can people do stuff like that?"

"No cruelty ever done in the world worse than what's done to animals every second of every day."

"I hear Aimee," said Jack.

"She loud."

A news announcement came through from the TV in her neighbor's yard about a missing teenage girl. While the mother begged for anyone with information to come forward, Estefan nodded knowingly. "Three days now. Almost zero chances a' finding her 'live."

A parrot squawked from somewhere in the house.

Jack remembered Elizabeth saying something about a missing child. And he'd found his Aimee—he'd been lucky. Lucky because he'd been so careless with the people who mattered the most.

A tall teenage boy crunched over the cat litter and put his head in the fridge. His hair was black, shiny and held back with the kind of headband Aimee used to wear for ballet class. He brought out a bag of bread and some dips. Jack made room for the boy to pass him on his way out by pressing himself against a stove, just managing to avoid a large pan of dark yellow oil.

"I'm feeling a lotta hostility from you," said Gloria, facing Jack with her back to the door, her red-black ringlets pressed against a wall calendar from 1997.

"What?"

"Kenzo just made her something to eat 'cause she was *starving*. She also had a shower."

They had running water?

"You know Aimee's only fourteen?"

"Do *you*? Your dumbass woman put her in a class of ten-year-olds! Dat's what the whole like problem was, mister!" She pinned back a strand of hair, causing her dress to ride up her thighs.

"Don't address my wife like that. It was a mistake."

"Your daughter was running away from the camp. She said she was gonna kill hesself. *Kill hesself!* Kenzo was 'fraid so he brought her here—he took a risk cause of her and he—" she prodded her finger in the air between them "—he *lost* his job!" She made the dolphin clicks again. "Lost his chance of good references for his college application. You know how serious that is for us, Mr. Mathews? Aimee said her brother's at San Diego State, they say you need a GPA of at least 4.0! Dat right?"

Jack drew back to avoid being sliced by her nails as her hands twisted and twirled in front of him.

"Your son could've called us."

"Don't you listen to nothin'? The minute my Kenzo was born and I was a single mom with nothing in the world but my baby, I said, *My boy's goin' to college*." She enunciated those two syllables as if they were sacrosanct. The hybrid dog thing squirmed on a laundry basket to get comfortable. "Every year of his life I been working day shifts and nights to pay for him to go to college. Maybe nothing to you but your daughter has taken that away from us and—"

"OK, listen. My wife is the principal at Orange Flower Park High, I'm sure she could help with the application…"

She scratched into her scalp with the scythes at the end of her fingers.

"My boy is all I got."

A dog came in, sniffed at the cats—one of them hissed at him until he leapt back.

"I guarantee we will do all we can to help with your son's application if I can just take my daughter home," Jack asked.

62

SUBJECT:
GOODNIGHT/MORNING

From: Neptune99

To: Salacia99

Date: Thursday October 8, 2020 at 10:44

My little mermaid, love the pics of Deauville! Very different from Kids Call, downtown SD! Al and I are just kicking back while I'm learning more French words. Saw the Instagram thing about the wallpaper company commissioning you to design a special collection. Felicitations! Can't wait for our rendezvous Saturday night 😊

———

AIMEE AND KENZO lay across each other, heads together watching a video on the boy's phone.

"Beanie, we gotta shoot."

Jack moved closer to Aimee, careful not to tread on a tortoise nibbling Kenzo's leftovers. The screen showed a piglet drinking frantically from a baby's bottle that a man was passing through cage bars. The man was Kenzo.

Aimee rolled over, letting the weight of her arms fall on either side of her. "Okaaaay, so this isn't at all awkward. K, this is dad." The boy nodded, not looking away from the screen.

"Where's your stuff, Beans?" Jack prodded her with his foot.

"I'm not going back so Mom can try and get rid of me again, leave me with a whole lot of dumb kids crying and puking?"

Kenzo laughed into his lettuce sandwich.

"You coulda called."

"Come on, Dad, it's not like you've been around—"

"That's not—" Jack was beginning to loathe the square jaw and long lashes of Aimee's accomplice. "Get off your ass now."

"Don't threaten us, Mr. Mathews."

"*Threaten you*? How is asking my underage daughter to come home anything to do with you?"

Estefan fanned out her nails and lunged towards him. "I am this close—" she pinched her thumb and index fingers in front of his eyes "—to callin' Child Protection on you."

Kenzo switched off the video and nodded to Aimee, releasing her.

Out on the street, mother, boy and Aimee held each other like they were hostages being torn apart.

"I'll call you, Apples," said Kenzo, kissing the tops of his fingers and settling them on Jack's daughter's lips.

"Sure you don't wanna sit up front with me?"

"Nope," she answered, belting herself up. "What did you think of Kenzo?"

"I think he's two years older than you."

"So? We're both vegan and he said he'd help me with Math. He's super focused on his goals and speaks three languages."

"The mother… on the other hand…" Jack chuckled.

Aimee's earphones were in and she was looking out of the window. Once on the freeway picking up speed, Aimee asked, "Elizabeth keeps calling you."

Jack looked at his phone on the passenger seat lighting up with Elizabeth's face and a banner announcing: Elizabeth: *3 missed calls.*

"You think I don't know who Elizabeth is? *Neptune 99.*"

Jack looked around for somewhere safe to stop the car.

"When you walked Tip you'd talk to her right under my window. When Mom was visiting Ma-May, sometimes I'd have to sign you out of that Gmail account you shared with her so no one else would read the stuff you sent."

Jack pressed his palms together, put them to his face.

"I'm so—"

"One Sunday, Mom had to go into the school and you said you'd take me to the Cine Complex. I waited all afternoon while you were on the phone—we missed the movie. Stuff like that happened *all the time.* Worst was last year when I did my show. You had your head down through the whole performance. Texting. I knew it was *her.*"

"Beanie, I'm just so sorry. I…"

All those weekends leaving Aimee in front a screen for hours because it freed him to contact Elizabeth. He'd lost Preston a place in student housing because he'd forgotten to post his application. And Jude—he stopped there—he couldn't start to measure the betrayal.

"I hated myself. I tried to stop it. Really."

"I hated you too. And I hated Mom more for being so nice to you."

"From now on I'm going to devote my life to making things right."

Mi tierra. Jack hummed the tune after Aimee settled her headphones back on in her ears.

63

SUBJECT: MESSAGE FROM CAMP JACK

From: Jack Mathews

To: Elizabeth Lambert

Date: Monday October 19, 2020 at 21:43

That TikTok reel of you and your daughter dancing to Dojo Cat in those silver hotpants—Wowza! You seen how many people watched it? We're at the lake house where Jude's running an entire school from the kitchen table. Dahlia's here from NY hoping they'll let her say goodbye to her mom. Only Tip is wi-fi free! I'll sneak out when the kids are watching *This Is Us* tonight and give you a private dance in my hotpants. Did those DNA test results come back?

———

It still stung when Elizabeth peed and it still hurt when she forced herself to realise that Jack was not coming back to make anything better. To quash any niggling optimism, he texted to say he was driving Aimee to the mountains and didn't know when he'd be back. Elizabeth drank two glasses of cranberry juice and lay in a bath, dipping her head in and out of the soundless space.

JACK PUTTING JUDE FIRST. Nothing had changed. Those hours in Jack's cabin, the boat's old oak, the polish, the golden glow inside and turquoise waters outside—so many times since she'd tried to capture how she'd felt for those few moments before she dressed and saw the note left for Jack from his dad on the back of a receipt. *Jack—Jude called. She can't wait to see you Saturday. Missing you and sends big kisses, etc. Be ready 6:30pm to leave and call mom.*

Elizabeth had left the boat, running out barefooted through the port until she realized she didn't have anywhere to go. She crouched behind a boat house to see Jack, moments later, come out searching for her. He called her name, ran out and along the quay to find her and when he was far enough away, she returned to the boat for Jack's savings. In two hours, Jack would be leaving for the mainland and she'd be gone. Only the worst was still ahead of her.

After her bath, Elizabeth passed the time grazing on social media feeds until it made her nauseous. It hadn't even come close to distracting her from the acute longing to hear Cosie's voice. She wanted to call but it was midnight in France. Elizabeth hadn't seen it coming, but now, curled up on her bed in the twilight, the transformation was almost complete: she had just walked slap bang right into becoming her mother. The woman who'd traded everything for a hit of pheromones.

"Lili?"

"Bruno," Elizabeth said. "I know it's late but I really need to speak to Cosie."

"I'm in Paris."

"With Cosie?"

"There's a heatwave so I left her with her mami and that pissing dog. I'm here for some days working."

Elizabeth stopped herself from asking what someone who'd inherited a hotel group meant by 'working.'

"How's Paris?"

"*Infernal.* But better than my mother's."

"So your mom' s driving you crazy?"

Bruno laughed. "She's mad at me for being a bad husband." Loaded pause before he chuckled. "And maybe she's right."

Elizabeth curled her legs under her. "But she hated me!"

"Not as much as me for losing you. *Et enfin*, was your American boy worth it?"

"None of your business."

"As you like. So I found a building—a Haussmann near the International School. There are two apartments for rent—one penthouse and another lower floor. It makes sense we take them."

"*Us?* In the same building—you for *real*?"

"Cosima starts school in September and we both need somewhere to live."

"I know, but—"

"*Écoute,* we share a daughter, *chérie.* It's nearly August. I send the details." She heard him light a cigarette. "We need to act fast because the properties are very interesting. OK, Lili, guess where I'm going now?"

"The Pigalle?"

"No, bad girl! I'm having breakfast at Les Deux Magots with Chrystelle. I'll send a selfie! Tomorrow my parents planned to take Cosie to the zoo so call early. Oh, and last thing, it's not my business but Céline wasn't impressed with your new man."

Elizabeth needed to pee again.

64

SUBJECT: IF A DOUBLE-DECKER BUS CRASHES INTO US...

From: Elizabeth Lambert

To: Jack Mathews

Date: Tuesday October 20, 2020 at 19:45

Thanks for turning me on to The Smiths—obsessed! Today's very much a Smithsonian day: gun-metal sky over a roiling Seine—but for me, nothing's been so clear. I want out of my marriage. This is about me—nothing to do with you. Call later.

————

"So tell me, what's the deal with you and Elizabeth?"

"I met her one summer when I was eighteen, she was fifteen."

"*O-M-G!* Like K and me!"

"We were older! Wait a sec." Text from Preston. Jack's contribution to his rent payment was late. Another message from Draxx: the garage was closed up but Bentley had still not returned the car. Should they report it as a theft?

"Dad! Go *on*."

"She had a difficult life, it didn't work out then I met your mom. Didn't hear from her again until the pandemic."

Welcome to Carmelito, California!

Just as Jack drove past the Italian restaurant where he'd asked Jude to marry him, a dark shape stepped out in front of the car. He had to break hard to stop in time. Both of them were thrown forward.

"Y'OK, baby?" Jack checked Aimee's head hadn't hit anything. She swallowed, nodding. They exchanged relieved smiles as their breathing kicked back in. When Jack looked back to the road, all he saw was a woman's face peering over the bonnet at him.

Once she was against the windshield, Aimee shouted, "Mommy!"

Jack felt the thump of Jude's hand on the metal. She pushed back spirals of hair from her face, swung her legs out in long strides to the driver's window.

"Liar! Liar! Liar! You goddamn lying son-of-a-bitch!"

The car behind tooted.

"How's 'time on my own'?"

The driver behind gestured at them to move out the way.

Jude's sienna-brown eyes were bloodshot, blackened, hateful until she heard, "Mommy?"

"Whataaru…?" Jude whispered.

"Jude, get in the back."

"I'm not sitting near you! Never. Never ever! You lying shit! Aimee, get over here."

The words came out with punches to the car, causing the groceries from the bag to roll out onto the road.

The owner of the La Familia came out with his son. He was about to say something but on recognizing Jude and Jack, treaded back.

"I wanna go with mommy!" said Aimee, getting out of the car.

"Stay. She's been drinking."

"I'm taking my daughter home!" Jude said, kicking the car as a jumbo-sized packet of potato chips fell out onto the road.

When Aimee freed herself and was by her mother's side, Jude reeled back, "Who is she?"

The driver behind leant out. "Hey lady! We all got dramas of our own to get to."

"I'll see you at the house," said Jack. "Beans, with me."

Jude clung to her daughter, shaking her head.

"Ju? Can we…?" He rolled the car forward a little.

"Beanie, in the back, honey."

Aimee buried her head into her mother's clothes; Jude fought her off to lean into Jack's window.

"You'll lose everything, Jack, everything. You'll be left with nothing because you are *nothing* without us."

Sorry you're leaving Carmelito, California!

Jack turned down a road behind the bus stop and waited for Jude to pass while he ripped through his phone deleting messages to Elizabeth. He didn't know why. But deleting the words was proof he wasn't a lying shit.

The MG chugged down the road, Jude's eyes scowling over the dashboard. Aimee sat behind her; the light from her phone turning her face phantom-white.

Jack followed them until he arrived at the cabin where Jude ditched the car on an angle, blocking the driveway. Mother and daughter crunched over the gravel to the front door, let Tip out, snapped the screen door shut. Lights came on.

They were just about to restart their life together, *there*, in the hills, overlooking the reeds and the herons and water voles. Jack hid across the road, watching the cabin through the trees until the stars pulsed over their roof—not for Jude and Aimee's safety, but for his.

65

SUBJECT: CAPTAIN, WE HAVE A MALFUNCTION

From: Elizabeth Lambert

To: Jack Mathews

Date: Thursday October 29, 2020 at 14:53

What's with the mixed messages you keep giving me? I shared something very personal with you and you return it with bumper-sticker psychology and shut me down. If you're so hot on communication—call me.

———

JACK DIDN'T USE his key, so Elizabeth had to come down and open the door to see him, arms heavy with flowers. She was in pink hot pants and a flimsy tank top, her body under the porch light was like sheet metal, lacquered by a jasmine and honey moisturizer.

"I'm sorry I haven't been here enough for you and wasn't sympathetic enough when you've missed your daughter. I'm sorry I didn't just tell Jude the truth instead of stalling. I was just trying to save people from pain—and hey," he raised his hands in surrender, "save myself too." Jack stepped towards Elizabeth until they were almost touching. "We're both in the dark here, but love is our lighthouse… and—that didn't sound so corny as when I was rehearsing it, but y'know what I mean."

Elizabeth had planned to turn him away forever, but he was there, and whatever he did, he just made her happy when he was there.

"And you promised to take me to the Fish Hook museum in Bay Tree!"

"It's a date! And I'll buy you anything you like from the gift shop."

Elizabeth nudged his shoulder with the crown of her head as he closed her into his arms, crushing the flowers against her hair. "Can we start again?" He presented the bouquet. "The 7/11 didn't have peonies, but they smell nice if you like the aroma of gasoline."

"Thank you. Maybe they'd look best on the outside terrace?"

"I know, mixed colors bother you, but they're symbolic."

"Come in, Matt's looking at us funny." Elizabeth waved at their nearest neighbor.

Jack followed her to the kitchen where Elizabeth searched for a vase.

"Listen, I don't wanna add to your troubles but someone keeps calling on the phone and hanging up, and I thought I saw someone trying to get over the wall."

"Jude," said Jack. "I told her about us and she's mad, hurt, crazy. But you OK?"

"I was feeling shitty, terrible actually, till Lindsay took me to a sunset yoga class run by this great teacher, Callie. I only got back a few minutes before you did. Esme's made some quesadillas." Elizabeth opened the fridge. "Hon, Jude's done a few things online, nothing serious, but embarrassing. This should be about you and her, not my business, or Bruno—I could lose Cosima."

Jack took off his jacket then washed his hands and face in the sink. "Aimee's with her, they're at the cabin, she'll calm down. I'm not hungry but can I have this beer?"

"Don't keep asking—it's your house too."

Elizabeth carried the 'symbolic' flowers—at arm's length—to the middle of the coffee table.

"That's a statement piece."

"The boy's catching on."

"It's a statement about how much I love you. But it's also a question."

Jack twirled her around, lowering her on the leather couch, and asked, "Will you marry me?"

"Now that's more like it."

66

SUBJECT: DIA DE LOS MUERTOS

From: Elizabeth Lambert

To: Jack Mathews

Date: Sunday November 1, 2020 at 10:32

Sorry I was grouchy when you called. I found out they'd got a second architect to verify our plans behind my back, such a diss. And I was hurt cause every time I talk about separating from Bruno you freak out. It's taken a pandemic to see my life differently, including my marriage. And before I'm forty I need to leave Bruno and find my dad.

———

TIP'S PAWS tapped over the wooden floor. There was birdsong, insects propelling themselves between the reeds, the splash of a frog. Mountain air toasting in the sun. It took Jude a while to get the glass of stale water from her bedside to her lips. That's when she realized her phone was still in her hand. Who'd she call? Nor did she remember shutting down the house or closing the windows. Or going to bed. A blurry image of Aimee pulling off her socks hovered in her throbbing head.

Tip began licking her ankle where it stung. She must have cut herself on something.

Jude was over the toilet bowl just in time.

Tip whined as her body heaved and she felt the spirit of her mother behind her, holding back her hair.

Worst over. Jude rested back on her heels, wiped her mouth and wished she could ask her mother how she'd coped during her father's drinking days, *that croupier from Atlanta*, the *tour guide in Hawaii*, being fired from his job on a newspaper that caused them to sell the town house. But somehow the turmoil and hurt had segued into the last twenty years of serenity by the lake once he got into AA and made every day a living amends to his family.

Jude retched again to the sound of her phone ringing. Dahlia.

"Remember calling me last night?"

Jude took two gulps of coffee and asked, "How bad?"

"The fact that you have to ask is your answer."

Jude sipped from an icy glass of water before pouring the rest into Tip's bowl, which was empty but for an entrepreneurial ant.

"Dad had blackouts when he drank."

"He also drove a fire engine when he drank." Dahlia's vape cigarette whistled.

"I've booked a flight out Thursday. Can you stay out of trouble till then?"

Aimee was on the porch letting Tip lick peanut butter from her fingers.

"Well someone had a party last night."

"I'm mortified. I was very upset, but everything's going to be fine now."

"Can we go home? The Biewers called, said Mouse was crying all night long to get into the house and there's a party tonight and—"

"—you only just arrived. I thought we could hang out, read, swim, and—"

"Bentley's on his way over to collect me."

"Does Bentley know?"

"Everybody knows, Mom, you announced it to the world: *my husband's a lying cheat!*"

"No way am I leaving you in town with Bentley."

"Like you're so sensible."

Jude dropped into the chair. Where was Aimee, and how come she'd lost the password to her?

"I don't feel well."

"It's called a hangover. Philly gets them all the time." Aimee looked at her phone. "People keep writing to me about Dad—everybody's saying what a shit he is and they'll never buy a car from him again."

"Text Bentley to pick up some dog food, bread and more painkillers and—" A black car screeched in the driveway, swerving around Jude's. "Too late."

67
SUBJECT: SOS

From: Jack Mathews

To: Elizabeth Lambert

Date: Monday November 2, 2020 at 18:43

Mermaid, PLEASE! We need to talk but I'm trapped in the house Aimee homeschooling, Bentley on Zoom with a psychologist 2 x week and Ma-May getting worse with the new shit they been giving her. I want you so bad I'm gonna explode. I'm also an Abba fan! If you want to blackmail me, now you got the dirt 😜

ESME DIDN'T COME in on Sundays so Elizabeth was the first to walk through the sunlight to make their pot of green tea. She stopped by the flowers Jack had brought her the night before. She would have liked to make a post announcing their engagement but not with that depressing collection of cellophane-wrapped weeds. Instead, she'd book that oceanside restaurant, have someone film Jack on one knee surprising her with a ring while a quartet—or how about a country 'n' western band? — played. A reel cut just before she answered him... A second post, maybe underwater? Mermaid and her sailor theme... She'd mood-board it later.

. . .

"How about a wedding on Catalina Island, right where you first asked me to marry you, with—"

Jack was pacing back and forth across the bedroom glaring at his phone.

"She sent an email to every person in my contact list saying I've abandoned three children and a wife for a woman I met on the internet." Jack ran his hands over his hair so often Elizabeth feared there wouldn't be any left. "Al—my so-called best friend —he's written to say this could jeopardize my work at Kids Call."

"That's a voluntary position."

"So? There's even an email from Mr. Applebaum asking why I'm sending him abusive messages. And on my website, some jerk I sold a car to five years ago: *Jack Mathews is a cheat at home and at the garage, dud guy, dud cars.* And listen to this—"

"You're shouting."

He waved his phone at her. "You bet I'm shouting!"

Elizabeth put down the teas to rush through her messages from friends, clients, people she hadn't communicated with for years, who'd all taken time out of their weekends to let her know how appalled they were that she was wrecking a beautiful family. She was so absorbed she hadn't even noticed that Jack was already dressed and at the bottom of the stairs.

"Smell the flowers!" he called up before slamming the door.

Shop bought flowers, she thought, reminding herself to get onto Megan again about the white peonies she'd ordered weeks ago.

Elizabeth sat crossed legged in the middle of her bed with her phone and laptop. After a short exchange with an excited Cosima who wanted to talk about her first horse jump, Elizabeth checked in with her team in London. Emily assured her they were all hands on deck finding a watertight narrative to plug Jude's barrage of sewage that was flooding Elizabeth's world of accent walls, stone bubblers and ambient lighting. 'We need you to look like the victim in this,' Magnus had said. 'I *am* the fucking victim!' cried Elizabeth. 'He wanted to marry me at fifteen and she stole him away and now she's trying to ruin everything. Again!' To which Magnus added that Jude had three children so it wouldn't be an easy clean up. 'Throw bleach at her,' she'd ordered.

Elizabeth would have to wait until the next day to reach her Paris office as there was no way they'd take a work call at the weekend.

She ached for her daughter, her office surrounded by familiar faces, to walk through drizzle, even public transport… *I'm homesick*—and it did actually make her feel sick. She lifted up her iPad and FaceTimed Bruno.

"Why didn't you tell me you were seeing someone—a new girlfriend who has cats?"

Bruno was laughing. "Hey, hey, Lili, you wake me up and I'm alone."

"Are those black satin sheets?"

"You gave them to me, remember? One Christmas—"

"The gift was ironic. A comment on the tacky girls you were fucking."

"But when I fucked them, Lili, it reminded me of how you were once just like that: so hungry and willing. And everything else was in the laundry. *Mais attends*, have you been on your Facebook page? Your Twitter? Instagram? *Chérie*, you see your webpage?" He was laughing. "Eh? You're in trouble. *You're* a bad girl—get some geek to change your settings, maybe get a lawyer too. *Bonne nuit.*"

When the call ended, she logged into her Facebook account.

The page unfurled with a photo of a group of people, smiling, tanned and half-dressed. Jack, with his hair messed up by the wind, was standing in front of a beach house by the sea. At first glance it looked like the Hamptons or Maine, somewhere east coast: pale sands and a turbulent sea. Jack had his arm around Jude, their three kids in front of them. Bentley wearing braces and holding a husky, Aimee still little. There were older people—parents and grandparents—and a dark, pretty woman. Above the photos was written:

This is my family. What kind of evil monster would break up this happy home? Do the right thing and leave my husband alone Elizabeth Lambert!

It had 857 likes. There were 369 comments, 58 shares.

Elizabeth's Twitter icon bounced with posts in which she'd been tagged. Instagram was the same. There were even posts about Elizabeth on Goodreads under the listings for her books. On Google reviews under her company's name, there was a message:

Hey Elizabeth Lambert, shouldn't you be making homes not breaking them?

The first response to the thread read:

Mrs Mathews: Elizabeth Lambert is a loving mother, a talented and respected designer. She also has a family and friends who love her and what you write hurts her and them. Stop and think about who the 'homewrecker' really is. Please defer and desist from these embarrassing public displays of hate and jealousy. Bruno Lambert.

Elizabeth half laughed and half cried at Bruno's defense. The weapon she'd used to fight her way clear of the marriage was sharpened every day by focusing on a picture of a man who was wholly repellent and dangerous to her. Now the separation was over, she could drop the gun, step back and see that Bruno had some redeeming qualities. Even ones she now missed. Even ones she saw lacking in Jack, and, like today, there were times in their near twenty years together, he really had been a friend. Ally, even, she thought, buzzing Lindsay through the gates.

Her neighbor hugged her while holding onto two bubble teas.

"I came as soon as I read those awful posts!" Lindsay sipped from her drink. "Nice flowers."

"We got engaged last night."

"Congrats. Matt's a killer lawyer. Here's his card."

After Lindsay left, the calls and messages kept coming in from strangers, old clients, friends of friends, and of course Céline.

"Darling, this is vulgar. You have to leave America and your mid-life crisis flirtation."

An editor of an online decorating magazine called to say that an article about a chateau Elizabeth had done up had been vandalized by obscene comments.

Then Megan called. "What have I done?"

68

SUBJECT: AND THE BEAT GOES ON!

From: Neptune99

To: Salacia99

Date: Monday November 16, 2020 at 22:59

Got ur message about using the secure emails . On it. Crazy about the headphones! Awesome quality. You'd laugh if you saw me now in my workshop, dead of night, listening to our latest playlist and working on a car I'm flipping. Tip keeps looking over, like, who's this guy? Who's this guy? *You see this guy, this guy's in love with you…*

———

ELIZABETH DROVE up to a café on the coast wearing a black dress and her trademark red lipstick. Megan was outside, pulling on an e-cigarette like it was life support.

"It's a vegan brunch place—I remembered you were vegetarian—I am too, well, almost. You look vegetarian, I mean, healthy and all. Can't believe you're my age. I just hate growing older, don't you? It feels like an illness and one morning I'll wake up and be myself again—thin and taut, no lines under my eyes—eyes that actually see anything. I didn't sleep at all night. I'm going to lose my job over this. It's a rule, never to mention clients to clients, cause they can make deals behind your back or whatever. You done micro-needling? Point at what you like."

"Just a black coffee."

"Really? Mind if I eat? I have viewings all afternoon and... She's even left messages on our work website—that table's free."

Minutes later, Megan placed the food tray in front of them.

"Jude Mathews needs to see how these attacks are extremely damaging to everybody, particularly her. Can you do that?"

"Is Mr. Mathews mad at me too?" Megan whimpered into her Buddha bowl.

They both looked up to see one of the servers standing by their table, glaring at Elizabeth.

"Elizabeth Lambert? Right?"

Elizabeth hadn't even had a chance to nod before the woman started: "Jude Mathews has been a super friend to me and a great boss where I work as a special ed. teacher. Y'know, she saved her husband from bankruptcy? And raises money for kids with leukaemia? And never once forgotten to send us a Christmas card."

She skittled behind the counter to make a call on her cellphone while pointing Elizabeth out to another woman who peered in her direction.

"She works in a school and she's serving food?"

Megan stared at the table. "They don't do that in France? In California, lot of teachers have second, third jobs. You know Chris? The guy who puts up the 'Sold' or 'For Rent' signs on our properties?"

"The guy with the beard and army fatigues? I wasn't sure if he was a hipster or homeless."

"Actually he's a history teacher, knows everything about the Civil War. They still talking about us? See, I'm conflict averse." Megan blew her nose. "Elizabeth, when can I start working with you?"

"When you get Jude to calm the fuck down. Leave this for the waitress."

Elizabeth walked out of the restaurant with Megan staring at a 100-dollar note just as her phone rang.

"What are you doing having lunch with *her?*" Jude asked.

"I'm not, I'm…"

"You are."

Megan glanced up to see clusters of people talking in low voices, looking over at her. One customer even pointed.

"Megan. You on my side or hers?"

"Yours. Definitely yours."

69

EL: TUES 17 NOV 2020

We need to talk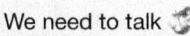

———

"I DON'T FEEL comfortable about this, Mom," said Bentley, shaking his head at the road in front of them. "Preston said wait till he comes home for the family strategy meeting."

"This is the family strategy meeting."

Bentley's palms slid around the steering wheel as he forced himself to defy the compulsion to veer into the barriers.

"You don't think I have a right to see where my husband is living? Huh? And how come Maxxie's not around these days?" asked Jude.

"She got extra hours at the doggy day-care center. What? What, Mom?"

"I just hope you're not cheating on Maxxie. Just hope you're not going to end up like him."

"Can someone please tell me what this is about?" asked Aimee, dabbing concealer to her chin.

"Left. You said Paloma Drive, that's a left."

"OK, OK," said Bentley.

"Second left." Jude pointed.

"I *know*."

"Of *course* you do!"

Jude crossed her arms, stared at him.

"I haven't done anything wrong!"

Jude gave a *humph*. She'd already got way more out of Bentley than he'd meant to tell. His mother had always been able to get anything out of him with just a look.

"I know a guy with a gun, you want me to get it, rough her up, shoot her?"

Aimee brought her fists to her temples, shook her head.

"Beans, he's kidding. No one's gonna hurt anybody. Your job is to film what happens."

"Is this going to be like Saturday when Mom screams in front of lots of people?" asked Aimee.

"No. Just one."

Bentley flicked the indicator; his eyes searched his mother's face for the slightest sign of prevarication.

"It's next on the right," she said as the house came into view.

"What if Dad's there?"

"Bradley says he's at the garage," said Jude.

"Bradley? The clown who washes the cars in the playground? *He's* your informant?"

The car hugged Paloma Hill as they approached the house.

Aimee peered over their heads. "Dad lives *here*?"

"Yup, baby. And I bet he makes sure her sprinkler system works."

Bentley had barely pulled up the handbrake when Jude was at the gates pressing on the buzzer with Aimee behind her, filming with her iPhone.

"Bentley, the code?"

70

You totally misunderstood everything I said. I can't live through 1999 again. CALL ME BACK!

———

ELIZABETH HAD FINISHED her fifty lengths of the pool and was drying off over a FaceTime call to Magnus to go over their Sapphire Group pitch, when she heard a car stop.

"Someone's outside the house."

"Don't you all have those private security firms over there? Call them," said Magnus.

"I'll call Jack."

"Him? The *police!*"

Elizabeth could see two people struggling against each other behind the windscreen.

"I think it's *her*... Definitely a woman. And others. They can't get in, there's a code—the gates are opening. It's her. With Bentley, and I don't know how many others."

"Call 911. Now!"

Elizabeth heard a car door slam. Footsteps.

Both Elizabeth and Magnus cried out when they heard the doorbell.

"Tits, stay calm, remember your black belt in aikido and grab a broom."

"Blue belt and that was fifteen years ago. They're walking around the house. They're—"

"Nice place. Elizabeth, right?"

In the last seventy-two hours Jude had done little else but study the life of Elizabeth Lambert, and now, approaching the woman she'd imagined her Jack wanting, she hurled herself towards her, a comet of hate.

Elizabeth held her towel up to her chest looking panicked at the dog behind Bentley and a teenage blonde behind them holding up a phone.

"I'm Jack's wife. This is Aimee, she is fourteen, Grade 9. You know Bentley, right? Just nineteen. He has additional needs. And there's Preston, he's in his last year of college, twenty-one years old."

Bentley wiped the corners of his mouth, looked away from Elizabeth's naked shoulders.

"Why are you telling her our ages, Mom?" asked Aimee.

"That's Tip. Go on, boy, take a good, long piss against those hydrangeas."

Jude was momentarily distracted by Aimee moving in close to film the silver ring on one of the woman's red-painted toes.

"We are—" Jude turned to Aimee and Bentley then back to Elizabeth "*Real*. We are *suffering* because of *him* and *you*! So we wanted to just ask nicely if you could just leave my husband alone."

"Jack can make his own decisions," said Elizabeth.

"Asking nicely for you to get the fuck out of our lives!"

"Mo-om!" Aimee sniggered.

"Have you asked Jack what *he* wants?" asked Elizabeth, finding herself strangely unshaken by the intrusion.

"What *Jack* wants? Jack *needs* us and we need him, my husband, the children's father! *Three* children!"

Elizabeth caught sight of Lindsay watching from her upstairs window, talking into a phone, making stay-calm gestures at Elizabeth.

"You messed with the wrong family, lady," said Bentley, his face twitching in all directions.

"What do you say, home-wrecker?" asked Aimee, moving close enough for Elizabeth to clutch her wrist. She grabbed the phone out of Aimee's hand and threw it far into the deep end of the pool.

"My phone!"

The first to go in after it was the dog but Bentley held him back at the same time as unlacing his shoes and getting ready to plunge in—Elizabeth called out to him to stop.

"Don't even think about it, Bentley. Now you leave *us* alone. You don't come here. You don't write shit about me on the internet and you stop calling. We clear?" Elizabeth glared at them.

"You threw my phone in the pool!" cried Aimee.

"He's my dad. He's married to my mom!" said Bentley, still pulling at Tip's collar.

"Wrong. I'm Jack's wife. *You* took him from *me*."

"What are you talking about?" Jude asked, so quietly she hardly made a sound.

Elizabeth folded her arms and spoke clearly, as if she were reading the day's news.

"Nineteen ninety-nine. He was just dating you when he met me that summer, in Avalon. We fell in love and Jack wanted to spend the rest of his life with me. He asked me to marry him and I said *yes*. We exchanged vows! But…something happened and I had to leave and when he couldn't find me, he settled with you. *Settled* with all of you. But he always loved me. You were just placeholders until we found each other again." Elizabeth soaked in the shock on Jude's face. "This is the last time I'm asking you to leave my property before I have you removed."

Aimee broke the deadlock by wiping her eyes on her mom's shirt sleeves. "But my phone!"

Bentley bounced on the balls of his feet about to say something but Elizabeth put up her hand.

Once Elizabeth was sure the car had driven away, she

returned to her laptop. She thought Magnus' face had frozen on the screen until he burst out laughing.

"Oh, Tits! Now I see that scrappy little trailer-park kid!"

71

SUBJECT: SEXY SIREN OF
THE SEA

From: Neptune99

To: Salacia99

Date: Thursday November 19, 2020 at 12:59

God bless technology and YOU!!! Can't stop thinking about last night… every time I see your face I just want to cum! Oh my sexy siren of the sea, BIG STONKING YES to our FUTURE! It's so clear that we have no choice but to live together. I agree the email/texts etc lead to miscommunication. Let's talk again when I'm back at the garage.

AUNT MARIBETH FELL ONTO ELIZABETH, squeezing her in warm, clammy, baby soft arms.

"You look just like 'er."

Maribeth opened a space between them to look at Elizabeth again.

"You know, she named you after me? The 'Beth' bit was 'cause a me."

Family. Just when Maribeth thought there was nobody.

Hands on hips, she stood shaking her bleached blonde hair with pink ends at how that tall scrawny little thing she hadn't seen for thirty years had turned out. Maribeth pulled up her elasticated jeans from under her once black—now gray—

sleeveless Bruce Springsteen tour vest and wriggled her bare bunioned toes, even the black Darth Vader-looking toenail.

"Come on in, kid, I made lemonade for ya—real lemonade like my Pa, yer grandpa, used ta—bet you never had that. I'll teach ya, then you'll have somethin' to pass on to your daughter. Myself, I might have a beer, but you're drivin' so, but if you prefer? Jesus, you do look like her—well, let's say, how she woulda ben, f'not for the drink and drugs and those dumb diets and even dumber men. That's Boadicea, our cat. Hog's out there somewhere," she said, flicking her hand towards the window. "Ben too hot last few days."

Elizabeth's aunt drew out a pitcher from her fridge while Elizabeth peered at the other side of the door covered in concert tickets.

"Any of my dad?"

"We'll get to him in a moment." Maribeth shook her head. "You sound like her. W'always said she had the voice of a dirty angel. And you, you got that same innocent face, dangerous combo."

She peered into Elizabeth's face again, red veins bordering her irises like ancient script.

"Can't believe you drove all the way out here." Maribeth wiped down two plastic chairs outside the kitchen and put the drinks on an upside-down bucket.

"I was the roadie for all the greats: Alice Cooper, The Boss," she lifted her vest to look at him, "REO Speedwagon, Melissa Etheridge... so I wouldn't see her for some time but ev'y time I did, she'd sunk further down. One time, so drunk and mouth smashed up she had to down vodka through a straw. I thought she had that Korsakoff's syndrome, ah. Then she met that grifter, Vince." Maribeth opened her beer, drank from it, licked her lips. "Only met him once, that place in Orange Country. A didn't know what to say, just dint. You kids were just playin' the dirt—beautiful kids, smart." Maribeth wiped a tear. "I used to send her money to a PO address but I know she didn't feed you—she goddamn fed her habit and his disgusting dog. And all that worried her was that *he* was gonna leave *her*. I regret till ma dyin' day—see, people talk of making amends, peace with God, all that, well, I needed to say it to your face: I'm really sorry, bottom of ma heart, I didn't do the right thing 'n' take you kids with me. A put maself first—thought about it—but see, a dint know nothin' 'bout child'en. But you got out, dintcha? And look at you! I tried my darndest to help Danny, but...you must never feel bad 'bout savin' y'self, man like Vince, bet he couldn't hold off a beautiful young girl, s'why you took off, huh? Never looked back."

Elizabeth watched a chicken pecking at some gravel, felt her aunt's hot palm on her shoulder.

"I told her it would happen, but ma sista in love, she woulda used anything or anyone to keep him. Even her own daughter."

Maribeth pinched some tobacco onto a cigarette paper and added in some homegrown grass. She didn't say anything, but she saw Elizabeth was shaking.

"So how's life with Romeo?"

"Not great," Elizabeth answered, rolling her eyes. "Here I am, divorced, my daughter in another country, my work on the line without me there, and y'know what? He never even got round to telling his wife."

Maribeth gave a tar-packed chuckle. "When I met Hog, she was the wife of a Seventh-Day Adventist minister. You know here in Arlington we got the Baptist University; he was big up there. Hog and I, we had a fight 'em all. Even today only two out of four of her kids talk to us—but hell, what the heart wants." Maribeth put her hand on Elizabeth's shoulder as the afternoon light dipped. "But what am sayin' is, it's hard enough with you both paddling upstream, but if he ain't feelin' it, that raft's goin' nowhere." They both looked at the bare horizon in front of them until Maribeth stood up. "Anyway, girl, I know you come over to see if you can track that bum of a father you got, at least you might get some answers. Follow me."

Maribeth went to the kitchen and returned holding a plastic crate filled with records. "So I knew him as the bass player for this terrible band, the *Cayotes*? You never heard of th' *Cayotes*?

Well, that's you and everybody else. Here he is. Granger Gallagher."

Maribeth passed the album cover to Elizabeth.

"Then he just disappeared off the scene, but last year, a girl-friend from those days called to say she'd seen him at a rebirthing ceremony in Carmel. Now his name's Zuni and he's a *shaman*."

Elizabeth stared at the record sleeve: four men in leather and denim carrying guitars with a backdrop of Las Vegas burning behind them.

"Your mom, she followed him everywhere. When she fell pregnant, I suspected he was the father. Them your eyes."

"What was he like?"

"He wasn't a Vince, not a bad motherfucker. He was… charismatic. Big talker, thinker-drinker, drug fiend—your mom had a type for sure."

The room filled with a honey light, same color as the mountain range through the windows, by the time Elizabeth got ready to leave for Long Beach where she was staying with friends.

"Beautiful child, you come back whenever. If me and my girl, Hog, ain't here just ask where the two dykes got to, someone'll tell ya."

72

SUBJECT: SYNCING NOW

From: Elizabeth Lambert

To: Jack Mathews

Date: Wednesday November 25, 2020 at 6:43

Back in Paris. Didn't win the award but being nominated was enough. Partied till the morning
—don't worry—all tested beforehand. Cosie is allowed back at school but if a kid gets sick, all
back home. Will call after meeting with my publisher.

———

"How about you run your car through our smog check station? Well, here's my card if—"

The man kept walking, didn't even acknowledge Bradley tipping his cap at him.

"Can you believe that guy?" Jack asked Traci. She shrugged, turned her back on him. Herpes was less of a turn off than someone in your sales team who couldn't hold a buyer's attention, and if it was your boss... Self-pity moved through Jack with peristaltic regularity. "T-Bird, it's been a minute—wanna grab a coffee?"

That shrug again, but half an hour later she sat down opposite him in his office.

"Did you manage to find a way of deleting some of the

comments?" he asked as his cursor buzzed around the Mathews Motors website.

"Marcie made herself Content Manager, can't she?"

Jack tapped at his keyboard. "We all need to protect this company's reputation. Hear this: 'Jack Mathews is a Nazi.' People with nothing better to do than post lies about others. Jude hasn't thought at all about how this could affect Aimee."

"Maybe we could talk about work sometime?" Traci, straight-backed, stared right at him.

"Jude's under a lot of a *strain,* she tends—"

"Your home life is not my business, but your *business* is my business. The person they're describing is my boss." She pointed at his screen. "As you know, I took a higher commission over salary."

"We agreed that—"

"So how come it feels like I'm the only one around here who gives a shit about selling cars? Look at this place! Since when did Marcie take three-hour lunches? My commission pays my rent, night school, living costs—we closed Saturday because Bentley didn't return a client's car and you just took off and, of all people, left Draxx in charge, *apparently.* The guys don't like him. *I* don't like him. I've only sold two cars this month because I'm doing other people's jobs—it's *July.* Gary worked his ass off on the Ford van, you know, the graffiti one, and you didn't even notice."

Jack looked puzzled.

"*Gary.* 'Good-Looking'—but he doesn't want to be called that anymore. His name is Gary Lord and he's only got Bradley to help him right now."

"Bradley's a smart kid."

"He's a child! You aware Marcie has been running Women's Empowerment Workshops after we close up?"

"I'm gonna fix this, how about—"

A white envelope appeared in her hand.

"Hey, Trace. Seriously? We can get the toilets cleaned and I'll—" Traci scratched her nose, waiting for him to finish.

"I'm out."

"Girl does an MBA and now she knows everything."

"That's exactly the kind of toxic-masculinity I can't work with anymore."

"It's a joke!"

"Jokes are meant to be funny."

"Ouch!"

Jack watched as she rode the little diamond pendant back and forth along the chain around her neck.

"I'm deeply sorry if I ever caused you offense. You mean a lot to me, T-Bird. Not just professionally. You know that."

Jack took the envelope and caught Draxx sneaking a look at them through the glass partition.

"Three months?"

"One *week*. And all my commissions up to date."

"We're pretty big around here, Mathews Motors is—"

"I know what Mathews Motors is. You sold the SL Mercedes you *knew* I wanted *and* the 'new guy' you keep referring to has been here for three months. You don't know his name but even he knows you spent six hundred on dinner the other night. You say this place is like your family, too fucking right."

"Pablo," said Jack after her. "The new guy is called Pablo."

But Traci was already out the room having passed Draxx on her way out.

"She's a..." Draxx sucked his teeth. "We need you at the body shop."

"Didn't I see a couple out front—did you ask if they needed help?"

Draxx clapped the monkey-wrench against his palm, he always had one in his hand, like some people have a cigarette, or a guitar.

"The Samurai—sold without air conditioning, Texas number plates, something's not right."

Draxx peeled himself off the wall, about to follow Jack out when he asked, "Those cops out there?"

Bradley brought the two men into the showroom. "I say, Mr.

Mathews, there appear to be two gentlemen on the premises asking to see you."

Jack heard the sound of a police walkie-talkie.

"Can I help you?" asked Jack.

"Jack Mathews? You own a black Nissan Frontier?"

"That's me."

"Sir, we have some questions to ask you."

"Shoot," said Jack, immediately regretting his turn of phrase. "I imagine this is about the car my son's borrowed, because he's—"

"We can't say."

"Aimee?"

"Who's Aimee?"

"Aimee's my fourteen-year-old daughter."

The two men looked at each other.

"Could you come with us to the station?"

73
SUBJECT: IMAGINE IT

From: Jack Mathews

To: Elizabeth Lambert

Date: Thursday November 26, 2020 at 9:03

You and me. Waking up every morning and going to bed every night in each others arms. Last night, after we talked, I rode my bike all around this beautiful city but it doesn't feel like home anymore because you're not in it. TBH, every day we're not together is a f'in wasted chance to live in love and I want that. Not this. I want you. Not anyone else. There. Said it.

————

GIDEON BROOKS HAD FIRST MET Elizabeth in Hong Kong where he, a struggling actor in his early twenties, had been having an on–off relationship with a much older decorator. Returning from LA after a series of failed auditions, he learnt his lover had a new project: a messed-up blonde call girl he'd taken on as an assistant. He set out to hate her but was won over by her talent, her sad backstory and ambition, while she appreciated the pretty boy with a predilection for cocaine had a gift for storytelling. It was Elizabeth who lent him the money for rehab and later, an MFA. Giddy paid her back after he sold his first film script, the same time she asked him to be godfather to Cosima.

Giddy had been a frequent visitor to the Lambert homes,

just as she'd spent many summers at his villa in Tuscany and, that afternoon, where he lived on Long Beach with his Italian partner, Fab.

For Elizabeth's arrival, they had planned a Botox afternoon. And as the nurse prepared the injections, Giddy tried to make sense of Elizabeth's love life.

"So now the Frying Pan has been arrested?" asked Giddy.

Elizabeth shrugged the shoulder she was rubbing sunscreen on. "For *three* years he filled my head with this amazing life we were going to have together… it did *not* look like this."

"Wouldn't surprise me if he were a criminal."

"All my life he's been at the back of my mind, I always thought—"

"We all have someone we think could have been 'the one.' Usually they only got the part because they didn't have enough time to disappoint us."

"Oh, he disappointed me alright. I wonder if it wasn't him I wanted. Maybe it was the picture of a home and a family and a dog. Being surrounded by people who were privileged enough to think the world was a good place."

"Sounds like Hell!"

Elizabeth's phone went, she put it on speakerphone between her and her friend. "Now what?"

"They cleared me of a little girl's murder," Jack shouted.

"Murder?" Elizabeth and Gideon locked eyes.

Whatever Jack said next was drowned out by the sound of a rattling truck in the background.

"Once they learned I hadn't raped and murdered a little girl, they were surprisingly nice. Told me that it's common for women to call the information line to say they suspected their exes of horrific acts. I'm at the station, can you get me?"

"I told you, I'm staying with friends outside LA. Since your family showed up at the house, I don't feel safe there."

"You don't think I'm not mad at her! I'm going straight there to—I don't know—but she won't come near us again. OK, I'll call Al to pick me up. Come home soon."

Gideon watched his friend put her phone back in her bag

and re-tie the little ponytail that swished across the blue sky and made her look about fourteen years old.

"Darling girl, I know something happened to you that made you leave California. I know you can't speak about it. But all I want to say is that re-enacting some kind of trauma is only going to destroy everything you've built for yourself. Don't go back there. Go home, leave all this crap behind."

"I loved him so much once, and he chose Jude. This time, he'll have no choice."

"Hmm. And his *wife* called the police about him abducting a little girl?" asked Gideon, catching her grin. "I know you too well, you terrible thing!"

Elizabeth sipped at her champagne. "Jack needs to be pinned right up against the wall with nowhere else to turn, then he'll find his way."

74

SUBJECT: 'TO LIVE IN LOVE'

From: Elizabeth Lambert

To: Jack Mathews

Date: Friday November 27, 2020 at 9:17

My hotel room is filled with red roses, thank you! Zoom later and I'll show you how they look on my naked body! Oh my darling Jack—*To live in love*. That's what we wanted all those years ago on Catalina Island, and now… that future will be ours!

––––––––

"Costa Rica?" asked Aimee.

"Your dad and I went there with Preston, he must've been—"

"OK, OK, don't bring us down."

Jude tried a smile at her daughter across the kitchen table.

"What about we drive to Ensenada?" asked Bentley, high-balling a can of Red Bull into the trash. "Then we can take you, Tip." He pulled the dog's ears. "Yes we can, we can take you on vacation."

"Who's for another waffle?" asked Preston. "Chad? More coffee?"

"Your father should have Tip for two weeks. See how the

inferior home-wrecker enjoys a big muddy dog all over her white furniture."

Bentley snapped his fingers. "We could feed him stuff that gives him the shits before we drop him off."

Aimee high fived her brother, clasped her hands to her chest, mimicking Elizabeth. "It's so vital every room has a unifying motif of doggy diarrhea."

"How I love muddy prints on my white pant-suit." Preston added, tapping his sister's head with a spatula.

"Hey, Kenzo texted…" squealed Aimee. "He said how 'bout Hawaii? He can surf there."

Jude looked up at the cupboards on the other side of the room and remembered the Sunday morning twenty years ago when Jack put them up: pencil behind his ear, his tongue between his teeth in concentration. How had they gone from building their first kitchen to planning a family vacation without him?

Jude swallowed down some painkillers with the dregs of her coffee.

"Check. It. Out, bitches!" Aimee slid the screen of her laptop to her mother. Jude nodded. "See if you can get a better deal. Whoa! There's—" Aimee stopped herself to nudge her mother's arm.

Tip charged from under the table to the hallway as Jack banged on the front door. Next thing, his face was level with Jude's.

"Six hours!"

"Daddy, don't shout," Aimee said.

Jack put out his arm to hold Aimee back. "Six hours they held me at the police station!"

Jude stared at Jack's cobalt eyes, his ruddy face and T-shirt ringed with sweat patches.

"Can we take this down a notch, Dad?" asked Preston.

"Your mother informed the police I'd killed that little girl, Chloe—the one they've been looking for all summer."

"What are you talking about?" cried Jude, noticing the dentist from across the road watching them from his driveway.

"How fucking crazy can you be? To tell the police you thought I had abducted a fifteen-year-old girl!" Jack's mouth moved with such rage his words seemed out of sync. "They came to my work! In front of everybody—and clients! I was taken away in a black and white! A *child* murderer?" He slapped the wall by her head. "That goes on my record and how's that gonna look for you? Principal with a child-killing husband?"

Jude remembered a night of drinking wine and making calls. She recalled watching an interview with the missing girl's parents. Chloe Lakes. It broke her heart. The family didn't live too far from Orange Flower Park, near Kids Call. The investigating officer put up a number for people to call if they had any information. Could she have called it?

"I'd never... I don't think I...?"

"Did they rough you up?" asked Bentley while Aimee googled *Chloe Lakes suspect*.

"I'd never call the cops but goddammit I should've." Jude's throat tightened. "That woman told us you were married!"

"What were you thinking going to Elizabeth's house?"

Aimee jumped in front of Jack. "And Daddy, she drowned my phone!"

Preston drew Aimee back when Bentley scraped a chair across the room. "They shoulda locked you up and never let you out."

"It's true. You're guilty," Jude said.

"Really? I killed a kid?" asked Jack, stepping back from Bentley.

"Killed our family,." murmured Jude.

"She said you were married?" asked Preston.

Jack slumped against the doorframe. "We knew each other before. It was the summer I was about to go to college, we got carried away. Jude, I—"

"You said you were meditating while you were fucking someone under two miles away!"

Preston put his hand on his mother's shoulder. "Dad, Marcie said you phoned this woman from work every day for—"

"Kids, this is a private conversation," said Jack, raising his palm at them.

"Private? You lied to *all* of us!" Jude slapped at her tears. "It's the cliché of it. We used to laugh at men like you! All these years, I've been so concerned recycling plastic, and paper, and glass, and making compost—"

"Compost?"

"I didn't want to waste anything, and yet—and yet I wasted myself on *you*! Can you imagine what it was like to have some moronic real estate agent tell me that she'd rented a home to you and your girlfriend? And then we go over there, and she says *I'm* the one breaking up *her* marriage?"

"How could you go to her house?"

As Jude spoke, she moved towards Jack forcing him to step back onto the doorstep. "You saying we aren't welcome at your mansion in the hills? You mean, we can't even use the pool, hot tub and any of the *five* bedrooms?"

Jack turned towards his car. "I thought I'd be in that jail cell forever," he said, avoiding eye contact with the people who were standing in their front gardens to watch the drama.

"When I'm through with you," Jude shouted, "you'll be begging for that jail cell!"

75

SUBJECT: STORM

From: Jack Mathews

To: Elizabeth Lambert

Date: Saturday November 28, 2020 at 17:46

There was a storm last night and all the power went out at the lake house. Me and the kids jumped into their grandmother's bed and told ghost stories under the quilt. The room in candlelight and rain hammering down on the roof—it was a beautiful moment. I made these people, this life, and what keeps it all together are the values of love and honesty. Whatever this is between us, it doesn't feel right.

————

JACK PRETENDED he hadn't seen Elizabeth by the pool talking to Flores who hung on her every word. He needed those few seconds dismounting his bike to get into character, shake himself off from the boy who'd sat behind his desk for the last two days gnawing at his nails and checking his phone compulsively since his incarceration.

Jack heaved his bike onto its stand in an exaggerated move to extend his biceps. As he peeled off his helmet, he shook out his hair, closed his eyes and braced himself for the 'talk' Elizabeth had said they had to have when she got back.

"And here she is!"

Elizabeth's arms sealed themselves around his waist, he squeezed his keys in one hand, placed the other over hers. After a minute like that, she lifted her head up and kissed his lips. His fingertips crawled under her white shirt and down to her cut-off shorts.

"So how was prison?"

"I gave it a 6.5 rating on Bookings.com. And how was your trip? Aunt Maribeth? Your friends?"

"All good. Gideon wanted me to stay for a party last night which was fun. No problems with the car." She laughed a little at how formal they were being. "I missed you."

"Jeez, how I missed you!"

Jack backed her through the door and lay her on the carpet by the fireplace where the two of them rolled around the floor in a cyclone of desire.

"I have some good news—and some bad news."

Elizabeth sat up expectantly. "Just the good news."

"Jude's taking the family for a week to Hawaii."

"How could there be bad news after that?"

"I'm paying for it."

"A whole week without your wife—bargain."

"I've made such a mess of us, I know, and I'm so sorry. Let's go to Carmel. Let's see if we can track down your dad—maybe I'll ask him for your hand in marriage."

Jack bunched up Elizabeth's hair in his fist, drew her close to him. He heard laughter from the house next door, he looked out the window to Lindsay and Matt and another couple cooking a BBQ. Why was everything so fucking easy for everyone else?

"If only I'd taken you with me that night, if only we'd run away together, if only…"

76

SUBJECT: REALITY CHECK

From: Elizabeth Lambert

To: Jack Mathews

Date: Sunday November 29, 2020 at 23:16

Thanks for taking my call. The video stuff maybe got out of hand. All I want is for you to be happy, never torn or guilty. One day, or one life, maybe we'll have better odds, until then, let's both focus on our families.

"I'M DISCO." The boy lifted Jude's arms into the sleeves of a black synthetic gown. "This way."

"I look like the last hangman," she mumbled.

The boy prodded his up-do with the sharp point of a comb then twirled it in the direction he was walking. Jude's bumpy landing into the chair gave her whiplash.

"Is Loretta your regular color consultant?"

"Maud was recommended to me?"

"Maud's the *styling* consultant," he said, close to her ear saving her from anyone overhearing her mistake. "But you want color too, right?"

"I don't know, I—"

"You need Loretta," Disco affirmed, examining a pimple

near the ring on his lower lip. "Som'ing a drink?" and with his other hand, he rested three of his fingers on her shoulder—his touch ignited a filament of warmth that shot through her.

"Vodka?" Jude laughed.

"Uh-uh. This here's an organic, vegan hairdressers." He continued placing pressure by her neck, leaving her dizzy. "Got detox smoothies, ice teas… or I can get one of the girls to run out for something across the road?"

"Water's fine," Jude said.

"What kind of water?"

"Wet?"

Disco tapped her shoulder twice and dropped a pile of magazines on her lap. "Right up."

Jude had no choice but to look at her own face from every angle. She remembered as a child staring into the mirror trying to imagine what she'd look like as an old person. Spoiler alert.

Jude arranged the folds of her dress to cover the cushioning of her belly. She patted hollows under her eyes and tried to stretch out the fine lines cutting across her neck, but her reflection confirmed, this was not going away.

The first magazine she opened promised readers a foolproof plan to be *Beach Ready in 14 Days!* Maybe, for once, it wasn't a bad thing that the print was too fuzzy to read.

Jude looked outside the window to see a mom walking by with a little girl in a ballet dress and boy in a buggy who was pointing at things, and she swallowed to stop the tears coming.

"Water, and a cucumber and mint dew. You're welcome."

Disco had gone before she'd a chance to thank him.

Last time she'd been to a hairdresser's was the weekend before her mother's funeral. Jack had driven her and Aimee into town to buy a black suit and hat. She'd got her hair colored and cut, and her nails done—black—and Aimee's, olive green. Jack had come to collect his girls from the salon and—

Tears boiled over the rim of her eyes, falling on a text from Dahlia reminding her, once again, she was arriving from NY the next day.

"Talk me through this," instructed the woman standing

behind Jude, hands on hips, pushing out her large breasts which were squeezed into a doctor's white coat. "I'm Loretta."

"I've been coloring it myself, using a product from Walmart," Jude confessed.

"*Color*? That's reaching." The woman dipped her fingers into the back of Jude's head.

A clump came out in the woman's hands.

"I've been losing a lot of hair recently."

In the mirror's reflection, Jude had a direct view of the street where she saw Jack driving a light-blue sports car. Next to him was Elizabeth. He was laughing at something she said, his head looking up to the sky. He stopped at the lights. Elizabeth put her hand on his thigh, opened the car door and stepped out. She was all in white, on the sidewalk, leaning in, saying something—he was still smiling—she held a straw hat to her head. Jack nodded, tapped his watch. The lights changed but before driving away, Jack made the shape of a heart with his hands. Elizabeth did the same, kissed her fingers and waved to him before turning to a waiting friend. The women joined each other, laughing, looking over at Jack. It was Callie. They both blew kisses at Jack as he drove off leaving them skipping into the shopping center together.

Jude fell forward, into her lap, holding her chest.

"Ma'am?" Loretta put her hand on Jude's shoulder. "Ma'am, you OK?"

"She alright?" another voice behind her.

Jude straightened up to meet Loretta's inked-on eyebrows. "I'm fine, sorry. I didn't catch—"

"These here are eggs, eggs from head lice. I'm sorry but we can't—hey Maxxie!"

Loretta held her arms open so Maxxie could snuggle in without being jousted by the scissors.

"Hi, Loretta. Mrs. M, I got you this—with a double shot of caffeine."

Jude gulped at the drink, shook her head.

Loretta waved her scissors in the air. "*You're* Jude Mathews! Why didn't you say? The school principal! Bentley's mom?"

"'S'right."

Loretta nodded her head knowingly.

"So you're Jack Mathews' wife! He sold us our coupé when we lived in Feliz. Had that car seven years—what a great guy—and handsome as hell." Loretta took a silver comb out of a back pocket. "Don't worry about these guys..." she pointed at Jude scalp. "We'll blitz 'em. Maxxie said you needed help, but..." her eyes widened, "*rescue* is more the word!"

Maud slid over. "So that's why your hair's falling out, girl! People say he left you and your kids to live up in the hills with a skinny hooker from France. She drives that old car, always shopping and meeting fancy people for lunch—"

"—she wears those tight yoga pants. Sick!" interjected the color technician.

Jude squeezed Maxxie's hand.

"That's rough," said Maud, "but there are worse things that can happen in a marriage than infidelity. Just sayin'."

"He's lied, cheated, stolen, betrayed her—there's worse?" asked Maxxie.

"One day I was cutting this woman's hair and the client starts on about the great weekend she had with her new guy—she goes on to describe my Brendan. I dropped the scissors, marched to my house and threw him out." Loretta paused. "Biggest mistake. Looking back, so what? We all mess up. He never stayed with her—now he's lonely, I'm lonely, the kids are mad at both of us all the time and the lawyers got richer. My advice? He'll get tired of blow jobs and fancy food. You fight for your family," she lowered her mouth to Jude's ear as she mixed the dye in its bowl, "and stay off the sauce."

77
SUBJECT: ALWAYS

From: Elizabeth Lambert

To: Jack Mathews

Date: Tuesday December 29, 2020 at 23:16

Still can't get over us calling each other at exactly the same time!!! The best Christmas gift I could ever hope for is you back in my life. This last month has proved we will ALWAYS find a way to be together 🦋 🦋 🦋

ELIZABETH AND JACK pulled up outside their house following an expedition in town to stock up on more sex toys. Elizabeth had hoped it would brighten Jack's black mood about Jude's profligate spending but it had only succeeded in giving her a migraine. As Jack took the keys out of the car, Elizabeth touched his hand.

"There's that kingbird."

The week before, Elizabeth had bought a tub of bird food in the health food store and set it up on the terrace. A few days later, Jack had bought her a *Guide to the Birds of California*. Elizabeth had mused cynically—but hopefully—that they might have found something in common outside issues with ex-partners and insatiable lust.

They held their breaths as the bird picked up a few grains before taking flight.

Jack took Elizabeth's hand, kissed the engagement ring.

"They say most car accidents happen within ten mile of the victim's house. Look at us, we're together. We're engaged. Soon taking a road trip to find your dad, maybe invite him to the wedding. Cosie's gonna love it here. Mermaid, it's almost a touch down."

Elizabeth slid his hand down inside her panties. His head dropped against her neck with a moan as he reached the trilling, rushing heat inside her. Jack nipped at her rib cage as she stretched out—he'd have to climb on her, do it there, her legs weren't solid enough to get in the house. He opened his zipper when Elizabeth put her hand on his.

"Flores. He's just there."

Inside the house, Jack staggered through the hall with Elizabeth clinging to him, nuzzling, muzzling, cooing. They made it up a few stairs until she gripped the banister to stop him. Jack came to a halt, pivoted, nearly dropped her. He was about to ask what was wrong, when he saw through their bedroom door a dark, unmoving bulk inside the four-poster bed.

"Se-cu-ri-ty," Jack mouthed at Elizabeth.

Elizabeth nodded, moved fast down the stairs while doing up the buttons on the front of her shirt. She skidded on the marble floor, opened the chest by the front door and took out the portable panic alarm. She held the button down for five seconds remembering Megan saying it would alert the home security firm.

Jack looked down at her from upstairs, she pressed the alarm for another five seconds to make sure.

Elizabeth remembered Bruno's warning, *Arm yourself, Lili. Any jealous wife can hire a hitman or buy a gun; it happens every day in the crazy USA.*

Elizabeth crept up the stairs until she was holding on to the back of Jack's T-shirt. They both looked into their bedroom at the draping curves of the white silk curtains around their bed. Through the gaps it looked like a black armchair had been upturned in the middle of the bed. But it was breathing in between snorts.

Jack's hand waved Elizabeth back down as he approached the bedroom. She tried to catch his fingers to pull him away from the door.

"Wait," she said.

There was a whimper coming from the bedroom. Elizabeth was ready to run out of the house when she heard Jack say, "Mom?"

Jack opened the bedroom door wide. All Elizabeth could see was his back lifting the curtains from the bed. There was a stench of shit in the room so pungent she could smell it from the hallway. Elizabeth advanced holding her collar up to her mouth. Jack was sitting opposite what looked like a heap of clothes but was an old lady of about 220 pounds. At the end of the bed was a wheelchair.

They both heard the body humming louder and louder as Jack advanced.

"It's OK, Mom. It's OK," he said, sitting on the bed by her. She didn't move. "It's Jack. Me. You're OK."

The old woman chomped on her lips. Jack turned to Elizabeth. "Glass of water."

Elizabeth sprang out of the room, opening every windows on the way to the kitchen. Running the faucet, she looked out for the gardener. Her lower back ached and her eyes stung. People had been in the house—her bedroom—her bed.

Taking the water to her bedroom, she was confronted again with the shock of how acidic the smell of human waste was.

"Mom, this is Elizabeth. Do you remember the girl I used to talk about when I was a boy?"

The woman's fingers twitched in her lap.

"Cunt," she said and continued to stare, transfixed, ahead of her.

"Mom! This is Elizabeth's house. Her—"

Jack and Elizabeth jumped at the sound of a long, loud fart forcing itself through the woman's thighs.

Jack held the glass of water to his mother's lips and she let the liquid run down her chin.

"Check in the wheelchair if there are diapers? And maybe medication? And bring up a bucket of warm water and a sponge."

"And how did she get in here?"

"I don't know! Esme maybe... Could you help?"

"Don't get cross at me!"

"Hey, Mom, it's OK." Jack stroked the few clumps of hair on her head, but she pulled away. "Stay here while I try the home again."

Once Jack was out of sight, Elizabeth snapped a photo of the old woman, the diapers and the feces-stained bed on her phone. She sent it to Giddy—*Meet the in-laws!*

Elizabeth listened from upstairs as Jack spoke with someone from Halcyon Days.

"Patricia Mathews' son... No. Wait. Sir, you can't put me through because my mother is sitting upstairs in my bed. No. *My* bed. What payment defaulted? What d'you mean my wife said I'd found other arrangements for her? What d'you mean you can't process this tonight?"

78
SUBJECT: RESOLUTIONS

From: Elizabeth Lambert

To: Jack Mathews

Date: Tuesday January 5, 2021 at 23:49

While Cosie was in ski class yesterday, I went off into the mountains and had a revelation. Heart and mind were one, sharp and ice clear. The pain of staying the same is worse than moving forward. I have two resolutions. First, get out of my marriage, and second, look my dad in the eye. When I called my aunt Maribeth to say merry Christmas, she told me she might have info on my dad. This is a sign and I have to follow it. And yes, you're right, that is Mont Blanc in the background! OK, there could be a third resolution, but that's up to you...

––––––––

DAHLIA HAD BOOKED a table at the Lakeside Inn which had turned from a beer and burger place into a boutique hotel with restaurant tables dotted all the way down to the jetty. Malone, Jude's dad's friend, who used to run it had been replaced by a woman in a black suit who took orders on an iPad.

Dahlia was seated at a table with a bottle of sparkling water and a gaudy gang of hibiscus flowers around her. Her neck smelled of body lotion and her hair rested against Jack's cheek when he kissed her.

Jude's sister had been hit the most by her father's drinking bouts and, unlike Jude, who fought for attention by bringing home straights As, Dahlia competed with black kohl eyes, pleather micro-skirts and thigh-high boots. She got drunk, smoked pot and stayed out late with older guys who had cars and could take her places. Even though she and Jack hooked up regularly through high school, she made it clear their secret trysts just filled time until someone substantial came along, and when he married her sister, part of him did it to hurt her back.

"Tom Ford," she said, stroking his jacket sleeve.

"No, Jack Mathews." She laughed. "Elizabeth upgraded my wardrobe. Turns out men's clothing's a lot more complicated than just having big enough pockets for keys."

"Go figure. And how did your views on menswear work out in jail?" she drawled.

"I still got PTSD from that. Seriously."

"Jude swears she never made that call."

"Did she tell you she took my mom out of her home and brought her to Elizabeth's house, put her in the bed?"

"Apparently you'd stopped paying the care home."

"I missed a payment cause things are pretty crazy at the moment, but I was straightening it. My mom! Jude used my mom to scare the hell out of us. Elizabeth was terrified, had to go to a hotel while I got my mom reinstated again and buy a new mattress. What's Jude gonna do next?"

"She's wildfire right now, but Jack, you lit the match."

Jack poured them both some mineral water while Dahlia drew on her e-cigarette. "So, handsome, what the fuck?"

"Remember our 21st anniversary, Hawaii, your mom, all the kids—you and Mitch came down? We had that big party at the beach. That last night, when Jude made that speech about our marriage, I just got this sense I was meant to be somewhere else, someone else."

"And?" Dahlia dampened her lips with a white wine.

"And I got an email from Elizabeth a few days later. We hadn't spoken since 1999. She was married, I was married, both had kids. It started out just two people catching up—I wasn't playing around and then... when we tried to cool it, we realized we couldn't live without each other." Jack smacked the menu against the table. "People split up all the time, why can't Jude be reasonable? Y'seen what she's been writing? She came to the house with the kids threatening Elizabeth! She left Mom in our bed!"

Dahlia looked up at the waiter. "The Nordic salad looks good."

"Steak. Medium rare."

They sat back wondering where and how deep to go in.

"Jude's lawyer advised her to sell the cabin so she can buy you out of the house. She's asking me to buy it, that way she can pay you off and keep it in the family. Thing is, *I* want to *sell* it. Your timing sucks, Romeo."

"Elizabeth and I plan to build eco-houses together, I want to play the guitar and travel and—hey, why d'you need money from selling the lake cabin? You and Mitch cool?"

"Cool like glaciers, y'mean?"

"I could tell something was up," said Jack, slicing up his steak.

"When he puts his hand in mine, it's like feeling the bottom of the garbage disposal. I have to get out of the marriage— that's why *I* need Jude to buy *my* share of the cabin."

"I'm sorry you're unhappy. I really am."

Dahlia dabbed her eyes with a neck scarf. "I'm not sad, I'm *angry.* Angry I let this go on so long because it convenienced *him.* Did you know he was so uptight? Neurotic? *Dull?*" Jack clicked his tongue. "He blows his nose in the morning—it goes on for *hours.*"

Jack wished Jude—who'd always been a little jealous of Dahlia's uptown New-York banker life—could hear Dahlia vent her unhappiness.

"I've got a Teams meeting in an hour and have to find a strong internet connection," Dahlia said, tapping his legs.

Jack sat back. "You've met someone else."

"How d'you...?" Dahlia looked down to her cleavage then back at him. "He's younger than me—so I need a *lot* of cash.

Maybe Elizabeth can give me some tips. Can we keep it between ourselves? I'll get this, expenses."

"Elizabeth works in New York a lot, so maybe we can have dinner together when this is all over. And don't worry about Jude, I'll make sure she's OK," said Jack.

"I never worry about Jude. I worry about you."

79

SUBJECT: LOVE LIVES

From: Jack Mathews

To: Elizabeth Lambert

Date: Thursday January 7, 2021 at 13:49

Me too, I wanna be one of those couples that never spend a night apart. I want to begin every day together in your arms and kiss each other goodnight—maybe kiss other parts too? We need to move quickly cause I want to be young enough to do so much stuff with you. Jude away this weekend on a field trip to Pasadena visiting jet propulsion labs so how about a virtual date-night together?

———

EVERYONE HAS A REFUGE, a sanctuary, a safe place. A tree house, beach cove, hotel room, ancient tree or seat in a café. Jack's was the metal scrapyard.

His dad had first taken him when he was a boy and he'd never lost his fascination with the mass graves of metallic exoskeletons. Since he'd been in charge of the garage, he didn't visit as often but that balmy evening, with the mechanics working through a backlog of repairs, he offered to drive to the dumpyard.

While they unloaded his truck, Jack rummaged through the parts, nodding to the folks, sometimes entire families, who spent their days picking out stuff that they could use. For a moment, he lost himself stepping over the glinting metals and softening rubber tires but his phone went as he was turning over a Ford's front axle.

"We've an early flight for Hawaii in the morning," said Jude. Jack could hear people in the background and could tell she'd had a few drinks. "Could you tear yourself away from your fantastic new life to say goodbye to your children?"

"I'm at the scrap—"

And she was gone.

Jack perched by the remains of a yellow Honda Civic staring at the dusty peeled-back Baby On Board sticker in the rear window. He took his baseball cap from his head and fell back onto an upturned passenger's seat. His chest heaved as sparks flew at him: the vacation he was about to go on at twelve years old when his mother had received the news that the biopsy results were bad. Bentley bouncing at the back of the car after school recounting adventures he'd had with friends when they'd been told he had none. The call that Preston had got into his first-choice college. Pizza nights. Tip as a puppy escaping out of Jude's bag at Clare's wedding. Gone. The family trips to Florida to visit his philandering dad, all of them singing to Britney Spears. Gone. Morning school runs. Sunday BBQs. Christmases and Father's Day. Gone.

All those moments more precious because he'd taken for granted there would always be more.

Jack's hands were so wet with tears his wedding ring slipped off easily. He climbed further up the heap to see the vistas of disembodied vehicles and flung his ring through the air. He didn't see it land but heard a ping somewhere down in the valley.

Jack and Jude. Gone.

80

SUBJECT: TESTING NEGATIVE, STAYING POSITIVE

From: Elizabeth Lambert

To: Jack Mathews

Date: Monday January 18, 2021 at 3:32

Hi from Dubai! I've never done a project like this before but whenever I feel scared of taking risks, thinking of you gives me courage. We have to stay here in this dystopian nightmare till we test negative after 5 days but my friend Gideon is here too going room-service crazy! Desperate 4 next video call and Yes! Let's plan a trip to NY. I'll get Emily to book somewhere—we'll all be vaxxed by then.

JACK WALKED through to the backyard where Jude was sitting under the pergola with a group of people around two large pitchers of Sangria, dipping tortillas into guacamole.

"Speaking of the infidel!" Jude said.

"See you started the vacation early," said Jack.

"Every day's a celebration without you, dearest." Jude lifted her sunglasses into her hair which was glossy, different some-how. "I see someone's wearing a new jacket," Jude said, winking at Carole who sucked on a pineapple slice. "You know everyone here: Dahlia, obviously, I think you dated her one time. Everyone's dated Jack, Carole, don't worry, he'll get around to you."

Carole snorted with laughter, slapped Jude's thigh.

"'Membah me?" asked Gloria, as Tip nuzzled into her lap.

"Kenzo's mom, sure."

"Beanie's upstairs with Savannah, they went to a party last night so she's zonked. The boys are at the home-brew beer garden."

Jack took the stairs to Aimee's room, two by two, to find her already asleep—arms outstretched, earphones buzzing, eyes flickering under the lids—her friend Savannah lay beside her. The last light of the day through the slatted blinds had cast long stripes across each wall, caging the girls in the hot room.

Jack caught snippets of the conversation below through the open window.

"*She* must have bought him that jacket—"

"Debbie saw them in Kennedy's—she's like freakishly skinny and had every kinda surgery, *ev-er-y-thing*."

"You didn't even know they were going away?"

Moving back to his daughter, Jack nudged Jude's old iMac set up on the plastic pink desk. The screen woke with Aimee's last conversation:

Ionfing6387:Bacon in yr PayPal acc for pix

Cupcake: Harley wants $100 if u want her ass in it 2

Ionfing6387:$50 w/black bitch fist

A screensaver of Kenzo kissing a pit bull's snout appeared.

Jack touched his not-so-little girl's shoulder, and for the first time noticed her torso was no longer flat but curved with the shape of her breasts under one of his old T-shirts.

"Have a great time in Hawaii, Aimee-B."

Aimee spoke without opening her eyes. "We gotta get up at five for the airport."

"I'll miss you," he said, unsure how to hold his hybrid girl-woman.

"We're gonna swim with dolphins."

"Beans, you been sending indecent photos of yourself to guys on the internet?"

Aimee rolled onto her elbows; half opened her eyes. "S'no biggie, everyone does and Kenzo's cool with it."

"It's illegal. Who is—"

"Sssh, Savannah's sleeping. Daddy, chill. They're just pervs."

"'They'?"

"I have an untraceable PayPal account."

"Bree works for the DA—she'd go nuts if her daughter—"

Her hand dropped on top of his. "When I'm back from the trip, can I come live with you?"

"Only if you promise to stop this photo thing. Hear me? Sleep tight, Beans."

Jack gripped the side of the sliding doors, gave Jude's party a wave, grateful the darkness had dimmed their faces.

Jude finished pouring a glass from the jug. "Take it."

"Thanks, but I've got the truck outside, had to take stuff to the dump, it's kind of... blocking..."

"*Blocking*? Jumpin' Jack Flash is dying to get outta here, aren't you?" The titters coming from Jude's gathering bolstered her on. "Got somewhere fancy to go? I hear you like Gatton's these days, but she has a private chef too, right?"

Gloria spat out a pip while Dahlia combed a tortilla through the dip.

"If you call returning the truck to the garage 'fancy'. Nice seeing y'all."

Jack trod back through the living room stepping over and around suitcases, shopping bags, boxes and piles of clothes until he was out in the night air. He was almost at the truck when he saw Jude standing by it, eclipsed by its size.

"I didn't mean to embarrass you," she said.

"I get it, you were just showing off in front of your friends. Your hair looks good."

Jude snorted, put her hands in her back pockets.

"Have a super time on the vay-cay I'm paying for."

"Oh, we *will*." This sounded like an exit quip, but Jude continued standing unsteadily in front of Jack, breathing out alcohol fumes. She half-smiled, "Kenzo's mother's a character, isn't she?"

"I'm not sure you should be encouraging that relationship. She's on the internet and—"

"Aimee and I, we're close. See I prefer transparency, y'know? I wouldn't want Aimee to feel she had to sneak around and lie. We're different, I guess."

Jack crossed his arms. "Wanna be transparent about how much money your spending?"

"Lambert Interiors can afford it."

"I'll take Tip then."

"No. Dahlia wants him with her at the cabin."

"And Mouse, who's feeding her?"

"Seems like you're not the only one with a second home; Mouse spends most of her time with the old lady on the corner."

"Enjoy Maui."

"Hope your road trip sucks."

"That's not nice."

"You're not nice, and *she* is certainly not nice."

"You don't know anything about Elizabeth, in fact—" he hadn't planned on saying it like that, standing on the street with her friends slowly appearing at the doorway, but he did. "For the sake of transparency, you should know we're getting married."

Jude put her hands up to her head as if she were lost and trying to remember the way back.

"My period's late."

Now it was Jack's turn to swoon.

As he tried to think what she was telling him, a group of

people turned into their street, one of them pointed at him. "Isn't that your dad?"

Under the streetlights, Jack made out Bentley walking in front of Preston and Chad, Kenzo and another boy.

Jack saluted them, though only Preston waved back.

"Hey, boys, d'you hear? Your daddy's getting married!"

Dahlia and Gloria came out to stand by Jude while the others hovered at the door.

"And d'you all know that Jack stayed over a few weeks ago?" Jude was shouting now. A few windows opened, someone even came out of their house to watch what was happening, phone in hand in case they needed to call the police. "Remember that night we ate out in the yard? He didn't go home to his precious Elizabeth, he fucked me—sorry for bad language, kids, but that's what he did."

Jack opened the truck door and climbed up. He turned the ignition and it began clanking loudly down the road. Looking in the rearview mirror, he saw a huddle around Jude, though Bentley stood apart, watching him back, his hand clenched in the air, his middle finger outstretched at his dad's reflection.

81

SUBJECT: LIFE AND LOVE DON'T MIX

From: Jack Mathews

To: Elizabeth Lambert

Date: Wednesday January 27, 2021 at 11:46

Out of the red zone but still have a stay-at-home order till they roll out the vaccine so when I'm not in touch, it's because Jude is standing next to me or I'm hustling for money to feed my family. Friends in Human Services say this thing is mutating and might get even worse. You really think you only mean something to me in a virtual world??? Bullshit. Jude's mom is unlikely to get outta hospital, alive that is, so Jude's working all day then up all night searching for trial drugs. Preston's college won't let them back IRL, Bentleys breeding axolotls in the basement and Aimee's just started her periods! so excuse me if I can't always take your calls!!!

———

A SWEET-SCENTED BREEZE lifted the skirts of the white lace curtains in the hotel room, the cooler air woke Elizabeth first.

Jack had originally booked a hotel at a chain where he collected loyalty points but when Elizabeth saw it, she refused to get out of the car. So while Jack talked the hotel out of charging him for the whole weekend, Elizabeth rebooked somewhere in Carmel where she wouldn't hear people's TVs through the walls and find hair in the bath drains.

The evening before they'd bought matching hoodies because the cool weather was a shock compared to San Diego, they'd climbed over rocks down to the sea, skimmed stones. They'd found a bistro to eat at, Elizabeth spoke French to the waiter, ordered Crème Brûlée. Just before going to sleep, Elizabeth had said, 'Today was perfect.'

It had been—*almost*—because before dinner Elizabeth had tried Cosima's phone and the moment she heard her daughter pick up, the line was disconnected.

'What if she's read some of the stuff Jude wrote about me?' It'd exhausted Jack's entire arsenal of reassuring arguments and whisky sours to convince Elizabeth everything would be alright if she just lay back in his arms and counted shooting stars.

But the fear was up and waiting for Elizabeth the next morning.

"What am I doing here?"

"Making me a coffee, I hope," moaned Jack.

Elizabeth planted little kisses in the dips between Jack's vertebrae down to where his buttocks began, she left feathery licks around his coccyx before opening out her palm and spanking him twice. He turned, grabbed her wrists, and, laughing, pulled her down with him, trapping her in his arms.

"How you feelin' about today?"

"Apprehensive."

"Can you use a coffee machine as well as them big words?" Jack rolled over as much as he could keeping his hand clamped over her ass.

"What if he's a bad person?"

Jack propped up his head with the pillow. "These last three years, I done things that I would despise in anyone else. Bad person, bad context. You making that coffee or what?"

Elizabeth went over to the kitchenette, set up the percolator and peed while picking up the sound of Jack's phone buzzing. Just for one day, she thought, she could do without his family monopolizing his attention.

"That was Dahlia. Jude and the kids arrived in Maui and are having a great time. They've booked a boat trip to a volcanic island." Jack stood in the bathroom. "See, I should be missing them, I should be wishing I was there with 'em, but I'm not. Does that make me a bad person?"

"That's not the same as having a daughter you've never once tried to make contact with?"

82

EL: MON 8 FEB 2021

Interesting how each time shit gets real,
you're too busy to talk.

JACK FOLLOWED the directions to Zuni's retreat somewhere in a redwood forest. One hand on the wheel, the other on the nape of Elizabeth's neck as she sat looking straight ahead, picking at her cuticles, in jeans and her new hooded fleece. It was almost like having Aimee with him.

"Y'know? This is the kind of place I often dreamt of living: creeks, giant trees, horse trails, and, oh, *another* organic café."

You have arrived at your destination, announced Jack's GPS.

"Thank you, Moneypenny," said Jack, Sean Connery-style. Elizabeth usually laughed at that, but not this time.

There was a cluster of tree houses raised on stilts, originally 1960s refuges from urban expansion but judging by the expensive cars and the security gates, they'd gradually been snapped up by tech millionaires. The *Rooms Available!* signs, however, were evidence of a few wily Woodstock remainders who'd managed to monetize their real-estate luck. Zuni was one of them.

The closing of the car doors unleashed a pair of birds from the trees. Elizabeth and Jack crunched over the path that lead to the lodge.

"That's cute," said Elizabeth, pointing to an old lion-foot bathtub filled with wildflowers. Next to it, a seating area had been created with snaggle-tooth decking lined with cacti, herbs and candle lanterns. There was a picnic table, a stool and Jack pointed to two seats pulled out of a car where someone must have been sitting under a broken parasol.

A breeze set off a chorus of wind chimes right through the forest.

"How do we greet him—we gotta kiss his ring, his didgeridoo?"

A door opened and a husky trotted out, reminding Jack of Tip. The dog looked straight at them and barked twice. A woman stood on the makeshift porch. She was small with a jet-black braid running down to her hips. She dropped into a squat, clasping the dog's neck.

"You come for healing?"

They stopped at the foot of the cabin.

"Is this where Zuni Gallagher lives?"

Jack could hear the unsteadiness in Elizabeth's voice and worried about how pale she was.

"Healing by appointment. You want rent room—money upfront." The woman turned her back to them, muttering as she picked up pieces of a broken flowerpot.

"Is Zuni here?"

"Spiritual consult next weekend better. Don't disturb. Making art." She crossed her arms to emphasize her role as human defense barrier. "You buy sculpture?"

"Not really, we—"

The woman tutted as a large crow settled on the nearest branch, shaking the leaves.

"When does he finish *making art*?"

"Sunset meditation." She waved a finger at them. "Next weekend. Better."

Elizabeth put her hands to her face and stretched out the skin under her eyes, something she did late at night after hours in front of her computer.

"I'm an interior decorator. I do a lot for the Sapphire Group, they have hotels all over the world. They're interested in some of Mr. Gallagher's larger pieces for their lobbies, but if he's too busy…"

The woman snatched Elizabeth's card from her fingers.

"Eleven. He has liver-cleansing drink."

"Tell him my name's Elizabeth. Elizabeth *Swanson*. He was a friend of my mother's, Annabeth Swanson—*Queenie*."

"Ah. No. Not this. Not good energy. Not this." The woman bustled back into the cabin she'd come out of.

"Wait!" Jack's voice echoed through the trees. The woman put her head around the doorframe. "We're driving back to San Diego today. If Zuni wants to meet his daughter, she came all the way from Paris to see him."

The woman looked at Elizabeth's card again.

"I take his juice. I ask, just *ask*. But," she leant forward, "no 'why no you send birthday present, where Christmas card, why you not at graduation, where child support?' Un'stand?"

"You get a lot of Zuni's kids turning up asking about lost Christmas presents?" asked Jack.

"He was rock star. Max Kansas City, 100 Club. His picture in the urinals of The Roxy. He met Steve Tyler and Kim Cattrall, lotta people. He… hmm…" she searched the trees for ways to describe him "…people come for healing, spiritual advices. Buy sculpture, seven hundred and fifty dollars."

Jack looked to Elizabeth. "We just wanted to say hi. That's all."

The woman sucked on her teeth. "Hi. OK. But he old man now," she conceded. "I take his juice. But if he no wanna come out, that's all, folks."

83

EL: TUES 16 FEB 2021

Sorry for the angry vocals. I understand why you could only send me emoji Valentine flowers but it still hurts. You have no idea what I'm going through. Cosie and her dad took off for the weekend without telling me as punishment for me seeing lawyers. Outmanoeuvring me is a big game to Bruno who has nothing else to do. I don't need you playing me as well!

———

SOME TIME LATER, the woman shuffled out of the cabin holding a tray with two bowls of something magenta colored and frothy. She made a point of ignoring them as she crossed to a corrugated-iron outhouse.

"What the fuck is that?" Elizabeth pointed to a totem pole on top of which was the decapitated head of a soft-toy jaguar.

The woman came out and positioned herself at the side of the door, hands clasped in front of her. The husky stood guard next to her.

A few seconds later, Zuni emerged in a long white robe and

matching bandana. He had a braided beard, dyed blue. He pressed his palms together and bowed, low, agile.

"Welcome to this space, a very small part on this rotating chunk of metals I am blessed to call my place of giving and receiving."

The man broke into a short jog down the stairs, his wrists jangling with bangles and strings of leather.

"Come here, darlin'." Zuni enclosed Elizabeth in the folds of his robe and held her long enough for Jack to start feeling uncomfortable. The man eventually relaxed his grip and searched Elizabeth's eyes.

"My mom says *zdravo,*" Zuni said, smiling into Elizabeth's face. "Cherry?" he called over to the woman, still holding Elizabeth's gaze. "Get the sage down, love—the one behind the wardrobe in the black case, the good stuff."

Cherry, who hadn't moved from her post, obeyed.

"So you met my girl, Cherry. My salvation and my rottweiler."

Elizabeth cleared her throat and said, "This is Jack."

Jack came forward, extending his hand. "Jack, more of a poodle really."

Zuni caught Jack's wrists and pulled him close, "Come 'ere, poodle."

Zuni released Jack and walked them to a group of carved-out tree trunks.

"Sit, sit. Man, those Slovenian cheekbones, gorgeous, ain't she?" he asked Jack, who was already agreeing though he didn't understand what *Slovenian* meant until Zuni added, "You don't look half look like my mom. And them's my eyes alright. My eyes without all the years of self-abuse: too much smack so now they're pinned forever—not great when going through airport security, I get the fuzz watching me, thinking, *I don't wanna go lookin' up that old geezer's arse.*" Zuni laughed. "So here's home for me, long way from the streets of Deptford."

Elizabeth smiled; her fingers tightly woven together. "Cherry tells me you're in the hotel business. Bloke who lives over that way owns the Holstar Suites. Big chain. He's got some of my pieces, never coughs up though."

"Elizabeth's done a bunch of celebrity houses, restaurants, yachts, but mainly hotels for the Sapphire Group. The Rivoli in Paris? The Church on 5th, New York?" asked Jack.

Zuni twirled his beard. "Can't say I been to none of those places."

"She speaks French, Japanese, she's written three books and designed a collection of wallpapers. She's writing another book, that's why she's in California. And Berkeley have asked her to—"

"Lot of external validation. I get it." Zuni smiled at Elizabeth. "I ain't no interior designer. This 'ere is nature's hotel. Cherry and I are the guests of the trees, the lichen, the mist, chipmunks, woodlice—so, Poodle, you her agent? Pal? Driver? Lover or somethin'?"

"I'm no one but a guy who loves Elizabeth and fixes up cars."

"Fixing up cars is a noble and necessary talent, don't put yourself down. See that Chevvy there? We done a four-hour luminal cleansing ritual on the fucker before I had to fork out 750 dollars for a bloke to come over and start it." He looked up to see Cherry walking towards them. "Didn't we, doll? Talkin' 'bout the truck."

Cherry placed bowls of stagnant-pond-colored liquid in front of them.

"Drink this up. 'Scuse bowls but I hate mugs, like breathin' through fuckin' tubes—be thankful you ain't inherited my snout."

"Drink," Cherry said, peering at Elizabeth over the rim of her bowl.

Elizabeth swallowed. "Tastes of… rosehip… cardamon?"

The rottweiler sniffed.

Jack could tell Elizabeth wasn't up to speaking much so he asked Zuni how long they'd been there although he was sure he wouldn't understand the answer.

"I was in Amsterdam before—one of the best places in the world—but I got fucked off with the cold winters, so I asked my spirit guide, 'Sort this out, mate, 'cause I gotta have me some sun and sea in my old age.' Few days later, this guy, Arne Shmidt, y'know, the billionaire? He lives up in that eco-palace in the hills. He brought his son—fentanyl fiend—to one of my detox weekends. The boy stayed with us for months, he really got it, didn't he, pet?" Cherry slurped her drink. "Arne was so grateful he gave us this plot of land to run workshops and mind his gaff."

"Zuni built irrigation system," said Cherry.

"We're fully self-sustainable. Dry toilets and that. Rent out those teepees. Last month, we had a family of Norwegians."

"From Norway," added Cherry, drawing her feet up into a cross-legged position. "They said water cold, go early, not *ready*."

"Lotta folk ain't woke to nature's lessons."

"Money upfront."

"So your mom was Queenie, eh? I just shivered so I assume she passed. Overdose? Suicide?" Elizabeth stared back at him. "Cherry, love, you wanna show this man the truck?"

Reluctantly, Cherry unfolded, tugged at Jack to follow her behind the lodges. He trod slowly, all the time checking if Elizabeth was alright with his leaving her.

Zuni grabbed the top of his garment, clutched at his throat. "Trapped. Walls too hot to touch. Black fumes."

Elizabeth whispered, "She was stoned, smoking, the bed caught fire."

"Woah!" Zuni said, flapping his wrists up and down. "I won't lie, that was a bad exit. You cold, love? I'm getting cold." He wrapped his arms around himself. "Freezing. This is something else—banging. Sealed in and can't get out." Elizabeth heard his teeth chattering. "Icy. Gimme your hand. You were not supposed to live, my child." Zuni's head moved from side to side as a crow glided past them and broke him out of his spell. He slapped his breastbone, his breathing calmed.

"Not surprising you like to build homes, make the safe nest

you never had. You flew away just in time. Burning up, she's still burning up. Not from the fire, but because she needs you to forgive her. You know what I'm talking about, don't you?"

Something passed between them. He had seen more, she knew it.

"Goosebumps—'aven't had that for a while." He finished his drink. "Thing is, love, I done you a favor by not being around. I was bad news back then, bad news. See I'd left South London and my cunt of a dad 'cause I had it hard too, darlin'. My life's been extreme, dangerous, but fucking awesome."

Elizabeth looked into her drink before asking, "Did you know about me?"

Zuni put down his bowl, licked his lips. "I met Queenie in Santa Monica. Right? Yeah. Blonde, skinny—we called her the *vacuum cleaner*."

"He say buy new truck," Cherry called over.

"Thought he might," winked Zuni.

Jack trudged back to the table, mouthing at Elizabeth, 'You OK?'

"I just said we called her mum the vacuum cleaner." He turned to Cherry. "Nothing to do with housework but the velocity with which she could suck up a line of coke. Crazy chick, blinding voice. We were knocking around the same clubs." Cherry looked away, tutting. "My girl don't like me talking about those days. Now I don't touch the drink or smoke nothin' except the pot we grow here, 'California sober' it's called. But them days, I had my fifteen minutes of bullshit. Then ended up in Peru where the Incas unlocked my demons, set me on the path to becoming a shaman."

"So you didn't know Annabeth—Queenie—had a child?"

"Over the years, people come out of the woodwork, like the twins, Harmony and Melody. Harmony rescues animals in SF, comes down here to vent 'bout what bastards all men are. Melody runs an online travel company. Lightning's from a bird I met in Bali. Things went down between us, we don't talk now." Zuni picked up Elizabeth's hand, closed his eyes. "Your brother's here. Something about you saving him that night."

Zuni brought his lips to Elizabeth's ear. "The spirits called you here for me to pass on their messages. You survived. That's all I can give, 'cause I ain't no Daddy Warbucks. What you're looking for, it ain't here, ain't me, and certainly not that cat who can't mend my car."

84

EL: MON 22 MARCH 2021

Jack, is everything going to be OK? Please, tell me everything is going to be OK even if you have to lie.

PS Private email and phones PLEASE!!!

———

"Mom, I'd like to use my hand again... kinda attached to it." Preston tugged his fingers out from where his mother had been fusing them together in a damp grip since the plane took off. "Look, all those little islands down there."

Jude pressed her palm onto the armrest between them, leant against his shoulder.

"Preston? Before, when I traveled, I used to worry I wouldn't get back home, now I'm scared of getting there."

"It's going to be OK." Not wanting to knock his generous optimism, Jude smiled back at his long dark eyelashes. "This plane, I mean, how come it's not falling out of the sky?"

"Bernoulli's principle."

"OK, *Professor Mom*, I was being metaphoric. I'm saying, just keep your engines turning, you'll rise above all this."

"Until then, they're coming round with the drinks, what do you want?"

"Coke'd be nice."

Jude plotted how to order something stronger without Preston commenting.

"What's Bentley doing?"

Preston turned around to see his brother at the back of the plane. "That weird bicep-flexing thing."

"He's not right, is he?"

"Nope. He's not."

"Excuse me," Jude asked the steward. "Could I have a Coke with ice and a white wine please?"

"Mom!"

"I'm still on vacation and I don't want to go home. But you know what's crazy? I'm looking forward to seeing him." Jude pawed at an opening at his elbow so she could thread her arm through his. "I heard she takes Callie's yoga classes, shops at Frank's Deli, they go to the golf club together and Carole's sister-in-law saw them at a Michelin-starred restaurant in Little Italy. I hate her Preston, and that's the truth."

"She's taken your husband, I get it. I do. But your integrity, your dignity and self-respect, that you're *giving* away."

Jude pulled away from him, leant back to glare at his face. "Where'd that come from?"

Preston spoke softly but he was clear. "The talking shit about Elizabeth to anyone who'll listen, the social media posts and making people take sides. You're acting like some deposed queen trying to rally an army against them, that's not you."

Jude caught the beverage cart and waved her credit card.

"A coke and two white wines please."

"Mom!"

"I don't know what else to do."

Preston squeezed her hand. "Just keep the engines turning."

85

SUBJECT: EVEN CAPTAINS GET THE BLUES

From: Neptune99

To: Salacia99

Date: Wednesday March 24, 2021 at 2:14

He can't listen to our phone convos but sure I'll cool off till ur back in London. Listen, if you feel threatened I've had to call on some pretty nasty guys who get stuff done when polite requests aren't respected. Let me know. Shit hit the fan big time after we got back from the mountains. Bentley got into a fight with another kid who's now in hospital. We're begging the parents not to press charges. J and I seeing a psychologist about him. Jude's mom no better and just for fun, my mother's care home's been taken over by a franchise who are hiking up the prices. Great about the vaccine—you're free!!! Safe flight xxx

———

MIKE WAS at the deli where he met Jack once a month. This lunchtime, unusually, Mike was not eating while Jack worked through a Magic Swirlz Ham and Cheese Sandwich.

"Whassup?" asked Jack, wiping mayonnaise from his lip.

"I'm a silent partner but I can't stay quiet over what's happening. You been on *another* vacation?"

"Just a long weekend up the coast so Elizabeth could meet her dad. He's like this witch doctor who—"

"Save it."

"This divorce, man—"

"I've been reading all about it on AutoTraders.com."

"That's Jude, she—"

"I'm mad about Traci leaving."

"After Covid, the car industry still—"

"—so you work *harder*. *Smarter*. Not check into the Four Seasons. I got a pacemaker, Jack, I can't get worked up. I can't be your partner anymore; my lawyers are onto it now."

"But Mike, hey, we've ridden out worse storms."

"This isn't just a storm, it's climate change. Have you looked at the accounts, bud? And who's the carrot-top kid blowing bubbles at the entrance?"

"Bradley. He does a hand car wash, customers love him."

"Why's he talk in that funny way? Wait—I don't wanna know." Mike gripped the table to steady himself. "You're off your game. And Bentley. Let's say, he's not an asset to the company. Draxx, he's on parole—"

"He's a good mecha—"

"Auditors are coming in."

"Hey, I have strategies in place. I'm negotiating higher holdbacks with Chrysler and an insurance company is getting back to me—"

"I don't know what this woman does for you but I hope she's worth it."

Mike turned his chair towards the door and in three bounces propelled himself through the exit.

"So good to hear your voice," Jack whispered to Elizabeth into his phone once he was back in the office. "Mike's pulling out of our partnership—we were in kindergarten together—I could be facing bankruptcy." He peeked through his blinds at the fore-court where Traci and Good-Looking were talking animatedly. "You there?"

"Uh-huh."

"I might have some luck though. I'm going to check out a

classic car in Bakersfield, already got two buyers lined up, could be good, huh?"

"I booked Katsumo's for eight. Dinner with Lindsay and Matt from next door. That a problem?"

Where could Jack start with his problems?

"No, of course not. But after Bakersfield I have to pick up Aimee from the lake house and bring her back to Savannah's."

Elizabeth cut the call. Jack was just about to press redial when he saw Draxx leaning against his doorframe, teeth and fists clenched.

"Seventeen thousand, three hundred and twenty dollars and I'm out of here."

"What?"

"Your boy's been slapping my sister around. Give me what you owe me or I'm reporting that monster to the cops."

Jack deliberated the odds of whether the son of an armed robber would be more or less likely to enlist the police's help on a domestic issue.

Draxx dropped a pen on Jack's desk. "My reference. Start writing. And these are my bank details."

86

SUBJECT: OLDER & BOLDER

From: Elizabeth Lambert

To: Jack Mathews

Date: Monday March 29, 2021 at 12:14

You remembered my birthday! Sorry I couldn't take your call, house full this weekend with friends. And guess what? I got the advance from my publishers for my next book idea, yay! Returning to Paris tomorrow with Cosie but busy week ahead xx

———

"DOOR'S OPEN. You don't have to just stand there," said Jude from inside the cabin. "You said you'd be here two hours ago."

"I came all the way from Bakersfield. This widow called saying she had a Jaguar F-Pace in great condition to sell. I took out the truck, got all the way there—in this heat, the traffic— the address she gave was a Weightwatcher's clinic and the phone number was a dud."

"Some people, eh?" said Jude, peering into the bottom of an empty glass before filling it with water and drinking it down.

Jack tugged at Tip's ears. "Beanie ready?"

"She gave up on you, champ," said Jude before shouting up the stairs, "Beanie? Your—" she eyed Jack, wrinkling her nose "—*father*'s here."

"Steak 'n' Shake!" Jack called up.

Aimee stood at the top of the stairs in a pink bikini. "Dad, I told you like three hundred times, I'm *vegan*."

Jude was about to roll her eyes at Jack but stopped herself. "They do salads."

"I made some iced tea, Mom's recipe," called Jude.

"I don't think she heard me." Jack called to Aimee again. "Ma-May's Iced tea, couldn't say no, thanks."

Jude waited a few seconds, deciding how generous she felt before opening the fridge door and lifting out the jug.

"Preston started his work-experience thing today," Jack said, leaning across the kitchen counter, putting the cold glass to his forehead before gulping the drink down. "First job, screens and masks, what a world." He let Jude refill his glass as he flapped a patterned shirt that Jude had never seen before against his chest. "So hot out there, bet you're happy to be out of the city."

"Thrilled."

They sat on chairs arranged over a square of lawn that Bentley had mowed before the Hawaii trip. Jude poured more iced tea into Jack's glass as he stroked Tip who'd flopped down in a patch of shade.

"I heard a disturbing thing about Bentley and Maxx."

"She called me when it happened. Who told you?"

"Draxx. He said if I didn't give him all his money upfront and write a reference they'd press charges."

"If you think Draxx is bad, wait till their dad gets out of prison. I invited Bentley to stay here but he sleeps at the gym now. I'm trying to get an appointment with a psychiatrist but the first one available is mid-October."

"Take it, you need someone to talk to."

"Not for *me*, asshole, for *Bentley*. He's bipolar. I read up on it."

"I want to be at that appointment."

"If you can spare the time."

"Hey, Jumping Bean, still not dressed?"

"Didn't Mom tell you? Savannah's dad came by their house before he goes to Syria so we're leaving tomorrow morning."

"Tomorrow? I nearly killed myself getting all the way out here!"

"But you wanted time with Beanie, right? Take her in the morning, what's the big deal?"

"I run a company—"

"Not from what I hear!" Jude looked away from Jack. "Stay with your daughter and leave in the morning, drop her off before work."

"Think you guys could quit screaming at each other for a few hours?"

"We're not screaming," Jack and Jude both said at the same time.

Aimee lay back in the hammock. "Mom, you go for your evening swim and Dad and I will get dinner. Deal?"

Jude emptied the pitcher of tea into Jack's glass. "If Daddy looks at that bathroom light—it keeps flickering."

After they'd eaten and Aimee had gone to bed, Jack cantered up the hill pulled by the force of the full moon over Hot Springs Mountain. He turned into the clearing where Bentley had learnt to ride a bike. On a large rock, Jack sat with his phone while Tip followed the trace of something in the dry bushes.

> Having post-dinner drinks at Juliana's. Where r u?

> No car at Bakersfield. At cabin with Beanie. Will return TMR. 🩶🩶🩶

> WTF???

87

SUBJECT: STILL MY LIL' CHATON?

From: Jack Mathews

To: Elizabeth Lambert

Date: Wednesday March 31, 2021 at 8:33

PLEASE CALL ME BACK!!! I know ur in meetings all day but am feeling very insecure not hearing from you especially after you saying what a great guy Bruno is all of a sudden. Be careful, babe, you know how manipulative he is. 4ever J xxx

———

TURNING IN HER SLEEP, the moonlight woke her, and Jude thought, *Jack's in the house.* She remembered laughing as he loaded the last spoonful of pie into his mouth before they'd washed up together while he'd talked about clearing out the barbecue area at the weekend. He'd fixed the bathroom light as she'd held the ladder for him, passing up his tools.

Tip was lying near Jack who was asleep, splayed out on the sofa, his legs over the edge, face illuminated by a rose-gold glow, his chin shaded by stubble. He was smiling. Jack's hands rested over the sheet as a breeze wafted through the open window. Hands that could weld large parts of metal together, throw children in the air and catch them, turn meat over on a spit-roast, and build something out of flat-packed furniture in the time it took to pour him a beer and say cheers. Hands on standby to make someone feel warm, feminine, wanted. Hinged to those industrial wrists were his forceful weighty arms, the left side always a little darker than the right because he liked to dangle it outside the truck as he drove.

Jude ran her fingers along the short strands of golden down on his forearms. Jack took her by the elbow and sunk his weight into the cushions, pivoting himself around, taking her with him until she was on the edge of the sofa pressed up against his back. Her lips prickled where she moved against the bristles at the base of his neck. Jude's nails traveled inside the creases of his boxers. Jack hummed a little, felt the weight of her breasts as she rolled him on his back. He spread a hand on either side of her hips, half opened his eyes.

"What the—" he said, pushing her away "—hell are you doing?"

"You looked cold."

Jack held his watch up to the moonlight while the other hand felt for his clothes.

"It's three thirty. What's… with you?"

Jude picked up a cushion, slapped it across the side of his head. "You can't do this!" She found a larger cushion and slammed it onto the top of his back. As she searched for another, he gripped her wrists, glared at her.

"I'm not coming back—don't you get that? Elizabeth and I are getting married and we're going to live in Paris. France."

"France? Wh—when?"

Jack was standing opposite her now, the front of his boxers extended.

"September, I think. Or October. I dunno."

"I won't let you."

"You can't stop us."

"I can, and so can her ex-husband, yeah, I've been talking to Bruno, he has emails and messages going way back and he's going after sole custody of their daughter. Don't underestimate me."

"Her ex…? Can't you see trying to hurt Elizabeth and me is

worse for you. Worse for the kids, for everyone. I know what you did—I worked it out. You invented the sale to drag me all the way out to Bakersfield—there was no car, was there? You set a trap so I'd be late and have to stay over."

"Not *me*—it was your stupidity, your greed, your self-ishness!"

"You callin' me selfish?" Jack grabbed his trainers, his keys and tumbled out the door.

Jude sat on the couch, panting. The cushion beneath her was still warm from his body. She felt for Jack's phone which she'd nudged under the armchair as he was storming out. He'd be back for it the moment he realized it was gone. She locked the door and sat out of sight from the windows.

When facial ID didn't recognize her, she pressed 0000—Jack's code since she'd first met him—and she was in.

Send SMS: All contacts.

> Hey guys! Jack here. Hope this finds you well and happy! Hate to trouble u but I really need $25,000. As you heard I been cheating on Jude and my 3 kids and now my business is going bust and I might lose my house 😕 Would really appreciate some financial support anything you can give 🙏

88

SUBJECT: KEEP SWIMMING LIL' MERMAID

From: Neptune99

To: Salacia99

Date: Tuesday June 15, 2021 at 6:33

Don't know if you check these emails anymore but my phone broke and things not private. Funeral's tomorrow. Jude's family all arriving so obvs won't be in contact. Good luck with the new lawyers.

———

JACK CUT the engine of his truck outside Savannah's home.

"Beans?"

His daughter was slumped against the passenger door as far from him she could get, her rose-gold ringlets flattened by her headphones. Jack gave her a playful poke; she nudged him off. She hadn't said a word to him since Jude had thrown his clothes, phone and Aimee's backpack through his truck window under a flame-red sky.

"I'll pick you up Friday, bring you and Savannah to the cabin."

"Dump me wherever so you can carry on with your super-fun summer."

"Didn't someone just get back from a great vacation in Hawaii?"

Aimee swung the door open and was about to jump down from the truck when Jack clasped her arm. "Come on, talk to me."

"Why? So you can tell me again it's OK you left us? Mom cries herself to sleep every night—forget it!"

Jack tried to grab hold of her jacket. "Get back here and—"

"Everything OK?" Standing by the truck was an elderly woman, staring at Jack, pushing her hands into the front pockets of her housecoat with such intensity she launched herself onto the balls of her feet. "Go on in, sugar," she said to Aimee.

"Jellybean, get back—" But Aimee darted into the house.

"Teenagers," said Jack, getting out of the truck and working up the smile that never failed to win over older clients. But not this one.

Jack walked into the hall just as Bree, dressed in a dark suit and high black shoes, cantered down the stairs. She picked up her car keys.

"My mother," she said, acknowledging Jack's *just-been-slapped-down* expression. "She's looking after Savannah 'til camp. I wasn't able to get time off and her dad's just been re-posted."

Bree's mom gave Jack the side-eye from the kitchen where the two girls watched her laying out ingredients for what Savannah announced would be Caribbean banana cake.

Bree unplugged her phone from the wall, spoke in a whisper. "I got your message. I understand things are hard, I'm sorry, but I can't help you out, it wouldn't be right. I love you guys—both of you."

"We love you too…" Jack said, wondering what message and noticing how pretty her mouth was in lipstick.

"Walk with me." She pointed the key fob at her navy-blue open-topped Mercedes. "I'm a friend but also a family lawyer and a woman who's *been* divorced. Marriage is like a country, y'know? There's a language, a history, culture, politics, definitely an economy, and a whole population of people who belong to it. And we all want vacations from where we live. We all want to explore other places, do new stuff, try out being someone else, but Jack, to emigrate? Leave your home forever? I see folks every day misjudging the loss it'll cost them and realising too late that they are forever in exile. It's brutal." Bree let her words hang in the air while a fat bee pillaged each lavender head for nectar. "So you'll pick them up Friday?"

89

SUBJECT: LOCKED AND LOADED

From: Jack Mathews

To: Elizabeth Lambert

Date: Thursday July 1, 2021 at 6:33

I'm NOT running away!!! You called when I was signing a purchase agreement. I'm happy you decided about your marriage—you crazy? Please understand Jude HAS JUST LOST HER MOTHER. I can't throw a grenade into our home and make a run for it. Of course I'm not saying her feelings are worth more than yours?!? Getting another burner phone tomorrow. Thanks, Homeland, for the vocab!

PS Email back ASAP coz we're gonna visit Clare and Kendall in BC.

———

"NEVER HEARD of anyone taking an Uber to a home invasion," said Megan. "You gonna barf?"

The driver peered at Jude from his rearview mirror.

"Drop us off here."

The Prius ground into the gravel as Jude opened the door, half falling out of the car.

Megan fast tracked a prayer that their driver was illegal so wouldn't be able to testify if it came to court.

"That view," said Megan.

Megan's mantra to herself was *Stop being nice* but she'd just gone and done it again: invited Jude out for Happy Hour at Bareback's. Actually, it *had* been fun. Jude had fit right in with her friends who were thrilled to crowd around their cocktails laughing about Lambert Interior*s* and taking turns to add insulting comments to Elizabeth's Instagram page. The fun had stopped when she agreed to break into the house.

"You have the keys *and* the new alarm code?"

Megan nodded.

"His secretary said they're eating in Oceanside. That's their bedroom, right?"

"Master bedroom, fifty-two meters squared, parquet floors, remote control day-and-night blinds, his and her walk-in wardrobes, outside waterfall and steam shower. But didn't you already leave his mom in their bed?"

"Bentley did—I stayed downstairs 'cause she kept grabbing me."

Megan rotated her shoulders. "Please don't take anything."

"*She* broke into my home. *She* stole my husband for Chrissakes."

"I could lose my real estate license—even go to jail." Megan pointed at the private security sign.

"Anything happens, you say you were concerned and checked on the house—you could even get promoted. Call the home line now to substantiate your story."

Megan's lips twitched. Jude put her hand on her shoulder. "You came down here to see everything was OK and when they didn't answer the phone you chased me off."

Megan hoped that someone who used words like *substantiate* knew better.

"It's ringing. No answer."

Jude nudged Megan forward to tap the code into the keypad. The side gate clicked and the two women walked through the courtyard to the house. Megan took out the key.

"They didn't put the alarm on. It's in the contract."

"Idiots," Jude murmured. She was about to put the lights on when Megan waved her away from the switch, "Neighbors."

Jude had a note in her hand in Jack's writing: *Babe-E, U looked so beautiful sleeping. Gone running, will be back 4 huevos rancheros, Captain Cock,* followed by a row of either poorly drawn hearts or vaginas.

"That's sweet," said Megan. "Sorry."

"Take me to the master bedroom."

"And then we go. *Please*?"

Megan led the way upstairs, lit by the domed skylight.

Megan's husband had cheated on her with their seventeen-year-old neighbor which, on many levels, was worse than Jude's experience, but at least she'd had the satisfaction of kicking him out and passing him every day when he was living in his car outside their home.

Out of habit she opened the door wide and flicked on the lights.

"The Lambert signature bed—Japanese simplicity with French Romanticism. See the recesses on either side for charging your phone, speakers, and the reading lights can be adjusted—you ok?"

Jude was holding Jack's San Diego State Aztecs T-shirt.

The bed was unmade, sheets piled up like waves in a high storm. In between the cotton folds were white lace suspenders, tissues, and a pair of Jack's boxers from a pack of three given to him at Christmas.

"You shouldn't see this," said Megan.

Jude spat on the bed.

Megan had expected worse. She'd driven back one night after a late viewing, seen Rick's car and set fire to it with him inside.

Megan and Jude froze when they heard the doorbell.

"Turn out the light," hissed Megan from the dressing-room window.

Jude went to the wall switches—the blinds came down and a TV screen lowered itself from the ceiling.

Megan closed her fists to her ears and squealed, "Fuck. Fuck. Fuck."

"Calm down. She's leaving."

Megan and Jude watched Lindsay jog off the drive and into the house next door.

"We have to go, now!"

"Alright already. Just—where would he keep his passport?"

90
EL: SUN 4 JULY 2021

Your sister sounds cool. Felt really warmed when you said we'd hit it off. Bruno's sister has completely frozen me out like so many people I thought were friends, she's just another spectator at the Roman arena. This divorce is killing me and it's not even got started. Am in London. Cosie in Paris with the summer nanny. Lawyers say this could take 2 years now. My independence day v far away. Living for the time we can be together 🩶🩶🩶

"You ladies alone? Could we buy you a drink?"

The voice came from behind Jude but she gathered the man must have been handsome judging by the flush in Megan's cheeks—though she probably grinned like that for anything male.

"We are not *alone,* we're *together* and we are not *ladies,*" snapped Jude, stirring her coffee.

Megan cleared her throat, shot Jude a stern look. "Thank you, but we just came to get our cars and have coffees."

"How about something sweet to go with them?"

Jude turned to the man, "How about you leave us alone?"

"Sorry to disturb you... Have a good evening, professional, adult people."

Jude felt the intruder leave her side, heard Megan giggle.

"He was just being *nice*," said Megan. "And it's singles' night." Megan pushed the coffee over to Jude. "Don't get bitter. It deepens the little lines around your mouth, can even give you cancer. I would've liked the salted-caramel sundae. And his friend's hot, too. Bet you they're SEALs. I can spot them a mile away."

"I can spot an asshole a mile away."

"Really?" said Megan, raising an eyebrow.

"Point made. I'll be back," said Jude.

When Megan looked up from checking her phone hoping the following day's viewing had been canceled, she didn't see Jude, but competition. Parting the Dames' salon-style doors, hair brushed out and loose on her shoulders, Jude was made up with her lips a particular, unmistakable shade of scarlet. *Well I'll be damned*, she thought. Jude had stolen Elizabeth's lipstick.

Jude rested her hand on each of the men's shoulders. "We like our coffees Irish, and the cheesecake's on me."

"Mrs Mathews?"

Jude peered at the speaker whose smile was breaking into a laugh.

"You taught science at Torres Pines? Daize Washington."

"Daize! Of the Washington brothers?"

Daize gestured to his friend. "I was just telling Jesse about me and my brothers. It's true, isn't it, Mrs. Mathews, we had to be put in different schools to separate us?"

"Absolutely true!"

The drinks came as the four took a fork each and dug into the dessert.

"That was my first teaching job. A long time ago—"

"Your reference got me into the navy after taking... let's say *a few wrong turns*. Now we're SEALs."

"I knew it!" said Megan with a clap.

"Wow." Jude sat back and looked at Daize. Her memories scrolled through what she remembered of the Washington family: dad in prison, mom working multiple jobs while taking care of five out-of-control boys.

"I really enjoyed your classes. In fact, I used to have a crush on you, Mrs. Mathews."

"*Jude*, please. But I was—"

"Easily the hottest teacher."

"Hey, sorry about earlier. It's been a weird day and—"

"She's going through a divorce," announced Megan. "We just broke into her husband's girlfriend's house and spat on her bed then we cast a spell on them that we saw on YouTube and Jude stole his passport so he can't go to Paris."

"Sounds like quite a night, *Jude*," said Daize, winking at his former teacher.

91

EL: WED 1 SEPT 2021

Your vocals keep cutting out. Could you record them when you're not running at the same time? My therapist says this is feeding into my abandonment issues. Every day I'm on the front line of this divorce and you clearly have other priorities.

———

JACK HAD BEEN in a deep sleep when a force possessed him from the arches of his feet through his perineum, gall bladder, epiglottis, his teeth and tingling each hair follicle. Currents of pleasure powered through his body every time Elizabeth's soft wet mouth enclosed the base of his cock, her fingers circling his anus and moving inside him. It took all he had to hold himself back to get one notch higher, one second longer—until his cellphone came alive, buzzing and bouncing around on the bedside table.

Elizabeth reached up and dropped it on his chest before walking to the bathroom.

"Marcie," he groaned.

"Then you *must* answer it."

"Come back, sweetheart. Marcie? ... No, I wasn't calling *you* sweetheart, I was—forget it—what?"

"It's Jude," announced his secretary. "*Something bad.* You gotta call her. Oh, and Achim, your 8 o'clock? He's here."

"Thanks—I have to go, there's another call waiting."

"Dad?" Preston. "I've been calling Mom for two days and there's no answer at the cabin."

"I got this."

Preston was quiet before asking, "You'll go and check on her? You won't forget?"

"No! Talk later. And good luck with your first presentation at—"

Another call joined the line.

Jack gave himself a moment's breath, noticing how the sunlight through the shutters made his sweaty body look like it'd been sliced into even pieces.

Bree's husky voice. "Aimee's gone. Savannah doesn't know where."

"OK. Thanks for the heads up," said Jack.

"Actually, that's not the real problem."

"Oh?"

"I called Jude about Aimee last night and she was hysterical, kept saying someone was dead. I tried to call you a few times—has something happened?"

"She likes to party up there in the hills."

"I'd go myself but I'm in court all day."

Aimee or Jude? Who to save first?

Elizabeth was sipping her iced green tea in the kitchen, staring at her iPad.

"I know you're pissed at me," he called out, hopping into his shorts. "But there's a big problem. In fact, *two* big problems."

"'Just *two*? That's a good day," Elizabeth said, flipping open a pot of vitamins.

As he entered the room, Jack gestured at Esme to bring him a coffee. "Aimee's disappeared—she could be with the guy she was sending those photos to—and Jude says someone's *died*. Don't make that face, these are circumstances beyond my control, this—"

"You have control, you just don't use it." Elizabeth opened her kimono then closed it, pulling tight on the ribbon.

Jack tucked his phone into his back pocket where it buzzed again.

"Take the call, Jack. I'll go back to reading about *the bitch* who lured you away from her happy home. The joke is, I haven't taken you anywhere. Go on, you're needed for your next bit-part in Jude's latest tragedy."

Jack sprung up and down on the spot waiting for the right words to come.

"We have each other, Jude has no one."

Elizabeth's eyes brimmed with tears. "You see it that way? Because I have never felt so alone in all my life."

92

SUBJECT: SNOW TO SLEET

From: Salacia99

To: Neptune99

Date: Wednesday December 29, 2021 at 1:45

This contact anorexia is killing me but my therapist says it's necessary to gain perspective. I actually think I could do with less 😊.

Spent Christmas alone but Cosima came for the weekend. Was so looking forward to seeing her but it was tough dealing with her anger without slinging shit back at Bruno. Meanwhile he's posting philosophical quotes on Facebook which all our friends are 'Liking'. I'm now in London putting my apartment on the market so I can buy Bruno out for the Paris home. There's no concession to the fact I've been subsidizing his life for the last two decades. Seems integrity is a sure-fire way to lose at the divorce game.

Out the window the snowflakes are landing on muddy slush banks and I'm thinking whatever we had is dying too.

———

"A COFFEE AND A BLUEBERRY MUFFIN?" Jack asked, taking the cup from Marcie. "You felt how hot it is outside?"

"Achim's in your office," she said. "Manage to get hold of Jude?"

Jack glanced at the title of the book on her desk: *How 2 B a Badass Boss Bitch.*

"No answer. Marcie, could you send some flowers—"

"She'd love that."

"Not *Jude*. To Paloma Drive. *Elizabeth*."

Marcie paused the TikTok reel on how to create the perfect kitten eyes. "Can you afford it?" She lowered her reading glasses over her nose. "The text message you sent?"

"What?"

"Never mind." She picked up a pink fluffy pen. "Shoot."

"Little Mermaid," he dictated. "Two months ago—"

"That a capital 'm'?"

"I'll write it."

Jack wrote: *Two months ago today you came to my land bringing love and light and since then, you've been dancing on knives—*

"That's *way* too long," said Marcie from over his shoulder. "Usually it's just like Happy Retirement or Get Better Soon or—"

"OK." Jack scrunched up the paper. "From an Admirer."

A message from Aimee came through recalibrating Jack's imminent crisis priority list.

> Dad! M fine! Stop worrying! K's mom in
> Ecuador so we r animal sitting.

"I'm going to the lake house. Re-schedule my appointment with Mr. Sanchez for—"

"Sanch… what? The midget? You have his number?"

"Mr. Sanchez—Citibank. You look up his number and you can't use that word anymore. And please, Marcie, don't let clients in my office without me there."

"*You're welcome* for the muffin."

. . .

Jack skidded his bike to a stop in front of the cabin's porch. When he removed his helmet, flies thronged above his head like zeppelins. He looked over the lake where the hot days incubated future generations of single-celled life forms in the gelatinous scum. Jude's MG was perched on the bank. Jack saw clothes draped over the barriers of the jetty, so she'd been swimming, and even though she was a strong swimmer, it was a reckless thing to do on her own. He blinked at what looked like a black mamba slithering to the house, but it was a thick cord of ants wriggling from the kitchen window to the bushes.

Jack called Jude's name as he pushed open the screen door.

The house was dark despite the morning sun. He heard scuffling and what sounded like an engine trying to start. The toilet upstairs flushed.

"Ju?"

Jude appeared at the top of the stairs, holding her stomach.

"You said someone had died."

Jack counted four empty bottles of wine on the kitchen worktop as he waited for her to land in the armchair. She drew her knees to her chest.

"D'you need a doctor?"

She shook her head. Jack put down his keys and said, "Aimee ran away again."

"That boy." Jude swept her matted hair off her face. "Why don't we run away, you and me?"

"Who *died*?"

Jude scratched at a border of gray roots behind her ear. "We said we'd sail down to Panama, remember?"

"Tell me what happened, then we'll talk tourism."

Jude curled up her fists and put them to her mouth. "Don't..."

"Juju... I have to get back to work." Jack poured a glass of water for her then he stopped. "Where's...?"

That's what was wrong with the place: no Tip.

Now Jude was crying loud and hard, one hand squeezing the other.

"*Where's* Tip?"

"*Now* I deserve what you've done to me."

"Tip! Here, boy!"

Jude sipped from the glass of water he'd passed her.

"Wednesday afternoon." She stopped, on the point of breaking down again. Jack put his hand on her shoulder. "We went to the store. It was so hot. So hot."

Jack took the glass from her with encouraging nods.

"I went in the house, did stuff. I must have fallen asleep until the next day and…" she swallowed another gulp of water "…Monday morning, about seven o'clock, usually he wakes me up, doesn't he? But he wasn't there. I didn't remember feeding him. Maybe you or Bentley or someone had come back. I started to look for him, calling him. I asked some hikers… after a few hours, I thought I'd drive to the vet, Dr. Dayton… Drayton… Denton…"

Jack picked up her keys and ran towards her car.

That's where the flies were coming from. Over, around, even inside the car hitting at the windows that were smeared white with dried saliva. The last cries of a dog trying to claw out of its metal coffin.

Jack opened the driver side door, beating off the insects that rushed at his face. He was knocked back by the stench of a decomposing carcass. The leather seats had been torn and the stuffing pulled up, but trapped halfway through the front seats was Tip's body.

Jack bent the seat down, crawled over it to the dog, wrapped his arms around him and tugged until the corpse was free enough to be pulled out. He took a few steps with the dead animal until they both collapsed on the grass.

In the workshop next to the garage, Jack found a roll of stiff mouse-chewed tarpaulin and masking tape. Rope. Saw. Spade.

93

SUBJECT: GOODBYE FROM SALACIA99

From: Salacia99

To: Neptune99

Date: Monday February 14, 2022 at 23:54

My bad. It was Bruno who sent me the flowers. Chrysanthemums on Feb 14th. Just in case you didn't get what kind of monster I was married to. Our IT team checked over all my comms and devices to find Bruno's been accessing everything for about a year. EVERYTHING! I'm devastated! Lot of damage done already but lawyers advised me to avoid any activity he could use against me. I said I had nothing to hide but didn't mention this Gmail account. I'm closing it down right now. Can't take much more of this.

———

JACK JABBED incisions into the ground. The summer sun had turned the earth to rock, the air was thick with a cloying sweetness and mosquitoes darted into his neck and ankles. But he wanted to bury Tip in this spot because that's where the dog liked to lay chewing bits of grass, half in the shade, half in the sun, with a lookout that covered most of the drive, cabin and Jack's workshop.

Jude appeared next to him, clutching some of Tip's toys.

"You can't bury pets in the ground. I read it on Google. You should take the body to a vet."

Jack stabbed into the widening crevice. "Wanna tell the vet that you left your Australian husky shepherd in a sports car on the hottest day in August with all the windows closed?"

Jude turned to retch, tripped over a branch. Jack walked around the three-inch-deep rectangle and stuck the pitchfork in again.

"Just leave me to do this."

Past midday Jack returned to the house, walked directly upstairs. Jude listened to the rush of water in the shower. Then his footsteps on the wooden boards. Cupboards opening, drawers. When he came down the stairs, he'd changed into one of her father's shirts, white and blue stripes, it suited him. Jude watched him towel dry his hair then fasten the clasp of his new watch.

Jude stood and dropped something on the table by Jack.

"What's that?"

"Your passport. Go wherever you want."

"You got this from the house, didn't you? This all stops now, right? And not one more bad word about Elizabeth."

Jude closed her eyes, nodded.

"I'll send one of the guys out to collect the car and leave a courtesy replacement. As for Aimee," he stretched out his arms, "probably best she stays with me."

Jude put her hands to her face and spoke through her fingers, "Please, no. Not with that woman. No!"

"You think she's better off here?"

Jack moved to the kitchen and poured two glasses of water. Drank one, refilled it and brought them to the living room.

"Here." Jude took the water, aware of his touch against the tips of her fingers. "I'll ask Aimee, let her decide. And Bentley, the boy has to get a job and start—"

"Please don't tell the kids what happened."

Jack stared into her pleading eyes, feeling a detachment he had never known before—as if somehow in the last hour the tectonic plates of Mr. and Mrs. Mathews had broken off into two separate continents.

"We'll say it was an accident. But you do anything to interfere with Elizabeth and me, and I'll tell them the truth. Understand?"

The two of them turned to the window as a jeep pulled into driveway. It stopped behind Jack's bike.

"Expecting somebody?"

"He's a—"

The screen door closed, cutting out her answer. Jude moved fast—almost skipped—towards the young man who took off his aviator glasses and hugged her.

Jack leant up to the window to hear what they were saying over the jeep's engine but they were too far. Jude was smiling as she listened to the man, her arm lifted over her forehead to block out the sunlight but the way she leant back, lifting up her breasts to him was not unconscious. The man enclosed her into his sleeveless T-shirt, his lips moving against Jude's ear as he said something that made her laugh. The pair let go of each other. Jude waved as her visitor hopped into his truck and reversed out.

Jude was back in the cabin, flushed, dashing around opening windows and picking up the glasses to wash—this time, keen for Jack to leave.

"Hello? You gonna tell me who that was?"

"A student."

"Seems a little old for private coaching," said Jack, letting the screen door slam behind him. "And way too young for you!"

94
SUBJECT: SAME QUESTION

From: Elizabeth Lambert

To: Jack Mathews

Date: Friday April 7, 2023 at 7:11

Are you *still* Jack Mathews? Jack, the man who used to email, make playlists, message and call me every day? What's with the monosyllabic WhatsApp messages and you sandbagging me with excuses. Three years on, I have to ask: do you still love me?

———

ELIZABETH HEARD Jack's bike in the driveway, then a slow, weighty tread over the gravel she didn't recognise.

"That you?" she called out once the front door closed.

"It's me, yeah."

Jack lingered at the bottom of the stairs like a mechanical device needing to be rewound.

"I'm up here."

Jack opened the bedroom door and keeled over on the bed.

"D'you get the flowers?"

"I gave them to Esme. You know my views on mixed flowers." Elizabeth spoke without taking her eyes from an American high school series that Cosie and she had been following. "I take it you found your daughter."

Jack reached for her with a hand serrated with cuts.

"Kenzo's dumbass mom left the country—father sick or something—she filled the kitchen with pet food but nothing for her kid. Can you believe that? I went to collect her, but…" he sighed "…they were so *happy*. They're turning the backyard into a theme park for the chinchillas. But we're still looking for Bentley."

Jack raked his fingers through his hair.

"Bentley out there, it scares me 'cause—" Elizabeth ricocheted back from him. "Where's all this dirt coming from?"

"I was digging."

Elizabeth started tugging at Jack's sneakers. "There's… *earth* everywhere. Take your pants off—not *here*, on the balcony—I'll get the vacuum cleaner. Don't touch anything. Go and—what?"

"Stop—" Jack took hold of her wrist and pulled her next to him. "I buried him." Seeing Elizabeth's panicked frown, he added, "Tip. Our dog. Jude left him locked in the car. Hottest day of the year…" Jack pressed his clenched fists into his eye sockets. "He's gone."

Elizabeth held Jack's body as the grief tore through him.

"The last few times I saw him, I just walked past him, I never even…"

Jack stood and fumbled in his back pocket, he brought out a bunch of twigs and his passport.

"But the war's over," Jack said, falling back on the bed. "All over. All I have left in the world is you."

He pulled her into him again, moved his face from side to side on her stomach before going into a deep sleep, snoring even.

All I have left is you. Elizabeth rubbed one foot over the other, watched a bat scoop up some water from the pool before twirling back into the black sky. She took the call before her phone even rang.

"Where are you, Lili?" asked Bruno.

"It's three in the morning and I'm sitting in the garden like I'm the only person in the world."

"No, *chérie*. Where are you in your head? Because you are not the only person in the world. You have a daughter. You have a company and clients and friends, and you have me."

"Why did you never tell me you loved me?"

It was a thought, from the darkness, and with almost all lost she could ask it now.

"*Hein?*" Elizabeth could hear his brain halt from whatever roster of activities he was jumping between. "*Bon alors.* Sometimes I read the messages you and that man wrote to each other. And I thought, does my Lili really think this is love? Songs, empty promises, heart emojis? That's not love, a home is love. And we had a home."

Bruno, firing his last shot.

The cold dense bullet went through her.

This wasn't about Jack.

"Lili, the reason I called was to remind you that Cosima isn't some DHL package you send for when you get bored. She starts at the International School of Paris in two weeks. I signed the lease on two connecting apartments—they call it a bird's nest divorce so you fly home very soon or I go back to the lawyer for sole custody and, thanks to your cowboy's wife, I'll get it."

And Elizabeth's world went silent again.

It was about Jude.

It was about having Jude's home.

It was about having Jude's love.

95

> Check out this view from Paloma Heights! Up here running with Tip. You can even see Mexico. Saw this house. Spanish colonial with pool and 'For Rent' sign. You said you needed us to move forward so how about us living here till we find somewhere to buy. Imagine you writing your book, me bringing you cocktails, massaging your ***?

———

ELIZABETH JUMPED as the grass around her lit up when her phone announced: *Lambert Interiors, London Office.* Twenty faces crammed themselves around Magnus' screen: "We got it!"

"The Sapphire Group! They've agreed!"

"Another three years!"

"To Titania Lambert!" They toasted. "Queen of the fairies!"

Emily jumped up and down behind the group to see Elizabeth. "You're the bestest!"

Elizabeth actually jigged from one foot to the other on the grass, twirling level with their faces. "They really? Agreed to re-sign? I'm so happy!"

At the end of every job Elizabeth had feared never being

offered work again, that the day would come she'd run out of ideas, originality and someone younger, brighter, hungrier would take her place, yet her proposal and pitch to the Sapphire Group had been underprepared and underwhelming. She'd been too distracted by winning Jack over. But fate had thrown her a lifeline; she was less celebratory than relieved.

"Come back soon!" begged Helena.

"How about you all come here?"

"Team trip! Team trip!" chanted Emily and Helena as the others joined in.

"More of a rescue mission!" Magnus announced.

Over the next few minutes, a trip to Los Angeles was organized to celebrate the contract and bring their boss back to Europe. After a few more rounds of tears and thank-yous, and someone announcing what time it was in California, they ended the call.

Elizabeth was about to go into the house to catch a few hours' sleep before morning when she saw someone moving inside the pool house. Through the window, she could make out the form of a man. Bare, white skin. A few steps closer and she could see it wasn't a stranger, yet her heart jumped.

"Bentley?"

It was, but it wasn't him. This bearded version didn't answer, didn't move, didn't seem to recognize her. But his eyes, under a hood of matted hair and the plane of his forehead, tracked her slightest movements as she came towards him. His hand stroking his penis, he opened his mouth, words scraped his throat.

"I saw you. Dancing. Laughing. Didn't know you laughed."

The tops of his thighs bulged, ready to pounce. Her instincts warned her to let the peak of his adrenaline die down, bolt when he was off guard. Not think what he might do to her; not fuel him with her terror.

"My dog died," he said. A shiver through his body entered hers.

"You need to leave."

It took everything in her to face him, palms upward.

"I'm sorry about Tip, you must be devastated. I know how much you—"

"Can we dance together?"

Elizabeth tightened her grip on her phone.

"Your dad's upstairs. Yes? Jack?"

"Shhhh." He stepped forward. She turned to the dark house, forced the quiver out of her voice when she said, "He's coming down now. Can you hear him?"

He snorted. "Dad's a very heavy sleeper."

"There are cameras all around watching the house."

"They're not activated and the alarm isn't on. Hey, I can actually see your heart beating." He stamped his foot towards her. "That time together, over there, when you let me show you who I am, I knew then."

"Bentley, I was wrong to play with you like that."

"You were *wrong*?"

Elizabeth moved back from his rancid breath as he leant in.

"Please. Go home. Let's talk tomorrow."

"I've no home left. Not since you bulldozed it down with your little kissy feet and blonde money. We been smashed up, burnt, razed to the ground." His face swirled into a grimace. "I heard you on the phone, you're leaving now, aren't you? You're done with us now there's nothing left."

Elizabeth stayed as still as she could while feeling around for a nearby chair with her fingertips.

"We'll be clearing up the wreckage of you for the rest of our lives, and you, you're just moving on to the next project."

"The security firm will be here any moment. Bentley, you are on my property illegally and—"

"Drive with me—the engine just purrs, it's like your voice. We can go places. See, Elizabeth, there's nothing in this world for me but you—"

Elizabeth's phone chimed. *Zuni.* As Bentley went to grab

Elizabeth's hand, she caught the chair and spun it into his legs. He cried out, there was a thud but Elizabeth didn't stop to see what happened as she raced back to the house and upstairs, bursting into the bedroom where Jack was still sleeping, earth in his hair and his phone flashing with messages.

"Jack, wake up. Jack! Bentley's outside."

"Wh—"

Outside they heard a shout: "Elizabeth! Come with me! Elizabeth!" The last 'Elizabeth' came out like a howl.

"Bentley?"

"Yes! He's outside!"

Jack crossed the hall to the landing window which looked over the front of the house. "He's bleeding."

They heard the roar of a car tearing down the hill.

"That's the Cobra."

"He was about to attack me. I was so—"

"I've got to get that car back."

"Listen to me—Bentley's been living in the pool house. I thought he was going to—and then Zuni called... If he hadn't..."

"Is he OK?"

"Is *he* OK?"

Elizabeth forced herself to move to the dressing room despite her entire body shaking. She dragged out her case, filling it with immediate clothes and stuff she might need. She crouched down to put on her running shoes, her fingers trembling like they didn't belong to her.

"Where are you going?"

"To a hotel. Anywhere away from you and your fucking family."

96

EL: WED 12 APR 2023

Call the agents. I'll take the house. It's a sign.

———

JUDE WAS SITTING with Maxxie in the cafeteria inside the hospital where Bentley had been for the last four days. Bentley's girlfriend was scrolling through reels on her phone while Jude watched Jack dismount his bike. He pulled off his helmet and unflattened his hair.

Maxxie nudged Jude. "O.M.G., he's wearing Nike SB Dunk Low 'Tokyos'. They cost a ton."

"And he can't afford to help Preston with his rental."

"And y'know I got this SMS from him asking me for money. Bentley too. Twenty-five large. Don't lose your shit, Mrs. M. So not worth it."

They watched Jack enter the hospital and stand, lost and diminutive, in the middle of the white-tiled foyer, until he spotted a sign for the café. Jude pushed a chair towards him with her foot. He sat down, cradling his helmet between his knees. He put his hand on Maxxie's shoulder, she showed him a smile, white teeth behind black lipstick.

"Think we'll get to see him?"

Jude shrugged.

Maxxie waved her phone. "There's a better signal outside."

Jude watched her leave and drank from a water bottle.

"Don't know why Bentley's having psychiatric evaluations and not her creepy brother," said Jack.

"Because Bentley drove a car off Coronado Bridge last Tuesday."

Jude squinted at Jack's black Linkin Park T-shirt and neon-blue jogging pants.

"What?" He looked down at his clothes. "I was running."

"From gang members?"

"*Balenciaga*," he said, pinching at the fabric on his thighs. "So I'm not allowed to exercise now?"

Jude gave a 'whatever' shrug while shifting her bag into the crook of her arm; same bag that Jack had bought her in San Miguel de Allende on their honeymoon.

Jude dropped back in the chair.

"You OK?" he asked.

"Woozy. Just give me…"

"Is she coming into the meeting with us?" Jack indicated to Maxxie who was sitting on a bench outside the hospital's entrance, talking on her phone.

"She really wanted to be here. I couldn't say no after all she's been through. She loves our boy, and—" she leant in close enough so that Jack felt the curls of her hair against his cheek "—her family still want to press charges."

"Mr., Mrs. Mathews, it's too early to give you a definitive outline of Bentley's mental state," began Dr. Luisa Angel. "You've cited incidents of behavioral issues in Bentley's history, depression, aggressive outbursts, intrusive thoughts but also stable periods. We need to explore if what happened last Tuesday was an isolated act or part of a pattern."

"You told her about your dad? They said he was bipolar—called it manic depressive then—great guy and super smart an' all, but when he drank, boy! Watch out! Remember that time, he—"

"This is helpful background information."

"And Maxxie, his girlfriend, she said he'd been taking these anabolic steroids to bulk and that was when he'd start, like, flying off the handle. And we just lost our family dog. Y'know he was watching my house, making threatening calls, he was driving a client's car."

It unnerved Jack that he was left to do the talking. Usually in these situations with professionals, Jude always took the lead, but this time, she seemed so small in her chair, quiet, defeated.

The doctor looked up from her notes and spoke, dividing her attention to each of them equally. "We'll work with Bentley at a time he's less sedated and in less pain."

"Can we see him?" ask Jude, about to take the doctor's arm.

"Yeah, we'd really like to see him," said Jack.

"Bentley expressed a desire to talk with his mother. I'm afraid Mr. Mathews, another time."

Jack sat back in the chair, crossed his arms over his chest.

"Tomorrow?"

"Let's see after my meeting with his care team tomorrow."

"My husband's in a hurry. He's fleeing to Paris with a call girl."

"She's a designer and I'll be back here all the time."

"It's best if we explore the relational dynamics in the family therapy sessions."

Jude sat on the toilet; eyes shut tight. The rapid inhalations did nothing to relieve the pain of seeing her son in bandages, staring up at the ceiling, so alone. Someone flushed in the next-door cubicle. Jude pressed the corner of the packed envelope full of hospital invoices into the palm of her hand. Only minutes before she'd dragged the bedside chair to his feet to rub his ankles, kneading into the arches, and closing her hand over his toes. Bentley had never liked people touching him, but as a child he let his mom hold his feet when no one else was looking.

Maxxie and Jack were talking, each had a fork digging into a piece of carrot cake, each had a can of Arizona tea and a packet of potato chips. When they'd gone to the movies as a family, Jack had always insisted they smuggled in drinks and candy from home so as not to pay the *extortionate* prices. She stared at this man with the big watch and designer clothes eating like a toddler at a birthday party while his son lay on a hospital bed a short elevator ride away.

"How was he?" asked Jack, wiping cream from his lips.

Jude motioned to Maxxie. "I'm leaving now if you wanna lift home. And you, get all your crap out of my house by midday tomorrow or I call junk haulers."

97
EL: THURS 18 MAY 2023

All documents signed and money wired over.
All those years ago we built castles in the air,
and now we're finally moving in! To live in
love! Forever starts today 🖤

———

"Le Grand Boss is in there," said Marcie, pointing at Jack's office. "If he hasn't fallen into one of those crates."

"My man Al, s'been too long." Jack cut some tape with his teeth, sealed a box. "Sorry I haven't been down to the center, you heard about Bentley."

"How's he doing?"

"They're easing up on the drugs. He's out next week. I'm trying to get Jude to send him to Elizabeth's dad—he's had crazy results with all kinds of mental illness."

"The witch doctor?"

"Shaman. Iced water? Coffee? Beer? We can toast me a *Bon Voyage*."

"That Spanish for sumthin'?" Al chuckled. "Hi, Marcie."

"Excuse me, boys. Al, could I ask a favor? Is there any chance Tammy could put some of my cards in her store window? It's not just Jack who's moving on, I just qualified as a life coach so gotta get the word out."

Once Marcie left, Al took out his pack of tobacco. "Can I?"

"Better out back."

Outside the workshop, under a cantaloupe-colored sky, Jack and his friend sat on upside-down metal containers. While Al lit his roll-up, Jack stared at the day's dirty overalls heaped up in the corner.

"Mike's guys move in tomorrow. Most of the team kept their jobs. I covered the floor debts—I'm broke but not bust."

"I wanted to help out when I got that text but we're going through hard times ourselves."

"People keep talking about a text, what text?"

Al took out his phone and showed Jack the message asking for money.

"I never wrote that. Goddamn Jude!" Jack looked to the sky, laughing in disbelief. "Can't wait to get out of this place. Negative vibes, man. We leave Friday morning for Paris. Elizabeth's in LA celebrating some big contract with a hotel group. They're all up at the Chateau Marmont..." Jack watched his friend flicking through a discarded Harley Davidson wall calendar. "The Bentley thing shook her up. Y'know, he'd been stalking her big time, she thought he was going to kill her."

Jack stopped his ramble to think about the last time he'd seen Elizabeth merging into the airport crowd in a blue dress that looked like it'd been ripped from a piece of sky, but the part he didn't want to remember was that she'd been so keen to get away, she hadn't even waved goodbye.

Al twisted the end of his mustache. "Was wondering if you could take the hatchback off me? We need the money to pay another two years on the store lease."

"But it was trade-in, for the truck—"

"S'right, but you said if ever...?"

Jack remembered what he'd said. It was what he said to all his clients, *Any problem, come by, and we'll give you your money back.*

"I looked it up, 1400 dollars sounds 'bout right."

"It's been kinda bashed around a bit. Why not leave it here tonight, I'll have one of the boys see what they can do tomorrow? Might be my last sale. You still coming Thursday, Gatton's? Bring Tammy, Elizabeth will love her."

"Maybe, I'll ask Tammy. Meanwhile, could you give me an advance on the car now?"

"Can't do, the books need to be watertight."

"A lift home?"

"I would, but I'm behind on the packing."

"Buddy, I'm all for love and new beginnings but no need to be an asshole."

As the cogs turned in Jack's brain for how to reply, Al was already walking along Pine Street, the sunset behind him.

Gary Lord, AKA Good-Looking, one of his longest-serving mechanics, came into view as he pulled up in his car, rolled down the window.

"So long and fuck you, Mathews Motors. Thanks to you, I gotta find a new job."

"Well fuck you too, *Not-So*-Good-Looking!"

As Jack watched him drive out onto the road, Bradley trailed his car wash cart into view.

"My, that's not a very gentlemanly thing to say, is it, Mr. M?"

His nose was peeling at the center of his glistening red face.

"Nope. And thank God I'm leaving this place for France. Guess you're starting back at school soon."

"Change of plans actually. I've been offered a full-time position here by the new management. And an assistant—rather hoped Traci would want the job but she's been made General Manager at Group 1 apparently."

"Stayin' here? Thought this was all to pay for college?" asked Jack, distracted by his last glimpse of Al fading into the shimmering smog.

"Queer thing, I've exceeded the cost of my tuition, which makes one wonder about the necessity of a degree somewhat, eh? Have a spiffing evening and send my regards to the marvelous Mrs. M."

98

JM: FRI 19 MAY 2023

> Couldn't talk this evening. Beanie's dance group needed someone to fix the sound system. Megan said the bed's arrived. She googled you and is now obsessed! You'll be super friends. So stop stressing—I'm telling Jude this weekend.

———

"MY, THIS IS FANCY!" said Tammy, as Jack led them through the doors of Gatton's. "Look at the view—even in this rain, gorgeous!"

"Dude, this ain't my scene," said Al. "Just give me what you owe me for the car then we'll scoot."

"Honey, lemme at least give Elizabeth my flowers. I'm dying to meet her."

"Don't be crazy," said Jack, looking around the restaurant. "I want my best bud here. There she is!"

Elizabeth was sitting at the helm of a long rectangular table at the back of the restaurant. She was wearing a bottle-green backless dress, her hair up apart from a symmetrical curl on either side of her face. Jack regretted that this dinner wasn't just for the two of them. They'd barely spoken since she'd returned from LA the day before, but she'd been so busy going through the proofs of her book and celebrating the new contract with Sapphire Group—this Jack gleaned from her TikTok account. She hadn't even been at the house to pack up, instead hiring a crew of professionals to do it.

On top of that, her team from London were staying with Gideon and Fabrizzio but Jack hadn't been invited to their lunches and furniture buying expeditions and events with people he was supposed to have heard of. That was fine, though, because he'd been caught up in the riptide of Bentley visits and packing up his own life. The lack of direct communication was off but when he asked her if anything was up, she just repeated that the week had been hectic. And now she wasn't making eye contact with him. Jack tried to get over to Elizabeth but his guests blocked the path. He shook hands with Matt, waved to Lindsay, fist bumped Fabrizzio.

"Hey, babe," he said, squinting to read the small print on the limbal ring of her verdigris eyes. Instead of returning his smile, Elizabeth's throat became taut when she asked, "What are you wearing that shirt for?"

"It's black. I thought all black. Kinda Alain Delon chic, *non*?"

"*No*. You look like a waiter." Elizabeth checked a message on her phone before announcing with strained alacrity, "So! Magnus, Emily, this is Jack."

"So the Brits brought the weather with them!" Jack laughed while realising that they had, originally, taken him for a waiter, "Emily, with that beautiful British accent. Great to finally meet you." The young brunette with a voice that either croaked or giggled at everything anyone said, pushed back his hug and kissed his cheeks. "The two kisses. I'm gonna have to get used to that. And, hey, Elizabeth's ride or die. Magnus! Silver pumps —this an Icelandic tradition?" asked Jack, stepping back to look at Magnus' footwear and deciding against saying anything about the man wearing glitter eye-shadow.

"The tackiness is all my own. Charmed," said Magnus, extending a hand weighed down by an enormous diamond-encrusted watch. Now that Jack had to present Tammy in her tie-dye tent dress and Al, with his rolled-up cigarette behind his ear and tangle-weed beard, he regretted insisting they come.

"So nice to meet you—and you are super cute! Just like Jack said. These are all the flowers indigenous to California," said Tammy, stabbing her bouquet at Elizabeth who had no choice but to grasp the sopping stems. The flower heads were heavy, already wilting. Magnus stepped back from them as Elizabeth looked to Jack, panicked, before Gideon ushered a waiter to take the flowers away. "Oh, did the eucalyptus scratch you—the ends can be spiky. If you cut their stems–"

"Jack, move up so your friends can sit at the head of the table next to me."

Jack tried to take Elizabeth's hand. "Shouldn't I be up with you?"

"It's best I keep them near me. Why don't—"

"Champagne! My Goodness!" exclaimed Tammy. "Grace Kelly. That's who you look like. I'd love to go to France, see the Eiffel Tower, eh, Al?"

"You guys gotta visit us," said Jack, pulling out Al's chair.

Elizabeth double blinked as she placed a menu in Tammy's hands how you might a *First Reader* for a child just beginning to sound out syllables.

"Jack, this is Mia. She's the amazing antique collector in La Jolla I've been raving about, and her partner, Hope." Hope, whose face was hidden behind thick yellow dreadlocks, didn't pause from listing the benefits of drinking crystal-infused water to Lindsay.

"If you like interesting stuff to buy, you should come visit my store, The Organic Orgasm, on Ryder Street in Feliz, we have—"

"The Organic Orgasm—I'd like to place a multiple order!" Gideon laughed.

"Shall we start?" asked Elizabeth. Lindsay pointed to Matt who was on the terrace taking a phone call in the rain.

When Elizabeth filled Al's glass with sparkling water, he said, "Jack told me about you, long time ago, the runaway he met and how much it affected him when you disappeared. And here you are."

"Here I am, with all I wanted at the age of fifteen."

"Reminds me of that film, *The Great Gatsby*," said Tammy with a flickering smile.

"Hope I don't get shot in our pool, be a nasty mess for Esme to clear up." Jack laughed.

"But I do have to say," said Tammy, flushing from her second glass of champagne, "Jude is a very special person too —you seem super nice but this is really hard for her."

"I appreciate your loyalty," Elizabeth said, gesturing to the waiter to start taking their orders.

"I'm vegan, so there's nothing here I can eat," said Tammy, closing the menu.

"They do a great truffle risotto."

"Rice and chocolate?"

"Truffles—like mushrooms but cost the same as gold nuggets."

"Huh. That then."

"Dad!"

Jack had almost not recognized Preston—the handsome young man in a suit. "Elizabeth, good evening. This is Chadiki. Sorry we're late, after work I went to see Bentley. So, all set?"

"Where's Aimee?"

Preston leant into his dad, "She... She didn't want to come. Sorry Elizabeth, but it's a lot for her, with her brother and... A *lot*."

"I get it. I have a daughter almost the same age," said Elizabeth. "But thank you both for coming. What handsome young men! Excuse me," Elizabeth moved away to rearrange the seating once again.

"I really wanted Aimee to meet Elizabeth. Why didn't she lemme know?"

"Dad, she's not OK about all this, it'd be really nice if you could spend some time with her before you go. Listen, when I was with Bentley, Mom was there—she asked why I was dressed up, and... I couldn't lie."

"It's not a secret, Marcie made the arrangements so it'll be all over social media by now. Hey, Mia, this is my son—he's a business student."

Jack winked at Elizabeth who was staring stoney-faced as Tammy recounted the details of her hysterectomy before she leapt out of her seat waving: "There's Marcie!"

Marcie waved back, "Sorry I'm late guys, y'know it's raining out there? This never happens here." Marci shuffled over in her heels and a black tuxedo dress with extended white wings at the neck. Jack didn't stop Elizabeth in time from introducing her to everybody as *Jack's secretary* which undermined the hours she'd spent dressing up so she wouldn't be viewed as such.

Al sucked his teeth, still staring at the menu, as Matt talked to him about the mooring costs for his boat. Jack texted Elizabeth to ask if he could borrow 1000 dollars cash to give Al for the car. He'd already heard Elizabeth promising Mia a few thousand for antiques. Jack saw her glance at her phone but she didn't reply or look at him. When he winked at Preston, his son just stared back at him, mouthing the word, *Mom*.

99
SUBJECT: CONGRATS SELLING YOUR HOUSE!

From: Jack Mathews

To: Elizabeth Lambert

Date: Monday May 22, 2023 at 9:02

Here's an email because you said you missed them. Now you don't have to be scared of anyone else reading them! Not the same for me. I couldn't talk to Jude over the weekend because Aimee had her friends over and Preston came by. But trust me!!! When we talked yesterday you said you didn't know what living with me will be like so instead of preparing Mike's budget forecast, I made a PowerPoint of how I imagine our future together. Open it and share your comments. Page 3 refers to division of labor—obviously I'm in charge of transportation. And I want a yacht! Massaging your feet three times a week is non-negotiable. We will live in love every day till we die XOX PS Don't worry about the peonies, Megan's on it.

———

AL HAD BEEN TWISTING the ends of his napkin when he looked up and saw Jude step into the restaurant. He leant back in his chair and thought now he might actually have some fun tonight.

Jack ducked behind the topiary of Marcie's hairstyle to watch the restaurant manager pick up a menu and lead Jude—wearing bright red lipstick—towards them.

Elizabeth was stroking her scallops with the back of her

343

fork, half listening to something Giddy and Céline were discussing.

"Hello, Jack. Hello, Elizabeth."

Elizabeth looked up as Jude sat in the chair that had been allocated for Megan.

"I'm Jude, Jack's wife. Hello, Preston, Chad, Marcie—oh, Tammy and Al—"

"What the—" Jack started, sinking onto a seat.

Elizabeth put up her hand to stop Jack from speaking.

"I'm Magnus, creative director of Lambert Interiors."

"I recognize you from the website."

"You need to—" Jack stood, scattering the silverware to the floor.

Elizabeth stared him down.

"Mrs. Mathews, let me pour you a glass of champagne." Magnus lifted a flute and poured.

"Just sparkling water for me, thanks, but everyone else, fill your glasses! I'd like to toast some great news." Jude looked around and asked, "But first, do you think they'd do a doggy bag so our son could be a part of this? The food in the psych ward is terrible."

Emily got up from her seat. "I'll just check…"

"That's Emily, my PA. Magnus, my everything," said Elizabeth. "This is Céline, Mia, Giddy and Fab, the rest of the people you know."

"Well, I *thought* I knew Jack!" Jude laughed. "After twenty-four years of marriage… seems not."

Jack moved towards Jude. "No one wants to hear your—"

As Magnus tipped a little more champagne into Jude's glass, Emily whispered into Elizabeth's ear, "She's wearing your lipstick."

"What are we celebrating again?" asked Jude.

The maître d' appeared at the table with Megan and her date, a man who came up to her shoulders in a pale purple velour tracksuit.

"Megan," said Jude before addressing the waiters, "the real

estate agent who found a married man a place to fuck his mistress."

"I didn't know! I said!" Megan chewed on her bottom lip.

"I know, Megs, you're only here for business. It's the same for Jack. I thought St. Jude was the 'patron saint of lost causes' but Elizabeth, you get the prize."

"You done trying to embarrass everybody?" asked Jack.

"I don't want to intrude, not at all, but as we're all here celebrating tonight, I just wanted to share my good news with you." Jude clinked Tammy's champagne glass.

The room went silent as Jude had their attention. She held her glass, looked to each of them all but stopped at Jack whose nostrils flared at her.

"I'd like to announce that Jack and I are having a baby!"

Jack moved behind Jude, pulling her away from the guests as her voice got louder.

"Elizabeth, it wasn't just me he was cheating on." Jude shook Jack off causing him to lose his balance. "Thank you, everybody. I can find my way back to my home. *Au revoir! Bon voyage!* "

100

> Take a beat, babe. I'm telling her tomorrow.
> It's a holiday weekend so we're going to the
> lake house away from the kids and everything.
> It'll be done by the time you land and I'll pick
> you up from the airport and take you to the
> house and you know the rest!!!

———

JACK TORPEDOED down the table as if he could tackle the information away from Elizabeth, but it had hit. As he passed Preston, his son muttered, "Baby?" before he and Chadiki walked over to Jude, turned, and made their way to the entrance where a man, only a few years older than Preston, pushed through the doors shaking an umbrella. The man with the truck Jack had seen talking to Jude at the cabin. Jack watched as the 'ex-student' hugged Jude. She said something, the man chuckled, bundled her towards the exit.

Once the doors closed on Jack's wife, Elizabeth's guests dropped their shoulders, leant back in their chairs and looked around at each other.

Elizabeth placed her napkin on the table. "Do you think the filet needs a little more salt?" The guests laughed, and didn't try to stop her when she added, "I have packing to do. Please excuse me."

Jack got up to follow her but she pressed her hand against his chest. "Stay here."

Jack fought against the distance between them, whispering, "She's crazy. She killed our dog for Chrissake. She's—"

"Goodnight, everybody." Elizabeth waved her hand.

Magnus jumped up to follow her. "Darling, I'll just get the car."

"No, I'll take her," said Jack.

Al grabbed Jack's arm. "Hey, man, you're driving Tammy and me back to—"

"Elizabeth, stop! What she said—"

"Is it OK if I order the *chocolate fondant*?" chirped Megan.

Céline and Giddy blew kisses as they refilled their glasses.

Jack jogged behind Elizabeth until Magnus gripped his shoulder.

"If she needs to be alone, then leave her *alone*."

Jack watched Elizabeth go, coatless, through the doors into the wet night.

"Hey! She forgot my flowers!" said Tammy.

101

EL: SAT 27 MAY 2023

It's happening, sailor boy—they're calling my flight! See you on the other side!

———

"Jude," Elizabeth called out.

Jude turned from the truck she was about to get into, walked towards Elizabeth, her eyes ablaze with nothing-left-to-lose ferocity.

"Congratulations. That baby is very lucky to have you as a mom."

"Congrats you too. You got your Jack."

Elizabeth smeared raindrops across her cheeks.

"It was a mistake, Jack and I. We got carried away thinking we were the stars in a perfect love story, couldn't see it for what it was." Elizabeth looked over to a shop door with a wide recess. "Can we talk?"

Jude looked to the man in the truck who gestured for her to go ahead before returning to a game on his phone.

Once out of the rain, Jude asked, "I don't get why, when you were fifteen and Jack cheated on you *and* me, you came back to him?"

"Something happened in Catalina which I've never got over. I went looking for Jack hoping he would cure me, but... here we are."

"What happened?"

Elizabeth shivered in her dress, wiped rain from her lips.

"When I found out about you, I stole Jack's college money to get away from my mother's boyfriend, Vince, but when I saw her, all beat up, I wanted us to leave together. But she didn't want to leave him—she was missing a tooth for fuck's sake. So to open her eyes, I told her how he'd tried stuff with me and how he'd said he was taking me with him off the island, leaving her behind. She went crazy, called me a liar, a slut, said I'd always been after her men. To calm her down, I showed her Jack's money and gave her an ultimatum, me or Vince. She went all calm, made Danny and me a hot chocolate, told us to watch TV while she packed up our stuff. When we were little she used to make us hot chocolates, stir in crushed sleeping pills so she could go out and we wouldn't wake up. I should've guessed."

Elizabeth's breath quickened, Jude rested a hand on Elizabeth's wrist, sensing her racing pulse.

"I woke up in the trunk. Freezing. Pitch dark. Danny lay beside me, ice-cold—I thought he was dead. She'd drugged us. Then the trunk opened. Every time I reached for my mother, she swatted me away. We were on the edge of a lake, behind us, forest. She had a gas canister and was pouring the fuel over us —it was burning, blinding. I couldn't wake Danny. Then something cold and metallic smashed into my face—the cigarette lighter Danny and I had stolen for her birthday. As the car began rolling toward the ravine, she was trying to set us alight."

Jude ran her eyes over Elizabeth's pearlized lips.

"I was screaming at her to help us when Vince and his friend appeared. That's when I was certain I'd die. But they started fighting. He was trying to stop her from killing us and all she could say was, 'We're better without them.' Vince and his friend got us away from her, took us to the mainland."

Elizabeth wrapped her arms around herself.

"I've never told anyone about that night. How could I be so bad that my own mother wanted me dead?"

"You were a child—Aimee's age!" said Jude. "How did you get away?"

"Danny's dad came for him. He'd just got married and they didn't have the space for us both. I stayed with Vince's friend in LA for two years—he was OK—and when he wasn't, I left for Europe. Never saw my mother or brother again, though Danny would call every once in a while before he overdosed."

Jude shook the rain from her head.

"I still don't understand why you came back?"

"I wanted what you had—a life of love. I wanted your home, your mom and your dad, a sister. Friends. Respect. No shame, no secrets. I wanted to feel I had the right to be loved, to be the girl Jack would marry not the one he'd just cheat on over a summer."

Jude stopped a raindrop snaking down the back of her cheek.

"You wrecked my home and now you're taking Jack off to Paris."

"No. I'm leaving tomorrow. He's not coming with me. It's over."

Jude flinched at a gust of wind.

"I want to go home, be with my daughter and my career. Jack needs you, his family—and now a baby! Jack loves you all so much, and this place, it's his home."

The rain started coming down harder as they looked to their cars.

"We'll have to make a run for it," Elizabeth smiled.

"First, let's… " Jude opened out her arms for Elizabeth to be closed into.

102

JM: SUN 28 MAY 2023

Megan coming to pick u up. Will explain later.

———

IT WAS past one in the morning when Jack set off all the motion detectors around the house as jumbo-sized raindrops drenched the Tom Ford suit Elizabeth had bought him. The alarm beeped until he tapped in *2020*: the year they'd re-found each other. He unpeeled his wet clothes in the dark hall, kicked them into a pile, his ears trained on movement in the master bedroom.

Jack, sensing the nerve-endings in his thighs spasm from cold, stood at the end of the four-poster bed which, for the first time, was completely closed. The getaway bed. He brushed his fingers over the white gauze curtains to find an edge to draw back. He felt Elizabeth's hand through the material and when she parted the curtains, he crawled into the tent, into the sheets and pulled her warm body into his.

"You'd only been here two weeks. It was that night we had a family BBQ. Jude and I slept in our bed, we were half asleep when we had sex. It was habit; it was goodbye."

"I don't care anymore."

"Megan told me this afternoon that you'd added a three-month break clause into the contract. Makes me think, were you really that serious?"

"I'm a businesswoman and it's a very expensive house—I wanted us to work more than anything! Why were you talking to Megan anyway?"

"She's selling the family home in the city to pay for Bentley's medical care." Elizabeth looked away, crinkling her nose. "Mermaid, we had everything."

"I remembered today that my mother once told me the story of the Little Mermaid, how she gave up her beautiful world in the sea to live on land with her sailor but every time she walked, it felt like her feet were treading over knives."

"We had the DVD of that, used to watch it with Aimee. It was Ariel, right? Definitely the hottest out of all the Disney princesses. He was a prince, not a sailor. And didn't the witch take out her tongue? Babe, what's it to do with us?"

Elizabeth spun to the edge of the bed, tussled with the curtain.

"Everything! We confused fact with fiction."

"What are you saying?"

"Tell me, you never thought I'd actually come out here, did you?"

"It's Magnus, isn't it? I could tell he didn't like me, and Céline—"

"It's *us*," Elizabeth said.

"But we were meant to be together. Avalon. 1999. Remember?"

"Maybe we *weren't*. Ever thought of that?"

Elizabeth's largest suitcase was spread-eagled on the floor, elastic belts fastening down her summer clothes. On the table she'd lined up her wallet, passport, phone charger and tickets. Everything matched, monogramed and labeled with her name and address printed out by Emily, her accomplice. From motel rooms to people's floors to the George V to wherever she'd go next, this mermaid didn't walk on knives, her feet didn't touch the ground long enough.

Elizabeth lay back down, opened up her arms for him to come into. Pressed up against each other, heartbeats synchronized and minds too tired to think. The rain stopped. They stayed like that until Elizabeth's phone beeped as the sun came up.

103

EL: FRI 1 SEPT 2023

So this is the end.

———

As Esme slowed her scooter to open the gates, Jack tugged the front door shut behind him.

The sun climbed over Paloma Heights, dabbing patches of yellow onto the highest trees where birds camped out like SWAT teams, their mission to raid the feast created by yesterday's rain. Jack's legs were achy from his walk the night before, a reminder that he had given his car to Al and his bike was still at the garage and that he had no wife, no girlfriend, no home, no job, no friends or nearby toilet.

Jack side-stepped around the back of the house, slunk behind the rose bushes, along the lines of palms, past the sun loungers to the pool house. He was surprised to find the door unlocked and went inside, stopping to look around at where Bentley had spent a few days while they'd all been looking for him. Since then, Flores and his team had cleaned it up, preparing it for the cooler climate. After using the bathroom, Jack made a lookout over the top of the stacked cushions and umbrellas.

Jack could see through the windows at where Esme and Elizabeth—both dressed in black—brought cases into the hall. A dark BMW slid up to the front of the house. The driver, wearing a chauffeur's hat, took sentry duty by the car.

Jack could hear Magnus' baritone commands to everyone around him and Emily standing on the terrace talking on the phone. Then Elizabeth came out, head down, stumbling a little in her dark glasses. The chauffeur took her arm and opened the passenger door. She got in, purse on her lap. Magnus was still talking as Elizabeth took out her phone and seemed to be writing something.

Jack's phone beeped. Elizabeth's last message.

The car rolled out of the driveway through the gates and down Paloma Hill. And she was gone.

Esme opened all the windows upstairs and shook out a rug from the balcony. Jack watched her lugging sheets to the laundry room, saw her spray something on the furniture and sweep the kitchen floor. The sound of her vacuuming made Jack sleepy so he dropped back on the pile of cushions and stared up at a spider tightening its web for the day's catch.

It was midday when Megan found Jack floating, face down, on top of the pool. She screamed, dropped her Lanvin purse, rushed to the side of the water. Megan teetered around the edge, half sobbing as she called Jack's name, each time more frantic. She deliberated rowing herself over on the inflatable unicorn but couldn't risk it capsizing. Then she saw the cleaning pole. Megan picked it up and leant out as far as she could, balancing the net over the top of the water but she only managed to push Mr. Mathews further away.

Even if Megan waded in, she'd never be able to drag a corpse twice her size out of the water and her memory of how to resuscitate someone was pretty hazy.

"Help!" Her arms swung from side to side as she looked around. "Flores? Esme? Help me! Anyone?"

Megan squatted down, opened her bag in search of her

phone to call 911, but her hands were so wet and shaky it squirmed out of her grip. "Please someone help!"

"It's beautiful. Wanna get in?"

Megan screamed, clutched at her heart, dropped her phone.

"Oh my God! Oh my—"

When she caught her breath, she laughed until tears ran down her cheeks. "I thought you were dead!"

Jack rolled over in the water, lay on his back.

"You *heard* me, didn't you?" Megan splashed him.

Jack slipped under the water only to reappear grinning at her from the shallow end.

"Not that you deserve to live, Mr. Mathews, after the way you treated your wife and Mrs. Lambert. I was only worried because it would have messed up my next viewing."

Jack wiped the water off his face, but not the smile.

"Now I'm alive, come on in. Let's be dead bodies together."

"I could..." She looked around. "Maybe just a little dip."

Megan slipped out of her shoes, lifted up her skirt and waded in up to her knees because she couldn't say no to a smile like that.

"Can you believe it rained last night?"

"Sure did!"

"Haha. Your own September storm. So Elizabeth left?"

Jack patted the top of the water. "It was just a summer thing, y'know?"

"I know *summer things*." Megan rolled her eyes, tilted her head at him, letting a tawny lock bounce at her cheek. "Y'know she never once tagged me when she took pictures of the house." Megan slapped the water. "She scared me."

"Well, you know what? She scared me too."

And Jack slapped the water back. And they laughed, the tops of their heads almost touching.

"And Jude. She made me break into the house and stuff. You caused me a lot of problems, Mr. Mathews! There. I said it."

"I'm sorry, really, that you got dragged into all my bullshit."

Megan nodded, closed her eyes, and felt the sun on her face.

"Look at the sky, the hills, the ocean, all warmed by that big ball of fire... and yet, we think we have control over anything..."

"Wow! That's beautiful." Jack panned the skyline, stopped. "Hey, there's a van at the gates. Expecting anybody?"

Megan peered around the front of the house, wetting her shirt as she bobbed over the water. The buzzer went. Once. Twice. Then the man got back in, drove away. Silence again until Megan started to laugh, pointing at the van, so much she held Jack's arm to steady herself. "It's Elizabeth's peonies!"

"Those flowers! Man, did she give me grief over that!"

"Do you know how hard I worked trying to find white peonies in Felicidad, in August? And he's just driven away with them!"

Every time they caught their breath, they'd set each other off giggling again, and maybe Megan was conscious that the water on her white shirt turned it so transparent that every detail of her bra was visible. Jack certainly was.

"Can I ask something indiscreet?"

"I insist, *only* indiscreet questions from now on."

Megan covered a grin behind her hand. "What will happen to that blue Mercedes-Benz Mrs. Lambert drove?"

"You liked that car?"

"Loved it." She ran her tongue over her top teeth, looked up at him.

"Always knew you had good taste." He winked. "So, first refusal goes to Traci, an ex-colleague, but, if she's still not speaking to me, I'll see what we can do for you."

Megan climbed out onto dry land, looked around for her things.

"By the way, Fridays me and my friends go to Barebacks Bar 'n' Grill—I know it's not Gatton's—but they do a great deal on cocktails. Maybe even tonight?"

Water rolled from Jack's torso. "I was going to visit my mom this afternoon. After that I'm free as a bird. Barebacks? On Bella Rosa beach? That still goin'? I haven't been since a bud of mine worked there, Axel."

"Axel's my brother!"

"No shit!"

"He works construction now. Shall I invite him too?"

Jack climbed out of the swimming pool shaking off drips of water from his ankles. "Do that. Haven't seen him in years." He slapped his chest as he walked towards the pool house. "You're a great agent, Megan. I'm sure you'll find someone to take this place in no time."

"You're paid up for another ten days if I don't."

"Just make sure you get rid of that ridiculous bed," he said, winking. "See you 'bout eight tonight."

"I'll be there!" Megan said, straightening her skirt and squeezing her purse against her.

The sun was at midpoint so all Megan could see was the dark outline of an unshaven man going into the pool house, picking up a towel and bending down to take off his boxers. Just the kind of man who would go so well in her new home, her new life.

ACKNOWLEDGMENTS

Special thanks to Deborah Paxford, my first reader, for her endless encouragement and perceptive feedback; Jon Bryant for his editorial advice and proofreading; Abbie Rutherford, for her extensive and painstaking editorial work. Amy Mugge, whose close reading, thoughtful suggestions, and insider's view into San Diego life were invaluable. Thanks also to Jessica Alexander for the reassurance that ordinary events in ordinary lives can still be extraordinary, and to Nancy Heslin, for her relentless support and generosity; Bella Shand, Claire McAlpine, Harriet Macaree, Rosa Jackson and Alison Jeremy. And, of course, thank you to everyone who's ever read this book!

ABOUT THE AUTHOR

Ruby Soames lives between London and France with her two children and journalist husband. She studied Literature and Theology at Bristol University, has an MA in Creative Writing from Manchester Metropolitan University and MSc in Psychology from the University of Liverpool. Ruby has published three novels, short stories, articles and works in adult education. For more information, please visit: www. rubysoames.com

- Seven Days to Tell You (Bloodhound Books, 2024)
- Mothers, Fathers & Lovers (Bloodhound Books, 2024)

Printed in Dunstable, United Kingdom